SONGMASTER

His weeping took Esste and Nniv by surprise.
This was not Mikal the Terrible. Could not be.
For Songbirds could only be fully appreciated
by people whose deepest places resonated with
that most powerful of musics. It was known that
a Songbird could never go to a person who
killed, to a person who loved power. But there
could be no doubt that Mikal had understood the
Songbird.

"You have damaged us," Nniv said, his voice
full of regret.

Mikal composed himself as best he could.
"How have I damaged you?"

"By proving to us that you do indeed deserve
a Songbird. But Mikal, you know also that we
must find the right Songbird for you, and if we
don't find one before you die, there can be no
complaint."

Mikal nodded. "But hurry. Hurry, if you
can."

SONGMASTER

Orson Scott Card

A Legend book
Published by Arrow Books Limited
20 Vauxhall Bridge Road, London SW1V 2SA

An imprint of Random Century Group

London Melbourne Sydney Auckland
Johannesburg and agencies throughout
the world

This edition first published 1987 by Tor Books, USA
Legend edition 1990

Printed and bound in Great Britain by
Courier International Ltd, Tiptree, Essex

ISBN 0 09 9638509

To Ben Bova,
a songmaster who takes as much care
to develop younger voices
as to sing his own songs

Prologue

Nniv did not go to meet Mikal's starship. Instead, he waited in the rambling stone Songhouse, listening to the song of the walls, the whisper of the hundred young voices from the Chambers and the Stalls, the cold rhythm of the drafts. There were few in the galaxy who would dare to make Mikal come to them. Nniv was not daring, however. It did not occur to him that the Songmaster needed to go meet anyone.

Outside the Songhouse walls the rest of the people on the planet Tew were not so placid. When Mikal's starship sent its savage pulses of energy onto the landing field and settled hugely and delicately to the ground, there were thousands waiting to see him. He might have been a well-beloved leader, come to hear the bands and see the cheering crowds that filled the landing field when it was cool enough to walk on again. He might have been a national hero, with flowers spread in his path and dignitaries bowing and saluting and struggling to cope with a situation for which no protocol had yet been learned on Tew.

But the motive behind the ceremonies and the outward adoration was not love. It was an uncomfortable memory of the fact that Tew had been slow to submit to the Discipline of Frey. That Tew's ambassadors to other worlds

1

had toyed with the plots and alliances that formed to make a last, pathetic resistance to the most irresistible conqueror in history. None of the plots came to anything. Too many greater leagues and nations had fallen, and now when Mikal's ships came no inner world resisted; no hostility was allowed to show.

To be sure, there was no great terror, either, in the hearts of the officials who fumbled their way through makeshift pomp. The days of ravaging conquered planets were over. Now that there was no resistance, Mikal proved that he could rule wisely and brutally and well, solidifying an empire from which he could reach farther out into the galaxy to the more distant worlds and confederations where his name was only a rumor. As long as the dignitaries were careful, Mikal's government on Tew would be reasonably fair, only mildly repressive, and disgustingly honest.

There were some who wondered why Mikal would bother with Tew at all. He seemed bored as he made his way along the flower-strewn path, his guards and retainers keeping the crowd a safe distance back. He did not look to the left or the right, and soon disappeared into the vehicles that rushed him to the government offices. And it was not Mikal but his aides who interviewed and fired and hired, who informed and explained about the new laws and the new order, who quickly revised the political system of the world to fit it into the pattern of Mikal's peaceful, well-governed empire. Why did Mikal need to come at all?

But the answer should have been obvious, and soon *was* obvious to those who were well-informed enough to know that Mikal had vanished from the building that was meant to house him. Mikal was really no different from the other tourists who came to Tew. The planet was pretty much a backwater, not important to any imperial plan. Except for the Songhouse. Mikal had come to see the Songhouse.

And for a man of wealth and power, there was only one reason, really, to visit there.

He wanted a Songbird, of course.

"You can't have a Songbird, sir," said the diffident young woman in the waiting room.

"I haven't come to argue with gatekeepers."

"Whom would you like to argue with? It will do you no good."

"The Songmaster. Nniv."

"You do not understand," the young woman explained. "Songbirds are given only to those who can truly appreciate them. We invite people to accept them. We do not take applications."

Mikal looked at her coldly. "I am not applying."

"Then what are you doing here?"

Mikal said no more. Merely stood, waiting. The young woman tried to argue with him, but he didn't answer. She tried to ignore him and go on with her work, but he waited for more than an hour, until she could stand no more. She got up and left without a word.

"What is he like?" sang Nniv, his voice low and comforting.

"Impatient," she said.

"Yet he waited for you." Correction did not give way to criticism in Nniv's voice. Ah, he is a kind master, the girl thought but did not say.

"He is stern," she said. "He is a ruler, and he will not believe there is anything he cannot get, anyone he cannot rule, anywhere he cannot fill with his presence."

"No man can travel through space," Nniv answered gently, "and not know there are places he cannot fill."

She bowed. "What do I tell him?"

"Tell him that I will see him."

She was startled. She was confused. She abandoned

words, and sang her confusion. The song was meek and uncontrolled, for she would never be a master, not even a teacher, but wordlessly she asked Nniv why he would even listen to such a man, why he would risk having the rest of mankind think, The Songhouse treats all men alike, judging only on merit, not on power—except for Mikal.

"I will not be corrupted," Nniv sang gently.

"Send him away," she pleaded.

"Bring him to me."

She broke Control and wept, then, and declared she could not do such a thing.

Nniv sighed. "Then send me Esste. Send me Esste, and be relieved of duty until Mikal leaves."

Mikal still stood in the gateroom an hour later, when the door opened again. This time it was not the gatekeeper. It was another woman, more mature, with darkness under her eyes and power in her bearing. "Mikal?" she asked.

"Are you the Songmaster?" Mikal asked.

"Not I," she said, and for a moment Mikal felt acutely embarrassed at having thought so. But why should I be embarrassed, he wondered, and shook off the feelings. The Songhouse weaves spells, said the common people on Tew, and it made Mikal uneasy. The woman led the way out of the room, humming. She said nothing, but her melody told Mikal he should follow, and so he pursued the thread of music through the cold stone halls. Doors opened here and there; windows let in the only light (and it was a dismal light of a gray winter sky); in all the wandering through the Songhouse they met no other person, heard no other voice.

At last, after many stairs, they reached a high room. *The* High Room, in fact, though no one mentioned it. Seated at one end of the room on a stone bench unsheltered from the cold breeze through the open shutters was Nniv. He was old, his face more sag than features, and Mikal was startled. Ancient. It reminded Mikal of mortality, which at the age of forty he was just beginning to be aware of. He had sixty years yet, but he was no longer young and knew that time was against him.

"Nniv?" Mikal asked.

Nniv nodded, and his voice rumbled a low *mmmmm*.

Mikal turned to the woman who had led him. She was still humming. "Leave us," Mikal said.

The woman stayed where she was, looking at him as if without comprehension. Mikal grew angry, but he said nothing because suddenly her melody counseled silence, insisted on silence, and instead Mikal turned to Nniv. "Make her stop humming," he said. "I refuse to be manipulated."

"Then," Nniv said (and his song seemed to shout with laughter, though his voice remained soft), "then you refuse to live."

"Are you threatening me?"

Nniv smiled. "Oh, no, Mikal. I merely observe that all living things are manipulated. As long as there is a will, it is bent and twisted constantly. Only the dead are allowed the luxury of freedom, and then only because they want nothing, and therefore can't be thwarted."

Mikal's eyes grew cold then, and he spoke in measured voice, which sounded dissonant and awkward after the music of Nniv's speech. "I could have come here in power, Songmaster Nniv. I could have landed huge armies and weapons that would hold the Songhouse itself for ransom to work my will. If I intended to coerce you or frighten you or abuse you in any way, I would not have come alone, open to assassins, to ask for what I want. I have come to you with respect, and I will be treated with respect."

Nniv's only answer was to glance at the woman and

say, "Esste." She fell silent. Her humming had been so pervasive that the walls fairly rang with the sudden quiet.

Nniv waited.

"I want a Songbird," Mikal said.

Nniv said nothing.

"Songmaster Nniv, I conquered a planet called Rain, and on that planet was a man of great wealth, and he had a Songbird. He invited me to hear the child sing."

And at the memory, Mikal could not contain himself. He wept.

His weeping took Esste and Nniv by surprise. This was not Mikal the Terrible. Could not be. For Songbirds, while they impressed everyone, could only be fully appreciated by certain people, people whose deepest places resonated with that most powerful of musics. It was known throughout the galaxy that a Songbird could never go to a person who killed, to a person of greed or gluttony, to a person who loved power. Such people could not really hear a Songbird's music. But there could be no doubt that Mikal had understood the Songbird. Both Nniv and Esste could hear his inadvertent songs too easily to be mistaken.

"You have damaged us," Nniv said, his voice full of regret.

Mikal composed himself as best he could. "I, damaged you? Even the memory of your Songbird destroys me."

"Uplifts you."

"Wrecks my self-composure, which is the key to my survival. How have I damaged you?"

"By proving to us that you do indeed deserve a Songbird. You know what that will do, I'm certain. Everyone knows that the Songhouse does not bend to the powerful where Songbirds are concerned. And yet—we will give *you* one. I can hear them now: 'Even the Songhouse sells out to Mikal.'" Nniv's voice was a raucous and perfectly accurate imitation of the speech of the common man, though of course there was no such creature in the galaxy. Mikal laughed.

"You think it's funny?" Esste asked, and her voice pierced Mikal deeply and made him wince.

"No," he answered.

Nniv sang soothingly, and calmed both Esste and Mikal. "But, Mikal, you know also that we set no date for delivery. We must find the right Songbird for you, and if we don't find one before you die, there can be no complaint."

Mikal nodded. "But hurry. Hurry, if you can."

Esste sang, her voice ringing with confidence, "We never hurry. We never hurry. We never hurry." The song was Mikal's dismissal. He left, and found his own way out, guided by the fact that all doors but the right ones were locked against him.

"I don't understand," said Nniv to Esste after Mikal had gone.

"I do," Esste said.

Nniv whispered his surprise in a steeply rising hiss that echoed from the stone walls and blended with the breeze.

"He's a man of great personal force and power," she told him. "But he has not been corrupted. He believes he can use his power for good. He longs to do it."

"An altruist?" Nniv found it difficult to believe.

"An altruist. And this," said Esste, "is his song." She sang, then, occasionally using words, but more often shaping meaningless syllables with her voice, or singing strange vowels, or even using silence and wind and the shape of her lips to express her understanding of Mikal.

At last her song ended, and Nniv's own voice was heavy with emotion as he sang his reaction. That, too,

ended, and Nniv said, "If he truly is what you sing him to
be, then I love him."

"And I," Esste said.

"Who will find a Songbird for him, unless it's you?"

"I will find Mikal's Songbird."

"And teach this bird?"

"And teach."

"Then you will have done a life's work."

And Esste, accepting the heavy challenge (and the possible inestimable honor), sang her submission and dedication and left Nniv alone in the High Room to hear the song
of the wind and answer as best he was able.

For seventy-nine years Mikal had no Songbird. In all
that time, he conquered the galaxy, and imposed the Discipline of Frey on all mankind, and established Mikal's
Peace so that every child born had a reasonable hope of
living to adulthood, and appointed a high quality of government for every planet and every district and every
province and every city there was.

Still he waited. Every two or three years he sent a
messenger to Tew, asking the Songmaster one question:
"When?"

And the answer always came back, "Not yet."

And Esste was made old by the years and the weight of
her life's work. Many Songbirds were discovered because
of her search, but none that would sing properly to Mikal's
own song.

Until she found Ansset.

ESSTE

1 There were many ways a child could turn up in the baby market of Doblay-Me. Many children, of course, were genuine orphans, though now that wars had ended with Mikal's Peace orphanhood was a social position much less often achieved. Others had been sold by desperate parents who had to have money—or who had to have a child out of their way and hadn't the heart for murder. More were bastards from worlds and nations where religion or custom forbade birth control. And others slipped in through the cracks.

Ansset was one of these when a seeker from the Songhouse found him. He had been kidnapped and the kidnappers had panicked, opting for the quick profit from the baby trade instead of the much riskier business of arranging for ransom and exchange. Who were his parents? They were probably wealthy, or their child wouldn't have been worth kidnapping. They were white, because Ansset was extremely fairskinned and blond. But there were trillions of people answering to that description, and no government agency was quite so foolish as to assume the responsibility of returning him to his family.

So Ansset, whose age was unknowable but who couldn't be more than three years old, was one of a batch of a dozen children that the seeker brought back to Tew. All the children had responded well to a few simple tests—

11

pitch recognition, melody repetition, and emotional response. Well enough, in fact, to be considered potential musical prodigies. And the Songhouse had bought—no, no, people are not *bought* in the baby market—the Songhouse had *adopted* them all. Whether they became Songbirds or mere singers, masters or teachers, or even if they did not work out musically at all, the Songhouse raised them, provided for them, cared about them for life. *In loco parentis,* said the law. The Songhouse was mother, father, nurse, siblings, offspring, and, until the children reached a certain level of sophistication, God.

"New," sang a hundred young children in the Common Room, as Ansset and his fellow marketed children were ushered in. Ansset did not stand out from the others. True, he was terrified—but so were the rest. And while his nordic skin and hair put him at the extreme end of the racial spectrum, such things were studiously ignored and no one ridiculed him for it, any more than they would have ridiculed an albino.

Routinely he was introduced to the other children; routinely all forgot his name as soon as they heard it; routinely they sang a welcome whose tone and melody were so confused that it did nothing to allay Ansset's fear; routinely Ansset was assigned to Rruk, a five-year-old who knew the ropes.

"You can sleep by me tonight," Rruk said, and Ansset dumbly nodded. "I'm *older*," Rruk said. "In maybe a few months or sometime soon anyway I get a stall." This meant nothing to Ansset. "Anyway, don't piss in your bed because we never get the same one two nights in a row."

Ansset's three-year-old pride was enough to take umbrage at this. "Don't piss in bed." But he didn't sound angry—just afraid.

"Good. Some of 'em are so scared they do."

It was near bedtime; new children were always brought

in near bedtime. Ansset asked no questions. When he saw
that other children were undressing, he too undressed.
When he saw that they found nightgowns under their
blankets, he too found a nightgown and put it on, though
he was clumsy at it. Rruk tried to help him, but Ansset
shrugged off the offer. Rruk looked momentarily hurt,
then sang the love song to him.

> *I will never hurt you.*
> *I will always help you.*
> *If you are hungry*
> *I'll give you my food.*
> *If you are frightened*
> *I am your friend.*
> *I love you now*
> *And love does not end.*

The words and concepts were beyond Ansset, but the
tone of voice was not. Rruk's embrace on his shoulder was
even more clear, and Ansset leaned on Rruk, though he
still said nothing and did not cry.

"Toilet?" Rruk asked.

Ansset nodded, and Rruk led him to a large room
adjoining the Common, where water ran swiftly through
trenches. It was there that he learned that Rruk was a girl.
"Don't stare," she said. "Nobody stares without permission." Again, Ansset did not understand the words, but
the tone of voice was clear. He understood the tone of
voice instinctively, as he always had; it was his greatest
gift, to know emotions even better than the person feeling
them.

"How come you don't talk except when you're mad?"
Rruk asked him as they lay down in adjoining beds (as a
hundred other children also lay down).

It was now that Ansset's control broke. He shook his

head, then turned away, buried his face under the blankets, and cried himself to sleep. He did not see the other children around him who looked at him with distaste. He did not know that Rruk was humming a tune that meant, ''Let be, let alone, let live.''

He did know, however, when Rruk patted his back, and he knew that the gesture was kind; and this was why he never forgot his first night in the Songhouse and why he could never feel anything but love for Rruk, though he would soon far surpass her rather limited abilities.

''Why do you let Rruk hang around you so much, when she isn't even a Breeze?'' asked a fellow student once, when Ansset was six. Ansset did not answer in words. He answered with a song that made the questioner break Control, much to his humiliation, and weep openly. No one else ever challenged Rruk's claim on Ansset. He had no friends, not really, but his song for Rruk was too powerful to challenge.

2   Ansset held on to two memories of his parents, though he did not know these dream people were his parents. They were White Lady and Giant Man, when he thought to put names to them at all. He never spoke of them to anyone, and he only thought of them when he had dreamed the dreams of them the night before.

The first memory was of the White Lady whimpering, lying on a bed with huge pillows. She was staring into nothingness, and did not see Ansset as he walked into the room. His step was unsure. He did not know if she would be angry that he had come in. But her soft, whipped cries drew him on, for it was a sound he could not resist, and he came and stood by the bed where she rested her head on her arm. He reached out and patted her arm. Even in the dream the skin felt hot and fevered. She looked at him, and her eyes were deep in tears. Ansset reached to the eyes, touched the brow, let his tiny fingers slide down, closing the eyes, caressing the lids so gently that the White Lady did not recoil. Instead she sighed, and he caressed all her face as her whimpers softened into gentle humming.

It was then that the dream went awry, ending in odd ways. Always Giant Man came in, but what he did was a mystery of rumbling voice, embraces, shouts. Sometimes he also lay on the bed with White Lady. Sometimes he picked Ansset up and took him on strange adventures that ended in waking. Sometimes the White Lady kissed him good-bye. Sometimes she did not notice him once the Giant Man came into the room. But the dream always began the same, and the part that never changed was memory.

The other memory was of the moment of kidnapping. Ansset was in a very large place with a distant roof that was painted with strange animals and distorted people. Loud music came from a lighted place where everyone was always moving. Then there was a deafening noise and the place became all light and noise and conversation, and White Lady and Giant Man walked among the crowd. There was pushing and jostling, and someone stepped between White Lady and Ansset, breaking their handhold. White Lady turned to the stranger, but at the same moment Ansset felt a powerful hand grip his. He was pulled away, bumping harshly through the crowd. Then the hand pulled him up, hurting his arm, and for a moment, lifted above the heads of the crowd, Ansset saw White Lady and Giant

Man for the last time, both of them pushing through the crowd, their faces fearful, their mouths open to cry out. But Ansset could never remember hearing them. For a blast of hot air struck him, and a door closed, and he was outside in a blazing hot night, and then he always, always woke up, trembling but not crying, because he could hear a voice saying Quiet, Quiet, Quiet in tones that meant fear and falling and fire and shame.

"You do not cry," said the teacher, a man with a voice that was more comforting than sunlight.

Ansset shook his head. "Sometimes," he said.

"Before," answered the teacher. "But now you will learn Control. When you cry you waste your songs. You burn up your songs. You drown your songs."

"Songs?" asked Ansset.

"You are a little pot full of songs," said the teacher, "and when you cry, the pot breaks and all the songs spill out ugly. Control means keeping the songs in the pot, and letting them out one at a time."

Ansset knew pots. Food came from a pot. He thought of songs as food, then, besides knowing they were music.

"Do you know any songs?" asked the teacher.

Ansset shook his head.

"Not any? Not any songs at all?"

Ansset looked down.

"Ansset, songs. Not words. Just a song that has no words but you just sing, like this, Ah——" and the teacher sang a short stretch of melody that spoke to Ansset and said, Trust, Trust, Trust.

Ansset smiled. He sang the same melody back to the teacher. For a moment the teacher smiled, then looked startled, then reached out with wondering eyes and touched Ansset's hair. The gesture was kind. And so Ansset sang the love song to the teacher. Not the words, because he had no memory for words yet. But he sang the melody as Rruk had sung it to him, and the teacher wept. It was Ansset's first lesson on his first day at the Songhouse, and the teacher wept. He did not understand until later that this meant that the teacher had lost Control and would be ashamed for weeks until Ansset's gifts were more fully appreciated. He only knew that when he sang the love song, he was understood.

3 "Cull, you're beyond this," said Esste, with grief and sympathy and reproach. "You're a good teacher, and that's why we trusted you with the new ones.

"I know," Cull said. "But, Esste——"

"You wept for minutes. Minutes before you regained Control. Cull, have you been ill?"

"Healthy."

"Are you unhappy?"

"I wasn't, not until after—after. I wasn't weeping for grief, Mother Esste, I was weeping for——"

"For what?"

"Joy."

Esste hummed exasperation and noncomprehension.

"The child, Esste, the child."

"Ansset, yes? The blond one?"

"Yes. I sang him trust, and he sang it back to me."

"He shows promise then, and you broke Control in front of him."

"You are impatient."

Esste bowed her head. "I am." Her posture said shame. Her voice said she was still impatient and only a little ashamed after all. She could not lie to a teacher.

"Listen to me," pleaded Cull.

I'm listening, said Esste's reassuring sigh.

"Ansset sang my trust back to me note for note, perfectly. Nearly a minute, and it wasn't easy. And he didn't sing just the melody. He sang pitch. He sang nuance. He sang every emotion I had said to him, except that it was stronger. It was like singing into a long hall and having the sound come back at you louder than you sang it."

Do you exaggerate? asked Esste's hum.

"I was shocked. And yet delighted. Because I knew in that instant that here we had a true prodigy. Someone who might become a Songbird——"

Careful, careful, said the hiss from Esste's mouth.

"I know it's not my decision, but you didn't hear his answer. It's his first day, his first lesson—and anyway, that was nothing, nothing at all to what came after. Esste, he sang the love song to me. Rruk only sang it to him once yesterday. But he sang the whole thing——"

"Words?"

"He's only three. He sang the melody and the love, and Esste, Mother Esste, no one has ever sung such love to me. Uncontrolled, utterly open, completely giving, and I couldn't contain it. I couldn't, Esste, and you know my Control has never faltered before."

Esste heard Cull's song, and the teacher wasn't lying to protect himself. The child was remarkable. The child was powerful. Esste decided she would meet the child.

After she met him, in a brief encounter at the Galley at breakfast, she reassigned herself to be his teacher. As for Cull, the consequence of his loss of Control was much lighter than the usual, and as Esste taught Ansset day after day, she sent word for Cull to be advanced step by step until within a few weeks he was a teacher of new ones again, and Esste put the word around so that none would criticize Cull: "With this child, any teacher would have lost Control."

And there was a dancing quality to her walk and a warmth to her voice that made every teacher and master and even the Songmaster in the High Room realize that Esste at last hoped, perhaps even let herself believe, that her life's work might be within reach. "Mikal's Songbird?" another Songmaster presumed to ask her one day, though his melody told her she need not answer if she didn't want to.

She only hummed high in her head and leaned her head against the stone, and laid her hand on her cheek so that the Songmaster laughed. But he had his answer. She could clown and play to try to hide her hopes, but the very clowning and playing were message enough. Esste was happy. This was so unusual it even startled the children.

4   It was unheard of for a Songmaster to teach new ones. The new ones did not know it, of course, not at first, not until they had learned enough of the basics to advance, as a class, to become Groans. There were other Groans, some as old as five or six, and like all children they had their own society with its own rules, its own customs, its own legends. Ansset's class of Groans soon learned that it was safe to be pugnacious and obstinate with a Belch, but never with a Breeze; that it meant nothing where you slept, but you sat at table with your friends; that if a fellow Groan sang you a melody, you must deliberately make a mistake in singing it back to him, or he'll think you're bragging.

Ansset learned all the rules quickly, because he was bright, and made everyone in his class think of him as a friend, because he was kind. No one but Esste noticed that he did not exchange secrets in the toilet, did not join any of the inner rings that constantly grew and waned among the children. Instead, Ansset worked harder at perfecting his voice. He hummed almost constantly. He cocked his head when masters and teachers talked without words, using only melody to communicate. His focus was not on the children, who had nothing to teach him, but on the adults.

While none of the children were conscious of his separation from them, unconsciously they allowed for it. Ansset was treated with deference. The hazing by the Belches (no, not in front of the teachers—in front of the teachers they're *Bells*), which was usually at the level of urinating on a Groan so he had to shower again, or spilling his soup day after day so that he got in trouble with the cooks—the hazing somehow bypassed Ansset.

And he entered the mythology of the Groans very quickly. There were other legendary figures—Jaffa, who in anger at her teacher burst one day into a Chamber and sang a solo, and then, instead of being punished, was advanced to be a Breeze without ever having to be a Belch at all; Moom, who stayed a Groan until he was nine years old, and then suddenly got the hang of things and passed through Bells and Breezes in a week, entered Stalls and Chambers and was out as a singer before he turned ten; and Dway, who was gifted and ought to have become a Songbird, but who could not stop rebelling and finally escaped the Songhouse so often that she was thrust out and put with a normal boarding school and never sang another note. Ansset was not so colorful. But his name passed from class to class and from year to year so that after he had been a Groan for only a month, even singers in Stalls and Chambers knew of him, and admired him, and secretly resented him.

He will be a Songbird, said the growing myth. And this was not resented by the children his own age, because while all of them could hope to be a singer, Songbirds only came every few years, and some children passed from Common Rooms into Stalls and Chambers without ever having known someone who became a Songbird. Indeed, there was no Songbird at all in the Songhouse now—the most recent one, Wymmyss, had been placed out only a few weeks before Ansset came, so that none of his class had ever heard a Songbird sing.

Of course, there were former Songbirds among the teachers and masters, but that was no help, because their voices had changed. How do you become a Songbird? Groans would ask Belches, and Belches would ask Breezes, and none of them knew the answer, and few dared hope that they would achieve that status.

"How do you become a Songbird?" Ansset sang to Esste one day, and Esste could not hide her startlement completely, not because of the question, though it was rare for a child to ask such an open question, but because of the song, which also seemed to ask, Were you a Songbird, Esste?

"Yes, I was a Songbird," she answered, and Ansset, who had not yet mastered Control, revealed to her that that *was* the question he had been asking. The boy was learning songtalk, and Esste would have to be careful to warn the teachers and masters not to use it in front of him unless they didn't mind being understood.

"What did you do?" Ansset asked.

"I sang."

"Singers sing. Why are Songbirds different?"

Esste looked at him narrowly. "Why do you want to be a Songbird?"

"Because they're the perfect ones."

"You're only a Groan, Ansset. You have years ahead of you." The statement was wasted, she knew. He could sing, he could hear song, but he was still almost an infant, and years were too long to grasp.

"Why do you love me?" Ansset asked her, this time in front of the class.

"I love all of you," Esste sang, and all the children smiled at the love in her voice.

"Why do you sing to me more than to the others, then?" Ansset demanded, and Esste heard in his song another message: The others are not my friends because you set me apart.

"I don't sing to anyone more than to anyone else," Esste answered, and in songtalk she said, I will be more careful. Did he understand? At least he seemed satisfied with her answer, and did not ask again.

Ansset became one of the great legends, however, when he was promoted from Groan to Belch earlier than the rest of his class—and instead of Esste remaining with the class, she moved with Ansset. It was then that Ansset realized that not only was it unusual for a Songmaster to be doing a teacher's job, but also Esste was teaching, not the class, but him. Ansset. Esste was teaching Ansset.

The other children noticed this at least as quickly as Ansset did, and he found that while all of them were nice to him, and all of them praised him, and all of them sought to be near him and eat with him and talk to him, none of them sang the love song to him. And none of them was his friend, for they were afraid.

5 A lesson.

Esste took her class of Bells out of the Songhouse. They rode in a flesket, so that all of them could see outside. It was always a wonder to them, leaving the cold stone walls of the Songhouse. Groans were never taken out; Breezes often were; and Bells knew that the trips in the flesket were only a taste of things to come.

They went through deep forests, skimming over the underbrush as they followed a narrow road cut between tall trees. Birds paced them, and animals looked up bemusedly as they passed.

To children schooled to singing, however, the miracle came when they left the flesket. Esste had the driver, who was only eighteen and therefore just returned from being a singer outside, stop them by a small waterfall. Esste led the children to the side of the stream. She commanded silence, and because Bells have the rudiments of Control, they were able to hold utterly still and listen. They heard birdsong, which they longed to answer; the gurgle of the stream as it slopped against the rocks and inlets of the shore; the whisper of breezes through leaves and grass.

They sat for fifteen minutes, which was near the limit of their Control, and then Esste led them closer to the waterfall. It wasn't a long walk, but it was slick and damp as they approached the mist rising from the foot of the falls. There had been a landslide many years before, and instead of falling into the pool it had carved out of rock, the cascade tumbled onto rock and sprayed out in all directions. The children sat only a dozen meters away, and the water soaked them.

Again, silence. Again, Control. But this time they heard nothing but the crash of the water on the rock. They could see birds flying, could see leaves moving in the wind, but could hear nothing of that.

After only a few minutes Esste released them. "What do we do?" asked one of the children.

"What you want," answered Esste.

So they gingerly waded at the edge of the pool, while the driver watched to make sure no one drowned. Few of them noticed when Esste left; only Ansset followed her.

She led him, though she gave no sign she knew he was following, to a path leading up the steep slope to the top of the falls. Ansset watched her carefully, to see where she was going. She climbed. He climbed after. It was not easy for him. His arms and legs were still clumsy with childhood, and he grew tired. There were hard places, where Esste had only to step up, while Ansset had to clamber over rises half as high as he was. But he did not let Esste out of his sight, and she, for her part, did not go too quickly for him. She had gathered her gown for the climb, and Ansset looked curiously at her legs. They were white and spindly, and her ankles looked too thin to hold her up. Yet she was nimble enough as they climbed. Ansset had never thought of her as having legs before. Children had legs, but masters and teachers rushed along with gowns brushing the floor. The sight of legs, just like a child's, made Ansset wonder if Esste was like the girls in the shower and toilet. He imagined her squatting over the trench. It was a sight that he knew was forbidden, yet in his mind he violated even good manners and stared and stared.

And came face to face with Esste at the top of the hill.

He was startled, and showed it. She only murmured a

few notes of reassurance. You were meant to be here, her song said. Then she looked out beyond the hill, and Ansset looked after her. Behind them was forest in rolling hills, but here a lake spread out to lap the edges of a bowl of hills. Trees grew right to the edge, except for a few clearings. The lake was not large, as lakes go, but to Ansset it was all the water in the world. Only a few hundred meters away, the lake poured over a lip of rock to make the waterfall. But here there was no hint of the violence of the fall. Here the lake was placid, and waterbirds skimmed and dipped and swam and dived, crying out from time to time.

Esste questioned him with a melody, and Ansset answered, "It's large. Large as the sky."

"That is not all you should see, Ansset, my son," she said to him. "You should see the mountains around the lake, holding it in."

"What makes a lake?"

"A river comes into this valley, pouring in the water. It has no place to go, so it fills up. Until some spills out at the waterfall. It can fill no deeper than the lowest point. Ansset, this is Control."

This is Control. Ansset's young mind struggled to make the connection.

"How is it Control, Ansset?"

"Because it is deep," Ansset answered.

"You are guessing, not thinking."

"Because," said Ansset, "it is all held in everywhere except one place, so that it only comes out a little at a time."

"Closer," said Esste. Which meant he was wrong. Ansset looked at the lake, trying for inspiration. But all he could see was a lake.

"Stop looking at the lake, Ansset, if the lake tells you nothing."

So Ansset looked at the trees, at the birds, at the hills. He looked all around the hills. And he knew what Esste wanted him to know. "The water pours out of the low place."

"And?" Not enough yet?

"If the low place were higher, the lake would be deeper."

"And if the low place were lower?"

"There wouldn't be a lake."

And Esste broke off the conversation. Or rather, changed languages, because now she sang, and the song exulted a little. It was low and it was not loud, but it spoke, without words, of joy; of having found after long searching, of having given a gift carried far too long; of having, at last, eaten when she thought never to eat again. I hungered for you, and you are here, said her song.

And Ansset understood all the notes of her song, and all that lay behind the notes, and he, too, sang. Harmony was not taught to Bells, but Ansset sang harmony. It was wrong, it was only countermelody, it was dissonant to Esste's song, but it was nevertheless an augmentation of her joy, and where a mere teacher, with less Control, might have been overcome by Ansset's echo of the deepest parts of her song, Esste had Control enough to channel the ecstasy through her song. It became so powerful, and Ansset was so receptive to it, that it overcame him, and he sobbed and clung to her and still tried to sing through his tears.

She knelt beside him and held him and whispered to him, and soon he slept. She talked to him in his sleep, told him things far beyond his comprehension, but she was laying pathways through his mind. She was building secret places in his mind, and in one of them she sang the love song, sang it so that at a time of great need it would sing back to him and he would remember, and be filled.

When he awoke, he remembered nothing of having lost

Control; nor did he remember Esste speaking to him. But he reached out and took her hand, and she led him down the hill. It felt right to him to hold her hand, though such familiarity was forbidden between children and teachers, partly because his body had vague memories of holding the hand of a woman whom he completely trusted, and partly because he knew, somehow, that Esste would not mind.

6   Kya-Kya was a Deaf. At the age of eight she had still not progressed beyond the Groan level. Her Control was weak. Her pitch was uncertain. It was not lack of native ability—the seeker who found her had not made a mistake. She simply could not pay attention well enough. She did not care.

Or so they said. But she cared very much. Cared when the children her age and a year younger and a year younger than that passed her by. All were kind to her and few despaired, because it was well known that some sang later than others. She cared even more when she was gently told that there was no point in going on. She was a Deaf, not because she could not hear, but because, as her teacher told her, "Hearing, you hear not." And that was it. A different kind of teacher, different duties, different children. There weren't that many Deafs, but there were enough for a class. They learned from the best teachers Tew could provide. But they learned no music.

The Songhouse takes care of all its children, she thought often, sometimes gratefully, sometimes bitterly. I am taken care of. Taught to work by being given duties in the Songhouse. Taught science and history and languages and

I'm damned good at it. Outside, outside they would consider me gifted. But here I'm a Deaf. And the sooner I leave the better.

She would leave soon. She was fourteen. Only a few months left. At fifteen she would be out, with a comfortable stipend and the doors to a dozen universities open to her. The money would continue until she was twenty-two. Later, if she needed. The Songhouse took care of its children.

But there were still these few months, and her duties were interesting enough. She worked with security, checking the warning and protective devices that made sure the Songhouse stayed isolated from the rest of Tew. Such devices had not always been needed, in the old days. There had even been a time when the Songmaster in the High Room ruled all the world. But it was still less than a century since the outsiders had tried to storm the Songhouse in a silly dispute over a pirate who wanted the Songhouse's reputed great wealth. And now the security devices, which took a year to patrol. The duty had taken her around the perimeter, a journey longer than circling the world, and all by skooter, so that she was alone in the forests and deserts and seacoasts of the Songhouse lands.

Today she was checking the monitoring devices in the Songhouse itself. In a way it made her feel superior, to know what none of the children and few of the masters and teachers knew—that the stone was not impenetrable, that, in fact, it was heavily strung with wires and tubes, so that what seemed to be a rambling, primitive stone relic was potentially as modern as anything on Tew. Possession of the wiring diagrams gave her information that would surprise any of the less-informed singers. Yet whenever she dwelt on her pride at having inside knowledge, she forced herself to remember that she was only allowed the knowledge so young because she was completely outside all the

discipline and study of the Songhouse. She was a Deaf—
she could know secrets because she would never sing and
so she didn't matter.

That was her frame of mind when she entered the High
Room. She knocked brusquely because she was feeling
upset. No answer. Good, the old Songmaster, Nniv, wasn't
in. She pushed open the door. The High Room was freezing, with all the shutters open to the wintry wind. It was
insane to leave the place like this—who could work here?
Instead of going to the panels where the monitors were
hidden, she went to the shutters of the nearest window,
leaned out to catch them, and found herself looking down
forever, it seemed, to the next roof below her. She hadn't
realized how high she really was. On the east side, of
course, the Songhouse was higher, so the stairs up to the
High Room were not so terribly long. But she was high,
and the height fascinated her. What would it be like to
fall? Would she feel it like flying, with the exhilaration of
the skooter rushing down a hillside? Or would she really
be afraid?

She stopped herself with one leg over the sill, her arms
poised to thrust her out. What am I doing? The shock of
realization was almost enough to throw her forward, out
the window. She caught herself, gripped the sides of the
window, forced herself to slowly pull her leg back inside,
withdraw from the window, and finally kneel, leaning her
head against the lip of rock at the base of the window.
Why did I do that? What was I doing?

I was leaving the Songhouse.

The thought made her shudder. Not that way. I will not
leave the Songhouse that way. Leaving the Songhouse will
not be the end of my life.

She did not believe it. And, not believing, she gripped
the stone and wanted not to ever let go.

The room was cold. It made her numb, motionless as

she was, and the whine of the wind through the spaces in
the roof and the rush of wind through the windows made
her afraid in a new way. As if someone were watching
her.

She turned. There was no one. Just the bundles of
clothing and books and stone benches and a foot sticking
out from under one of the bunches of clothing and the foot
was blue and she went over to it and discovered that this
bundle of clothing was the misshapen, incredibly thin body
of Nniv, who was dead, frozen in the wind from the winter
outside. His eyes were open, and he stared at the stone in
front of his face. Kya-Kya whimpered, but then reached
down and pulled on his hip, as if to wake him. He rolled
onto his back, but an arm stuck up in the air, and the legs
moved only a little, and she knew he was dead, that the
entire time she had been in the room he had been dead.

The Songmaster in the High Room died only rarely. She
had never known another. It was Nniv who had ultimately
decided her fate. He had declared her Deaf and decided
she would leave the Songhouse without songs. She had
hated him in her heart, though she had only talked to him a
few times, ever since she was eight. But now she only felt
repulsed by the corpse, and more than that, disgusted at
the way he had died. Was the room always kept this
bitterly cold? How had he lived so long! Was this some
part of the discipline, that the ruler of the Songhouse lived
in such squalor and misery?

If this emaciated, frozen corpse was the pinnacle of
what the Songhouse could produce, Kya-Kya was not
impressed. The lips were parted and the tongue lolled
forward, blue and ghastly. This tongue, she thought, was
once part of a song. Reputed to be the most masterful song
in the galaxy, perhaps in the universe. But what had the
song been, if not the throat and lips and teeth and lungs,
all now cold; if not the brain, that now was still?

She could not sing because of lips and teeth and throat and lungs and because in her own mind she was not so single-minded that she could be what the Songhouse demanded. But did it matter?

She did not feel triumphant that Nniv was dead. She was old enough to know that she, too, would be dead, and if she had a century ahead of her, it only meant time in which she might end up just as accidently cruel as Nniv had been. Kya-Kya did not pretend to unusual virtue. Just unusual value, which no one but her recognized. And it occurred to her that Nniv's failure to recognize who and what she was (or had he, indeed, recognized it?) did not *change* her.

She left him, went downstairs to find the Blind in charge of maintenance, an old man named Hrrai who rarely left his office. "Nniv is dead," she told him, wondering if her happiness sounded in her voice (but knowing that Hrrai would not be likely to read her very well, being a Blind). Can't let anyone hear that I'm happy, she thought. Because I'm not rejoicing at his death. Only at my life.

"Dead?" Imperturbable Hrrai only sounded mildly surprised. "Well, then, you must go tell his successor."

Hrrai leaned down over his table and began worrying his pen back and forth across a page.

"But Hrrai . . ." Kya-Kya said.

"But what?"

"Who is Nniv's successor?"

"The next Songmaster of the High Room," he said. "Of course."

"Of course nothing! How should I know who that is? How am I supposed to figure it out if you don't tell me?"

Hrrai looked up, more surprised this time than he had been at the news of Nniv's death. "Don't you know how this works?"

"How should I? I'm a Deaf. I never got past Groan."

"Well, you needn't act so upset about it. It isn't exactly a secret, you know. Whoever finds the body will know, that's all. Whoever finds that the Songmaster in the High Room is dead will know."

"How will I know?"

"It will be obvious to you. Just go and tell him or her that he or she is supposed to take care of funeral arrangements. It's all that simple. But you really ought to act quickly. The Songhouse shouldn't be long without someone in the High Room."

He turned back to his work with a finality that told Kya-Kya she must leave, must be about her business, certainly must not bother him anymore. She left. And wandered the halls. She had thought to be quit of the Songhouse in a matter of months, the least important person ever to have been there, and suddenly she was supposed to choose the leader of the place. What kind of crazy system is this? she thought. And what the hell kind of rotten luck for me, of all people!

But it was not rotten luck, and as she wandered through the stone corridors, all of them chilly with the winter outside, she realized that no one ever came to the High Room unbidden except maintenance people, and all the maintenance people were Deafs or Blinds, those who had not made it into the highest reaches of the singing folk. They could not sing, they could not teach—and so it was left to one of them to stumble across the body and, being impartial, not a member of the eligible group, choose fairly the person who obviously should be the Songmaster in the High Room.

Who?

She went to the Common Rooms and saw the teachers moving among the classes and knew that she could not suddenly elevate a teacher above his rank; it was tempting to be whimsical, to take vengeance on the Songhouse by

naming an incompetent to head it, but it would be cruel to
the incompetent so called, and she couldn't destroy someone that way. She knew enough to know that it was just as
cruel to lift someone above where he ought to be as it was
to force him to stay below his true station. I won't cause
misery.

But the Songmasters, the logical group to choose from—
she knew none of them, except by reputation. Onn, a
gifted teacher and singer, but always assigned as a consul-
tant to everybody because he couldn't live with the necessity of keeping a fixed schedule, meeting with obnoxious
people, and making, of all things, decisions. Much better
to give advice. No, Onn was not the one anyone would
expect, though he was by far the nicest. And Chuffyun
was too old, far too old. He would not be long behind Nniv.

In fact, just as Hrrai had told her, the choice was
obvious. But not one she enjoyed, not at all. Esste, who
was cold to everyone except for the little boy she was
promoting as a possibility for Mikal's Songbird. Esste,
who had reached down into the Common Rooms and
lowered herself to be a teacher when she had been administrator of half the Songhouse, all for the sake of a little
boy. No one made such great sacrifices for me, Kya-Kya
thought bitterly. But Esste was a great singer, one who
could light fires in every heart in the Songhouse—or quench
those fires, if she wanted to. And Esste was above the
petty jealousies and competitions that were endemic to the
Songhouse. Esste was above such things in her attitude—
and now she would be above them in station, too.

Kya-Kya stopped a master (who was quite surprised at
having a Deaf interrupt her) and asked where she might
find Esste.

"With Ansset. With the boy."

"And where is he?"

"In his stall."

Stall. The boy had been promoted. He couldn't be more than six yet, and he was already in Stalls and Chambers. It turned Kya-Kya's mouth down, her stomach dull. But in a moment she brightened again. The boy had been advanced by Esste, that's all. He would be in the Songhouse all his life, except for a few years as a performer. While she would be free, could see all of Tew—more, could see other planets, could go, perhaps, to Earth itself where Mikal ruled the universe in indescribable glory!

A few questions. A few directions. She found Ansset's stall, identical to all the others except for a number on the door. Inside she could hear singing. It was conversation— she knew when it was songtalk. Esste was inside, then. Kya-Kya knocked.

"Who?" came the answer—from the boy, not from the Songmaster.

" Kya-Kya. With a message for Songmaster Esste."

The door opened. The boy, who was far smaller than Kya-Kya, let her in. Esste sat on the stool by the window. The room was bleak—bare wooden walls on three sides, a cot, a stool, a table, and the stone wall framing the single window that opened onto the courtyard. Every stall was interchangeable with any other. But Kya-Kya would once have given her soul to have a stall and all that it implied. The boy was six.

"Your message?"

Esste was as cold as ever; her robe swirled around her feet as she sat absolutely erect on the stool.

"Esste, I have come from the High Room."

"He wants me?"

"He is dead." Esste's face betrayed nothing. She had Control. "He is dead," Kya-Kya said again. "And I hope you will take care of the funeral arrangements."

Esste sat in silence for a moment before she answered.

"You found the body?"

"Yes."

"You have done me no kindness," Esste said, and she rose and left the room.

What now? Kya-Kya wondered, as she stood near the door of Ansset's stall. She had not thought beyond informing Esste. She had expected some reaction; expected at least to be told what to do. Instead she stood here in the stall with the boy who was the opposite of her, the epitome of success where she had met nothing but failure.

He looked at her inquiringly. "What does this mean?"

"It means," said Kya-Kya, "that Esste is Songmaster in the High Room."

The boy showed no sign of response. Control, thought Kya-Kya. That damnable Control.

"Doesn't it mean anything to you?" she demanded.

"What should it mean?" Ansset asked, and his voice was a web of innocence.

"It should mean a little gloating, at least, boy," Kya-Kya answered, with the contempt the hopelessly inferior can freely use when the superior is helpless. "Esste's been pampering you every step of the way. Leading you up without having to go through the pain everyone goes through. And now she has all the power it takes. You'll be a Songbird, little boy. You'll sing for the greatest people in the galaxy. And then you'll come home, and your Esste will see to it you never have to bother with being a friend or a tutor, you'll just step right into teaching, or being a master, or perhaps—why not?—a high master right from the start, and before you're twenty you'll be a Songmaster. So why don't you forget your Control and let it show? This is the best thing that's ever happened to you!" Her voice was bitter and angry, with no hint of music in it, not even the dark music of rage.

Ansset regarded her placidly, then opened his mouth, not to speak but to sing. At first she decided to leave immediately; soon she was incapable of deciding anything.

Kya-Kya had heard many singers before, but no one had sung to her like this. There were words, but she did not hear words. Instead she heard kindness, and understanding, and encouragement. In Ansset's song she was not a failure. She was, in fact, a wise woman who had done a great favor for the Songhouse, who had earned the love of all future generations. She felt proud. She felt that the Songhouse would send her out, not in shame, but as an emissary to the worlds outside. I will tell them of the music, she thought, and because of me the Songhouse will be held in even greater esteem by everyone who knows of it. For I am as much a product of the Songhouse as any singer or Songbird. She was bursting with joy, with pride. She had not been so happy in years. In her life. She embraced the boy and wept for several minutes.

If this is what Ansset can do, he is worth all the praise he has been given, she thought. Why, the boy is full of love, even for me. Even for me. And she looked up into his eyes and saw—

Nothing.

He regarded her as placidly as he had before. Control. He had let out the Song, and that was all. There was nothing human about him when he wasn't singing. He knew what she wanted to hear, he had given it to her, and that was all he needed to do.

"Do they wind you up?" she said to the blank face.

"Wind me up?"

"You may be a singer," she said angrily, "but you aren't human!"

He began to sing again, the tones already soothing, but Kya-Kya leaped to her feet, backed away. "Not again! You can't trick me again! Sing to the stones and make them cry, but I won't have you fooling me again!" She fled the room, slamming shut the door on his song, on his empty face. The child was a monster, not real at all, and she hated him.

She also remembered his song and loved him and longed to return to his stall to hear him sing forever.

That very day she pleaded with Esste to let her go early. To let her leave before she ever had to hear Ansset sing again. Esste looked confused, asked for explanation. Kya-Kya only insisted again that if she wasn't allowed to go, she'd kill herself.

"You can go tomorrow, then," the new Songmaster in the High Room said.

"Before the funeral?"

"Why before the funeral?"

"Because he'll sing then, won't he?"

Esste nodded. "His song will be beautiful."

"I know," Kya-Kya said, and her eyes filled with tears at the memory. "But it won't be a human being singing it. Good-bye."

"We'll miss you," Esste said softly, and the words were tender.

Kya-Kya had been leaving, but she turned to look Esste in the eye. "Oh you sound so sweet. I can see where Ansset learned it. A machine teaching a machine."

"You misunderstand," said Esste. "It is pain teaching pain. What else do you think the Control is for?"

But Kya-Kya was gone. She saw neither Esste nor Ansset again before the tram took her and her luggage and her first month's money away from the Songhouse. "I'm free," she said softly when she passed the gate leading to Tew and the farms opened before her.

You're a liar, you're a liar, answered the rhythm of the engines.

7 A machine teaching a machine. The words left a sour memory that stayed with Esste through all the funeral arrangements. A machine. Well, true enough in a way, and completely untrue in another. The machines were the people who had no Control, whose voice spoke all their secrets and none of their intentions. *But I am in control of myself, which no machine can ever be.*

But she also understood what Kya-Kya meant. Indeed, she already knew it, and it frightened her how completely Ansset had learned Control, and how young. She watched him as he sang at Nniv's funeral. He was not the only singer, but he was the youngest, and the honor was tremendous, almost unprecedented. There was a stir when he stepped up to sing. But when he was through singing, no one had any doubt that the honor was deserved. Only the new ones, the Groans and a few of the Bells were crying—it would not be right at a Songmaster's funeral to try to get anyone to break Control. But the song was grief and love and longing together, the respect of all those present, not just for Nniv, who was dead, but for the Songhouse, which he had helped keep alive. *Oh, Ansset, you're a master,* thought Esste, but she also noticed things that most did not notice. How his face was impassive before and after he sang; how he stood rigidly, his body focused on making the exact tone. *He manipulates us,* Esste thought, *manipulates us but not half so perfectly as he manipulates himself.* She noticed how he sensed every stir, every glance in the audience and fed upon it and gave it back a hundred-fold. He is a magnifying mirror, Esste thought. You are a magnifying mirror who takes the love you've been given and spews it out stronger than before, but with none of yourself attached to it. You are not whole.

He came to where Esste sat, and sat beside her. It was his right, since she was his master. She said no words, but only sighed in a way that said to Ansset's sensitive ears,"Fair, but flawed." The unexpected and undeserved criticism did not cause his expression to change. He only answered with a grunt that meant, "You hardly needed to tell *me*, I knew it."

Control, thought Esste. You have certainly learned Control.

8 Ansset did not sing again for an audience in the Songhouse. At first he did not notice it. It was simply not his turn to solo or duo or trio or quarto in Chamber. But when everyone in his chamber had performed twice or three times, and Ansset had not been asked to sing, he became puzzled, then alarmed. He did not ask because volunteering simply was not done. He waited. And waited. And his turn never seemed to come.

It was not long after he noticed it that the others in Chamber began commenting on it, first to each other, finally to Ansset. "Did you do something wrong?" they asked him, one by one at mealtime or in the corridors or in the toilet. "Why are you being punished?"

Ansset only answered with a shrug or a sound that said, How should I know? But when his ban from performing continued, he began to turn away the questions with coldness that taught the questioner quickly that the subject was forbidden. It was part of Control for Ansset, not to let himself become part of speculation about this mysterious ban. Nor would his Control allow him to ask. Esste could continue as long as she liked. Whatever it meant, whatever she hoped to accomplish, Ansset would bear it unquestioning.

She came to his stall every day, of course, just as before. Being Songmaster in the High Room meant additional duties, not relief from her previous ones. Finding and training Mikal's Songbird was her life's work, chosen freely decades ago. It would not end, the burden would not be lifted, just because Nniv died and that damned fool Kya-Kya had had the temerity to afflict her with his office. She said as much to Ansset, hoping to reassure him that he would not be losing her. But he took the news without any sign that he cared either way, and went on with the day's lessons as if nothing were wrong.

And why should he do anything else? Until Kya-Kya had said her say just before leaving, Esste had not worried particularly. If Ansset was superb at Control, he was superb at everything else, too, and so it was not to be remarked upon. But now Esste noticed the Control as if each example of Ansset's apparent unconcern were a blow to her.

As for Ansset, he had no idea what was going on inside Esste's mind. For Esste's Control was also superb, and she showed nothing of her worry or reasoning to Ansset. That was as it should be, Ansset assumed. I am a lake, he thought, and all my walls are high. I have no low place. I grow deeper every day.

It did not occur to him that he might drown.

9 A lesson.

Esste took Ansset to a bare room with no windows. Just stone, a dozen meters square, and a thick door that admitted no sound. They sat on the stone floor, and because all the floors were stone, they found the floor comfortable, or at least familiar, and Ansset was able to relax.

"Sing," said Esste, and Ansset sang. As always, his body was rigid and his face showed no emotion; as always, the song was intensely emotional. This time he sang of darkness and closed-in spaces, and he sounded mournful. Esste was often surprised by the depth of Ansset's understanding of things he surely, at his age, could not know firsthand.

The song resonated and echoed back from the walls.

"It rings," Esste said.

"Mmmm," Ansset answered.

"Sing so it doesn't ring."

Ansset sang again, this time a wordless and essentially meaningless song that danced easily through his lowest notes (which were not very low) and came out more as air than as tone. The song did not echo.

"Sing," Esste said, "so that it is as loud to me, here by the wall, as it is right next to you, but so that none of it echoes."

"I can't," Ansset said.

"You can."

"Can you?"

41

Esste sang, and the song filled the room, but there was no echo.

And so Ansset sang. For an hour, for another hour, trying to find the exact voice for that room. Finally, at the end of the second hour, he did it.

"Do it again."

He did it again. And then asked, "Why?"

"You do not sing only into silence. You also sing into space. You must sing exactly for the space you have been given. You must fill it so that no one can fail to hear you, and yet keep your tone so clear and free of echo that all they can hear is exactly what your body produces."

"I have to do this every time?"

"In a while, Ansset, it becomes reflex."

They sat in silence for a moment. And then, softly, Ansset asked, "I would like to try to fill the Chamber this way."

Esste knew what he was asking, and refused to answer his real question. "I believe the Chamber's empty right now. We could go there."

Ansset struggled with himself for a moment—Esste assumed, anyway, for though he was silent for a time, his face showed nothing. "Mother Esste," he finally said, "I don't know why I've been banned."

"Have you been?"

Mildly: "You know I have."

It was a minor victory. She had actually forced him to ask. Yet the victory was an empty one. He had not lost Control; he simply had found it unproductive to remain silent about it. Esste leaned back on the stone wall, not realizing that she herself was bending to his rigidity by relaxing her own.

"Ansset, what is your song?"

He looked at her blankly. Waited. Apparently he did not understand.

"Ansset, you keep singing our songs back to us. You keep taking what people feel and intensifying it and shattering us with it, but child, what song is yours?"

"All."

"None. So far I have never heard you sing a song that I knew was only Ansset."

He did not lose Control. Surely he should be angry. But he only looked at her with empty eyes and said, "You are mistaken." The child was six, and said *you are mistaken*.

"You will not sing before an audience again until you have sung for me a song that is yours."

"How will *you* know?"

"I don't know, Ansset. But I'll know."

He continued to regard her steadily, and she, because of her own Control, did not break her gaze. Some children had taken to Control very badly before, and usually they ended up as Deafs. Control was not easy for anyone, but essential for the songs. Yet here was a child who, like most really good singers and Songbirds, had learned Control quickly, lived with it naturally. *Too* naturally. The object of Control was not to remove the singer from all human contact, but to keep that contact clear and clean. Instead of a channel, Ansset was using Control as an impenetrable, insurmountable wall.

I will get over your walls, Ansset, she promised him silently. You will sing a song of yourself to me.

But his blank, meaningless face said only, You will fail.

10 Riktors Ashen was angry when he got to the High Room. "Listen, lady, do you know what this is?"

"No," Esste answered, and her voice was calculated to soothe him.

"It's a warrant of entry. From the emperor."

"And you've entered. Why are you upset?"

"I've entered after four *days*! I'm the emperor's personal envoy, on a very important errand——"

"Riktors Ashen," Esste interrupted (but quietly, calmly), "you are on an important errand, but this is not it. This is just a stop along the way——"

"Damn right," Riktors said, "and this petty errand has put me four days behind schedule."

"Perhaps, Riktors Ashen, you ought to have *asked* to see me.

"I don't have to ask. I have the emperor's warrant of entry."

"Even the emperor asks before he enters here."

"I doubt that."

"It's history, my friend. I myself brought him to this room."

Riktors was less agitated now. Was, in fact, embarrassed at his outburst. Not that he hadn't the right—this was a man, Esste knew, who could use rage to good effect. He hadn't risen to high rank in the fleet without reason. He was embarrassed because the rage had been real, and over a matter of pride. This was a young man who was learning. Esste liked him. Even though he was also a young

44

man who would kill anyone to get what he wanted. Death waited in his calm hands, behind his boyish face.

"History is shit," Riktors said mildly. "I'm here to find out about Mikal's Songbird."

"The emperor has no Songbird."

"That," said Riktors, not without amusement, "is precisely the problem. Do you realize how many years have passed since you promised him a Songbird? Mikal is a hundred eighteen years old this year. Naturally it's polite to suppose the emperor will live forever, but Mikal himself told me to tell you that he is aware of his mortality, and he hopes he will not die without having heard his Songbird sing."

"You understand that Songbirds are matched very carefully to their hosts. Usually we *have* the Songbird and work to place him or her properly. This was an unusual case, and until now we haven't had the right Songbird."

"Until now?"

"I believe we have the Songbird who will be Mikal's."

"I will see him now."

Esste chose to smile. Riktors Ashen smiled back. "With your permission, of course," he added.

"The child is only six years old," Esste answered. "His training is far from complete."

"I want to see him, to know that he exists."

"I'll take you to him."

They wound their way down the stairs, through passages and corridors. "There are so many corridors," Riktors said, "that I don't see how you have any space left for rooms." Esste said nothing until they reached the corridors of Stalls, where she paused for a moment and sang a long high note. Doors closed in the distance. Then she led the emperor's personal envoy to Ansset's door, and sang a few wordless notes outside.

The door opened, and Riktors Ashen gasped. Ansset

was thin, but his light complexion and blond hair were given a feeling of translucence by the sun coming in his window. And the boy's features were beautiful, not just regular; the kind of face that melted men's hearts as readily as women's. More readily.

"Was he chosen for his voice, or his face?" Riktors Ashen asked.

"When a child is three," answered Esste, "his future face is still a mystery. His voice unfolds more easily. Ansset, I have brought this man to hear you sing."

Ansset looked blankly at Esste, as if he did not understand but refused to ask for explanation. Esste knew immediately what Ansset planned. Riktors did not. "She means for you to sing for me," he said helpfully.

"The child needs no repetition. He heard my request, and chooses not to sing."

Ansset's face showed nothing.

"Is he deaf?" asked Riktors.

"We will go now," answered Esste. They went. But Riktors lingered until the last possible moment, looking at Ansset's face.

"Beautiful," Riktors said, again and again, as they walked through more passageways toward the gatehouse.

"He is to be the emperor's Songbird, Riktors Ashen, not the emperor's catamite."

"Mikal has a large number of offspring. His tastes are not so eclectic as to include little boys. Why wouldn't the boy sing?"

"Because he chose not to."

"Is he always so stubborn?"

"Often."

"Hypnotherapy would take care of that. A good practitioner could lay a mental block that would forbid resistance—"

Esste sang a melody that stopped Riktors cold. He

looked at her, not understanding why suddenly he was afraid of this woman.

"Riktors Ashen, I do not tell you how to move your fleets of starships between planets."

"Of course. Just a suggestion——"

"You live in a world where all you expect of people is compliance, and so your hypnotherapists and your mental blocks accomplish all your ends. But here in the Songhouse, we create beauty. You cannot force a child to find his voice."

Riktors Ashen had regained his composure. "You're good at that. I have to work a little harder to force people to listen to me."

Esste opened the door to the gatehouse.

"Songmaster Esste," Riktors said, "I will tell the emperor that I have seen his Songbird, and that the child is beautiful. But when can I tell him the child will be sent?"

"The child will be sent when I am ready," Esste replied.

"Perhaps it would be better if the child were sent when *he* was ready."

"When *I* am ready," Esste said again, and her voice was all pleasure and grace.

"The emperor will have his Songbird before he dies."

Esste hissed softly, which forced Riktors to come closer, to bring his face near enough that only he could hear what Esste said next:

"There is much for *both* of us to do before Mikal Imperator dies, isn't there?"

Riktors Ashen left quickly then, to finish his business for the emperor.

11

Brew takes your mind,
Bay takes your life
Bog takes your money,
Wood takes your wife.
Stivess is cold,
Water is hot,
Overlook wants you,
Norumm does not.

"What song is that?" asked Ansset.

"Consider it a directory. It used to be taught to the children of Step, to make fun of the other great cities of Tew. Step is no longer a great city. But the ones they made fun of still are."

"Where will we go?"

"You are eight years old, Ansset," Esste answered. "Do you remember any life, any people outside the Songhouse?"

"No."

"After this, you will."

"What does the song mean?" asked Ansset. The flesket stopped then, at the changing place, where Songhouse vehicles always stopped and commercial transport took over. Esste led Ansset by the hand, ignoring his question for the moment. There was business at the ticket counter, and their luggage, slight as it was, had to be searched and itemized and fed into the computer, so that no false insurance claims could be made. Esste knew from her memories of her first venture outside the Songhouse lands that Ansset understood almost nothing of what was going on. She tried explaining a few things to him, and he seemed to pick it up well enough to get along. The money, and the idea of money, he took in stride. The clothing he found uncomfortable; he kept taking the shoes off until she insisted that they were essential. She did not look forward to his getting accustomed to the food. There would be diarrhea for days—at the Songhouse he had never acquired a taste or a tolerance for sugar.

She was not surprised at his quiet acceptance of everything. The trip meant that he was within a year of placement, yet he showed no excitement or even interest in his ultimate destination. Over the last two years he had finally begun to show a little human emotion in his face, but Esste, who knew him better than any other, was not fooled. The emotion was placed there in order to avoid exciting comment. None of it was real. It was nothing more or less than what was expected and proper at the moment. And Esste despaired. There were paths and hidden places that she herself had put in Ansset's mind, but now she could not reach him at all. She could not get him to speak of himself; she could not get him to show even the slightest inadvertent emotion; and as for the closeness they had felt on the hill overlooking the lake, he never betrayed a memory of it but at the same time never allowed her to get even a few steps into the path she could follow to put him into a light trance, where she might have accomplished or at least discovered something.

When the business at the changing place was finished, they sat to wait for the bus, a flesket that anyone with the money could ride. It was then that Esste whiled away the time by answering Ansset's question. If he was surprised or gratified that she had remembered it, he did not show any sign.

"Brew is one of the Cities of the Sea—Homefall, Chop, Brine, and Brew—all of which are famous for beer and ale. They also have a reputation for exporting very little of their product because they are such prodigious drinkers. Beer and ale contain alcohol. They are enemies of Control, and you cannot sing when you've been drinking them."

"Bay takes your life?" Ansset prompted, having memorized the song, as usual.

"Bay used to have the unfortunate habit of holding public executions every Saturday whether anyone was sentenced to death or not. To avoid using up too many of their own citizens, they used strangers. The practice has, in recent years, been stopped. Wood had a sort of mandatory wifemarket. Very odd things. Tew is a very odd planet. Which is why the Songhouse was able to exist here. We were more normal than most cities, and so we were left alone."

"Cities?"

"The Songhouse began as a city. It began as a town of people who loved to sing. That's all. Things grew from there."

"The rest of the cities?"

"Stivess is very far to the north. Water is just as far to the south. Overlook is a place whose only product is the beauty of its scenery, and it lives off the people of wealth who go there to end their days. Norumm has four million people. It used to have nine million. But they still feel crowded and refuse to let more than a few people visit them every year."

"Are we going there?"

"We are not."

" 'Bog takes your money.' What does that mean?"

"You'll find out for yourself. That's where we're going."

The bus arrived, they boarded, and the bus left. For the first time in memory, Ansset saw people outside the milieu

of the Songhouse. There were not very many people on the
bus. Though this was the main highway from Seawatch to
Bog, most people took the expresses, which didn't stop at
the Songhouse changing place—or even at Step, usually.
This bus was not an express—it stopped everywhere.

Directly in front of them were a mother and father and
their son, who must have been at least a year older than
Ansset. The child had been riding far too long, and could
not hold still.

"Mother, I need to go to the toilet."

"You just went. Stay in your seat."

But the child whirled around and knelt on the bench to
stare at Esste and Ansset. Ansset looked at the boy, his
gaze never wavering. The boy stared back, while wagging
his backside impatiently. He reached out to bat at Ansset's
face. It might have been meant as a friendly gesture, but
Ansset uttered a quick, harsh song that spun the boy
around in his seat. When the mother took the boy to the
bathroom at the back of the bus, the child looked at Ansset
in terror and stayed as far from him as possible.

Esste was surprised at how frightened the child had
become. True, the music had been a rebuke. But the
child's reaction was far out of proportion to Ansset's song.
In the Songhouse, anyone would have understood Ansset's
song, but here the child should have understood it only
vaguely—that was the purpose of the trip, to learn to adapt
to outsiders. Yet somehow Ansset had communicated with
the boy, and done it better than he had with Esste.

Could Ansset actually *direct* his music to one particular
person? Esste wondered. That went beyond songtalk. No,
no. It must have been just that the boy had been paying
closer attention to Ansset than she had, so that the song
struck him with more force.

And instead of worrying, she made the incident give her
more confidence. In his first encounter with an outsider,

Ansset had done far better than he should have been able
to. Ansset was the right choice for Mikal's Songbird. If
only.

Though the forest was not so lush as the deep woods in
the Valley of Songs, where all Ansset's excursions had
taken him before, the trees were still tall enough to be
impressive, and the lack of underbrush made for a different kind of beauty, a sort of austere temple with trunks
extending into the infinite distance and the leaves making a
dense ceiling. Ansset watched the trees more than the
people. Esste speculated as to what was going on in his
impenetrable mind. Was he deliberately avoiding looking
at the others? Perhaps he needed to avoid their strangeness
until he could absorb it. Or was he truly uninterested,
more drawn to the forest than to other human beings?

Perhaps I was wrong, Esste thought. Perhaps my intui-
tion was a mistake, and I should have let Ansset perform.
For two years he has had no audience but me. If his
preferred treatment before kept the other children from
being close to him, his ban had made him a pariah. No one
knew what his error had been, but after that triumphant
song at Nniv's funeral Ansset's voice had gone unheard,
and everyone concluded the disgrace must be punishment
for something terrible. Some had even sung of it in chamber. One child, Ller, had even had the temerity to protest,
to sing angrily that it was unjust to ban Ansset for so long,
so unfairly. Yet even Ller avoided Ansset as if the future
Songbird's suffering were contagious.

If I was wrong, Esste concluded, the damage has been
done. In a year Ansset will go to Mikal, ready or not.
Ansset will go as the finest, most exquisite voice we have
sent from the Songhouse in living memory. But he will go
as an inhuman creature, unable to communicate the normal
human feelings with others. A singing machine.

I have a year, Esste thought. I have one year to break down his walls without breaking his heart.

The forest gave way to wooded prairie, the desolate land where wild animals still roamed. Population pressure on Tew had never been great enough to drive many settlers to this plateau where winters were impossibly cold and summers unbearably hot. They were an hour reaching the Rim, a great cliff thousands of kilometers long and nearly a kilometer high. Here, however, the rift had split in two parts, and between them other cliffs took the descent more gradually. The city of Step had grown up at the front of the jumble of rock, where river traffic had to end and transfer to roads. Few of the farmers could afford fleskets. Even when Step ceased to be a major city, it remained important locally.

The bus followed the switchback road carved centuries ago in the rock. It was rough, but the bus never felt it, except when sudden dips forced it to drop a bit in altitude. Ansset still watched the scenery, and now even Esste gazed at the huge expanse of farmland at the base of the descent. What fell as snow on the plateau came as rain below the Rim, and the farmers here fed the world, as they liked to say.

Step itself was boring. All the buildings were old, and decay was the loudest message shouted by the shabby signs and the nearly empty streets. Nevertheless, lessons had to be learned. Esste took Ansset into a dismal restaurant and ordered and paid for a dinner. "Even the prices are depressed here," she commented. Ansset ignored her.

The restaurant was no more crowded than the streets. Wherever all the people were, it wasn't here. And the food came quickly. It was not bad, but the flavor had left it somewhere between the farm and the table. Ansset ate some, but not much. Esste ate less. Instead, she looked around at the people. At first she got the impression that they were all old, but because she didn't trust impressions, she counted. Only six were gray-haired or balding—the other dozen were middle-aged or young. Some were silent, but most conversed. Yet the restaurant felt old, and the conversations sounded tired, and it all made Esste vaguely sad. The songs of the place were gone, if there had ever been songs. Now only moans were appropriate.

And, as soon as Esste thought that, she realized that Ansset was moaning. The sound was soft but penetrating, almost like the background noise of the kitchen machines that processed the food. Control allowed Esste to refrain from glancing at Ansset. Instead she listened to the song. It was a perfect echo of the mood of the place, a perfect understanding of the, not misery, but weariness of the people. But gradually Ansset built a rising tone into his melody, a strange, surprising element that made it interesting, or at least that made a person hearing it want to be interested in something. Esste knew immediately what Ansset was doing. He was breaking the ban. He was performing. And once again the song was not his own—it was what every person in the restaurant, including Esste, wished to hear, wished to be made to feel.

The lilting quality of his song became more pronounced. People who had not been conversing began to talk; conversations already in progress became more animated. People smiled. The ugly young woman at the counter began talking to the waiter. Even joking. No one seemed to notice Ansset's song.

And Ansset faded, softened the song, let it die in mid-note so that it seemed to continue into the silence. Esste was not sure, in fact, when the song was over, even though she was the only person who had been carefully listening to it. Yet the effect of the song lingered. Deliberately Esste waited, watched to see how long the people would remain cheerful. They left the restaurant smiling.

"I congratulate you," said Esste, "on your superb performance."

Ansset's face did not respond. His voice did. "They're harder to change than Songhouse people."

"Like trying to move through water, yes?" asked Esste.

"Or mud. But I can do it."

Not even smugness. Just a recognition of fact. But I know you, boy, Esste thought. You are enjoying yourself immensely. You are having a hilarious time outsmarting me and at the same time proving that you can handle any situation. As long as it's outside of you.

The bus took them through the night back up the Rim, but to the west this time, and it was still dark when they reached Bog. The sky was dark, that is. The lights of the city filled the land to the edge of the sea. It seemed in places that there were no breaks between the lights, as if the city were a carpet of pure light, a fragment of the sun. The clouds above the city glowed brightly. Even the sea seemed to shine.

The streets were so crowded, even in the last hours before dawn, that buses and fleskets and even skooters had to use overhead ramps that wound among the buildings. It was dazzling. It was exciting. The crush of humanity was frantic, desperate, exhilarating, even from the inside of a bus. Ansset slept through it, after waking for a moment when Esste tried to get him to look. "Lights," he said, in a tone of voice that said, I'd rather sleep.

"Might as well go upstairs and sleep," said the clerk at the hotel. "Nothing happens during the day here. Not even business. Can't even get a decent meal except at one of those junky all-day diners."

But after only a few hours of sleep, Ansset insisted that they go out.

"I want to see the city now."

"It looks better by electric light," Esste told him.

"So." So that's why I want to see it.

"So?" I'd rather rest.

"The beds here are too soft," Ansset said, "and my back is sore. The food we ate in Step has sent me to the toilet four times, and it looked better than it did on the table. I want to see outside. I want to see it when it isn't dressed up to fool people."

You are eight years old, Esste said silently. You might as well be a crusty old eighty.

They saw Bog by daylight.

"Name?" asked Ansset.

"The city is on the estuary of the River Salway. Most of the land is only a few centimeters above sea level, and it is constantly trying to sink into the sea." She showed him how architecture had adapted to the conditions. Every building had a main entrance opening onto air on every floor. As the building sank, the entrance on the next floor up came into use. There were buildings whose tops were only a few feet above street level—usually, other buildings had already been built atop them.

The lighted signs were off in the daytime, and very few people were on the streets. "As dismal as Step," Ansset said.

"Except that it comes alive at night."

"Does it?"

Litter was inches deep on the streets in some places. Sweepers sucked their way through the city, roaring as they chewed up the trash. The few people on the streets looked as if they had had a hard night—or were up after very little sleep. It had been a carnival the night before; today the city was a cemetery.

A park. They sat on a massit that contoured itself to fit their bodies within a few moments. An old woman sat not far off, dangling her feet in a pond. She was holding a string that led off into the water. Beside her an ugly eel occasionally twitched. She was whistling.

Her melody was harsh, untuneful, repetitive. Ansset began singing the same tune, in the same pitch—high, wavering, uncertain. He matched her, waver for waver, sour note for sour note. And then, abruptly, he sang a dissonance that grated painfully. The old woman turned around, heaving her huge stomach off her lap as she did. She laughed, and her breasts bounced up and down. "You know the song?" she called.

"Know it!" cried Ansset. "I wrote it!"

She laughed again. Ansset laughed with her, but his laugh was a high imitation of hers, great gasps and little, loud bursts of sound. She loved hearing his laugh as much as her own—since it was her own. "Come here!" she called.

Ansset came to her, and Esste followed, unsure whether the old woman meant well for the boy. Unsure until she spoke again.

"New here," she said. "I can tell who's new here. This your mother? A beautiful boy. Don't let go of him tonight. He's pretty enough to be a catamite. Unless that's what you have in mind, in which case I hope you turn into an eel, speaking of which would you like to buy this one?"

The eel, as if to display its charms, twisted obscenely.

"It isn't dead yet," Ansset commented.

"They take hours to die. Which is fine with me. The longer they wiggle the more they pee and the better they taste. This pond's full of them. Connects right up with the sewer system. They live in the sewer. Along with worse things. Bog produces more turds than anything else, enough to keep a million of these things alive. And as long as they're around, I won't starve." She laughed again, and Ansset laughed with her, then briefly took her laugh and turned it into a mad song that made her laugh even harder. It took Control for Esste not to laugh with her.

"The boy's a singer."

"The boy has many gifts."

"Songhouse?" asked the woman.

Better to lie. "They wouldn't take him. I told them he had talent, genius even, but their damned tests wouldn't find a genius if he sang an aria."

"That's fine enough. Plenty of market for singers around here, and not the Songhouse type, you can bet. If he's willing to take off his clothes, he can make a fortune."

"We're just visiting."

"Or there are even places where he could earn plenty by putting them on. All kinds here. But you *are* from out of town. Everybody knows you don't go into the parks in the daytime. Not enough police to patrol them. Even the monitors do no good—only a few men and women to watch them, and they're sleepy from the night before anyway. The night's alive, but the daytime's deadly. It's a saying."

The singsong in her voice had said as much. But Ansset apparently couldn't resist. He took the words and sang them several times, each time funnier than the last. "The night's alive, but the daytime's deadly."

She laughed. But her eyes got serious quickly. "It's all right here on the edge. And they never bother me. But you be careful."

Ansset picked up the eel, looked at it calmly. The eel's eyes looked desperate. Ansset asked, "How does it taste?"

"How else? All it eats is shit. It tastes like shit."

"And you eat it?"

"Spices, salt, sugar—I can take eel and make it taste like almost anything. Still terrible, but at least not eel. Eel's a flexible meat. You can bend it and twist it into whatever you want."

"Ah," said Ansset.

To the old woman, his *ah* meant nothing. To Esste, it

said, I am an eel to you. It said, You can bend me, but I will strain against the bending.

"Let's go," said Esste.

"A good idea," said the old woman. "It isn't safe here."

"Good-bye," said Ansset. "I'm glad I met you." He sounded so glad to meet her that she was surprised, and smiled with more than mirth as they left.

12 "This is boring," Ansset said. "There must be more to see than this."

Esste looked at him in surprise. When she had come here as an incipient Songbird, the shows with their dancing and singing and laughing were a marvelous surprise to her. She had not thought Ansset would be so easily satiated.

"Where should we go, then?"

"Behind."

"Behind what?"

He did not answer. He had already left his seat and was sliding out between the rows. A woman reached out and patted his shoulder. He ignored her completely and moved on. Esste tried to catch up, but he fit better through the crowds in the aisles as people constantly moved in and out. She saw him dart out the door where the waiters came and went. Esste, having no choice, followed. Where was the fear and shyness of strangers that normally kept children from the Songhouse in line?

She found him with the cooks. They laughed and joked with him, and he echoed their laughs and their mood and made it happier as he talked virtual nonsense to them. They loved it. "Your son, lady?"

"My son."

"Good boy. Wonderful boy."

Ansset watched as they cooked. The heat in the kitchen was intense. The cook explained as he worked. "Most places use quick ovens. But here, we go for the old flavors. The old ways of cooking. It's our specialty." Sweat dripped from Ansset's chin; his hair stuck to his forehead and neck in sweaty curls. He seemed not to notice it, but Esste noticed, and in tones that meant she intended to be obeyed she said, "We're going."

Ansset offered no resistance, but when she started leading him to the door they had entered from, he unerringly headed toward another exit. It led to a loading dock. Loaders looked at them curiously, but Ansset was humming a mindless tune and they left him alone.

Beyond the dock an indoor street serviced all the buildings of that area. It was a city within the city: all the fronts outside glittering for the visitors, the gamers, the funseekers, while behind the buildings, within the buildings the loaders, the cooks, the waiters, the servants, the managers, the entertainers passed back and forth, rode in shabby taxis, emptied garbage. It was the ugliness that all the pleasure of Bog generated, hidden from the paying customers behind walls and doors that said Employees Only.

Esste could barely keep up with Ansset. She made no pretense of directing him now. He had found this place, and it was his music that kept at bay those who might have stopped them. She had to stay with him; wanted to stay with him, for she was excited by the discoveries he made, much more excited than he let himself appear to be.

A garbage-processing station; a whoreshop; an armored car loading that hour's receipts from a gambling establishment; a dentist who specialized in fixing the teeth of those who had to smile and didn't want to take more than a few minutes off work; a rehearsal for a slat show; and a thousand loaders bringing in food and taking out garbage.

And a morgue.

"You're not allowed in here," said the embalmer, but Ansset only smiled and said, "Yes we are," and sang unshakable confidence. The embalmer shrugged and went on with his work. And soon he began talking as he went. "I clean 'em," he said. The bodies came in on a conveyor. He rolled them off onto a table, where he slit the abdomen and removed the guts. "Rich folks, poor folks, winners, losers, players, workers, they dies a hundred a night in this city, and here we cleans 'em up pretty so they'll keep. All the guts is the same. All the stinks is the same. Naked as babies." The guts went into a bag. He filled the cavity with a stiff plastic wool and sewed up the skin with a hooked needle. It took only ten minutes for one body. "Another one does the eyes, and another one does visible wounds. I'm a specialist."

Esste wanted to leave. Pulled on Ansset's arm, but Ansset wouldn't go. He watched four bodies come by. The fourth one was the old woman from the park. The embalmer had just about run out of chat. He cut open the huge stomach. The stench was worse. "I hate the fat ones," said the embalmer. "Always having to hold the fat out of the way. Slows me down. Gets me behind." He had to reach over mounds of flesh to reach the bowels, and he swore when he broke them. "Fat ones makes me clumsy."

The woman's face was set in a grimace that might have been a grin. Her throat had been slit.

"Who killed her?" asked Ansset, his face and voice showing no emotion beyond curiosity.

"Anyone. How should I know? Just a deader. Could have been killed for anything. But she's a poor one, all right. I know the smell. Eats eels. If the killers hadn't got her, the cancer would've. See?" He pulled up the stomach, which was distended and putrified by a huge tumor. "So fat she didn't know she had it. Would have finished her off soon enough."

It took the embalmer several tries and stronger thread
before he could tie the abdomen back together again. In
the meantime another body passed on the conveyor.
"Damn," he said. "There'll be complaints tonight, that's
for sure. Another missed quota. I hate the fat ones."

"Let's go *now*," said Esste, deliberately letting her
Control slip enough that he would be surprised into moving. He let her lead him to the indoor street.

"Enough," Esste said. "Let's go."

"She was wrong," Ansset answered.

"Who?"

"The woman. She was wrong. They wouldn't let her
alone."

"Ansset."

"This has been a good trip," Ansset said. "I've learned
a lot."

"Have you?"

"Pleasure is like making bread. A lot of hot, nasty work
in the kitchen for a few swallows at the table."

"Very good." She tried to lead him away.

"No, Esste. You can ban me at the Songhouse, but you
can't ban me here." And he broke away from her and ran
to the backstage entrance of a theatre. Esste followed, but
she was not young, and though she had made an effort to
stay in shape, a woman of her age could not hope to
overtake a child determined to escape. She was lucky to
stay close enough to see where he went.

An orchestra was playing to a full hall, and a woman on
the stage was dancing nude. An equally naked man waited
in the wings. Ansset stood behind one of the illusions,
rigid as he sang. His voice was clear and loud, and the
woman heard it and stopped dancing, and soon the members of the orchestra began hearing it and stopped playing.
Ansset stepped through the illusion and walked out onto
the stage, still singing.

Ansset sang to them what they had been feeling, what the orchestra had been pathetically incompetent to satisfy. He sang lust to them, though he had never experienced it, and they grew passionate and uncontrollable, audience and orchestra and the naked woman and man. Esste grieved inwardly as she watched it. He will give them everything they want.

But then he changed his song. Still without words, he began telling them of the sweating cooks in the kitchen, of the loaders, of the dentist, of the shabbiness behind the buildings. He made them understand the ache of weariness, the pain of serving the ungrateful. And at last he sang of the old woman, sang her laugh, sang her loneliness and her trust, and sang her death, the cold embalming on a shining table. It was agony, and the audience wept and screamed and fled the hall, those who could control themselves enough to stand.

Ansset's voice penetrated to the walls, but did not echo.

When the hall was empty, Esste walked out onto the stage. Ansset looked at her with eyes as empty as the hall.

"You eat it," said Esste, "and you vomit it back fouler than before."

"I sang what was in me."

"In you? None of this ever got in you. It came to the walls and you threw it back."

Ansset's gaze did not swerve. "I knew you would not know it when I sang from myself."

"It was you that did not know," Esste said. "We're going home."

"I was to have a month."

"You don't need a month here. Nothing here will change you."

"Am I an eel?"

"Are you a stone?"

"I'm a child."

"It's time you remembered that."

He offered no resistance. She led him to the hotel, where they gathered their things and left Bog before morning. It all failed, Esste thought. I had thought that the mixture of humanity here would open him. But all he found was what he already had. Inhumanity. An impregnable wall. And proof that he can do to people whatever he wants.

He had read the audience of strangers too well. It was something that had never happened at the Songhouse before. Ansset was not just a brilliant singer. He could hear the songs in people's hearts without their having to sing; could hear them, could strengthen them, could sing them back with a vengeance. He had been forced into the mold of the Songhouse, but he was not made of such malleable stuff as the others. The mold could not fit.

What will break? Esste wondered. What will break first?

She did not for a moment believe it would be the Songhouse. Ansset, for all his seeming strength, was far more fragile than that. If he goes to Mikal like this, Esste realized, he will do the opposite of all my plans for him. Mikal is strong, perhaps strong enough to resist Ansset's perversion of his gift. But the others: Ansset would destroy them. Without meaning to, of course. They would come to drink again and again at his well, not knowing it was themselves they drank until they were dry.

He slept in the bus. Esste put her arms around him, held him, and sang the love song to him over and over in his sleep.

13 "I haven't time for this," Esste said, allowing her voice to sound irritated.

"Neither have I," Kya-Kya answered defiantly.

"The schools on Tew are excellent. Your stipend is more than adequate."

"I have been accepted at the Princeton Government Institute."

"It will cost ten times as much to support you on Earth. Not to mention the cost of getting you there. And the inconvenience of having to give it to you in a lump sum."

"You earn ten times that amount from a single year's payment on a Songbird."

True enough. Esste sighed inwardly. Too much today. I was not ready to face this girl. What Ansset has not taken from me, exhaustion has. "Why Earth?" she asked, knowing that Kya-Kya would recognize the question as the last gasp of resistance.

"Earth, because in my field I'm a Songbird. I know that's hard for you to admit, that someone can actually do something excellent that isn't singing, but——"

"You can go. We will pay."

The tone of voice was dismissal. The very abruptness and unconcern of it made her victory feel almost like a letdown. Kya-Kya waited for a few moments, then went to the door. Stopped. Turned around and asked, "When?"

"Tomorrow. Have the bursar see me."

Esste turned back to the papers on her table. Kya-Kya took advantage of her inattention to look around the High Room. I chose you for this place, Kya-Kya thought, trying to feel superior. It didn't work. It was as Hrrai had said— she made the obvious choice. Anyone who knew the Songhouse would have named Esste to the office.

The room was cold, but at least all the shutters were closed. There were drafts, but no wind. Apparently Esste did not intend to die soon. Kya-Kya looked at the window where she had almost fallen out. With the shutters closed, it was just another window, or part of the wall. The room was not kilometers above the ground; it was as low as any other building; the Songhouse was just a building; she did not care whether she never saw it again, felt no lingering fondness for its stone, refused to dream of it, did not even demean herself by disparaging it to her friends at the university.

Her fingers brushed the stone walls as she left.

Esste looked up at the sound of Kya-Kya's leaving. Finally gone. She picked up the paper that concerned her far more than the needs of a Deaf who was trying to avenge her failure.

Songmaster Esste:
Mikal has called me to Earth to serve in his palace guard. He has also instructed me to bring his Songbird back with me. It is my understanding that the child is nine. I have no choice but to obey. I have arranged my route, however, so that Tew is my last stop. You have twenty-two days from the date of this message. I regret the abruptness of this, but I will carry out my orders. Riktors Ashen.

The letter had been transmitted that morning. Twenty-two days. And the worst of it is, Ansset is ready. Ready. Ready.

I am not ready.

Twenty-two days. She pushed a button under the table. "Send Ansset to me."

14 Rruk had just entered Stalls and Chambers, right on schedule. She had no power in her voice, but she was a sweet singer, and pleased everyone who heard her. Still, she was afraid. Stalls and Chambers was a greater step than those between Groan and Bell or Bell and Breeze. Here she was one of the youngest, and in her chamber she *was* the youngest. Only one thing helped her forget her timidity—this was the seventh chamber. Ansset's chamber.

"Will Ansset come?" Rruk asked a boy sitting near her.

"Not today."

Rruk did not show her disappointment; she sang it.

"I know," said the boy. "But it hardly matters. He never sang here anyway."

Rruk had heard rumors of that, but hadn't believed them. Not let Ansset sing? But it was true. And she murmured a song of the injustice of Ansset's banning.

"Don't I know it," said the boy. "I once sang just such a song in Chamber. My name's Ller."

"Rruk."

"I've heard of you. You're the one who first sang the love song to Ansset."

It was a bond—they both had given something, even dared something for Ansset. Chamber began then, and their conversation ceased. Ller was part of a trio that day. He took the high part, and did a thin high drone that changed only rarely. Yet it was still the controlling voice in the trio, the center to which the other two voices always returned. By subordinating his own virtuosity, he had made the song unusually good. Rruk liked him even more, for his own sake now, not just for Ansset's.

After Chamber, without particularly deciding it, they went to Ansset's stall. "He was called to the Songmaster in the High Room just before Chamber. Perhaps he'll be back now. Usually Esste comes to him as master, so it may be that she called him up there to lift the ban."

"I hope so," Rruk said.

They knocked at Ansset's door. It opened, and Ansset stood there regarding them absently.

"Ansset," Ller said, and then fell silent. Any other child they could have asked directly. But Ansset's long isolation, his unchildlike expression, his apparent lack of interest—they were difficult obstacles to surmount.

When the silence had lasted too long, Rruk blurted, "We heard you went to the High Room."

"I did," Ansset said.

"Is the ban lifted?"

Ansset again looked at them in silence.

"Oh," said Rruk. "I'm sorry." Her voice told how sorry.

It was then that Ller noticed that Ansset's blankets were rolled together.

"Are you leaving?" Ller asked.

"Yes."

"Where?" Ller insisted.

Ansset went to the blanket, picked it up, and came back to the door. "The High Room," he said. Then he walked by them and headed down the corridor.

"To live there?" Ller asked.

Ansset did not answer.

15

"This was not a job for a seeker," the seeker said.

"I know," Esste answered, and she sang him an apology that pleaded the necessity of the work.

Mollified, the seeker made his report. "I spent the income from a decade of singers getting into the secret files of the child market. Doblay-me is a simple place to do business. If you have enough money and know whom to give it to, you can accomplish anything."

"You found?"

"Ansset was kidnapped. His parents are very much alive, would pay almost anything to get him back. And when he was taken, he was old enough to know his parents. To know they didn't want him to go. Stolen from them at a theatre. The kidnapper I talked to is now a petty government official. Taxes or something. I had to hire some known killers in order to scare him into talking to me. Very unpleasant business. I haven't been able to sing in weeks."

"His parents?"

"Very rich. The mother a very loving woman. The father—his songs are more ambiguous. I'm not a great judge of adults, you know that. I haven't needed to be. But I had the feeling there were guilts in him that he was afraid of. Perhaps he could have done more to get Ansset back. Or perhaps the guilts are for other things entirely. Completely unrelated. According to the law, now that you and I know this, it's a capital offense not to give the boy back."

Esste looked at him, sang a few notes, and both of them laughed. "I know," the seeker said. "Once in the Songhouse, you have no parents, you have no family."

"The parents don't suspect?"

"To them their little boy is Byrwyn. I told them that the psychotic child in our hospital on Murrain had the wrong blood type to be their son."

A knock on the door.

"Who?"

"Ansset," came the answer.

"May I see him?" the seeker said.

"You may see him. But don't speak to him. And when you leave, bar the door from the other side. Tell the Blind that I'll be taking my meals through the machines. No one is to come up. Messages through the computer."

The seeker was puzzled. "Why the isolation?"

"I am preparing Mikal's Songbird," Esste said.

Then she arose and went to the door and opened it. Ansset came in, holding his blanket roll unconcernedly. He looked at the seeker without curiosity. The seeker looked at him, too, but not so unemotionally. Two years of tracing Ansset's past had given the boy unusual importance in the seeker's eyes. But as the seeker watched, and saw the emptiness of Ansset's face, he let himself show grief, and he sang his mourning to Esste, briefly. She had told him not to speak. But some things could not. Should not go unsaid.

The seeker left. The bar dropped into place on the other side of the door. Ansset and Esste were alone.

Ansset stood before Esste for a long time, waiting. But this time Esste had nothing to say. She simply looked at him, her face as blank as his, though because of age some expression was permanently inscribed there and she could not look as empty of personality as he. The wait seemed interminable to Esste. The boy's patience was greater than most adults'. But it broke, eventually. Still silent, Ansset went to the stone bench beside one of the locked shutters and sat down.

First victory.

Esste was able, now, to go to the table and work. Papers came from the computer; she wrote by hand notes to herself; wrote by keys messages into the computer. As she worked, Ansset sat silently on the bench until his body grew tired and cold. Then he got up, walked around. He did not try the door or the shutters. It was as if he already grasped the fact that this was going to be a test of wills, a trial of strength between his Control and Esste's. The doors and windows would be no escape. The only escape would be victory.

Outside it grew dark, and the light from the cracks in the shutters disappeared. There was only the light over the table, which almost no one ever saw in use—the illusion of primitiveness was maintained before everyone possible, and only the staff and the Songmasters knew that the High Room was not really so bare and simple as it seemed. The purpose of it was not really illusion, however. The Songmaster of the High Room was invariably someone who had grown up in the chilly stone halls and Common Rooms and Stalls and Chambers of the Songhouse. Sudden luxury would be no comfort; it would be a distraction. So the High Room seemed bare except when necessity required some modern convenience.

Ansset sat in the gloom in a corner of the High Room as Esste finally closed the table and laid out her own blankets on the floor. Her movement gave him permission to move. He spread out his own blankets in the far corner, wrapped himself in them, and was asleep before Esste.

The second day passed in complete silence, as did the

third, Esste working most of the day at the computer, Ansset standing or walking or sitting as it pleased him, his Control never letting a sound pass his lips. They ate from the machine in silence, silently went to the toilet in a corner of the room, where their wastes were consumed by an incredibly expensive disturbor in the walls and floor.

Esste found it hard, however, to keep her mind on her work. She had never been so long without music in her life. Never been so long without singing. And in the last few years, she had never passed a day without Ansset's voice. It had become a vice, she knew—for while Ansset was banned from singing to others in the Songhouse, his voice was always singing in his stall, and they had conversed for hours many times. Her memory of those conversations, however, maintained her resolution. An intellect far beyond his years, a great perception of what went on in people's minds, but no hint of anything from his own heart. This must be done, she said. Only this can break his walls, she said to herself. And I must be strong enough to need him less than he needs me, in order to save him, she cried to herself silently.

Save him?

Only to send him to the capital of mankind, to the ruler of humanity. If he has not found a way to tap the deep wells of himself by then, Ansset will never escape. There his very closedness would be applauded, honored, adored. His career would be made, but when he came back to the Songhouse at the age of fifteen there would be nothing there. He would never be able to teach; only to sing. And he would be a Blind. That would kill him.

That would kill me.

And so Esste remained silent for three days, and on the fourth night she was wakened from her sleep by Ansset's voice. He was not awake. But the voice had to come out. In his sleep he was singing, meaningless, random ditties, half of them childish songs taught to new ones and Groans. But in his sleep his Control had broken, just a little.

The fourth day began with complete silence again, as if the pattern could be repeated forever. But sometime during the day Ansset apparently reached a decision, and, when the High Room was warmest in the afternoon, he spoke.

"You must have a reason for your silence, but *I* don't have a reason for mine except that you're being silent. So if you were just trying to get me to stop being stubborn and talk, I'm talking."

The voice was perfectly controlled, the nuances suggesting a *pro forma* surrender, but no real recognition of defeat. A slight victory, but only a slight one. Esste showed no notice of the fact that Ansset had spoken. She was grateful, however, not so much because it was another step forward as because it meant she could hear Ansset's voice again. Ansset speaking with perfect Control was only slightly closer to her objective than Ansset silent with perfect Control.

When she did not answer, Ansset fell silent again, occasionally exercised as before, said nothing for several hours. But at nightfall, when Esste laid out her blanket and Ansset laid out his, he began to sing. Not in his sleep, this time. The songs were deliberately chosen, gentle melodies that pleased Esste very much. They made her feel confident that everything would work out fine, that her worries were meaningless, that Ansset would be fine. After a while they even made her feel that Ansset was already fine, and she had been exaggerating her fears because of her concern for him in the frightening placement he would be facing.

She startled. Her Control gave no outward sign, but

inwardly she was furious with herself. Ansset was using his voice on her, using his gift. He had sensed her mood of worry and her wish for peace and was playing on it, trying to put her off her guard.

I'm out of my class, she realized. I'm a Groan trying to sing a duet with a Songbird. How can my silence compare to his singing as a weapon in this battle?

He sang that night for hours, and she lay awake resisting him by concentrating on the problems and concerns of the Songhouse. The pressure from Stivess to open the northwest section, which the Songhouse almost never used, to oil exploration. The complaints by Wood that pirates were using the desert islands in the southwest as bases from which to pillage shipping in the gulf. The question of where to invest the incredible amount the emperor would pay each year to have a Songbird. The damage that would be done when Mikal the Terrible actually received a Songbird and the rest of mankind, to whom the Songhouse had seemed like the one inviolable institution left in the galaxy, lost faith and supposed that for money, or under pressure, even the Songhouse had lowered its standards.

All these thoughts were enough to occupy days and weeks under normal circumstances. But Ansset's songs played around the edges and while she was no longer trapped by them, she also could not completely escape them. Even after Ansset gave up and went to sleep, she lay awake, dreading the next day. I was worried about how this would affect the boy, she thought ironically. It's my Control that's in danger, not his.

Ansset sang to her sporadically through the next day, and she found that, awake, she could resist him better than in the weariness of evening. Yet the resistance took effort, and when evening came she was even more tired than before, and the ordeal was even harder.

But her Control did not break, and while Ansset could sense emotions that her Control hid from others, he apparently did not realize how close he had come to success. On the sixth day he fell silent again, much to her relief. And he showed signs of the tension on him. He exercised more often. He looked at her more often. And he touched the door twice.

16 Is she insane? It occurred to Ansset more than once. He could conceive of no reason for her to have locked him up in absolute silence. Neither silence nor singing did any good. What did she want?

Does she hate me? That question had arisen often enough in the last few years. During his ban he had found the pressure almost unendurable. But he trusted her—whom else could he trust? It was terrible to know that everyone was wondering what he had done wrong, when he knew but could not tell them that he had done *nothing* wrong. And her mad ideas about his mind—often he could not understand what she was getting at, but sometimes he felt he was getting closer. She accused him of not singing from himself. And yet he knew that his singing was exhilaration, the one great joy of his life. To look at people and understand them and sing to them and change them; he almost re-created them, almost felt as if he could take them and make them over, make them better than they were. How could this not be coming from himself?

And now silence. Silence until his head ached. In all his life there had been no such silence, and he didn't know what to make of it. Why did you become so close to me, if you only meant to cut me off? And yet she wasn't cutting him off, was she; here he was in the High Room, spending every moment with her. No, she wasn't just trying to hurt him. There was a purpose in this. Some insane purpose.

Somehow she has misunderstood me. It made Ansset sad that everyone so consistently failed to understand him. The children couldn't be expected to; the masters and teachers hardly knew him; but Esste. Esste knew him as completely as anyone could. I have sung every song I have to her, and she has refused them all. I showed her that I could sing to a theatre of strangers and change them, and she told me I had failed. She can't admit that I can do any good.

Is she jealous? She was a Songbird herself. Can she see that I'm better than her, and does that make her want to hurt me? This thought appealed to him because it offered some rational explanation. It *might* be true, while insanity was clearly out of the question no matter how often he tried to persuade himself of it. Jealousy.

If she realized it, she wouldn't persecute him anymore. They could be friends again, like that day on the mountain by the lake, when she taught him Control. He had not understood it before then. But the lake—that was clear, that had told him the *reason* for Control. It wasn't just a matter of *not* crying, of *not* laughing, of holding still when told to, all the meaningless things that he had struggled with and hated and resented as he studied in the Common Rooms. Control was not to tie him down, but to fill him up. And the very day of that lesson, he had relaxed, had allowed Control to become, not something outside himself that pressed him in, but something inside himself that kept him safe. I have never been happier. Life has never been easier, he thought at the time. It was as if the anger and fear that had constantly plagued him before had disappeared. I became a lake, he thought, and only when I sing does anything come out. Even then, the singing is easy, it

comes lightly and naturally. Because of Control I can see
sorrow and know its song. It doesn't make me afraid as it
did before—it gives me music. Death is music, and pain,
and joy, and everything that people feel—it is all music. I
let it all in and it fills me up and only music comes out.

What is she trying to do? She doesn't know.

I have to help her. I have used my music to help strangers
in Step, to awaken sleeping souls in Bog. But I have never
used it to help Esste. She's troubled and doesn't know why,
and thinks that it's my fault. I will show her what it is she
really fears, and then perhaps she will understand me.

When I sang before, I tried to calm her fear. This time I
will show it to her more clearly than she has ever seen it.

And with that decision made, Ansset slept on the eighth
night of his stay in the High Room. He gave no outward
sign, of course, of what had passed through his mind. His
body had been as rigid as when he sang, as when he slept.

17 Ansset did not sit on the periphery of the room or
exercise periodically as he had before. On the eighth day
of the confinement he sat in the middle of the floor,
directly before the desk, and looked at Esste as she worked.
He is going to attack today, Esste immediately concluded,
and braced herself inwardly. But she was not ready. There
was no brace to cope with what Ansset did to her today.

His singing was sweet, but not reassuring. Instead the
song kept forcing memories into her mind. He had found
the melody of nostalgia. She struggled (outwardly placid)
to keep working. But as she went over reports of lumbering operations in the White Forest she no longer felt like
Esste, the aging Songmaster of the High Room. She felt

like Esste, Polwee's Songbird, and instead of stone walls she saw crystal out of the corners of her eyes.

Crystal of the palace Polwee had built for his family on the face of a snow-covered granite mountain, a palace that looked more like nature's work than the mountain around it. All the world seemed artificial once she had seen Polwee's home. But she remembered it better from inside than out. The sun shining through a thousand prisms into every room, a hundred moons rising wherever she looked at night, floors that seemed invisible, rooms whose proportions were all wrong and yet completely perfect, and more than all the beauty of the place, the beauty of the people.

Polwee was the easiest placement anyone could remember. He had come to the Songhouse to apply for a Songbird or a singer only a few weeks before Esste was ready to be placed. He had talked to Songmaster Blunne and in the first minute she had said, "You may have a Songbird." He had never asked the price, and when it came time to pay, he never minded that it was half his wealth. "All my wealth would have been worth it," he told her when she left to return to the Songhouse at the age of fifteen. Only good people had come, only kind people, and in Polwee's palace there was always love and joy to sing about.

Love and joy and Greff, Polwee's son.

(I cannot remember this, said a place in Esste's mind, and she tried to continue with her work, but now it was the High Room that was at the periphery of her vision and the reality was all crystal and light. She sat stiffly at the table, her Control keeping her from betraying any emotion, but utterly unable to work or pretend to work because Ansset's song carried too far, deeply into her.)

Greff was his father's son. Concerned more for her happiness than his from the moment she arrived. He was ten and she was nine; and the last year the drug's effects began to wane and Esste reached puberty only a few months ahead of schedule. It had no effect on her voice yet, and showed only slightly in her body. But Greff was growing an adolescent mustache, and he was even more tender than before, touched with shyness that made her feel an infinite fondness, and they had made love quite by accident as snow fell on the crystal one winter.

It was not forbidden, was not really even a failure of Control—she had sung throughout, and learned new melodies as she did. But she did not want to leave him. She realized that Greff was more important to her than anybody in the Songhouse. Who had ever loved her like this? Whom had she ever loved? She tried to be rational, to tell herself that she had been nearly seven years, almost half her life with Greff as her closest friend, that, no matter how she felt about him, she was a creature of the Songhouse and would not be happy living outside forever.

It made no difference. The Songmaster came to take her home, and she refused to come.

The Songmaster was patient. He was still in middle age; it would be years before he would be named Songmaster of the High Room, and Nniv had not learned the brusqueness that enabled him to bear later, heavier responsibilities. So instead of arguing, Nniv merely asked Polwee if he could stay for a while. Polwee was concerned. "I didn't know anything about it," he kept saying, but as Nniv later sang to Esste, "It wouldn't have mattered if he knew, would it?" Of course it wouldn't. Esste was in love with Greff from their first childish romps through the crystal the year she arrived.

The longer Nniv stayed, the more patiently he waited, the more the memory of the Songhouse became important to her. She began to remember her teachers, her master, singing in Chamber. She began to spend more time with Nniv. One day she sang a duet with him. The next day she came home.

(Ansset's song did not relent. Esste had not remembered this day in years. And had never remembered it with such clarity. But she could not resist him, and she lived through it again.)

"I'm going, Greff."

And Greff looked at her with surprise on his face, hurt in his voice as he spoke. "Why? I love you."

What could she explain? That the children of the Songhouse needed other singers as much as they needed to sing? He'd never understand that. She tried to tell him anyway.

"Esste, Esste, *I* need you! Without your songs——"

That was another thing. The songs—she would always have to perform, forever if she stayed with Greff. She could not refuse to sing, but already, after only seven years, singing for people whose only songs were coarse approximations of what they thought and felt, or (worse yet) lies, she was weary of it.

"You don't have to sing if you don't want to!" Greff cried, desperation in his voice, tears on his face. "Esste, what has this Songmaster done to you? You were prepared to defy armies in order to stay with me, and suddenly today you don't care about any of that, you're ready to leave me without a second thought."

She remembered his embrace, his kisses, his pleading, but even then her Control had worked, and he finally backed away, hurt beyond describing because her body had been cold to him. Patiently she explained the one reason he would understand. She told him about the drug that put off puberty for years, how the drug had no permanent effect beyond the one that counted—singers and Songbirds were sterile for life. "Why else do you think we bring children in from outside? It wouldn't do for children to be born in the Songhouse. We'd be more concerned with being parents than with being singers. I can't marry you. There'd be no children.''

But he insisted, demanded. He didn't care about children, just cared about her, and she finally realized that love wasn't just giving, it was also——

(I don't want to remember this! But Ansset's song did not give up——)

It was also possession, ownership, dependence, self-surrender. She turned and walked out of the room, went to Nniv, told him she was going with him back to the Songhouse. Greff stormed into the room, a bottle of pills in his hand, threatening to kill himself if she left. She had no answer for him, only wished that he had been able to take it with grace, only wished that people outside the Songhouse could also learn Control, for it smoothed pain as nothing else in life could. So she told him, ''Greff, I'm going because Nniv and I sang a duet last night. You can never sing with me, Greff. So I can't stay with you.''

She turned and left. Nniv afterward told her that Greff swallowed the poison. Of course he was saved—in a house full of servants suicide is difficult to accomplish and Greff had no real intention of dying, just of forcing Esste to stay with him.

It had taken all of Esste's Control, however, not to turn back, not to change her mind at the entrance of the starship and plead for a chance to stay with Greff.

Control had saved her. And Ansset's song insisted:

Leave me in Control. Do not break my Control.

It was night. She sat by the table, the electric light on overhead. Ansset was asleep in his corner of the room. She did not know how long ago he had gone to sleep, how long ago his song had ended, or how long she had sat stiffly by the table. Her arms hurt, her back ached, the tears that her Control had barely contained pressed behind her eyes and she knew that the victory today had been

Ansset's. There was no way he could know what parts of
her past were most painful—but his singing could evoke
those memories anyway, and she dreaded the morning.
Dreaded the morning and the songs Ansset would sing, but
she lay down anyway, slept instantly, dreamed nothing,
and the night passed in a moment.

18 Riktors Ashen arrived unannounced on the planet
Garibali, his last stop but one before Tew. He preferred to
arrive unannounced on Mikal's errands. Yet there was no
sign that he had flustered anyone; there was no panic when
he presented his credentials at customs. The official there
had simply bowed, asked him his preference of hotel, and
arranged a private car to take him there. It disturbed
Riktors because it meant that things here were worse than
reports had hinted. The problem might be just the nation of
Scale, where he had landed, or it might be the whole
world, but they had been expecting an imperial messenger—
and on a nominally free world, that meant that they knew
there was some reason an imperial messenger ought to
come.

Someone had been busy calling. The hotel staff was
ready for him when he arrived. Riktors watched with
amusement as the elaborate courtesy occasionally gave
way to terror—in the hotel, at least, Mikal's emissary had
not been looked for.

There was a woman waiting for him in his room.

Riktors closed the door. "Are you an official or a
whore?" he asked.

She shrugged. "An official whore, perhaps?" She smiled.
She was nude.

Riktors was unimpressed. However efficient they were in Scale, they certainly had no taste. "Talaso," he said.

"Yes?" she asked, puzzled.

"I want to see him."

"Oh, no," she said helplessly. "I can't do *that*."

"I think you can. I think you will."

"But no one sees him without an appoint—"

"I have an appointment." He reached out his hand, touched her neck almost affectionately. But there was a small dart in his hand, and though she winced at the sudden, sharp sting, the drug worked quickly.

"Talaso?" she asked sleepily.

"Immediately."

"I don't know," she said.

"But you know who *does*."

She led him out of the hotel. He did not bother dressing her; she was incapable of feeling any shame under the drug, and Riktors felt it appropriate. Symbolic, perhaps, that the entire world stood naked before him.

It required the drugging of another confused official before Riktors Ashen stood outside the door of Talaso's office. Talaso's receptionist called the guard, of course, and there were three soldiers with weapons leveled, prepared to kill Riktors before he was allowed to enter. But then the door opened and Talaso himself stood there, poised and self-assured.

"Let Mr. Ashen come in, please. I meant to see him tomorrow, but since he is so impatient I will see him now."

Reluctantly the guards let him by, and Riktors entered the room. He immediately began the formal accusation. "You are known to be constructing starships capable of military activity. You are known to be overtaxing. You are suspected of having a police force three times the legal maximum, and you are accused of dominating and requiring tribute from at least four other nations on Garibali. The facts, the suspicions, and the accusations are enough to bring you to trial before the emperor. If you resist arrest, I am authorized to pass judgment and execute sentence myself. The charge is treason; you are under arrest.''

Talaso did not lose his smile. Perhaps, Riktors thought, perhaps he does not realize the danger. Or he thought that because my tone was so matter-of-fact he could resist or delay or argue.

''Mr. Ashen, these are serious charges.''

''You will come with me immediately,'' Riktors said.

''Of course I honor the emperor, but—''

''This is not your trial, I have no time to listen to your protests, and it will do you no good. Come along, Talaso.''

''Mr. Ashen, I have responsibilities here. I can't just leave them on a moment's notice.''

Riktors looked at his watch. ''Any further delay or attempt at delay will constitute the treasonous crime of resisting the emperor's arrest, for which the penalty is death.''

''You forget,'' said Talaso, ''that I have three guards standing behind you and you made the foolish mistake of coming to my nation, to my city, alone.''

''Whatever gave you the idea that I am alone?'' Riktors asked mildly.

Talaso looked irritated; this, Riktors knew, was his first realization that he just might have been too confident. ''You are the only passenger who debarked from a registered passenger ship.''

''The emperor's soldiers have already won complete control of the port, Talaso.''

''It's a passenger ship!'' Talaso said angrily. ''You can't fool me. The sealed identifier declares it to be a passenger ship! The identifiers are absolutely tamperproof—''

''By the emperor's own decree,'' Riktors said.

"Shoot him," Talaso said to the guards, who stood with their lasers in hand. But they were already collapsing from the drug Riktors had released by clamping the muscles of his buttocks tightly while scuffing his boot along the floor. Talaso's terror suddenly won out, and he was trembling and shouting for help as he fumbled for a weapon in his desk.

"Talaso, you are guilty of treason, sentenced to death; look at me."

Talaso tried to hide behind the desk; but he did look at Riktors, just for a moment. Just long enough for Riktors's dart to strike him in the eye.

Talaso clutched at his face; then the poison struck. He vomited violently, so violently that his jaw dislocated. He sprawled on the desk until the spasms began. His muscles contracted sharply. He jerked and flopped over like a fish drowning in air, until one of the spasms struck with such force that his neck broke. Then he lay still, his hair matted with his own vomit, his face turned at an angle from his shoulders that it could never have assumed in life.

Riktors grimaced. It was an unpleasant business, serving as Mikal's emissary. Still, he had done it well enough these past years, and at last he had been promoted to the palace guard. He could have been moved into the job of assassin, an ugly business of stealth and well-contrived natural deaths, a dead-end assignment. Riktors was sure he would have been a good assassin, and he had good friends among that most private group—but much better to govern. That was the part of his job that Riktors actually liked, and thank God the emperor had chosen to let him follow that path instead of the other.

He turned and opened the door. More guards had just arrived. Riktors killed them all, along with Talaso's receptionist and the official whore and the confused official who had led him here.

Then he called in other bureaucrats from nearby rooms. He brought them into Talaso's office and showed them the corpse. "I assume there was holographic recording equipment running," he said. There was. "Duplicate it and broadcast it immediately throughout Scale and all over the world." The official he looked at was confused. "My friend," Riktors said, "I don't care much what your job has been before. I am the government of Scale now, in the name of the emperor Mikal, and you will do what I say or you will die."

The corpses around him were proof enough of power. The official left quickly, and Riktors continued giving orders, already setting in motion the changes that had to be complete in a week for him to stay on schedule, that had to be so thorough that no new dictator could spring up on Garibali for centuries. He picked up the phone and called the port. His second-in-command had been waiting for his call.

"Proceed," Riktors said. "I have Talaso here, dead of course, and we're moving well."

"And I have a message for you from the emperor. His agents on Clike have found that the rumors were unfounded and your visit there has been canceled. He orders you to proceed to Tew when this work is accomplished."

Tew. The Songhouse, and Mikal's Songbird. "Then would you please inform the Songhouse we will be arriving a week earlier than we anticipated." Courtesy could not be forgotten, not if the machinery of government were to run smoothly. The Songhouse. That frozen, frightening woman, Esste, and the beautiful child who would not sing for him. Petty politicians and adventurers like Talaso were easy to handle. But how to fight with singers, how to win a gift that could only be given freely—those were questions whose answers could not be found. That was an assignment that could not be handled routinely, and if he

succeeded it would be because they let him succeed, and if
he failed it would mean the end of his career, the whimsical end to his ambition because he had once happened to
be the soldier nearest to Tew that Mikal Imperator could
trust.

Damnable bad luck.

He sat down at the receptionist's desk and began to
reorganize the government of Scale while his soldiers took
control of every other government on Garibali, one by
one, and placed the rule of two billion people in Riktors's
hands. In the delight of power, Riktors soon put the Songbird far into the back of his mind, where he need not
worry. Not just yet, anyway.

19 It was the fourth day that Ansset had tormented
Esste. It was near dark outside, and the High Room was
growing cold. He had stopped singing an hour ago, but he
could not move. He sat in the middle of the floor and
looked at Esste and was afraid.

She sat still, her eyes open, looking forward but seeing
nothing. Her hands rested on the table in front of her. She
had not moved from that position since Ansset began his
song in the morning.

And now he was full of doubt. He did not understand
what was happening to her. The first time he had been
excited because he had actually changed her. While her
Control had held and she still remained silent, she had
stopped work, had lost her struggle to concentrate on the
computer in the table. He had thought the end would come
the next day. But the next day she had held on, and the
next, and today he realized that she was not going to

break. He knew that these were the songs that would make her afraid. But he had no idea what fears he had summoned up.

Each night he had gone to sleep with her frozen at the table; each morning he had awakened to find her asleep in the blankets. When she woke she said nothing, hardly looked at him, just got up, ate, went to the table, and began work. Each day he had started to sing and, each time a little sooner, she had stopped working and taken her day-long pose of studied inattention.

What am I doing to her behind her face?

Ansset felt restless, felt that he had to move. He delayed (Control) and when he got up he got up slowly (Control) and did not walk back and forth but instead headed directly for a shutter and tried to open it and realized that the very attempt was a sign that his Control was slipping. At the thought he was instantly aware of the walls of rock inside him, the deep placid lake that grew ever deeper within them. But something was stirring at the bottom of the lake.

He touched the cold stone wall between the windows and heard the whine of wind outside. Perhaps the first storm of fall was coming. Why had she brought him here? What was she trying to achieve?

What have I done to her?

He looked into the lake, looked deep and began to understand what was happening to him. After eleven days in the High Room he was beginning to be afraid. Things were out of his control. He could not leave. He could not force Esste to speak to him, or even to weep or show any sign that she felt anything at all. (Why is it so important that she show a sign of feeling?) And now he was feeling things within the walls of his Control that did not belong there. Fear stirred at the bottom of his calm. Fear, not just of what would happen to him in the High Room, but of what he might have done to Esste. He could not put it into

words, but he realized that if something happened to her,
something would happen to him. There was a connection.
They were linked somehow, he was sure of it. And by
raising her fears he had raised his own. They lurked. They
waited. They were inside his walls and he did not know
how he would be able to control them.

Speak to me, Esste, he said silently. Speak to me and be
angry with me and demand that I change, abuse me or
praise me or sing idiotic songs about the cities of Tew but
stop hiding from me!

She did not look alive or human, her face empty like
that, her body motionless. Human beings moved, their
faces expressed things.

I will not break Control.

"I will not break Control," he sang softly. But in the
moment of singing he knew it was not true, and the fear
moved sluggishly within him.

20 It was her childish nightmare that held her. A
roaring in her ears and a vast invisible globe that grew and
grew and rolled toward her to crush her swallow her fill
her empty her. . . .

And the globe reached her, roaring like a storm at sea.
She was a little girl holding the blanket up tight to her
neck, lying on her back, her eyes wide open, seeing and
not seeing the ceiling of the Common Room, seeing and
not seeing the vast roar that had filled the hall. She opened
her hands to press against the globe, but it was too heavy
and she could not lift her hands against the weight. She
closed her hands into fists, but the stuff of the globe could
not be shut out so simply, and it squeezed in between her

fingers and into her fist so that instead of shutting it out
she was holding it in. If she opened her mouth it would
enter and fill her. If she closed her eyes it would be able to
change without her seeing. And so she lay there hour after
hour until sleep overcame her or until she screamed and
screamed and screamed.

But no one ever came, because she never made a sound.

The stone wall emerged from the shadows. It was dark
night, and the light through the cracks in the shutters was
gone. Ansset was no longer in the middle of the room. She
could see him asleep sitting up in the corner, his blanket
wrapped around him. The wind whistled outside; it was
cold. She reached stiff and painful fingers down to the
computer and made the room warmer. She was inured to
cold, but Ansset was still young. Freezing him to death
would accomplish nothing.

She got up slowly, so that her body could adjust to
movement. Her back protested. But the pains of her body
were nothing. Today had been worse than ever, not a
memory of the past at all, but the terrors of childhood
returned with a vengeance. I cannot last another day of
this.

She had said the same thing to herself yesterday, and yet
she had lasted.

How am I different from him, she wondered. I, too, am
hiding behind my Control. I, too, am unreachable, express
nothing to anyone but what I choose to express. Perhaps if
I unbent, if I broke Control just a little, he, too, would
come out and be human again.

But she knew she would not try the experiment. He
would have to open first. If she moved first it would all
have been wasted, and he would be stronger and she
weaker the next time it was tried. If there was a next time.
Twenty-two days. It was the twelfth night, tomorrow would
be the twelfth day, they were more than halfway through

the time and she had accomplished nothing of importance except that her own strength was flagging and she wondered if she could last another day.

She walked to her blanket roll, and spread the blankets on the floor and bent over to lie down. But in the bending she glanced at the corner where Ansset was sleeping, and she quickly looked up again and stared and realized that Ansset was not asleep as he had been every other time. His eyes were open. He was watching her.

Don't sing! she cried out silently. Let me have peace!

He did not sing. He just watched. And then, in a controlled, quiet voice that expressed no emotion whatsoever he said, "Can we stop now?"

Can we stop now? If it hadn't been for Control she would have laughed hysterically. *He* asks *her* for mercy? His voice was still ice; the battle was still going on; but he had asked for it to end, and somehow that made her feel that she had, after all, made some progress. No. *She* hadn't made the progress. *He* had. It was a sign that maybe this would end.

She slept a little better that night.

In the morning a message waited on the computer. Riktors Ashen had sent a regretful note that the emperor had canceled several of his errands and he would be arriving on Tew a week ahead of schedule. The emperor had been most explicit. The Songhouse had promised him a Songbird. He needed the Songbird now. If the Songbird did not come with Riktors Ashen immediately, Mikal would know that the Songhouse did not intend to keep the promise made by Songmaster Nniv.

A week early. Three days from now.

She ate breakfast with Ansset, silently, and wondered if there was any hope of finishing this now.

Sitting for her day's work at the table, Esste steeled herself for Ansset to sit in the middle of the floor and start

to destroy her with a song. Today it did not happen. Today
Ansset walked around aimlessly, stroking the rock, sitting
down and standing up again almost immediately, trying
the door, trying the shutters. He hummed as he did, but
the humming expressed almost nothing, a hint of impatience, and under that an even fainter hint of fear, but he
was not trying to manipulate her with his voice. At first she
was relieved beyond expression, but soon, as she began to
pursue the work that had gone undone for three days, she
began to worry about Ansset again. Now that he was
giving her a rest from fearing for herself, she could care
about him.

The strain was beginning to show in his face. His eyes
were not empty. They darted back and forth, unable to rest
on one object for long. And he was biting his cheek
occasionally. Control was breaking down. Why now? What
had happened to *him*?

I have to watch him now, very carefully. I'm playing
with fire, playing along the rim of his destruction, I must
know the moment when I can speak to him. He must not
be allowed to pass into despair.

Three days.

In the afternoon Ansset's aimless humming turned into
speech. At first Esste could hardly hear him and wondered
if he was even talking to her. But soon the words became
clearer and, she noticed, he was exactly filling the High
Room with his voice and speaking no louder. The voice
was still under Control; it expressed, but only what he
wanted it to express. "Please please please," said the
controlled careful meticulous voice, "please please please
I've had enough can I please go or will you please say
something to me I don't know what you're trying to
accomplish I don't understand any of this but please I can't
stand it anymore please please please. . . ."

Ansset's voice droned on and he didn't look at Esste,

looked instead at the walls and the windows and the floor and his own hand, which did not tremble when he looked at it but wavered ever so slightly when he did not. She had not seen him move a muscle when he sang in years. This movement was not voluntary, but it was *movement*, and the very involuntariness of it spoke of terrible things going on inside Ansset's mind. She wanted to reach out and comfort him and stop the muscles from trembling. She did not, however. She stayed at the computer and worked as she listened to his voice drone on.

"I'm sorry I made you afraid I'm sorry I'm sorry I'm sorry please can this be over I'm afraid of you I'm afraid of this room let me hear your voice Esste Esste Esste please. . . ."

His voice finally faded into silence again and he sat by the door, his face pressed into the heavy wood.

21 I have begged and she hasn't answered. The whales are swimming deep inside me and she doesn't help. I need help. All the monsters in the world are inside me instead of outside me I've been tricked and trapped and they are inside my walls not outside my walls inside with me and she won't help me. When I stop thinking about a muscle it shakes. When I stop thinking about a fear it leaps at me. I'm drowning but the lake keeps getting deeper and deeper and deeper and I don't know how to get out the walls go up forever and I can't climb over and I can't break through and she won't talk to me.

Ansset pressed his face into the wood of the door until it hurt terribly, and the pain helped.

He remembered. He remembered singing. He could hear

all the voices. He heard Esste's voice criticizing his songs.
He heard the other children in Chamber. He heard the
voices in his class of Breezes and his class of Bells and his
class of Groans. Voices at meals. Voices in the toilet. The
voices of the strangers in Step and Bog. Rruk's voice as
she helped him learn how things were done in the
Songhouse. All the voices sang at once to him but there
was only one voice that he could not recognize, that he
could not hear clearly, a dim and distant voice that he did
not understand.

But it was not a Songhouse voice. It was coarse and
crude and the song was meaningless and empty. But it was
not empty, it was full. It was not meaningless, for he knew
that if he could once hear the song, really hear it through
the din of the other voices, that it would help him, that the
song would mean something to him. And as for coarseness
and crudeness, the song he tried to hear did not jar on him
at all. It made him feel as comfortable as sleep, as comfortable as eating, as the satisfaction of all the miserable
desires. He strained to hear, he pressed his face into the
wood, but the voice would not come clear.

Not for hours, and he rubbed his face back and forth
against the wood, and threw himself to the stone floor, so
the pain would drive all the other voices out of his mind,
would let him hear the one voice he searched for, because
that was the voice that would save him from the terror that
swam every moment closer to the surface where he watched
and waited helplessly.

22 The vigil lasted all night. Esste watched as Ansset drove the splinters of the door into his nose and brow and cheeks until blood flowed. She watched as he tried to grip and tear the stone until his nails broke. She watched as he slammed his face into the rock walls until he bled and she feared he would cause permanent damage. It seemed he would never sleep. And in between the self-mutilation he would, in a wooden, controlled voice, his body held as rigid as he could hold it for all the trembling, say, "Now please. Now please. Help me." There was Control, but that was all. No music. His songs were gone.

Just for the moment, she told herself. Just for now. His songs, his good songs, will come back if I just wait for this to run its course, like a fever that has to break.

Morning came and Ansset was still awake. He had stopped thrashing, and Esste went to the machines for food. She set it in front of him, but he did not eat. She reached a piece of it to his mouth, but instead of taking the food he bit her, he set his teeth into her fingers with all his strength. The pain was excruciating, but Esste's Control was not even tested by this—physical pain, at her age, was the least of her weaknesses. She waited patiently, saying nothing. Blood from her fingers drooled out of Ansset's mouth for minutes as both silently looked at each other. And it was Ansset who made the first sound, a moan that sounded like the slow breaking of rock, a song that spoke only of agony and self-hatred. Slowly he released his bite on her fingers. The pain rushed up her arm.

Ansset's eyes went blank. He did not see her.

Esste went to the machine and covered her fingers with salve. She was exhausted after a night of no sleep, and Ansset's savage bite had disturbed her far more than the mere pain. I will stop. This has gone too far, she decided. Her hand shook, despite Control, despite the calm she tried to enforce on herself. I can't do this anymore, she said silently.

But for twelve days she had been silent, and sound did not come easily to her throat. Came with such difficulty, in fact, that as she looked at Ansset's blank face she could not make any sound come. Instead she lay down on her blanket, unused that night, and slept.

She awoke to the sound of wind howling through the High Room. It was cold, icy even under the blanket. It took only a few moments for her to realize what that meant. She leaped up from the floor. It was afternoon, but dark with wind and clouds. The clouds were so low that mist trailed into the High Room with every gust of wind, and the ground was invisible. Every shutter of every window was open, some of them banging against the stone walls outside.

He has jumped from the tower. The thought screamed in her mind, and she gasped aloud.

Her gasp was answered by a moan. She whirled and saw Ansset lying on the table, curled up with the thumb and little finger of his right hand in his mouth, the other fingers pressed into his forehead and eyes like an infant's involuntary pose. The relief that swept over her forced her to lean on the table, taking her breath in great gasps. Any illusion of Control was gone now. Ansset had won, forcing her to break before her task was completed.

The cold forced her to take action again. She went to the windows and closed them all, leaning out over the sills to catch the handles of the shutters and pull them closed. The mist was so dense that it seemed to swallow up her hand as she reached into it. But inside she was singing. Ansset had not jumped.

The windows closed, she returned to the table, and only now realized that Ansset was asleep. He trembled with cold and, probably, exhaustion, but he had not seen her panic, her relief, had not heard her gasp. Her first thought was gratitude, but she realized that it might have been good for him to see that fear for his safety could overcome even Esste's iron reserve. It is as it is, she told herself, and looked in his left hand for the key to the shutters, found it, and went around and locked them all, then replaced the key on the chain which had fallen to the floor after he took it from her neck in her sleep.

She went to the computer and turned up the heat in the High Room. Instantly the stones under her feet grew warm.

Then she took her blanket and Ansset's and covered the boy where he lay on the table. He stirred slightly, moaned and whimpered, but did not awaken.

23 Ansset's face was stiff when he awoke. He was not cold anymore. His head ached, and where the splinters had been driven into his face, the stinging was a constant undercurrent. But he felt something cool touching his face, and wherever it touched, the stinging went away. He opened his eyes just a little. Esste leaned over him, dabbing salve on his face. For the moment Ansset forgot everything bad and carefully said to her, "I didn't jump. They told me to jump and I didn't."

She said nothing. She said nothing at all, nothing at all, and her silence was a blow that knocked him back in on himself, and his struggle returned. The water was rushing up to meet him, a vast whirlpool sweeping higher and higher and Ansset was at the top and there was nowhere higher that he could go to escape it. He looked inside himself and there was no escape and as the water touched him, swept his feet out from under him, bore him in fast, dizzying circles around and around, he screamed. His scream was a voice that filled the High Room and echoed from the walls and shattered the stillness of the mist outside.

He was no longer in the High Room. He was being sucked down into the maelstrom. The water closed over his head. Spinning faster and faster he plunged deeper and deeper toward the mouths of the waiting terrors below. One after another they swallowed him up. He felt himself being swallowed, the massive peristalsis driving him into gullet after gullet, hot warm places where he could not breathe.

And he was walking into a room. Walking and walking but getting no farther into the room than he had been before. And all alone, no other sound, he heard the song he had been searching for. Heard the song and saw the singer, but could not hear and could not see, not really, because the singer had no face that he could recognize, and the song, no matter how carefully he listened, kept escaping the moment after he heard it. He could not hear the melody in his memory, only in the moment, and as he looked at an eye, the other eye vanished, and when he looked for the mouth, the eye he had seen before disappeared.

He was no longer walking, though he had no memory of reaching the woman who lay on the bed. He reached out. He was touching her face. He was stroking her face so very gently, tracing the features, the eyes, the mouth, and the voice sang, "Bi-lo-bye. Bi-lo-bye," but the moment

he understood the words he lost them. Lost them, and the
mist came and swallowed up the face. He clutched for it,
held it, held it tight; she could not disappear from him in
the mist which was all white invisible faces that swallowed
her up. This time he held on tightly and he would not let
go, nothing could pull him away.

He heard the song again, heard the song and it was
exactly the same song and this time the words were:

> *I will never hurt you.*
> *I will always help you.*
> *If you are hungry*
> *I'll give you my food.*
> *If you are frightened*
> *I am your friend.*
> *I love you now*
> *And love does not end.*

He knew where he was now. Somehow he had been
pulled from the lake. He lay on the shore of the lake and
he was dry and safe and the song he had been searching
for had at last been found. He still gripped the face tightly,
clinging to the hair, holding the face close over his own as
he lay there, and he knew her at last, and cried for joy.

24 Ansset lay across Esste's lap, his hands frantically gripping her hair, when at last his violent shaking stopped, and his jaw slackly opened, and his eyes at last focused and he saw her.

"Mama," he cried, and there was no song but childhood in his voice.

Esste opened her mouth, and tears poured from her eyes and flew as she blinked to Ansset's cheeks, and she sang from the deepest part of her heart. "Ansset, my only son."

He wept and clung to her, and she babbled meaningless words to him, sang her most soothing songs to him, and held him tightly. They lay on the blankets in the warm High Room as the storm raged outside. As she held his bruised and cut face into her shoulder, she also wept; for two hidden places had been plumbed, and she did not know or care which had been the greater achievement. She had locked him into silence in the High Room in order to cure him; he had returned the favor, and she, too, was healed.

25 It was the afternoon of the fourteenth day. Sunlight streamed through the cracks on the western shutters. Ansset and Esste sat on the floor of the High Room, singing to each other.

Ansset's song was halting, though the melody was high and fine, and his words were all the agony of loss and loneliness as he grew up; but the agony had been transformed, was transformed even as he sang, by the harmony and countermelody of Esste's wordless song which said not to fear, not to fear, not to fear. Ansset's hands danced as he sang, played gently along Esste's arms, face, and shoulders, kept capturing her hands and letting them go. His face was alight as he sang, the eyes were alive, and his body said as much as his voice did. For while his voice spoke of the memory of fear, his body spoke of the presence of love.

26 Riktors Ashen was not sure what to do. Mikal had been emphatic. The Songbird was to return with Riktors Ashen. And yet Riktors knew that he could not achieve anything by blustering or threatening. This was not a national council or a vain dictator on an unsophisticated planet where the emperor's very name could inspire terror. This was the Songhouse, and it was older than the empire, older than many worlds, older than any government in the galaxy. It recognized no nationality, no authority, no purpose except its songs. Riktors could only wait, knowing that delay would infuriate Mikal, and knowing that haste would accomplish nothing in the Songhouse.

At least the Songhouse was taking him seriously enough that they left a full-fledged Songmaster with him, a man named Onn whose every word was reassurance, though in fact he promised nothing at all.

"We're honored to have you here," Onn said.

"You must be," Riktors answered, amused. "This is the third time you've said so."

"Well, you know how it is," Onn said with good cheer. "I meet so few outsiders that I hardly know what to say. You'd hardly enjoy hearing the gossip of the Songhouse, and that's all I know to talk about."

"You'd be surprised at how much interest I'd have in gossip."

"Oh, no. We have singularly boring gossip," Onn said, and then changed the subject to the weather, which had been alternately rainy and sunny for days. Riktors grew impatient. Weather mattered a great deal, he supposed, to the planetbound. To Riktors Ashen weather of any kind was just one more reason to be in space.

The door opened, and Esste herself entered, accompanied by a boy. Blond and beautiful, and Riktors recognized him instantly as Ansset, Mikal's Songbird, and almost said so. Then he hesitated. The boy looked different somehow. He looked closely. There were scratches and bruises on his face.

"What have you been doing to the boy?" asked Riktors, appalled at the thought that the child might have been beaten.

It was Ansset himself who answered, in tones that inspired absolute confidence. The boy could not lie, said his voice: "I fell on the woodpile. I knew better than to play there. I was lucky not to break a bone."

Riktors relaxed, and then realized another, more important reason why the child looked different. He was smiling. His face was alert, his eyes looked warm and friendly. He held Esste's hand.

"Are you ready to come with me?" Riktors asked him.

Ansset smiled and sighed, and both melted Riktors's normal reserve. He liked the boy immediately. "I wish I could come," Ansset said. "But I'm a Songbird, and that means that I must sing to the whole Songhouse before I go." Ansset turned to Esste. "May I invite him to attend?"

Esste smiled, and that surprised Riktors more than the change in Ansset. He hadn't thought the woman knew how to seem anything but stern.

"Will you come?" Ansset asked.

"Now?"

"Yes, if you like." And Ansset and Esste turned and left. Riktors, unsure of himself, looked at Onn, who blandly returned his gaze. I was invited, Riktors decided, and so I can follow them.

They led him to a large hall which was filled with hundreds and hundreds of children who sat on hard benches in absolute silence. Even their bare feet on the stone made little noise as the last of them filed into place. Scattered among them were many teen-agers and adults, and on the stone platform at the front of the hall sat the oldest of them. They were all dressed alike in the drab robes that reached the floor, though none of the children seemed to have clothing that exactly fit. The impression was of poverty until he looked at their faces, which looked exalted.

Esste and Ansset led him to the rear of the hall, at the end of the center aisle. Riktors was surprised to have been given such a poor seat; he did not know, and no one at the Songhouse ever told him, that he was the first outsider in centuries to witness a ceremony in the great hall of the Songhouse.

He did not even know it was a ceremony. Ansset and Esste merely walked, hand in hand, to the front of the hall. Esste stepped onto the platform, then reached down a hand to bring Ansset up. Then the Songmaster retired to a chair on the platform while Ansset stood alone in front, at the head of the aisle, where Riktors could see him clearly.

And he sang.

His voice filled every part of the hall, but there was no resonance from the walls to distort the tone. He rarely sang words, and those he sang seemed meaningless to Riktors. Yet the emperor's envoy was held spellbound. Ansset's hands moved in the air, rising, falling, keeping time with odd rhythms in the music. His face also spoke with the song so that even Riktors, at a distance, could see that the song came from Ansset's soul.

No one in the hall wept, not even the youngest Groans with the least Control. Control was not threatened by Ansset's song, and it did not reflect the feelings of the audience. Indeed, the song divided the audience into every separate individual, for Ansset's song was so private that no two people could hear it the same way. The song made Riktors think of plunging down between planets, though the child could not possibly have experienced a pilot's thrill of vertigo. And when Ansset at last fell silent, the song lingered in the air and Riktors knew he would never forget it. He had shed no tears, felt no terrible passions. Yet the song was one of the most powerful experiences of his life.

Mikal has waited a lifetime for this, Riktors thought.

All the children and adults in the hall arose, though he had seen no cue given. And all of them began to sing, one by one, then all together, until the sheer weight of sound made the air in the hall feel thick and aromatic with melody. They were saying good-bye to Ansset, who alone was silent, who stood without weeping on the platform.

They were still singing as Ansset stepped from the platform, and without looking to the left or the right walked down the aisle to where Riktors waited. Ansset held out his hand. Riktors took it.

"Take me with you," Ansset said. "I'm ready to go."

And Riktors's hand trembled as he led Ansset from the hall, as he took him to the flesket waiting outside that would carry them both to Riktors's starship. Riktors had seen wealth, had seen the opulence of Mikal's palace at Susquehanna, had seen the thousand most beautiful things that people made and bought and sold. None of them was worth the beauty that walked beside him, that held his hand, that smiled at him as the Songhouse door closed behind them.

MIKAL

1   Susquehanna was not the largest city on Earth; there were a hundred cities larger. Perhaps more. But Susquehanna was certainly the most important city. It was Mikal's city, built by him at the confluence of the Susquehanna and West Susquehanna rivers. It consisted of the palace and its grounds, the homes of all the people who worked at the palace, and the facilities for handling the millions of guests every year who came to the palace. No more than a hundred thousand permanent residents.

Most government offices were located elsewhere, all over Earth, so that no one spot would be the center of the planet more than any other. With instant communications, no one needed to be any closer. And so Susquehanna looked more like a normal suburban community—a bit richer than most, a bit better landscaped, better paved, better lit, perhaps, with no industrial wastes whatsoever and utterly no poverty or signs of poverty or even, for that matter, decay.

It was only the third large city Ansset had ever seen in his life. It lacked the violent, heady excitement of Bog, but neither was it weary, as Step had been. And the vegetation was a deeper green than any on Tew, so that while the forest did not tower, and the mountains were sleepy and low, the impression was of lushness. As if the world that had spawned mankind was eager to prove that she was still fecund, that life still oozed out of her with plenty to spare, that mankind was not her only surprise, her only trick to play on the universe.

"It's a proud place," Ansset said.

"What, Earth?" Riktors Ashen asked.

"What have I seen of Earth?"

"The whole planet's like this. Mikal didn't design this city, you know: It was a gift to him."

"The whole planet's like this? Beautiful?"

"No. Trimmed. With its nose in the air. People on Earth are very proud of their place as the 'heart of humanity.' Heart, hell. On the fringe, that's all they are, an insane fringe, too, if you ask me. They cling to their petty national identities as if they were religions. Which they are, I think. Terrible place for a capital—this planet is more fragmented than the rest of the galaxy. There are even independence movements."

"From what?"

"From Mikal. His capital planet, and they think that just a piece of a planet should be free of him." Riktors laughed.

Ansset was genuinely puzzled. "But how can they divide it up? Can they lift a piece of the world up and put it in space? How can they be independent?"

"Out of the mouths of babes."

They rode in a flesket, of course, all transparent except for the view of the road beneath their feet, which would have made them sick to see. It was an hour from the port to the city, but now the palace was in view, a jumble of what seemed to be stone in an odd, intricate style that looked lacy and delicate and solid as the planet itself.

"Most of it's underground, of course," Riktors said.

Ansset watched the building approach, saying nothing. It occurred to Riktors that perhaps the boy was nervous, afraid of the coming meeting. "Do you want to know what he's like?"

Ansset nodded.

"Old. Few men in Mikal's business live to be old.

There have been more than eight thousand plots against the emperor's life. *Since* he got here on Earth."

Ansset did not register emotion until a moment later, and then he did it in a song, a short wordless song of amazement. Then he said, so Riktors could understand, "A man that so many people want to die—he must be a monster!"

"Or a saint."

"Eight thousand."

"Fifty of them actually came close. Two of them succeeded in injuring the emperor. You'll understand the security arrangements that always surround him. People go to great lengths to try to kill him. Therefore we must go to great lengths to try to protect him."

"How," Ansset asked, "did such a man ever earn the right to have a Songbird?"

The question surprised Riktors. Did Ansset really understand his own uniqueness in the universe right now? Was he so vain about being a Songbird that he marveled that the emperor should have one? No, Riktors decided. The boy was only just made a Songbird at the beginning of the flight that brought him here. He still thinks of Songbirds as other, as outside himself. Or does he?

"Earn the right?" Riktors repeated thoughtfully. "He came to the Songhouse years and years ago, and asked. According to the story I heard, he asked for anything—a Songbird, a singer, anything at all. Because he had heard a Songbird once and couldn't live without the beauty of such music. And he talked to the old Songmaster, Nniv. And the new one, Esste. And they promised him a Songbird."

"I wonder why."

"He'd already done most of his killing. His reputation preceded him. I doubt that they were fooled about that. Perhaps they just saw something in him."

"Of course they did," Ansset said, and his voice chided

gently so that suddenly Riktors felt young and vaguely patronized by the child beside him. "Esste wouldn't make a mistake."

"Wouldn't she?" Devil's advocate, Riktors thought. Why do I always play such opposite roles? "There's more than a little grumbling throughout the empire, you know. That the Songhouse has been sold out, sending you to Mikal."

"Sold out? For what price?" Ansset asked mildly. And Riktors resented the scorn in the question.

"Everything has a price. Mikal's paying more for you than for dozens of ships of the fleet. You came for a high price."

"I came to sing," Ansset said. "And if Mikal had been poor, but the Songhouse had decided he should have a Songbird, they would have paid him to take me."

Riktors raised an eyebrow.

"It has happened," Ansset said.

"Aren't you a bit young to know history?" Riktors asked, amused.

"What family doesn't know its own past?"

For the first time Riktors realized that the Songhouse's isolation was not just a technique or a façade to raise respect. Ansset, and by extension all the singers, didn't really feel a kinship with the rest of humanity. At least not a close kinship. "They're everything to you, aren't they?" Riktors asked.

"Who?" Ansset answered, and they arrived. It was just as well. Ansset's *who* was frigid and Riktors could not have pursued the questioning had he wanted to. The child was beautiful, especially now that the scars and bruises had healed completely. But he was not normal. He could not be touched as other children could be touched. Riktors had prided himself on being able to make friends with children easily. But Ansset, he decided, was not a child.

Days together on the flight, and the only thing their relationship had disclosed to Riktors was the fact that they had no relationship. Riktors had seen Ansset with Esste, had seen love as loud as the roar of engines in atmosphere. But apparently the love had to be earned. Riktors had not earned it.

Riktors had been hated by many people. It had never bothered him before. But he knew that, more than any other thing, he wanted this boy to love him. As he had loved Esste.

Impossible. What am I wishing for? Riktors asked himself. But even as he asked himself, Ansset took his hand and they walked off the flesket together, walked into the gate, and Riktors felt what little closeness they had had slipping away from him. He might as well still be on Tew, Riktors decided. He's lightyears away, even holding my hand. The Songhouse has a hold on him that will never let go.

Why the hell am I jealous?

And Riktors shook himself inwardly, and condemned himself for having let the Songhouse and this Songbird weave their spells around him. The Songbird is trained to win love. Therefore, I will not love him. And, once decided, it became very nearly true.

2   The Chamberlain was a busy man. It was the most noticeable thing about him. He bounced slightly on the balls of his feet when he stood; he leaned forward as he walked; so anxious was he to reach his destination that even his feet could not keep up with him. And while he was graceful and interminably slow during ceremonies, his normal conversation was quick, the words tumbling out so

that you dared not let your attention flag for a moment or you would miss something, and to ask him to repeat himself—ah, he would fly into a rage and there would be your promotion for the year, utterly lost.

So the Chamberlain's men were quick, too. Or rather, seemed to be quick. For it did not take long for those who worked for the Chamberlain to realize that his quickness was an illusion. His words were rapid, but his thoughts were slow, and he took five or six conversations to finally get to a point that might have been said in a sentence. It was maddening, infuriating, so that his underlings went to infinite pains to avoid speaking to him.

Which was precisely what he wanted.

"I am the Chamberlain," he said to Ansset, as soon as they were alone.

Ansset looked at him blankly. It took the Chamberlain a bit by surprise. There was usually some flicker of recognition, some half-smile that betrayed nervous awareness of his power and position. From the boy? Nothing.

"You are aware," he went on without waiting any longer for a response, "that I am administrator of this palace, and, by extension, this city. Nothing more. My authority does not extend any farther. Yet that authority includes you. Completely, utterly, without exception. You will do what I say."

Ansset looked at him unblinkingly.

Damn, but I hate dealing with children, the Chamberlain thought. They aren't even the same species.

"You're a Songbird. You're incredibly valuable. Therefore you will not go outside without permission. *My* permission. You will be accompanied by two of my men at all times. You will follow the schedule prepared for you, which will include ample opportunity for recreation. I cannot have you out of my ken at any time. For the price paid for you, we could build another palace like this one and have room left over to outfit an army."

Nothing. No emotion at all.

"Have you nothing to say?"

Ansset smiled slightly. "Chamberlain, I have my own schedules. Those are the ones I will keep. Or I cannot sing."

It was unheard of. The Chamberlain could say nothing, nothing at all as the boy smiled at him.

"And as to your authority, Riktors Ashen already explained everything."

"Did he? What did he explain?"

"You don't control everything, Chamberlain. You don't control the palace guard, which has its own Captain appointed by Mikal. You don't control any aspect of imperial government except palace administration and protocol. And no one, Chamberlain, controls me. Except me."

He had expected many things. But not to have a nine-year-old boy, however beautiful, speak with more command than an admiral of the fleet. Yet the boy's voice was an admirable lesson in strength. The Chamberlain, who was never confused, was thrown into confusion.

"The Songhouse said nothing of this."

"The Songhouse doesn't speak, Chamberlain. I must live in certain ways to be able to sing. If I can't live as I must, then I will go home."

"This is impossible! There are schedules that must be followed!"

Ansset ignored him. "When do I meet Mikal?"

"When the schedule says so!"

"And when will that be?"

"When *I* say so. I make the schedule. I give access to Mikal or I deny access to Mikal!"

Ansset only smiled and hummed soothingly. The Chamberlain felt very much relieved. Later he tried to think why, but couldn't.

"That's better," the Chamberlain said. He was so relieved, in fact, that he sat down, the furniture flowing to fit him perfectly. "Ansset, you have no idea what an incredible burden the office of Chamberlain is."

"You have a lot to do. Riktors told me."

The Chamberlain had very good self-control. He prided himself on it. He would have been distressed to know that Ansset read the flickers of emotion in his voice and knew that the Chamberlain had little love for Riktors Ashen.

"I wonder," the Chamberlain said. "I wonder if perhaps you might just sing something now. Music soothes the savage breast, you know."

"I would love to sing for you," Ansset said.

The Chamberlain waited a moment, then gazed questioningly at Ansset.

"But, Chamberlain," said Ansset, "I'm Mikal's Songbird. I can't sing for anyone until I've met him and he's given his consent."

There was just enough of mockery in the Songbird's voice that the Chamberlain went hot inside, embarrassed, as if he had tried to sleep with his master's wife and found that she was merely amused at him. The child was going to be a horror.

"I'll speak to Mikal about you."

"He knows I'm here. He was quite impatient to have me come, I heard."

"I said that I would speak to Mikal!"

The Chamberlain whirled and left, a quick, dramatic exit; but the drama was spoiled when Ansset's voice came gently after him, gently and yet exactly loud enough that it could have been whispering in his ear: "Thank you." And the *thank you* was full of respect and gratitude so that the Chamberlain couldn't be angry, indeed could think of no reason for anger. The boy was obviously going to be compliant. Obviously.

The Chamberlain went straight to Mikal, something that

only a few were allowed to do, and told him that the Songbird was there and eager to meet him, and was definitely a charming boy, if a bit stubborn, and Mikal said, "Tonight at twenty-two," and the Chamberlain left and told his men what to do and when to do it and adjusted the schedules to fit that appointment and then realized:

He had done exactly what the boy had wanted. He had changed everything to fit the boy.

I have been outclassed, said the sickening feeling in the pit of his stomach.

I hate the little bastard, said the hot flush in his cheeks a moment later.

The contract said he'd be here for six years. The Chamberlain thought of six years and they were long. Terribly, terribly long.

3   The palace had no music.

Ansset finally realized it with relief. Something had been nagging him since he arrived. It was not the impersonal search by the security guards or the casual way that he seemed to be fit into a machine and processed. He expected things to be different, and since everything was strange compared to life in the Songhouse, none of it should have felt "wrong." He had a far from cosmopolitan outlook, but the Songhouse had never allowed him to think that the Songhouse way was "right" and all other ways were not. Rather the Songhouse was home, and this was merely a different place.

But the lack of music. Even Bog had had music, even lazy Step had its own songs. Here the artificial stone that was harder than steel carried little sound; the furniture was

silent as it flowed to fit bodies; the servants went silently
about their business, as did the guards; the only sounds
were of machines, and even they were invariably muffled.

On his visit to Step and Bog, he had had Esste with
him. Someone to whom he could sing and who would
know the meanings of his songs. Someone whose voice
was full of inflection carefully controlled. Here everyone
was so coarse, so unrefined, so careless.

And Ansset felt homesick as he ran his fingers along the
warm stone that was so unlike the cold rock of the walls of
the Songhouse. He hummed in his throat, but these walls
absorbed the sound, reflected nothing. Also, he was hot.
That was wrong. He had been raised in a slightly chilly
building since he was three. This place was warm enough
that he could cast away his clothing and still be a little too
warm. How can they be comfortable?

His unease was not helped by the fact that he had been
alone ever since the obsequious servant had led him to a
room and said, "This is yours." No window, and the door
had no device that Ansset could see for opening. So he
waited and did not sing because he was not sure someone
would not be listening—that much Riktors Ashen had
warned him of. He sat alone in silence and listened to the
utter lack of music in the palace, unwilling to make any of
his own until he had met Mikal, and not knowing when
that would be, or if it would happen at all, or if he would
be left forever in a place where he might as well be deaf.

No.

That is also wrong.

There *is* music here, Ansset realized. But it was cacoph-
ony, not harmony, and so he had not recognized it. In Step
and Bog the moods of the cities had been uniform. While
individuals had had their own songs, they were only variations on a theme, and all had worked together to give the
city a feeling of its own. Here there was no such harmony.

Only fear and mistrust to such a degree that no two voices worked together. As if the very melding of speech patterns and thought patterns and ease of expression might somehow compromise a person dangerously, bring him close to death or darker terrors. That was the music, if he could call it music, of the palace.

What a dark place Mikal has made for himself. How can anyone live in such deafening silence and pain?

But perhaps it is not pain to them, Ansset thought. Perhaps this is the way of all the worlds. Perhaps only on Tew, which has the Songhouse, have voices learned to meet and mix harmoniously.

He thought of the billions of pinpoint stars, each with its planets and each of those with its people, and none of them knew how to sing or hear anyone else's song.

It was a nightmare. He refused to think of it. Instead he thought of Esste, and at the thought of her felt again the wonder of what he held inside himself that she had finally compelled him to find. Remembering her, he could not really see her face—he had left her too recently to be able to conjure her like a ghost. Instead he heard her voice, heard the huskiness of her morning speech, the force in her normal expression. She would not have been made uneasy. She wouldn't have let the silly Chamberlain force her into saying more than she ought. And if she were here, he thought, I would not feel so——

If she were here, she would not let herself feel any of these things. Some Songbirds had had difficult assignments before. Esste, whom he loved and trusted, had put him here. Therefore this was where he belonged. And so he would look for ways to survive, to put the palace to use in his songs, instead of wishing that he were in the Songhouse instead. For this he had been trained. He would give his service and then, when they came for him, he would return.

The door slid open and four security guards came in. They were in different uniforms from those men who had searched him before. They said little, only enough to direct Ansset to take off his clothing. "Why?" Ansset asked, but they only waited and waited until at last he turned his back and stripped. It was one thing to be naked among the other children in the toilets and showers, and something else again to be nude in front of adult men, all there for no other purpose than to watch. They searched every crevice of his body, and the search, while not overly rough, was also not pleasant. They were intimate with him as no one had ever been intimate before, and the man who fondled his genitals, searching for unfathomably arcane items— Ansset could think of nothing that could be hidden there— held and touched a little too long, a little too gently. He did not know what it meant, but knew that it was not good. The man's face was outwardly calm, but as he spoke to the others, Ansset detected the trembling, the faint passion suppressed in the interstices of his brusque speech, and it made him afraid.

But the moment passed, and the guards gave him back his clothes, and they led him out of the room. They were tall; they towered over him, and he felt awkward, unable to keep step with them and afraid of somehow getting under their feet, between their legs. The danger was more their anger if he tripped them up than any damage their legs might do to him. Ansset was still too hot, hotter now because he was moving fast and because he was tense. In the Songhouse his Control had been unshakable, except to Esste. But there he had been familiar with everything, able to cope with changes because everything but the change was what he had known all his life. Here he began to realize that people acted for different reasons, that they followed different patterns or no patterns at all; and yet.

He had been able to control the Chamberlain. It had

been crude, but it had worked. Human beings were still human beings. Even if they were large soldiers who trembled when they touched a naked little boy.

The guards touched the sides of doors, and the doors opened. Ansset wondered if his fingers, too, could open doors by touching them. Then the guards reached a door they could not open, or at least didn't try to open. Was Mikal on the other side?

No. The Chamberlain was, and the Captain of the guard, and a few other people, none of whom looked imperial. Not that Ansset had any clear idea of what an emperor would look like, but he knew almost immediately that none of these people was sure of power or enough in control of himself to rule on the strength of his own authority. In fact, Ansset had only met or seen one outsider who could—Riktors Ashen. And that was probably because Riktors was a starfleet commander who had almost bloodlessly quelled a rebellion. He knew what he could do. These palace-bound people did not know anything about themselves.

They asked questions. Seemingly random questions. About his training at the Songhouse, his upbringing before he got to Tew, and dozens of questions that Ansset could not begin to understand, let alone answer.

How do you feel about the four freedoms?

Did they teach you in the Songhouse about the Discipline of Frey?

What about the heroes of Seawatch? The League of Cities of the Sea?

And, finally: "Didn't they teach you *anything* at the Songhouse?"

"They taught me," Ansset said, "how to sing."

The questioners looked at each other. The Captain of the guard finally shrugged. "Hell, he's a nine-year-old kid. How many nine-year-old kids know anything about history? How many of them have any political views?"

"It's the Songhouse I'm worried about," said a man whose voice sang death to Ansset.

"Maybe, just maybe," said the Captain, and his voice was oiled with sarcasm, "the Songhouse is as apolitical as they claim."

"Nobody's apolitical."

"They gave Mikal a Songbird," the Captain pointed out. "It was a very unpopular thing to do, in the empire at large. I heard that some pompous ass on Prowk is returning his singer to them as a protest."

The Chamberlain raised a finger. "They did not *give* Mikal a Songbird. They charged a great deal."

"Which they didn't need," said the man whose voice sang death. "They have more money than any other institution in the empire except the empire itself. So the question remains—why did they send this boy to Mikal? I don't trust them. It's a plot."

A quiet man with large, heavy eyes left the edges of the room and touched the Chamberlain on the shoulder. "Mikal is waiting," he said softly, but his message seemed to settle gloom on everyone.

"I had begun to hope the Songhouse would actually delay long enough that——"

"That what?" asked the Captain of the guard, belligerently daring the Chamberlain to speak treason.

"That we wouldn't have to put up with all this fuss."

The man whose voice sang death came over to Ansset, who sat with a blank face, watching him. He looked Ansset coldly in the eyes. "I suppose," he finally said, "you might just be what you seem to be."

"What do I seem to be?" Ansset asked innocently.

The man paused before answering.

"Beautiful," he finally said, and there were tremolos of regret in his voice. He turned away, turned away and left the room through the door Ansset had entered by. Everyone seemed to be relieved. "Well, that's that," said the Chamberlain, and the Captain of the guard visibly relaxed. "I'm supposed to command every starship in the fleet, and I spend an hour trying to get inside a child's head." He laughed.

"Who was that man who left?" asked Ansset.

The Chamberlain glanced at the Captain before answering. "He's called Ferret. He's an outside expert."

"Outside of what?"

"The palace," answered the Captain.

"Why were you all so glad to have him leave?"

"Enough questions," said the large-eyed man, his voice gentle and trustworthy. "Mikal is ready for you."

So Ansset followed him to a door, which led to a small room where guards passed wands over their bodies and took samples of blood, then to another door which led to a small waiting room. And at last an old, gritty voice came over a speaker and said, "Now."

A door slid upward in what looked like a section of wall, and they passed from the false stone to a room of real wood. Ansset did not yet know that this, of all things, was a mark of Mikal's wealth and power. On Tew, forests were everywhere and wood was easy to get. On Earth, there was a law, punishable by death, against poaching wood from the forests, a law which had been made perhaps twenty thousand years before, when the forests had almost died. Only the poorest exempt peasants in Siberia could cut wood—and Mikal. Mikal could have wood. Mikal could have anything he wanted.

Even a Songbird.

There was a fire (*burning* wood!) in a fireplace at one end of the room. By it, on the floor, lay Mikal. He was old, but his body was lithe. His face was sagging but his arms were firm, bare to the shoulder with no hint of the loss of muscle.

The eyes were deep, and they regarded Ansset steadily. The servant led Ansset partway into the room, and then left.

"Ansset," said the emperor.

Ansset lowered his head in a gesture of respect.

Mikal rose from his lying position to sit on the floor. There was furniture in the room, but it was far back at the walls, and the floor was bare by the fire. "Come," Mikal said.

Ansset walked toward him, stopped and stood still when he was only a meter or so away. The fire was warm. But, Ansset noticed, the room was otherwise cool. Mikal had said only two words, and Ansset did not know his songs, not from that little bit. Yet there had been kindness, and a feeling of awe. Awe, from the emperor of mankind toward a boy.

"Would you like to sit?" Mikal asked.

Ansset sat. The floor, which had felt rigid to his feet, softened when his weight was distributed over a larger area, and the floor was comfortable. Too comfortable— Ansset was not used to softness.

"Have you been treated well?"

For a moment Ansset did not answer. He was listening to Mikal's songs, and did not realize that a question had been asked, not until he had begun to understand a little of the reason a Songbird had been sent to a man who had killed so many millions of human beings.

"Are you afraid to answer?" Mikal asked. "I assure you, if you've been mistreated in any way——"

"I don't know," Ansset said. "I don't know what passes for good treatment here."

Mikal was amused, but showed it only warily. Ansset admired his control. Not Control, of course, but something akin to it, something that made him hard to hear. "What passes for good treatment in the Songhouse?"

"No one ever searched me in the Songhouse," Ansset said. "No one ever held my penis as if he wanted to own it.

Mikal did not answer for a moment, though the pause was the only sign of emotion Mikal let himself show. "Who was it?" Mikal asked calmly.

"It was the tall one, with the silver stripe." Ansset felt a strange excitement in being able to name the man. What would Mikal do?

The emperor turned to a low table, and pressed a place on it. "There was a tall guard, a sergeant, among those who searched the boy."

A moment of silence, and then a soft voice answering— the Captain's voice, Ansset realized, but muted somehow, all harshness sifted out and softened. Was it the machinery? Or did the Captain speak this tenderly to Mikal? "Callowick," said the Captain. "What did he do?"

"He found the boy tempting," Mikal said. "Break him and get him off planet somewhere." Mikal took his hand from the table.

For a moment Ansset felt a thrill of delight. He did not really understand what the guard had done, this Callowick, except that he had not liked it. But Mikal refused to let it happen again, Mikal would punish those who offended him, Mikal would keep him as safe as he had been in the Songhouse. Safer, for in the Songhouse Ansset had been hurt, and here no one would dare hurt him for Mikal's sake. It was Ansset's first taste of the power of life and death, and it was delicious.

"You have power," Ansset said aloud.

"Do I?" asked Mikal, looking at him intently.

"Everyone knows that."

"And do you?" Mikal asked.

"A kind of power," Ansset said, but there had been something in Mikal's question. Something else, a sort of plea, and Ansset searched in his memory of this new, strange voice, to hear what the question was really asking. "A kind of power, but you see the end of it. It makes you afraid."

Mikal said nothing now. Just looked carefully at Ansset's face. Ansset was afraid for a moment. Surely this was not what Esste had urged him to do. *You* must make friends, she had said, because you understand so much more. Do I? Ansset wondered now. I understand some things, but this man has hidden places. This man is dangerous, too; he is not just my protector.

"You have to say something now," Ansset said, outwardly calm. "I can't know you if I don't hear your voice."

Mikal smiled, but his eyes were wary, and so was his voice. "Then perhaps I would be wise to be silent."

It was enough of Mikal's voice, and held enough of the emperor's emotion that Ansset could reach a little further. "I don't think it's the loss of your power that you fear," Ansset said. "I think—I think——" And then words failed him, because he did not understand what he saw and heard in Mikal, not in a way he could express in words. So he sang. With some words, here and there, but the rest melodies and rhythms that spoke of Mikal's love of power. You don't love power like a hungry man loves food, the song seemed to say. You love power like a father loves his son. Ansset sang of power that was created, not found; created and increased until it filled the universe. And then Ansset sang of the room where Mikal lived, filled it to the wooden walls with his voice, and let the sound reverberate in the wood, let it dance and become lively and, though it distorted his tone, come back to add depth to the song.

And as he sang the songs he had just learned from Mikal, Ansset became more daring, and sang the hope of friendship, the offer of trust. He sang the love song.

And when he had finished, Mikal regarded him with his careful eyes. For a moment Ansset wondered if the song had had any effect. Then Mikal reached out a hand, and it trembled, and the trembling was not from age. Reached out a hand, and Ansset also held out a hand, and laid it in the old man's palm. Mikal's hand was large and strong, and Ansset felt that he could be swallowed up, seized and gathered into Mikal's fist and never be found. Yet when Mikal closed his thumb over Ansset's hand, the touch was gentle, the grip firm yet kind, and Mikal's voice was heavy with emotion when he said, "You are. What I had hoped for."

Ansset leaned forward. "Please don't be too satisfied yet," he said. "Your songs are hard to sing, and I haven't learned them all yet."

"*My* songs? I have no songs."

"Yes you have. I sang them to you."

Mikal looked disturbed. "Where did you get the idea that they were——"

"I heard them in your voice."

The idea surprised Mikal, took him off guard. "But there was so much beauty in what you sang——

"Sometimes," Ansset answered.

"Yes. And so much—what, I don't know. Perhaps. Perhaps you found such songs in me." He looked doubtful. He sounded disappointed. "Is this a trick you play? Is this all?"

"A trick?"

"To hear what's going on in your patron's voice and sing it back to him? No wonder I liked the song. But don't you have any songs of yourself?"

Now it was Anssets's turn to be surprised. "But what am I?"

"A good question," Mikal said. "A beautiful nine-year-old boy. Is that what they were waiting for? A body that would make a polygamist regret ever having loved women, a face that mothers and fathers would follow for miles, coveting for their children. Did I want a catamite? I think not. Did I want a mirror? Perhaps when I met the Songmaster so many years ago he was not so wise as I thought. Or perhaps I've changed since then.''

"I'm sorry I disappointed you." Ansset let his real fear show in his voice. Again, it was what Esste had told him: Hide nothing from your patron. It had been easy, after the ordeal in the High Room, to open his heart to Esste. But here, now, with this strange man who had not liked the song even though it had moved him deeply—it took real effort to keep the walls down. Ansset felt as vulnerable as when the soldier had fondled him, and as ignorant of what it was he feared. Yet he showed the fear, because that was what Esste had told him to do, and he knew she would not be wrong.

Mikal's face set hard. "Of course you didn't disappoint me. I told you. That song was what I hoped for. But I want to hear a song of yourself. Surely you have songs of your own."

"I have," Ansset answered.

"Will you sing them to me?"

"I will," said Ansset.

And so he sang, beginning timidly because he had never sung these songs except to people who already loved him, people who were also creatures of the Songhouse and so needed no explanation. But Mikal knew nothing of the Songhouse, and so Ansset groped backward with his melody, trying to find a way to tell Mikal who he was, and finally realizing that he could not, that all he could tell him was the meaning of the Songhouse, was the feel of the cold stone under his fingers, was the kindness of Rruk when he had wept in fear and uncertainty and she had sung confidence to him, though she herself was only a child.

I am a child, said Ansset's song, as weak as a leaf in the wind, and yet, along with a thousand other leaves I have roots that go deep into rock, the cold, living rocks of the Songhouse. I am a child, and my fathers are a thousand other children, and my mother is a woman who broke me open and brought me out and warmed me in the cold storm where I was suddenly naked and suddenly not alone. I am a gift, fashioned by my own hands to be given to you by others, and I don't know if I am acceptable.

And as he sang, he found himself inexorably heading toward the one song he would never have thought to sing. The song of the days in the High Room. The song of his birth. I can't, he thought as the melodies swept into his throat and out of his teeth. I can't bear it, he cried to himself as the emotions came, not in tears, but in passionate tones that came from the most tender places in him. I can't bear to stop, he thought as he sang of Esste's love for him and his terror at leaving her so soon after having learned to lean on her.

And in his song, too, he heard something that surprised him. He heard, through all the emotion of his memories, a thread of dissonance, a thread that spoke of hidden darkness in him. He searched for that note and lost it. And gradually the search for the strangeness in his own song took him out of the song, and brought him to himself again. He sang, and the fire died, and his song at last died, too.

And it was then that he realized that Mikal lay curled around him, his arm embracing Ansset, the other arm covering his face, where he wept, where he sobbed silently. With the song over, the sparks were the only music in the room as the last fusses of flame kept trying to revive the fire.

Oh, what have I done? Ansset cried to himself as he watched the emperor of mankind, Mikal the Terrible, weeping into his hand.

"Oh, Ansset," said Mikal, "what have you done?"

And then, after a moment, Mikal stopped crying and rolled over onto his back and said, "Oh, God, it's too kind, it's too cruel. I'm a hundred and twenty-one years old and death lurks in the walls and floor, waiting to catch me unawares. Why couldn't you have come to me when I was forty?"

Ansset did not know if an answer was expected. "I wasn't born then," he finally said, and Mikal laughed.

"That's right. You weren't born yet. Nine years old. What do they do to you in the Songhouse, Ansset? What terrible squeezing they must do, to wring such songs out of you."

"Did you like my song this time?"

"Like?" Mikal asked, wondering if the boy was joking. "Like?" And he laughed a long time, and laid his head on Ansset's lap. The two of them slept there that night, and from then on there were no more searches, no more questions. Ansset was free to come to Mikal, because there was no time when Mikal did not long to have him there.

4 "You're in luck," their guide told them, and Kya-Kya sighed. She had been hoping that they would be lucky enough to get out of Susquehanna after only the normal five-hour tour. But she was sure that was not what the guide had in mind. "The emperor," said the guide, "has asked to meet with you. This is a very great honor. But, as the Chamberlain told me just a few moments ago, you students from the Princeton Government Institute are the future administrators of this great empire. It is only just that Mikal should meet with his future aides and helpers."

Aides and helpers, hell, Kya-Kya thought. The old man will die before I graduate, and then we'll be aiding and helping somebody else—probably the bastard who killed him.

She had work to do. Some of the trips and tours were worthwhile—the four days they spent at the computer center in Tegucigalpa, the week observing the operation of a welfare services outlet in Rouen. But here at Susquehanna they were shown nothing of any importance, just as a matter of form. The city existed to keep Mikal alive and safe—the real government work went on elsewhere. Worse, the palace had been designed by a madman (probably Mikal himself, she thought) and the corridors were a maze that doubled back constantly, that rose and fell through meaningless ramps and stairways. The building seemed to be one vast barrier, and her legs ached from the long walk between one exhibit and another. Several times she could have sworn that they walked up one corridor, lined with

131

doors on the left, and then turned 180 degrees and walked down a parallel corridor with doors on the left that led only to the corridor they had just traveled. Maddening. Wearying.

"And what's more," said the guide, "the Chamberlain even hinted that you might get a chance usually granted only to distinguished offworld visitors. You may get to hear Mikal's Songbird."

There was a buzz of interest among the students. Of course they had all heard of Mikal's Songbird, at first the scandalous news that Mikal had forced even the Songhouse to bend to his will, and then the spreading word from those privileged few who had heard the boy sing: that Mikal's Songbird was the greatest Songbird ever, that no human voice had ever done what he could do.

Kya-Kya felt something entirely different, however. None of her fellow students knew she was from the Songhouse, or even from Tew. She had been discreet to the point of aloofness. And she did not long to see Ansset again, not the boy who had been Esste's favorite, not the boy who was the opposite of her.

But there was no escape from the group. Kya-Kya was systematically being a model student—creative but compliant. Sometimes it nearly killed her, she thought, but she made sure there would be glowing recommendations from every professor, a perfect record of achievement. It was hard for a woman to get a job in Mikal's government at all. And the kind of job she wanted usually came to a woman only as the climax of her career, not at the beginning.

So Kya-Kya said nothing, as they filed into the seats that formed a horseshoe whose open end framed Mikal's throne. Kya-Kya took a seat near one end, so that she would be looking at Mikal's profile—she preferred to study someone without direct eye contact. Eye contact allowed them to lie.

"You should stand," said the guide deferentially, and

of course they all took the suggestion and stood. A dozen uniformed guards entered the hall and fanned out to positions along the walls. Then the Chamberlain entered and announced in slow, ceremonial tones, "Mikal Imperator has come to you." And Mikal came in.

The man was old, the face lined and creased and sagging, but his step was bright and quick and his smile seemed to come from a light heart. Kya-Kya of course rejected that first impression, for it was obviously the public relations face that Mikal wore to impress visitors. Yet he seemed to be in undeniably good health.

Mikal came to the throne and sat, and it was then that Kya-Kya realized that Ansset had come into the room with him. Mikal's presence was so overpowering that even the beautiful Songbird had not been able to distract. Now, however, Mikal took the boy's hand and gently pulled him forward, sent him a few steps ahead of the throne, where he stood alone and looked at everyone in the small audience.

Kya-Kya did not watch Ansset, however. She watched the other students watching him. They all wondered, of course, if a boy of such great beauty had found his way into Mikal's bed. Kya-Kya knew better. The Songhouse would never tolerate it. They would never send a Songbird to someone who would try such a thing.

Ansset turned all the way to look at the end of the row of chairs, and his eyes met Kya-Kya's. If he recognized her, he gave no sign. But Kya-Kya knew enough about Control to know that he could well have recognized her—in fact, probably had.

And then he sang. The song was powerful. It was all the hopes and finest ambitions of the students there, a song of serving mankind and being honored for it. The words were simple, but the melody made all of them want to shout for the excitement of their own futures. All except Kya-Kya, who remembered gatherings in the great hall of the

Songhouse. Remembered hearing others sing there, and how she had felt at the first gathering after she had been declared Deaf. There was no hope in the song for her. And in a way her own bitterness at Ansset's song was a pleasure. He obviously was singing what the students most wanted to hear, trying to touch everyone in the audience. But he would never touch her.

When Ansset finished, the students did stand, did clap and cheer. Ansset bowed shyly, then walked from the place in front of Mikal's throne and came to stand near the wall. Not two meters from Kya-Kya. She glanced at him when he came. It hurt her to see up close how beautiful he was, how kind and happy his face seemed in repose. He did not seem to look at her, so she looked away.

Mikal began to speak then, the usual things about how important it was for them to study hard and learn how to cope with all the known problems, yet develop themselves so that they had the deep inner resources to cope with the unexpected. And so on, thought Kya-Kya, and on and on and on and on.

"Listen," said a voice in Kya-Kya's ear. She whirled and saw only Ansset, still a couple of meters off, still not looking at her. But she had been forced out of her reverie; she heard Mikal.

"You will naturally rise quickly to important positions, with many people under you. Often you'll become impatient with the sluggish people under you. The petty bureaucrats who seem to love to own every piece of paper that crosses their desks for as long as they possibly can before passing it on. They seem to have tiny minds, no ambitions, no vision of what the government ought to be doing. You'll long to take a heavy broom and sweep the bastards out. God knows I've wanted to often enough."

The students laughed, not because of what he said, but

because they were immensely flattered that Mikal Imperator would speak so casually, so openly to them.

"But don't do it. Don't do it unless you absolutely have to. The bureaucrats are our treasures, the most valuable part of the government. You who have great ability, you'll rise, you'll change, you'll get bored, you'll move from job to job. If you had a different kind of emperor, some of you would get removed from time to time and sent to— Well, I haven't the kind of imagination to conjure up the sort of places offensive administrators might get sent." Again a laugh. Kya-Kya was digusted.

"Listen," said the voice again, and this time when Kya-Kya turned, Ansset was looking at her.

"I know it's treason to speak of it, but I doubt that any of you have failed to notice that I'm old. I've ruled a long time. I'm past a man's normal life expectancy. Someday, I have reason to believe, I will die."

The students sat stiffly, unsure of what this had to do with them, but certain that they wished they were not hearing such things.

"When that happens, someone else will take my place. I don't come from a particularly long dynasty, and there may be some question as to who is my legitimate heir. There may even be some nastiness over the question. Some of you will be tempted to take sides. And those who choose the wrong side will pay for your mistake. But while all the storms rage, those paper-pushing bureaucrats will go on their stodgy, incompetent way, running the government. Already they have such inertia that I couldn't possibly change them even if I wanted to. Here and there, a few changes. Here and there an improvement, or a brilliant bureaucrat who deserves and damn well better get a promotion. But most of them will go on doing things in the same infinitely slow way, and that, my young friends, will be the salvation and the preservation of this empire.

Rely on the bureaucracy. Depend on the bureaucracy. Keep it, if you can, under control. But never weaken it. It will save mankind when every visionary has failed, when every utopia has crumbled. Bureaucracy is the one eternal thing mankind has created.''

And then Mikal smiled, and all the students laughed again, because they realized that he knew he was exaggerating. But they also knew that he meant much of what he said, and they understood his vision of the future. That it didn't matter who was at the helm, as long as the crew knew how to run the ship.

But no one understood him so well as Kya-Kya. There was no time-honored system of succession to the throne, as there had been in the Songhouse, where the choice of the Songmaster of the High Room had been left up to a Deaf and no one had even protested her choice. Instead, the rule of the empire would pass to whoever was strongest and most determined at the time of Mikal's death. In history, far too many sovereigns had destroyed their empires by trying to promote a favorite or a relative as successor. Mikal had no such intention. He was announcing to the students from the Princeton Government Institute that he was going to leave the succession up to the law of natural selection, while trying to build institutions that would survive the turmoil.

The first few years after Mikal's death will be interesting, Kya-Kya decided, and wondered why, when those years were bound to be miserable and full of slaughter, she was so glad to know she would be alive and working in government during them.

Mikal stood, and so everyone stood, and when he had gone they erupted into dozens of different conversations. Kya-Kya was amused at how effectively Mikal had taken everyone in with his warmth and casualness. Had they forgotten that this man had killed billions of people on burned-over worlds, that only brute force and utter callousness had brought him to power? And yet she also had to admire the fact that after a life like the one Mikal had led, he was able to so conceal his viciousness that everyone in the room but her—no, be honest, everyone in the room—now thought of him as grandfatherly. Kind. A gentleman and gentle man. And wise.

Well, give the old bastard that. He was smart enough to stay alive as the number one target in the galaxy. He'd probably die in bed.

"Contempt is so easy," said Ansset's voice beside her.

She spun to face him. "I thought you were gone. What did you mean, telling me to listen?" She was surprised that she spoke angrily to him.

"Because you weren't." The boy's voice was gentle, but she heard the undertones of songtalk.

"Don't try it with me. I can't be fooled."

"Only a fool can't be fooled," Ansset answered. He had grown, she noticed. "You pretend not to like Mikal. But of all the people here, you're the one most like him."

What did he mean? She was infuriated. She was flattered. " Do I look like the killer type?" she asked.

"You'll get what you want," Ansset answered. "And you'll kill to get it, if you have to."

"Not just songs but psychology, too. How far-reaching your training must have been."

"I know your songs, Kya-Kya," Ansset said. "I heard your singing when you came to Esste in my stall that day."

"I never sang."

"No, Kya-Kya. You always sang. You just never heard the song."

Ansset started to turn away. But his air of confidence, of superiority, angered Kya-Kya. "Ansset!" she called, and he stopped and faced her. "They're using you," she said. "You think they care about you, but they're only using you. A tool. A foolish, ignorant tool!'' She had not spoken loudly, but when she turned she realized that many of the other students were looking back and forth between her and Ansset. She walked away from the boy and threaded her way through the students, who knew enough not to say anything, but who no doubt wondered how she had gotten into a conversation with Mikal's Songbird, and no doubt marveled that she had been able to bring herself to be angry at him.

That had been enough to keep the students gossiping for days. But before she reached the door, she heard all the conversations fall silent, and Ansset's voice rose above the fading chatter to sing a wordless song that she, alone of all the students, knew was a song of hope and friendship and honest good wishes. She closed her mind to the boy's Songhouse tricks and left the room, where she could wait outside in silence with the guards until the guide came to lead them all away.

The buses, all fleskets from the Institute, took them home to Princeton with only one stop, in the ancient city of Philadelphia, where one of the older men students was kidnapped and found, mutilated terribly, near the Delaware River. He was the fifteenth in a wave of kidnap murders that had terrorized Philadelphia and many other cities in the area. The rest of the students returned in utter gloom to Princeton and resumed their studies. But Kya-Kya did not forget Ansset. Could not forget him. Death was in the air, and while Mikal could not be responsible for the mad killings in Philadelphia, she could not help but believe that he, too, would die mutilated. But the mutilation had been going on for years, and she thought of Ansset, and how he, too, might be twisted and deformed, and for all that she cared nothing for the Songhouse and even less for Mikal's Songbird, she could not help but hope that somehow the beautiful boy who had remembered her after all these years could emerge unsullied from Susquehanna and go home to the Songhouse clean.

And she fretted, because she was in school and the world was passing on quickly toward great events that she would not be part of unless she hurried or the world waited just a little bit for her. She was twenty years old and brilliant and impatient and frustrated as hell. She cried for the Songhouse one night when she went to bed especially tired.

5   Ansset walked in the garden by the river. In the Songhouse, the garden had been a patch of flowers in the courtyard, or the vegetables in the farmland behind the last chamber. Here, the garden was a vast stretch of grass and shrubs and tall trees that stretched along the two forks of the Susquehanna to where they joined. On the other side of both rivers was dense, lush forest, and the birds and animals often emerged from the trees to drink or eat from the river. The Chamberlain had pleaded with Ansset not to wander in the garden. The space was too large, kilometers in every direction, and the wilderness too dense to do any decent patrolling.

But in the two years he had lived in Mikal's palace, Ansset had tested the limits of his life and found they were broader than the Chamberlain would have liked. There were things Ansset could not do, not because of rules and schedules but because it would displease Mikal, and displeasing Mikal was never something Ansset desired. He could not follow Mikal into meetings unless he was specifically invited. There were times when Mikal needed to be alone—Ansset never had to be told, he noticed the mood come over Mikal and left him.

There were other things, however, that Ansset had learned he *could* do. He could enter Mikal's private room without asking permission. He discovered, by trial and error, that only a few doors in the palace would not open to his fingers. He had wandered the labyrinth of the palace and knew it better than anyone; it was a way he often amused himself, to stand near a messenger when he was being sent on an errand, and then plan a route that would get him to the destination long before the messengers. It unnerved them, of course, but soon they got into the spirit of the game and raced him, occasionally reaching the end before Ansset.

And Ansset could walk in the garden when he wanted to. The Chamberlain had argued over it with Mikal, but Mikal had looked Ansset in the eye and asked, "Does it matter to you, to walk in the garden?"

"It does, Father Mikal."

"And you have to walk alone?"

"If I can."

"Then, you will." And that was the end of the argument. Of course, the Chamberlain had men watching from a distance, and occasionally a flit passed overhead, but usually Ansset had the feeling of being alone.

Except for the animals. It was something he hadn't had that much experience with at the Songhouse. Occasional trips to the open country, to the lake, to the desert. But there had not been so many creatures, and there had not been so many songs. The chatter of squirrels, the cries of geese and jays and crows, the splash of leaping fish. How could men have borne to leave this world? Ansset could not fathom the impulse that would have forced his ancient ancestors into the cold ships and out to planets that, as often as not, killed them. In the peace of birdsong and rushing water it was impossible to imagine wanting to leave this place, if it was your home.

But it was not Ansset's home. Though he loved Mikal as he had loved no one but Esste, and though he understood the reasons why he had been sent to be Mikal's Songbird, he nevertheless turned his back on the river and looked at the palace with its dead false stone and longed to be home again.

And as he faced the palace, he heard a sound in the river behind him, and the sound chilled him like a cold wind, and he would have turned to face the danger except that the gas reached him first, and he fell, and remembered nothing of the kidnapping.

6 There were no recriminations. The Chamberlain didn't dare say I told you so, and Mikal, though he hid his grief well, was too grieved and worried to bother with blaming anyone except himself.

"Find him," he said. And that was all. Said it to the Captain of the guard, to the Chamberlain, and to the man he called Ferret. "Find him."

And they searched. The news spread quickly, of course, that Mikal's Songbird had been kidnapped, and the people who read and cared at all about the court worried also that the beautiful Songbird might have been a victim of the mutilator who still went uncaught in Philadelphia and Manam and Hisper. Yet the mutilator's victims were found every day with their bodies torn to pieces, and never was one of the bodies Ansset's.

All the ports were closed, and the fleet circled Earth with orders to take any ship that tried to leave the planet and stop any ship that tried to land. Travel between districts and precincts was forbidden on Earth, and thousands of flits and flecks and fleskets were stopped and searched. But there was no sign of Ansset. And while Mikal went about his business, there was no hiding the circles under his eyes and the way he bent a little as he walked and the fact that the spring was gone from his step. Some thought that Ansset had been stolen for profit, or had been kidnapped by the mutilator and the body simply had not been found. But those who saw what the kidnapping did to Mikal knew that if someone had wanted to weaken Mikal, hurt him as deeply as he could be hurt, there could have been no better way than to take the Songbird.

7 The doorknob turned. That would be dinner.

Ansset rolled over on the hard bed, his muscles aching. As always, he tried to ignore the burning feeling of guilt in the pit of his stomach. As always, he tried to remember what had happened during the day, for the last heat of day always gave way to the chill of night soon after he awoke. And, as always, he could neither explain the guilt nor remember the day.

It was not Husk with food on a tray. This time it was the man called Master, though Ansset believed that was not his name. Master was always near anger and fearsomely strong, one of the few men Ansset had met in his life who could make him feel as helpless as the eleven-year-old child his body said he was.

"Get up, Songbird."

Ansset slowly stood. They kept him naked in prison,

and only his pride kept him from turning away from the harsh eyes that looked him up and down. Only his Control kept his cheeks from burning with shame.

"It's a good-bye feast we're having for you, Chirp, and ye're going to twitter for us."

Ansset shook his head.

"If ye can sing for the bastard Mikal, ye can sing for honest freemen."

Ansset let his eyes blaze. His voice was on fire as he said, "Be careful how you speak of him, traitor!"

Master advanced a step, raising his hand angrily. "My orders was not to mark you, Chirp, but I can give you pain that doesn't leave a scar if ye don't mind how ye talk to a freeman. Now ye'll sing."

Ansset had never been struck a blow in his life. But it was more the fury in the man's voice than the threat of violence that made Ansset nod. But he still hung back. "Can you please give me my clothing?"

"It an't cold where we're going," Master said.

"I've never sung like this," Ansset said. "I've never performed without clothing."

Master leered. "What is it then that you *do* without clothing? Mikal's catamite has no secrets we can't see."

Ansset didn't understand the word, but he understood the leer, and he followed Master out the door and down a dark corridor with his heart even more darkly filled with shame. He wondered why they were having a "good-bye feast" for him. Was he to be set free? Had Mikal paid some unimaginable ransom for him? Or was he to be killed?

Ansset thought of Mikal, wondered what he was going through. It was not vanity but recognition of the truth when Ansset concluded for the hundredth time that Mikal would be frantic, yet bound by pride and the necessities of government to show nothing at all. Surely, though, surely Mikal would spare no effort hunting for him. Surely Mikal would come and take him back.

The floor rocked gently as they walked down the wooden corridor. Ansset had long since decided he was imprisoned on a ship, though he had never been on a boat larger than the canoe he had learned to row on the pond near the palace. The amount of real wood used in it would have seemed gaudy and pretentious in a rich man's home. Here, however, it seemed only shabby. Peasant rights and nothing more.

Far above he could hear the distant cry of a bird, and a steady singing sound that he imagined to be wind whipping through ropes and cables. He had sung the melody to himself sometimes, and often harmonized to it.

And then Master opened the door and with a mocking bow indicated that Ansset should enter first. The boy stopped in the doorframe. Gathered around a long table were twenty or so men, some of whom he had seen before, all of them dressed in one of the strange national costumes of the past-worshipping people of Earth. Ansset couldn't help remembering how Mikal mocked such people when they came to court to present demands or ask for favors. "All these ancient costumes," Mikal would say as he lay with Ansset on the floor, staring into the fire. "All these ancient costumes mean nothing. Their ancestors weren't peasants, most of them. Their ancestors were the wealthy and effete from boring worlds who came back to Earth hunting for some meaning. They stole the few peasant customs that remained, and did shoddy research to discover some more, and thought that they had found truth. As if shitting in the grass is somehow nobler than doing it into a converter."

The great civilizations such people claimed to be heirs to

were petty and insignificant to those who had come to think on a galactic scale. But here, where Ansset looked closely into their rough faces and unsmiling eyes, he realized that whatever these people's ancestors might have been, they had acquired the strength of primitiveness, and they reminded him of the vigor of the Songhouse. Except that their muscles were massive with labor that would have astonished a singer. And Ansset stood before them soft and white and beautiful and vulnerable and, despite his Control, was afraid.

They looked at him with the same curious, knowing, lustful look that Master had given him. Ansset knew that if he allowed the slightest hint of cringing into his manner, they would be encouraged. So he stepped farther into the room, and nothing about his movement showed any sign of the embarrassment and fear that he felt. He seemed unconcerned, his face as blank as if he had never felt any emotion in his life.

"Up on the table!" roared Master behind him, and hands lifted him onto the wood smeared with spilled wine and rough with crumbs and fragments of food. "Now sing, ye little bastarrd."

And so he closed his eyes and shaped the ribs around his lungs, and let a low tone pass through his throat. For two years he had not sung except at Mikal's request. Now he sang for Mikal's enemies, and perhaps should have torn at them with his voice, made them cringe before his hatred. But hatred had not been born in Ansset, nor had his life bred it into him, and so he sang something else entirely. Sang softly without words, holding back the tone so that it barely reached their ears.

"Louder," someone said, but Ansset ignored him, and soon the jokes and laughter died down as the men strained to hear.

The melody was a wandering one, passing through tones and quartertones easily, gracefully, still low in pitch, but rising and falling rhythmically. Unconsciously Ansset moved his hands in the strange gestures that had accompanied all his songs since he had opened his heart to Esste in the High Room. He was never aware of the movements—in fact, he had been puzzled by a notice in a Philadelphia newspaper that he had read in the palace library: "To hear Mikal's Songbird is heavenly, but to watch his hands dance as he sings is nirvana." It was a prudent thing to write in the capital of Eastamerica, not two hundred kilometers from Mikal's palace. But it was the vision of Mikal's Songbird held by all those who thought of him at all, and Ansset did not understand, could not picture what they saw.

He only knew what he sang, and now he began to sing words. They were not words of recrimination, but rather the words of his captivity, and the melody became high, in the soft upper notes that opened his throat and tightened the muscles at the back of his head and tensed the muscles along the front of his thighs. The notes pierced, and as he slid up and down through haunting thirdtones, his words spoke of the dark, mysterious guilt he felt in the evenings in his dirty, shabby prison. His words spoke of his longing for Father Mikal (though he never spoke his name, not in front of these men), of dreams of the gardens along the Susquehanna River, and of lost, forgotten days that vanished from his memory before he awoke.

Most of all, though, he sang of his guilt.

At last he became tired, and the song drifted off into a whispered dorian scale that ended on the wrong note, on a dissonant note that faded into silence that sounded like part of the song.

Finally Ansset opened his eyes. Even when he sang for an audience he neither liked nor wanted to sing for, he could not help but give them what they wanted. All the men who were not weeping were watching him. None seemed willing to break the mood, until a youngish man down the table said in a thick accent, "Ah but thet were better than hame and mitherma." His comment was greeted by sighs and chuckles of agreement, and the looks that met Ansset's eyes were no longer leering and lustful, but rather soft and kind. Ansset had never thought to see such looks in those coarse faces.

"Will ye have some wine, boy?" asked Master's voice behind him, and Husk poured. Ansset sipped the wine, and dipped a finger in it to cast a drop into the air in the graceful gesture he had learned in the palace. "Thank you," he said, handing back the metal cup with the same grace he would have used with a goblet at court. He lowered his head, though it hurt him to use that gesture of respect to such men, and asked, "May I leave now?"

"Do you have to? Can't you sing again?" It was as if the men around the table had forgotten that Ansset was their prisoner. And he, in turn, refused them as if he were free to choose. "I can't do it twice. I can never do it twice." Nor for them, anyway. And for Mikal, all songs were different, and every one was new.

They lifted him off the table then, and Master's strong arms carried him back to his room. Ansset lay on the bed after the door locked shut, his Control easing, letting his body tremble. The last song he had sung before this had been for Mikal. A light and happy song, and Mikal had smiled the soft, melancholy smile that only touched his face when he was alone with his Songbird. And Ansset had touched Mikal's hand, and Mikal had touched Ansset's face, and then Ansset had left to walk along the river.

Ansset drifted off to sleep thinking of the songs in Mikal's gray eyes, humming of the firm hands that ruled

an empire and yet could still stroke the forehead of a
beautiful child and weep at a sorrowful song. Ah, sang
Ansset in his mind, ah, the weeping of Mikal's sorrowful
hands.

8   Ansset awoke walking down a street.

"Out of the way, ya chark!" shouted a harsh accent
behind him, and Ansset dodged to the left as a cart zipped
passed his right arm. "Sausages," shouted a sign on the
case behind the driver.

Then Ansset was seized by a terrible vertigo as he
realized that he was not in the cell of his captivity, that he
was fully dressed, though not in the clothing of the
Songhouse. He was alive and free of his captors and the
quick joy that realization brought was immediately soured
by a rush of the old guilt, and the conflicting emotions and
the suddenness of his liberation were too much for him,
and for a moment too long he forgot to breathe, and the
darkening ground slid sideways, tipped up, hit him——

"Hey, boy, are you all right?"

"Did the chark slam you, boy?"

"I got the number of the car. We can get him!"

"He's comin' around and to."

Ansset opened his eyes. "Where is this place?" he
asked softly.

Why, this is Northet, they said.

"How far is the palace?" Ansset asked, vaguely remembering that he had heard of Northet as a suburb of
Hisper.

"The palace? What palace?"

"Mikal's palace—I must go to Mikal—" Ansset tried to

get up, but his head spun and he staggered. Hands held him up.

"The kit's kinky, that's what."

"Mikal's palace."

"It's only sixty kilometer, boy, should I have 'em hold supper for you?"

The joke brought a burst of laughter, but Ansset had regained Control and he pulled away from the hands holding him and stood alone. Whatever drug had kept him unconscious was now nearly worked out of his system. "Find me a policeman," Ansset said. "Mikal will want to see me immediately."

Some still laughed, but others looked carefully at Ansset, perhaps noticing that he spoke with precision, an offworld accent, that his bearing was not that of a streetchild. "Who are you boy?" one asked.

"I'm Ansset. Mikal's Songbird."

They looked, realized that the face *was* the one pictured in the papers; half of them ran off to find authorities who could handle the situation, while the other half stayed to look at his face, to realize how beautiful his eyes were, to hold the moment so they could tell about it to their children and grandchildren. I saw Ansset himself, Mikal's Songbird, they would say, and when their children asked, What was Mikal's Songbird? they would answer, ah, he was beautiful, but was the most valuable of all the treasures of Mikal the Terrible, the sweetest face you ever saw, and songs that could bring rain out of the sky or a flower from the deep of the snow.

They reached out, and he touched their hands, and smiled at them, and wondered how they wanted him to act—embarrassed at their awe, or accustomed to it? He read the songs in their voices as they murmured, "Songbird," and "Thank you," and "Lovely." And decided that they wanted him to be poised, to be beautiful and

gracious and distant so their worship would be uninterrupted. "Thank you," Ansset said, "thank you. You've
all helped me. Thank you."

The policemen came, apologizing effusively for how
dirty their flesket was, that it was the only one in the
station, and please take a seat. They did not take him to
the station; rather they took him to a pad where a flit from
the palace waited. The Chamberlain got out. "Yes, it's
him," he said to the police, and then reached for Ansset's
hand. "Are you all right?" he asked.

"I think so," Ansset said, suddenly aware that something might be wrong with him. He was inside the flit; the
doors closed; the ground seemed to push up on him and he
was airborne, heading for the palace. For Mikal.

9   "The child is becoming impatient," said the Captain.
"I really don't give a damn," said the Chamberlain.

"And Mikal is also impatient."

The Chamberlain said nothing, just stared back at the
Captain.

"All I'm saying, Chamberlain, is that we have to hurry."

The Chamberlain sighed. "I know. But the child's a
monster. I was married once, you know."

The Captain hadn't known, but did not care. He shrugged.

"I had a boy. When he was eleven he was mischievous,
a little devil, but so transparent you could see through him
no matter how he tried to deceive. Even when he tried to
conceal his feelings, you could tell exactly what he was
trying to conceal. But this boy."

"They train them to school their emotions in the
Songhouse," the Captain said.

"Yes, the Songhouse. I marvel at their teaching. The child can hide any emotion he wants to. Even his impatience—he chooses to show it, and then shows nothing else."

"But you *have* hypnotized him."

"Only with the aid of drugs. And when I start mucking around in his mind, Captain, what do I find?"

"Walls."

"Walls. Someone has built blocks in his mind that I can't get through."

The Captain smiled. "And you insisted on conducting the interrogation yourself."

The Chamberlain glared. "To be frank, Captain, I didn't trust your men. It was *your* men who were supposed to be guarding him that day."

It was the Captain's turn to get angry. "And you know who ordered them to keep completely out of sight! They watched the whole thing through ops and couldn't get there before they had taken him off underwater. The whole search was just a second too late all the way!"

"That's the problem," the Chamberlain said. "A second too late."

"You've failed at the interrogation! Mikal wants his Songbird back! I *will* interrogate the boy!"

The Chamberlain glowered a moment, then turned away. "All right. And much as it pains me to say so, I honestly hope you succeed."

The Captain found Ansset sitting on the edge of a couch that flowed aimlessly around him. The boy looked up at him without interest.

"Again," the Captain said.

"I know," Ansset said. The Captain had brought a tray of syringes and slaps. As he prepared the first slap, he talked to Ansset. Trying, he supposed, to put the boy at ease, though whether the boy was nervous or not was impossible to tell.

"You know that Mikal wants to see you."

"And I want to see him," Ansset said.

"But you were held for five months by someone who was probably not a friend of the emperor."

"I've told you everything I know."

"I know it. We have recordings. I think we know everything about what you did in the evenings. Every word the crew of the boat spoke to you. You're a marvelous mimic. Our experts are studying the accent of the crew right now. Your memory of the faces has our artists busy reconstructing them. Everything you've told us has been in perfect detail. You're an ideal witness."

Ansset showed no emotion, not even a sigh. "Yet we go through this again."

"The trouble is, Ansset, what went on during the days. You have blocks——"

"The Chamberlain's told me. I knew it already."

"And we must get behind them."

"I want you to. You have to believe me," Ansset said. "I want to know. I don't want to be a threat to Mikal. I'd rather die than harm him. But I'd also rather die than leave him."

The words were song. The voice was flat and empty. Not even a song in it. "Is that because of a commitment from the Songhouse? I'm sure they'd understand."

Ansset looked at him. "Captain. The Songhouse would accept me back at any time."

"Ansset, one of the reasons we can't get through the blocks in your mind is because you aren't helping."

"I'm trying to."

"Ansset, I don't know how to say this. Most of the time your voice is natural and human and you react like any other person might. But now, when we need to communicate with you more than ever before, you are frozen. You're completely unreachable. You haven't shown an emotion since I came in here.''

Ansset looked surprised. The very fact of even that mild reaction made the Captain's breath quicken in excitement. ''Captain, aren't you using drugs?''

''The drugs are the last resort, Ansset, and you can still resist them. Perhaps whoever put the blocks in your mind gave you help in resisting them. The drugs can only get us partway into you. And then you resist us every step of the way.''

Ansset regarded him a little more, as if digesting the information. Then he turned away, and his voice was husky as he said, ''What you're asking me to do is lose Control.''

The Captain knew nothing of Control. He only heard *control,* and did not understand the difficulty of what he was asking.

''That's right.''

''And it's the only way to find out what's been hidden in my mind?''

''Yes,'' said the Captain.

Ansset was silent a moment more. ''Am I really a danger to Mikal?''

''I don't know. Perhaps whoever took you found you as hard to cope with as we have. Perhaps there's nothing hidden in your mind, except a memory of who the kidnappers were. Perhaps they had meant to hold you for ransom, then realized they'd never get away with it alive and spent the rest of the time trying to conceal who they were. I don't know. But perhaps behind those blocks are instructions for you to kill Mikal. If they wanted to pick a perfect assassin, they couldn't do better than you. No one but you sees Mikal every day in intimate circumstances. No one has his trust. The very fact that he pleads with us to bring you to him, to hurry the interrogation and let him see you—You can see what a danger you might be to him.''

''For Mikal's sake, then,'' Ansset said. And the Captain was astounded by how quickly Ansset's Control broke. ''Tell Mikal,'' said Ansset, as his face twisted with emotion and tears began to flow, ''that I'll do anything for him. Even this.'' And Ansset wept, great sobs wracking his body, weeping for the months of fear and guilt and solitude. Weeping at the knowledge that he might never see Mikal again. The Captain watched, incredulous, as for an hour Ansset could not communicate at all, just lay on the couch like a little child, babbling and rubbing his eyes. He knew that from the observation stations the other interrogators would be watching in awe at how quickly the Captain had broken through barriers that even drugs had not been able to breach. The Captain felt a delicious hope that the Chamberlain had been watching, too.

And then Ansset became relatively calm, and the Captain began the questioning, using every clever trick he could think of to get behind the barriers. He tried every indirection he had ever heard of. He tried all the dazzling thrusts that had shattered walls before. But even now, with Ansset cooperating fully, nothing could be done at all. Not even in the deepest trance was Ansset able to speak what had been hidden in his mind. The Captain learned only one thing. He asked, while questioning around the skirts of one block, ''Who placed this barrier here?''

And Ansset, so deep in the trance that he could hardly speak, said, ''Esste.''

The name meant nothing to the Captain at the time. But that name was all he got. An hour later he and the Chamberlain stood before Mikal.

''Esste,'' Mikal said.

''That's what he said.''

"Esste," Mikal said, "is the name of the Songmaster of the High Room. His teacher in the Songhouse."

"Oh."

"These blocks you have so lovingly spent four days trying to break were placed there years ago by his teachers! Not by kidnappers only in the last few months!"

"We had to be sure."

"Yes," Mikal said. "You had to be sure. And we're not sure now, of course. If the barriers were placed in his mind by his teacher, why can't he remember how he spent his days during his captivity? We can only conclude that some blocks come from the Songhouse, and some blocks from his captors. But what can we do about it?"

"Send the boy back to the Songhouse," said the Chamberlain.

Mikal's face was terrible. It was as if he wanted to shout, but dared not say what he would say if he surrendered himself to passion that much. So he did not shout, but after a moment of struggle said, "Chamberlain, that's a suggestion I *will* not hear again. I know it may be necessary. But as for now, I will have my Songbird with me."

"My Lord," the Captain said, "you've stayed alive all these years by not taking such chances."

"Until Ansset came," Mikal answered painfully, "I did not know what I was staying alive *for*."

The Captain bowed his head. The Chamberlain thought of another argument, almost said something, and then thought better of it.

"Bring him to me," said Mikal, "in open court, so that everyone can watch me accept my Songbird again. I'll have no taint on him. In two hours."

They left, and Mikal sat alone on the floor in front of his fireplace, resting his chin on his hands. He was getting old, and his back hurt, and he tried to hum a tune the Songbird had often sung. The voice was old and creaky, and he couldn't do it. The fire spat at him, and he wondered what it would be like to have beautiful Ansset hold a laser and aim it at his heart. He would not know what he was doing, Mikal reminded himself. He would be innocent in his heart.

But I would still be dead when he was through.

10   The Captain and Chamberlain came together to take Ansset from the cell where he had spent the last four days.

"He wants you to come."

Ansset had Control again. He showed little emotion as he asked, "Am I ready?"

They said nothing for a moment, which was answer enough.

"Then I won't go," Ansset said.

"He commands it," the Chamberlain said.

"Not if we don't know what's been hidden in my head."

The Captain patted Ansset's shoulder. "A loyal attitude. But the only thing we could find was that at least some of the blocks were laid by your teacher."

"Esste?"

"Yes."

Ansset smiled, and suddenly his voice radiated confidence. "Then it's all right. She wishes nothing but good for Mikal!"

"Only some of the blocks."

And the smile left Ansset's face.

"But you will come. He's expecting you in court in less than two hours."

"Can't we try again?"

"Trying again would be pointless. Whoever laid the blocks in your mind laid them well, Ansset. And Mikal won't be put off any longer. You have no choice. Please come with us now." And the Captain stood. He expected to be obeyed, and Ansset followed. They wound their way through the palace to the security rooms at the entrances to the court. There Ansset insisted on their most thorough search, every possible poison and weapon checked for.

"And tie my hands," Ansset said.

"Mikal wouldn't stand for it," the Captain said, but the Chamberlain nodded and said, "The boy's right." So they clamped manacles onto Ansset's forearms. The manacles quickly fit snugly from elbow to wrist. They were held by metal bars exactly twenty centimeters apart behind his back, which was uncomfortable at first and steadily more uncomfortable the longer he had to hold the position. They also hobbled his legs.

"And keep guards with lasers far enough from me that there's no chance of my taking a weapon."

"You know," said the Captain, "that we might still find your kidnappers. We've identified the accent now. Eire."

"I've never heard of the planet," said the Chamberlain.

"It's an island. Here on Earth."

"Another group of freedom fighters?" asked the Chamberlain, scornfully.

"With more gall than most."

"An accent isn't much to go on."

"But we're going on it," the Captain said, with finality.

"It's time," said a servant at the door.

They left the security room and passed through the ordinary security system, detectors that scanned for metal and the more ordinary poisons, guards who frisked everyone, including Ansset, because they had been told to make no exceptions.

And then Ansset passed between the doors and walked into the great hall. When the students had visited, most of the hall had been empty, their chairs gathered up near the throne. Now the full court was in session, with visitors from dozens of planets waiting along the edges of the room to present their petitions or make gifts or complain about some government policy or official. Mikal sat on his throne at the end of the room. He needed nothing more than a simple if elegant chair—no raised platform, no steps, nothing but his own bearing and dignity to raise him above the level of everyone around him. Ansset had never approached the throne from this end of the room. He had always stood beside Mikal, had always entered from the back, and now he knew why so many who walked up this long space were trembling when they reached the end. Every eye was upon him as he passed, and Mikal watched him gravely from the throne. Ansset wanted to run to him, embrace him, sing songs, and find comfort in Mikal's acceptance. Yet he knew that in his mind might hide instructions to kill the old man on the throne.

He came within a dozen meters of the throne and knelt, bowing his head.

Mikal raised his hand in the ritual of recognition. Ansset had heard Mikal laugh at the rituals when they were alone together, but now the majesty of set forms helped Ansset maintain his calm.

"My Lord," said Ansset in clear, bell-like tones that filled the room and stopped all the whispered conversations around the walls. "I am Ansset, and I have come to ask for my life." In the old days, Mikal had once explained to Ansset, this was the ritual for rulers of hundreds of worlds, and it had meant something. Many a rebel lord or soldier had died on the spot, when the sovereign denied the petition. And even Mikal took the *pro forma* surrender of life seriously. It was one of many constant reminders he used to help his subjects remember that he had power over them.

"Why should I spare you?" Mikal asked, his voice old but firm. To anyone else, he would have seemed a model of poise. But Ansset knew the voice, and heard the quaver of eagerness, of fear and gentle trembling on the edges of the tones.

The ritual required Ansset to simply state his accomplishments, something modest yet impressive. But Ansset left the ritual here, and fervently sang to Mikal, "Father Mikal, you should not!"

The crowd around the walls began whispering again. The sight of the Songbird in manacles and hobbled was shocking enough. But for the Songbird to plead for his own death—

"Why not?" Mikal asked, seeming impassive (but Ansset knew that he was warning him, saying, "Don't push, don't force me").

"Because, my Lord Mikal Imperator, things were done to me that are now locked in my mind so that neither I nor anyone can find them. I therefore have secrets from you. I'm a danger to you, Father Mikal!" Ansset deliberately broke with formality in his last sentence, and the threat in his voice struck fear in everyone in the room.

"None of that," Mikal said. "You think you're acting for my good, but you don't know my good. Don't try to teach me to fear you, because I will not." He raised his hand. "I grant you your life."

And Ansset, despite the strain it caused on his bound arms, leaned down and kissed the floor to express his gratitude for Mikal's clemency. It was a gesture that only pardoned traitors used.

"Why are you bound?" asked Mikal.

"For your safety."

"Unbind him," Mikal said. But Ansset noticed with relief that the Captain of the guard disarmed the men who came out to untie the hobble and break open the manacles. When they were removed, Ansset stood. He raised his now-free arms over his head, lifted his gaze to the great vaults of the ceiling, and sang his love for Mikal. But the song was full of warning, though there were no direct words, and the song also sang of Ansset's regret that because of Mikal's wisdom and for the sake of the empire Ansset would now be sent away.

"No!" cried Mikal, interrupting the song. "No! My Son Ansset, I won't send you away! I would rather meet death at your hands than receive gifts from any other's. Your life is more valuable to me than my own." And Mikal reached out his arms.

Ansset came to him, and embraced him before the throne, and together they left the hall, with legend already growing behind them. In a week all the empire would know that Mikal had called his Songbird *My Son Ansset;* the embrace would be pictured in every newspaper; storytellers would repeat over and over again the words, "Your life is more valuable to me than my own."

11   The door to Mikal's private room closed, and Ansset
stood only a few steps into the room. Mikal was ahead of
him, stopped, looking at nothing, his back to Ansset.

"Never again," Mikal said.

The voice was husky with emotion, and the back was
bent. Mikal turned around and faced Ansset, and it shocked
the boy how old Mikal's face had become. The creases
were deeper, and the mouth turned more sharply down,
and the eyes were deep with pain. They lay in the sunken
sockets like jewels in dark velvet, and Ansset suddenly
realized that Mikal might someday die.

"Never again," Mikal said. "This can never happen
again. When you pleaded with me for freedom from guards
and rules and schedules, I said, 'That's right, you can go,
a Songbird can't be caged.' To me, to my friends, you're a
beautiful melody in the air. To my enemies, who far
outnumber my friends, you're a tool. The very taking of
you might have killed me, Ansset. I'm not young. I can't
take such things."

"I'm sorry."

"Sorry. How could you have known? Raised in that
damnable Songhouse with no exposure to life at all, how
could you have known what kind of hate propels the
animals who walk on two legs claiming to be intelligent? *I*
knew. But ever since you came, I've been a fool. I've
lived for it feels like a thousand years, a million years, and
never made so many mistakes as I have since you came."

"Then send me away. Please."

Mikal looked at him closely. "Do you want to go?"

Ansset wanted to lie to him, to say yes, I must go, send me home to the Songhouse. But he couldn't lie to Mikal. "No," he finally said.

"Then there we are. But from now on, you'll be guarded. It's too damned late, but we'll watch you and you'll let me and my men protect you."

"Yes."

"Sing to me, dammit! Sing to me!" And Mikal strode across the floor, lifted the eleven-year-old boy in his arms, carried him to the fire, and held him as Ansset began to sing. It was a soft song, and it was short, but at the end of it Mikal was lying on his back looking at the ceiling. Tears streamed out from his eyes.

"I didn't mean the song to be sad. I was rejoicing," Ansset said.

"So am I."

Mikal's hand reached out and gripped Ansset's. "How was I to know, Ansset, how was I to know that now, in my dotage, I'd do the foolish thing I've avoided all my life? Oh, I've loved like I've done every other passionate thing, but when they took you I discovered, my Son, that I need you." Mikal rolled over and looked at Ansset, who was gazing at the old man adoringly. "Don't worship me, boy," Mikal said. "I'm an old bastard who'd kill his mother if one of my enemies hadn't already done it."

"You'd never harm me."

"I harm everything I love." His face relaxed from bitterness into the memory of fear. "We were afraid for you. At first we were afraid you were another victim of this madman who's been terrorizing the citizens. The audacity of it was incredible. I expected to learn they'd found your body torn to pieces——" His voice broke. "But then we didn't, and we didn't, and we kept finding more and more bodies, but none of them was yours. We even had to fingerprint some, or use their teeth, but none of them was you and we realized that whoever had taken you had picked his time well. We had wasted weeks trying to fit you in with the other kidnappings, and by the time we realized that was all wrong, the trail was cold. There were no ransom notes. Nothing. I lay awake at night, hours on end, wondering what they were doing to you.''

"I'm all right."

"You're still afraid of them."

"Not of them," Ansset said. "Of me."

Mikal sighed and turned away. "I've let myself need you, and now the worst thing anyone can do to me is take you away. I've grown weak."

And so Ansset sang to him of weakness, but in his song the weakness was the greatest strength of all.

Late in the night, when Ansset had thought Mikal was drifting off to sleep, the old emperor flung out his hand and cried in fury, "I'm losing it!"

"What?" asked Ansset.

"My empire. Did I build it to fall? Did I burn over a dozen worlds and ravage a hundred others just to have the whole thing fall in chaos when I die?" He leaned close to Ansset and whispered to him, their eyes only centimeters apart, "They call me Mikal the Terrible, but I built it all so it would stand like an umbrella over the galaxy. They have it now: peace and prosperity and as much freedom as their little minds can cope with. But when I die they'll throw it all away."

Ansset tried to sing to him of hope.

"There's no hope. I have fifty sons, three of them legitimate, all of them fools who try to flatter me. They couldn't keep the empire for a week, not all of them, not any of them. There's not a man I've met in all my life who could control what I've built in my lifetime. When I die, it all dies with me." And Mikal sank to the floor wearily.

For once Ansset did not sing. He reached out to touch Mikal, rested his hand on the old man's knee, said, "For you, Father Mikal, I'll grow up to be strong. Your empire will not fall!" He spoke so intensely that both he and Mikal, after a moment's surprise, had to laugh.

"It's true, though," Mikal said, tousling Ansset's hair. "For you I'd do it, I'd give you the empire, except they'd kill you. And even if I lived long enough to train you to be a ruler of men, to put you on the throne and force them to accept you, I wouldn't do it. The man who will be my heir must be cruel and vicious and sly and wise, completely selfish and ambitious, contemptuous of all other people, brilliant in battle, able to outguess and outmaneuver every enemy, and strong enough inside himself to live utterly alone all his life." Mikal smiled. "Even *I* don't fit my list of qualifications, because now I'm not alone."

"Neither," said Ansset, "am I." And he sang Father Mikal to sleep.

And as he lay in the darkness, Ansset wondered what it would be like to be emperor, to speak and have his words obeyed, not just by those close enough to hear, but by billions of people all over the universe. He imagined great crowds of people moving to his song, and worlds moving in their paths around their suns according to his word, and the very stars moving left or right near or far as he wished it. His imaginings became dreams as he drifted off to sleep, and he felt the exhilaration of power as if he were flying, the whole of Susquehanna spread below him, but at night, with the lights shining like stars.

Beside him someone else was flying. The face was familiar, but he did not remember why. The man was tall, and in a sergeant's uniform. He looked at Ansset placidly, but then reached out and touched Ansset, and suddenly Ansset was naked and alone and afraid, and the man was fondling his crotch, and Ansset didn't like it and struck out at the man, struck out with all the power of an emperor, and the sergeant fell from the air with a look of terror, fell and was smashed on one of the towers of the palace. Ansset stared at the broken body, the crumpled, bleeding body, and he suddenly felt the terrible weight of responsibility. He looked up, and all the stars were falling, all the worlds were plunging into their suns, all the crowds were marching over a huge and terrible cliff, and however much he wept and cried out for them to stop, they would not listen; until his own screaming woke him up, and he saw Mikal's kind face looking at him with concern.

"A dream," Ansset said, not really awake. "I don't want to be emperor."

"Don't be," Mikal answered. "Don't ever be." It was dark, and Ansset slept again quickly.

12 If the Freemen of Eire had not been guilty, would they have fired on the first imperial troops to come questioning them at their supposedly secret base in Antrim? Some said not. But the Chamberlain said, "It's too stupid to believe."

The Captain of the guard held his temper. "It all fit. The accent pinpointed them to Antrim. Seventeen members of the group had been in Eastamerica for one reason or another during most or all of the time Ansset was kidnapped. And they opened fire the moment they saw the troops."

"There isn't a nationalist group that wouldn't have opened fire."

"There are many nationalist groups that haven't."

"Too convenient, I think," the Chamberlain insisted, not looking at Mikal because he had long since learned that looking at Mikal did not help at all to persuade him. "Every damn one of the Freemen of Eire were killed. Every one!"

"They started killing themselves, when they saw they would lose."

"And I think that Ansset is still a danger to Mikal!"

"I've found the conspiracy and destroyed it!"

And then silence, as Mikal considered. "Has Ansset been able to recognize any of the men you killed?"

The Captain turned a little red in the face. "There was a fire. Few of the bodies were recognizable. I showed him pictures, and he thinks that two or three might have been——"

"Might have been," scoffed the Chamberlain.

"Might very well have been members of the crew on the ship. I did the best I could. I command fleets, dammit, not small mop-up crews!"

Mikal looked at him coldly. "Then, Captain, you should have let someone command who knew what he was doing."

"I wanted to make—to make sure there weren't any mistakes."

Neither Mikal nor the Chamberlain needed to say anything to that. "What's done is done," said the Chamberlain. "But I don't think we ought to get complacent. The enemy was clever enough to get Ansset in the first place and keep him for five months where we couldn't find him. I suspect that even if some or all of the crew were Freeman of Eire, the conspiracy didn't originate with them. They were too easy to find. From the accent. Remember, the kidnapper was able to hide every single day from Ansset's memory and our best probing. If he hadn't wanted us to find the Freemen, he would have blocked those memories, too."

The Captain was not one to cling to defeated arguments. "You're exactly right. I was taken in."

"So were we all, at one time or another," Mikal said, which did much to ease the Captain's discomfort. "You may leave," Mikal told him, and the Captain bowed his head and got up and left. The Chamberlain was alone with Mikal in the meeting room, except for the three trusted guards who watched every movement.

"I'm concerned," said Mikal.

"And so am I."

"No doubt. I'm worried because the Captain is not a stupid man, and he has been behaving stupidly. I assume you've been having men follow him ever since he was appointed."

The Chamberlain tried to protest.

"If you haven't been following him, you haven't been doing a very good job."

"I've been having him followed."

"Get the records and correlate them with Ansset's kidnapping. See what you find."

The Chamberlain nodded. Waited a moment, and then, when Mikal seemed to have lost interest in him, got up and left.

When Mikal was alone (except for the guards, but he had learned to dismiss them from his mind, except for the constant watch against an unwary word), he sighed, stretched his arms, heard his joints pop. His joints had never popped until he was over a hundred years old. "Where's Ansset?" he asked, and one of the guards answered, "I'll get him."

"Don't get him. Tell me where he is."

And the guard cocked his head, listening to the constant

stream of reports coming into his ear implant. "In the garden. With three guards. Near the river."

"Take me to him."

The guards tried not to betray their surprise. Mikal hadn't gone outside the palace in years. But they moved efficiently, and with five guards and an unseen hundred more patrolling the garden, Mikal left the palace and walked to where Ansset sat on the riverbank. Ansset arose when he saw Mikal coming, and they sat together, the guards many meters off, watching carefully, as imperial flits passed overhead.

"I feel like an invader," Mikal said. "I have to take two guards with me when I take a shit."

"The birds of Earth sing beautiful songs," Ansset answered. "Listen."

Mikal listened for a while, but his ear was not so finely tuned as Ansset's, and he grew impatient.

"There are plots within plots," Mikal said. "Sing to me of the plans and plots of foolish men."

So Ansset sang to him a story he had heard only a few days before from a biochemist working in poison control. It was about an ancient researcher who had finally succeeded in crossing a pig with a chicken, so that the creature could lay ham and eggs together, saving a great deal of time at breakfast. The animals laid plenty of eggs, and they were all the researcher had hoped they'd be. The trouble was, the eggs didn't hatch, so the animal couldn't reproduce. The blunt-snouted pickens (or chigs?) couldn't break the eggs, and so the experiment failed. Mikal was amused, and felt much better. "But you know, Ansset, there was a solution. He should have taught them to screw out with their tails."

But Mikal's face soon grew sour again, and he said, "My days are numbered, Ansset. Sing to me of numbered days.'' For all his attempts, Ansset had never understood mortality in the way the old understand it. So he had to sing Mikal's own feelings on the matter back to him. They were no comfort at all. But at least Mikal thought that he was understood, and he felt better as he lay in the grass, watching the Susquehanna rush by.

13 ''We have to take Ansset along. He's the only one who might recognize anyone.''

''I won't have any chance of Ansset being taken away from me again.''

The Chamberlain was stubborn on this point. ''I don't want to leave it to chance. There are too many ways evidence can be destroyed.''

Mikal was angry. ''I won't have the boy caught up in any more of this. He came to Earth to sing, dammit!''

''Then I refuse to try anything more,'' the Chamberlain said. ''I can't accomplish the tasks you set for me if you tie my hands!''

''Take him, then. But you'll have to take me, too.''

''You?''

''Me.''

''But the security arrangements——''

''Damn the security arrangements. Nobody expects me to be along on something like this. Surprise is the best security of all.''

''But, my Lord, you'd be risking your life——''

''Chamberlain! Before you were born I had risked my life in far more dangerous circumstances than these! I bet my own life that I could build an empire and I damn near lost the bet a hundred times. We're leaving in fifteen minutes.''

"Yes, my Lord," said the Chamberlain. He left quickly, to get everything ready, but as he walked out of Mikal's room, he was trembling. He had never dared argue with the emperor that way before. What had he been thinking of? And now the emperor was going with him. If anything happened to Mikal while he was in the Chamberlain's care, the Chamberlain was doomed. No one would agree on anything after Mikal's death except that the Chamberlain must die.

Mikal and Ansset came to the troop flesket together. The soldiers were petrified about going on an operation with the emperor himself. But the Chamberlain noticed that Mikal was buoyant, excited. Probably remembering the glories of past days, the Chamberlain supposed, when he had conquered everybody. Well, he's not much of a conqueror now, and I wish to hell he had let me handle this. One of the dangers of being so close to the center of power—one had to accept the whims of the powerful.

The child, however, seemed to feel nothing at all. It wasn't the first time the Chamberlain had envied Ansset his iron self-control. The ability to hide every feeling from one's enemies and friends—the group was often undistinguishable—would be a greater weapon than any number of lasers.

The flesket went down the Susquehanna River at an unusually high speed, which took it over the normal river traffic. They reached Hisper in an hour, then went another hour beyond, left the river, and crossed farmland and marshes until they reached a much broader river. "The Delaware," the Chamberlain whispered to Mikal and Ansset. Mikal nodded, but said, "Keep your esoterica to yourself." He sounded irritable, which meant he was enjoying himself immensely.

It wasn't long before the Chamberlain had the lieutenant pull the flesket to the shore. "There's a path here that leads where we want to go." The ground was soggy and two soldiers led the column along the path, finding firm ground. It was a long walk, but Mikal did not ask them to go slowly. The Chamberlain wanted to stop and rest, but did not dare ask the column to halt. It would be too much of a victory for Mikal. If the old man can keep it up, thought the Chamberlain, so can I.

The path led to a fenced field, and beyond the field was a group of farmhouses. The nearest house was a colonial revival, which made it about a hundred years old. Only a hundred meters off was the river, and moored to a pile there was a flatboat rocking gently with the currents.

"That's the house," said the Chamberlain, "and that's the boat."

The field between them and the house was not large, and it was overgrown with bushes, so that they were able to reach the house without being too easily noticeable. But the house was empty, and when they rushed the flatboat the only man on board aimed a laser at his own face and blasted it to a cinder. Not before Ansset had recognized him, though.

"That was Husk," Ansset said, looking at the body without any sign of feeling. "He's the man who fed me."

Then Mikal and the Chamberlain followed Ansset through the boat. "It's not the same," Ansset said.

"Of course not," said the Chamberlain. "They've been trying to disguise it. The paint is fresh. And there's a smell of new wood. They've been remodeling. But is there anything familiar?"

There was. Ansset found a tiny room that could have been his cell, though now it was painted bright yellow and a new window let sunlight flood into the room. Mikal examined the windowframe. "New," the emperor pronounced. And by trying to imagine the interior of the flatboat as it might have been, unpainted, Ansset was able to find the large room where he had sung on his last evening in captivity. There was no table. But the room seemed the same size, and Ansset agreed that this could very well have been the place he was held.

Down in Ansset's cell they heard the laughter of children and a flesket passing on the river, full of revelers singing. "Ouite a populated area," Mikal said to the Chamberlain.

"That's why I had us come in through the woods. So we wouldn't be noticed."

"If you wanted to avoid being noticed," Mikal said, "it would have been better to come in on a civilian bus. Nothing's more conspicuous than soldiers hiding in the woods."

The Chamberlain felt Mikal's criticism like a blow. "I'm not a tactician," he said.

"Tactician enough," said Mikal, letting the Chamberlain relax a bit. "We'll go back to the palace now. Do you have anyone you can trust to make the arrest?"

"Yes," the Chamberlain said. "They're already warned not to let him leave the palace."

"Who?" Ansset asked. "Who are you arresting?"

For a moment they seemed reluctant to answer. Finally Mikal said, "The Captain of the guard."

"He was behind the kidnapping?"

"Apparently so," said the Chamberlain.

"I don't believe it," Ansset said, for he had thought he knew the Captain's voice, and hadn't heard any songs except loyalty in it. But the Chamberlain wouldn't understand that. It wasn't evidence. And this was the boat, which seemed to prove something to them. So Ansset said nothing more about the Captain until it was too late.

14 As prisons went, there had been worse. It was just a cell without a door—at least on the inside. And while there was no furniture, the floor yielded as comfortably as the floor in Mikal's private room.

It was hard not to be bitter, however. The Captain sat leaning on a wall, naked so that he couldn't harm himself with his clothing. He was more than sixty years old, and for four years had been in charge of all the emperor's fleets, coordinating thousands of ships across the galaxy. And then to get caught up in this silly palace intrigue, to be the scapegoat—

The Chamberlain had plotted it, of course. Always the Chamberlain. But how could he prove his innocence without undergoing hypnosis; and who would conduct that operation, if not the Chamberlain? Besides, the Captain knew what no one else alive did—that while a serious probe into his mind would not prove that he was at all involved in kidnapping Ansset, it would uncover other things, earlier things, any one of which could destroy his reputation, all of which together would result in his death as surely as if he had captured Ansset himself.

Forty years of unshakable loyalty, and now, when I'm innocent, my old crimes stop me from forcing the issue. He ran his hands along his aging thighs as he sat leaning against a wall. The muscles were still there, but his legs felt as if the skin were coming loose, sagging away. A man should live to be a hundred and twenty in this world, he thought. I won't have had much more than half that.

What had prompted them to imprison him? What had he done that was suspicious? Or had there been anything at all?

There must have been something. Mikal was not a tyrant; he ruled by law, even if he was all powerful. Had he talked to the wrong people too often? Had he been in the wrong cities at the wrong time? Whoever the real traitors were, he was sure the case they had set up against him looked plausible.

Abruptly the lights dimmed to half strength. He knew enough about the prison from the other end of things to know that meant darkness in about ten minutes. Night, then, and sleep, if he *could* sleep.

He lay down, rested his arm across his eyes, and knew that the fluttering in his stomach would be irresistible. He wouldn't sleep tonight. He kept thinking—morbidly let himself think, because he had too much courage to hide from his own imagination—kept thinking about the way he would die. Mikal was a great man, but he was not kind to traitors. They were taken apart, piece by piece, as the holos recorded the death agony to be broadcast on every planet. Or perhaps they would only claim he was peripherally involved, in which case his agony could be more private, and less prolonged. But it wasn't the pain that frightened him—he had lost his left arm twice, not two years apart, and he knew that he could bear pain reasonably well. It was knowing that all the men he had ever commanded would think of him from then on as a traitor, dying in utter disgrace.

That was what he could not bear. Mikal's empire had been created by soldiers with fanatic loyalty and love of honor, and that tradition continued. He remembered the first time he had been in command of a ship. It was at the rebellion of Quenzee, and his cruiser had been surprised on planet. He had had the agonizing choice of lifting the cruiser immediately, before it could be damaged, or waiting to try to save some of his detachment of men. He opted for the cruiser, because if he waited, it would mean nothing at all would be saved for the empire. But the panicked cries of *Wait, Wait* rang in his ears long after the radio was too far to hear them. He had been commended, though they didn't give him the medal for months because he would have found a way to kill himself with it.

I thought so easily of suicide then, he remembered. Now, when it would really be useful, it is forever out of reach.

I will only be paying for my crimes. They don't realize it, but even though they think they're setting up an innocent man, I deserve exactly the penalty I'm getting.

He remembered—

And the lights went out—

He tried to sleep and dream, but still he remembered. And remembered. And in every dream saw her face. No name. He had never known her name—it was part of their protection, because if a name was never known, it could never be found by the cleverest probe, no matter how hard he tried. But her face—blacker than his own, as if she had pure blood descending from the most isolated part of Africa, and her smile, though rare, so bright that the very memory brought tears to his eyes and made his head swim. She was supposed to be the real assassin. And the night before they had planned to kill the prefect, she had brought him to her house. Her parents, who knew nothing, were asleep in the back; she had given herself to him twice before he finally realized that this was more than just release of tension before a difficult mission. She really loved him, he was sure of it, and so he whispered his name into her ear.

"What was that?" she asked.

"My name," he answered, and her face looked as if she was in great pain.

"Why did you tell me?"

"Because," he had whispered as she ran her fingers up his back, "I trust you." She had groaned under the burden of that trust—or perhaps in the last throes of sexual ecstasy. Whatever. He would never know. As he left, she whispered to him at the door, "Meet me at nine o'clock in the morning, meet me by the statue of Horus in Flant Fisway."

And he had waited by the statue for two hours, then went looking for her and found her house surrounded by police. And the houses of two other conspirators, and he knew that they had been betrayed. At first he thought, had let himself think that perhaps *she* had betrayed them, and it was to save his life that she asked him to meet her at the time she knew the police would come. Either way, though, even if she was innocent, he read in the papers that she had killed herself as the police came into her house, had blasted her head off with an old-fashioned bullet pistol right in front of her parents as they sat in the living room wondering why the police were coming to the door. Even if she had betrayed the group, she had refused to betray him—knowing his name, she had preferred death to the possibility of being forced to reveal it.

Scant comfort. He had killed the prefect himself, then left the planet he had been born on and never returned. Spent a few years, until he was twenty, trying to join rebellions or foment rebellions or even uncover some serious discontent somewhere in Mikal's not-very-old empire. But gradually he had come to realize that not that many people longed for independence. Life under Mikal was better than life had ever been before. And as he learned that, he began to understand what it was that Mikal had achieved.

And he enlisted, and used his talents to rise in the military until he was Mikal's most trusted lieutenant, Captain of the guard. All for nothing. All for nothing because of an ambitious civil servant who was having him die, not with honor, as he had dreamed, but in terrible disgrace.

I deserve that, too, he thought. Because I told her my name. All my fault, because I told her my name.

He had been dozing, because the sudden draft of cooler air startled him into wakefulness. Had they come for him? But no—they would have turned on a light. And there was no light, not even in the hall, if his impression was right and the door was open.

"Who is it?" he asked.

"Shhh," came the answer. "Captain?"

"Yes." The Captain struggled to remember the voice. "Who are you?"

"You don't know me. I'm just a soldier. You don't know me. But I know you, Captain. I brought you something." And the Captain felt a hand grope along his body until it found his arm, his hand, and pressed into it a slap with a syringe mounted on it.

"What is it?"

"Honor," said the soldier. The voice was very young.

"Why?"

"You couldn't have betrayed Mikal. But they'll get you, I know it. And make you die—as a traitor. So if you want it—honor."

And then the touch of wind as the soldier left in the darkness; the gathering heat as the door closed and the breeze stopped. The Captain held death in his hand. But he hadn't much time. The soldier was brave and clever, but the prison security system would soon alert the guards—had probably already alerted them—that someone had broken in. Perhaps they were already coming for him.

What if I actually *do* prove my innocence, he wondered. Why die now, when I might be exonerated and live the rest of my life?

But he remembered what the Chamberlain's drugs and questions would uncover, and he could see only her black, black face in his mind as he slapped the stick on his stomach, hard, and the impact broke the seal and allowed the chemicals to open his skin to the poison in the syringe. Normally he would have been counting seconds, to take away the drug when the proper dose had been achieved, but this time the only proper dose was everything the syringe might contain.

He was still holding the slap to his stomach when the lights dazzled on and the door opened and guards rushed in, pulled the syringe off his stomach and out of his hand, and started picking him up to rush him out of the cell. "Too late," he said weakly, but they carried him just the same, half-dragged him down a corridor. The Captain's limbs were completely dead; he recognized the poison and knew that this was a sign that death could not be delayed, no matter what the treatment. They passed through another door, and there he saw the back of a young soldier being forced by three others into an examination room. "Thank you," the Captain tried to say to the boy, but he could not make enough sound to be heard over the footfalls and the rushing of uniforms through the halls.

They laid him on a table and the doctor leaned over him, shook his head, said it was too late.

"Try anyway!" cried a voice that the Captain dimly recognized as the Chamberlain's.

"Chamberlain," the Captain whispered.

"Yes, you bastard!" said the Chamberlain, his voice a study in anguish.

"Tell Mikal that my death frees more plotters than it kills."

"Do you think he doesn't know it?"

"And tell him—tell him——"

The Chamberlain leaned closer, but the Captain died not knowing if he had been able to give his last message to Mikal before he was silenced forever.

15   Ansset watched as Mikal raged at the Chamberlain. Ansset knew Mikal's voice well enough to know that he was lying somehow, that the rage was, at least partly, a sham. Did the Chamberlain know it? Ansset suspected that he did.

"Only a fool would have killed that soldier!" cried Mikal.

The Chamberlain, acting frightened, said, "I tried everything—drugs, hypnosis, but he was blocked, he was too well blocked——"

"So you resorted to old-fashioned torture!"

"It was one of the penalties for treason. I thought that if I began it he'd confess to the rest of the conspiracy——"

"And so he died and now we have no hope of discovering——"

"He was blocked, I tell you, what could I do?"

"What could you do!" Mikal turned away. Ansset heard a hint of pleasure in his voice. At what? It was a grim pleasure, certainly, nothing that Mikal could let himself openly rejoice about.

"So he got poison to the Captain despite our best efforts."

"At least it proves the Captain's guilt," the Chamberlain said.

"At least it proves nothing!" Mikal snarled, turning back to face down the Chamberlain's attempt at brightening the prospects. "You betrayed my trust and failed your duty!"

It was the start of a ritual. The Chamberlain obediently began the next step. "My Lord Imperator, I was a fool. I deserve to die. I resign my position and ask you to have me killed."

Mikal followed the ritual, but angrily, gracelessly, as if to make sure the Chamberlain knew that he was pardoned but not forgiven. "Damn right you're a fool. I grant you your life because of your infinitely valuable services to me in apprehending the traitor in the first place." Mikal cocked his head to one side. "So, Chamberlain, who do you think I should make the next Captain of the guard?"

Ansset was even more confused. The Chamberlain and Mikal were lying about something, withholding something from each other—and now Mikal was asking the Chamberlain for advice on a subject that was absolutely none of his business. And the Chamberlain was actually going to answer.

"Riktors Ashen, of course, my Lord."

Of course? The attitude was impertinent, the very fact of giving advice downright dangerous. The Chamberlain did not do dangerous things. A safe answer would have been to say that he had never given the matter any thought and wouldn't presume to advise the emperor on such a vital matter. And here he had said *of course*.

Ordinarily, Ansset would have expected Mikal to grow cold, to dismiss the Chamberlain, to refuse to see him for days. But Mikal defied everything Ansset thought he knew about him and simply answered, with a smile. "Why of course. Riktors Ashen is the obvious choice. Tell him in my name that he's appointed."

Even the Chamberlain, who had mastered the art of blandness, at will, looked surprised for a moment. And the

Chamberlain's surprise made the connection in Ansset's mind. The Chamberlain had named the one man he definitely did not want as Captain of the guard, sure that Mikal would immediately reject any man the Chamberlain suggested. Instead, Mikal had chosen him, knowing the man would be the one most independent of the Chamberlain's influence.

And Ansset couldn't help but be pleased. Riktors Ashen was a good choice—the fleet would approve, of course, because Riktors Ashen's reputation as a fighter was the best in years. And the empire would approve because Riktors Ashen had proved in the rebellion of Mantrynn that he could deal mercifully with people. Instead of retribution and destruction, Riktors had investigated the people's complaints against their rapacious planet manager, tried the fellow, and executed him. Along with the leaders of the rebellion, of course, but he had governed the planet himself for several months, rooting out corruption in the upper levels of the government and installing local people in high positions to continue the work after he was gone. There was not a more loyal planet in the galaxy than Mantrynn, and no name in the fleet better loved by the common people than that of Riktors Ashen.

But more than any of those good reasons for the appointment, Ansset was glad because he knew the man and liked him and trusted him. Esste herself had told him that Riktors Ashen was the man most like Mikal in the universe. And now that Ansset knew Mikal and loved him, that was the highest praise he could think of.

While Ansset had reflected on the appointment, the Chamberlain had left, and Ansset was startled out of his reverie by Mikal's voice. "Do you know what his last words to me were?"

Ansset knew without being told that Mikal was talking about the Captain.

"He said, 'Tell Mikal that my death frees more plotters than it kills.' And then—and then he said he loved me." Mikal's voice broke. There were tears in his eyes. "Imagine, that cagey old bastard saying he loved me. Did you know that forty years ago he was involved in a conspiracy to overthrow my government? A pathetic thing—his lover betrayed the conspiracy and eventually he grew out of it. He never knew that I knew it. But maybe he wasn't lying. Maybe he did love me, after a fashion."

"Did you love him?"

"I damn well never trusted him, that's for sure. I never trust anybody. Except you." Mikal smiled at Ansset, roughed his hair. His tone was flippant, but Ansset knew the sorrow that lay behind it. "But love him? Who can say. I know I feel like hell knowing he's dead. Loves me. Loved me. Yes, as much as I could love anybody I suppose I loved him. At least I'm glad he found a way to die with honor." Mikal laughed. "Sounds odd, doesn't it? His death leaves the conspiracy covered, and yet I'm glad of it. Since you came here, Ansset, I've forgotten my dedication to my own self-interest.

"Then I should leave."

Mikal sighed. "La la la. One of your most boring songs, Ansset, forever singing the same note."

Mikal settled deeply into the chair. It flowed to support his shift of weight. But his face also sagged into a morose expression.

"What's wrong?" Ansset asked.

"Nothing," Mikal said. "Oh, it does no good to lie to you. Let's just say I'm tired and affairs of state get heavier the older I become."

"Why," Ansset asked, to change the subject—and to satisfy his own curiosity, he was willing to admit to himself, "why was the Captain arrested? How did you know?"

"Oh, that. The Chamberlain's men had been watching

the Captain. He visited that place regularly. He claimed to his friends that he was seeing a woman who lived there. But the neighbors all testified under drugs that a woman never lived there. And the Captain was a master at establishing mental blocks. Still, it all would have been circumstantial, even the ship being similar, if you hadn't identified that man who killed himself there. Husk?"

"Husk." Ansset looked down. "I don't like knowing I affirmed the Captain's destruction."

"It wasn't pleasant for anybody."

"At least the conspiracy is broken," Ansset said, glad for the relief it would bring him from the constant surveillance of the guards.

"Broken?" Mikal asked. "The conspiracy is barely dented. The soldier was able to get poison to the Captain. Therefore there are still plotters within the palace. And therefore I'll instruct Riktors Ashen to keep a close watch on you."

Ansset did not try to hide his disappointment from Mikal.

"I know," Mikal said wearily. "I know how it grates on you. But the secrets are still locked in your mind, Ansset, and until they come out, what else can I do?"

16 The secrets came out the next day.

Mikal held court in the great hall, and at his request Ansset stood with the Chamberlain not far from the throne. Sometime in the afternoon Mikal would have Ansset sing. The rest of the time Ansset resigned himself to watching the boring procession of dignitaries paying their respects to the emperor. They would all be ritually respectful and solicitous and swear their undying love and loyalty to Mikal. Then they would all go home and report how soon they thought Mikal the Terrible would die, and who might succeed him, and what the chances were for grabbing a piece of the empire.

The order of the dignitaries had been carefully worked out to honor loyal friends and humiliate upstarts whose inflated dignity needed puncturing. A minor official from a distant star cluster whose innovations in welfare management had been adopted throughout the empire was officially honored, the first business of the day, and then the real boredom set in. Princes and presidents and satraps and managers, depending on what title had survived the conquest seventy or eighty or ninety years before, all proceeded forward with their retinue, bowing (and their bows showed how afraid they were of Mikal, or how much they wanted to flatter him, or how proud and independent they wanted to seem), uttering a few words asking for a private audience or a special favor, and then backing away to wait along the walls as Mikal put them off with a kind or curt word.

To particularly humiliate the satrap from Sununuway, he was preceded by a delegation of Black Kinshasans attired in their bizarre ancient Earth costumes. Kinshasa insisted, ridiculously, that it was a sovereign nation, though the Chamberlain whispered in Ansset's ear that they hadn't even got their country in the right place, that ancient Kinshasa had been in the Congo River Valley, while these benighted peasants lived at the southern tip of Africa. Still they thumbed their nose at Mikal, calling their representative an ambassador, and they were so ridiculous that giving them precedence over anyone was a gross insult.

"Those toads from Sununuway," said the Chamberlain, "will be madder than hell." He chuckled.

They were picturesque, after a fashion, their hair piled

high with bones and decorations holding it all in place, vast piles of beads across their chests and only the tiniest of loincloths keeping them decent. But picturesque or not, Mikal was bored with them already and signaled for wine.

The Chamberlain poured, tasted it, as was the custom, and then took a step toward Mikal's throne. Then he stopped, beckoned to Ansset. Surprised at the summons, Ansset came to him.

"Why don't *you* take the wine to Mikal, Sweet Songbird?" the Chamberlain said. The surprise fell away from Ansset's eyes, and he took the wine and headed purposefully toward Mikal's throne.

At that moment, however, pandemonium broke loose. The Kinshasan envoys reached into their elaborate headdresses and withdrew wooden knives—which had passed the metal detectors and the frisking—and rushed toward the throne. The guards fired quickly, their lasers dropping five of the Kinshasans, but all had aimed at the foremost assassins, and three continued unharmed. They raced on toward the throne, arms extended so the knives were already aimed directly at Mikal's heart. There were shouts and screams. A guard managed to shift his aim and get off a shot, but it was wild, and the others had exhausted their charges on the first shot. They were struggling to recharge their lasers, but knew even as they tried that they would be too late, that nothing would be fast enough to stop the wooden knives from reaching Mikal.

Mikal looked death in the eye and did not seem disappointed.

But at that moment Ansset threw the wine goblet at one of the attackers and then leaped out in front of the emperor. He jumped easily into the air and kicked the jaw of the first of the attackers. The angle of the kick was perfect, the force sharp and incredibly hard, and the Kinshasan's head flew fifty feet away into the crowd, as his body slid forward until the wooden knife still clutched in his hand touched Mikal's foot. Ansset came down from the jump in time to bring his hand upward into the abdomen of another attacker so sharply that his arm was buried to the elbow in bowels, and his fingers crushed the man's heart.

The third attacker paused just a moment, thrown from his relentless charge by the sudden onslaught from the child who had stood so harmlessly by the emperor's throne. That pause was long enough for recharged lasers to be aimed, to flash, and the last Kinshasan assassin fell, dropping ashes as he collapsed, flaming slightly.

The whole thing, from the appearance of the wooden knives to the fall of the last attacker, had taken five seconds.

Ansset stood still in the middle of the hall, entrails on his arm, blood splashed all over his body. He looked at the gory hand, at the body he had pulled it out of. A rush of long-blocked memories came back, and he remembered other such bodies, other heads kicked from torsos, other men who had died as Ansset learned the skill of killing with his hands. The guilt that had troubled him when he awakened in the evenings on the boat swept through him now with greater force than ever, for now he knew why he felt it, what the guilt was for.

The searches had all been in vain. The precautions were meaningless. Ansset could not have used a weapon, did not need a weapon—Ansset *was* the weapon that was to have been used against Father Mikal.

The smell of blood and broken intestines combined with the emotions sweeping his body. He would have vomited. Longed to vomit. But Control asserted itself—it had been instilled in him for such unbearable moments as this. And he stood, his face an impassive mask, waiting.

The guards approached him carefully, unsure what they should do.

But the Chamberlain was sure. Ansset heard the voice, trembling with fear at how close the assassination had come and how close Mikal had been to assassination ever since Ansset had been restored to him, as the Chamberlain shouted, "Keep him under guard. Wash him. Never let him be out of a laser's aim for a moment. Then bring him to the council chamber in an hour."

The guards looked toward Mikal, white-faced and shaken on the throne, and he nodded to them.

17   Mikal sat staring into the fire, remembering the first man he had ever killed. Mikal had been a mere child, only ten, younger than Ansset—no. Mustn't think of Ansset.

Only ten, and upstairs asleep. It was in the years of terror on the worlds of the Helping Walk, and that night it was their turn. There was no knock on the door, no sound outside, just the crash of the door blowing in, the scream of Mikal's mother, who had not yet gone to bed, the shriek of Mikal's sister as she awakened across the small room from him. Mikal had not had to wonder what it was. He was only ten, but such things could not be kept from children in those years, and he had seen the women's corpses, taken apart and strewn along the street; had seen the male genitals nailed to the walls as the corpse of the man who had owned them leaned below them, leering madly at the fire that had turned his bowels to ashes.

The marauders traveled in small groups, and were said to be irresistible, but Mikal knew where the hunting gun was kept and how to aim it true. He found it in his parents' room, loaded it carefully while his mother kept on screaming downstairs, and then waited patiently while two sets of footsteps came up the stairs. He would have only one shot, but if he chose the right moment, it would be enough—the gun was strong enough to shove a charge through one man and kill another behind him.

The men loomed at the top of the stairs. Mikal had no angst at the thought of killing. He fired. The recoil of the gun knocked him down. When he got up, the two men were gone, having tumbled down the stairs. Still his poise did not leave him. He loaded again, then walked carefully to the top of the stairs. At the bottom, two men knelt over the corpses, then looked up. If Mikal had hesitated, they would have killed him—lasers are quicker than any projectile, and these men knew how to use them. But Mikal did not hesitate. He fired again, and this time held his ground against the recoil, watching as the two men dropped from the explosion as the shell hit one man in the head. It was a lucky shot—Mikal had been aiming for the other man's belly. It made no difference. Both were dead.

Mikal did not know how he would get down the stairs under fire to finish off the rest, but he intended to try. It turned out that he didn't need to. His father was being held, forced to watch as the second man began raping his wife. When four of the marauders were suddenly dead, Mikal's father didn't hesitate to tell the other three, "You haven't got a chance. There are four of them upstairs and another dozen outside."

They believed him; but they were marauders, and so they slit his throat to the bone, and stabbed Mikal's mother eight times, and only then did they turn their lasers on themselves, knowing that there would be no mercy if they surrendered, not even a trial, just the brief ceremony of tearing them to pieces. Mikal's father died even as they did. But Mikal's mother lived. And at the age of ten Mikal became something of a hero. He organized the villages into a strong resisting force, and when the word spread that no marauders could get into that village, other villages pleaded with Mikal to lead them, too, though he was just a child. By the age of fifteen, he had forced the marauders to accept a treaty that, in essence, kept them from landing on Mikal's planet, and over the next few years Mikal taught them that he had the power and the will to enforce it.

Yet in the moments when he first came downstairs and saw the four men he had killed, saw his father gouting blood through the gaping smile in his throat, saw three charred corpses already stinking of half-cooked meat, saw his mother lying naked on the floor with a knife in her breast, he had felt an agony that powered all his actions ever since. Even remembering that night left him sweating, more than a century later. And at first it had been hate that propelled him, forced him to take a fleet out to the marauders' own worlds and subdue them, brought him to be the head of a strong, tough group of men all older than him and willing to follow him to hell.

But somewhere along the way the hate had left him. Not until after they had finally succeeded in killing his mother with poison, decades after she had survived the knives—he had hated then, surely. Perhaps it was gradual, as the night of death faded into memory and he began to feel the responsibility of caring for the billions of people who depended on him for law, for peace, for protection. Somewhere along the way his goals had changed. He was no longer out to punish the wicked, as he had once thought his mission in life to be. Now he was out to establish peace throughout the galaxy, to protect mankind from mankind, even though it meant more bloody war to force the quarreling worlds and nations and leagues of worlds to accept what they all claimed to want. An end to death in battle.

I did it, Mikal told himself, staring into the flames. I did it.

And yet not well enough. Because after all of this a boy had to stand there tonight with blood on his hands, looking at the corpses of the men he had killed. I started all this so that no boy would ever have to do that again.

Mikal felt a pain inside himself that he could not bear. He put his hand into the fire until the pain of his body forced the pain of his heart to recede. Then he wrapped the hand, salved it, and wondered why inward wounds could not be so easily healed.

18   "Songbird," Riktors Ashen said, "it seems that someone has taught you new songs."

Ansset stood among the guards, who all held lasers trained on him. Control kept him from showing any emotion at all, though he longed to cry out with the agony that tore at him inside. My walls are deep, but can they hold this? he wondered, and inside his head he heard, faintly, a voice singing to him. It was Esste's voice, and she sang the love song, and that was what allowed him to contain the guilt and the grief and the fear and keep Control.

"You must have studied under a master," Riktors said.

"I never," Ansset started, and then realized that he could not keep on speaking, not and keep Control.

"Don't torture the boy, Captain," said Mikal from where he sat in a corner of the council room.

The Chamberlain launched into his *pro forma* resignation. "I should have examined the boy's muscle structure and realized what new skills he had been given. I submit my resignation. I beg you to take my life.''

The Chamberlain must be even more worried than usual, Ansset realized, for he had prostrated himself in front of the emperor.

"Shut up and get up," Mikal said. The Chamberlain arose with his face grey. Mikal had not followed the ritual. The Chamberlain's life was still on the line.

"Apparently," Mikal said, "we've broken through some of the barriers laid in my Songbird's mind. Let's see how many."

Ansset stood watching as Riktors took a packet off the table and spread pictures for Ansset to look at. Ansset looked at the first one and felt sick. He did not know why they were making him look until he saw the third one and gasped, despite Control.

"You know this one," Riktors said.

Ansset nodded dumbly.

"Point to the ones you know."

So Ansset pointed to nearly half of them, and Riktors checked them against a list he held in his hands, and when Ansset was through and turned away (slowly, slowly, because the guards with the lasers were nervous), Riktors smiled grimly at Mikal.

"He picked every single one kidnapped and murdered after he himself was kidnapped. There was a connection after all."

"I killed them," Ansset said. and his voice was not calm. It shook as no one in the palace had ever heard it shake before. Mikal looked at him, but said nothing, gave no sign of sympathy. "They had me practice on them," Ansset finished.

"Who had you practice?" Riktors demanded.

"They! The voices—from the box." Ansset struggled to hold onto the memory that had been hidden from him by the block. Now he knew why the block had been so strong—he could not have borne knowing what was hidden in his mind. But now it was in the open, and he had to bear it, at least long enough to tell. He had to tell, though he longed to let the block slide back to hide these memories forever.

"What box?" Riktors would not let up.

"The box. A wooden box. Maybe a receiver, maybe a recording. I don't know."

"Did you know the voice?"

"Voices. Never the same. Not even for the same sentence. The voices changed for every word. I could never find any songs in them."

Ansset kept seeing the faces of the bound men he was told to maim and then kill. He remembered that though he cried out against it, he could not resist, could not stop himself.

"How did they force you to do it?" Riktors asked, and though his voice was soft, the questions were insistent, had to be answered.

"I don't know. I don't know. There were words, and then I had to."

"What words?"

"I don't know! I never knew!" And Ansset began to cry.

Mikal spoke softly. "Who taught you to kill that way?"

"A man. I never knew his name. On the last day he was tied where the others had been. The voices made me kill him." Ansset struggled with the words, the struggle made harder by the realization that this time, when he had killed his teacher, he had not had to be forced. He had killed because he hated the man. "I murdered him."

"Nonsense," the Chamberlain said, trying to sound sympathetic. "You were a tool."

"I told you to shut up," Mikal said curtly. "Can you remember anything else, my son?"

Ansset nodded, took a breath, knowing that though he had lost the illusion of Control, still it was the walls of Control that kept him from screaming, from charging a guard and dying in the welcome flame of a laser. "I killed Master, and all of the crew that was there. Some were missing. The ones I recognized from the pictures from Eire. And Husk. But I killed all the rest, they were all there in the room with the table, and all alone I killed them. They fought me as hard as they could, all except Master, who just stood there like he couldn't believe that I could be doing what he saw me do. Maybe they never knew what it was I was learning to do on deck."

"And then?"

"And then when they were all dead I heard footsteps above me on the deck."

"Who?"

"I don't know. The box told me to lie down on my stomach, and I did, and the box told me to close my eyes, and I did, and I couldn't open them. Then footsteps down the stairs and a slap on my arm and I woke up walking down a street."

Everyone was silent then, for a few moments. It was the Chamberlain who finally spoke first. "My Lord, it must have been the Songbird's great love for you that broke through the barriers, despite the fact that the Captain was already dead——"

"Chamberlain!" Mikal interrupted. "Your life is over if you speak again before I address you." He turned to Riktors Ashen. "Captain, I want to know how those Kinshasans got past your guard."

Riktors Ashen made no attempt to excuse himself. "The guards at the door were my men, and they gave them a routine check, without any effort to investigate the possibility of unusual weapons in those unusual headdresses. They've been replaced with more careful men, and the ones who let them by are in prison, waiting for your pleasure.''

''My pleasure,'' said Mikal, ''will be a long time coming.''

Ansset was regaining Control. He listened to the songs in Riktors Ashen's voice and marvelled at the man's confidence. It was as if none of this could touch Riktors Ashen. He knew he was not at fault, knew that he would not be punished, knew that all would turn out well. His confidence was infectious, and Ansset felt just a little better.

Mikal gave clear orders to his Captain. ''There will be a rigorous investigation of Kinshasa. Find any and every link between the Kinshasan assassination attempt and the manipulation of Ansset. Every member of the conspiracy is to be treated as a traitor. All the rest of the Kinshasans are to be deported to a world with an unpleasant climate, and every building in Kinshasa is to be destroyed and removed and every field and orchard and animal is to be stripped. I want every bit of it on holo, to be distributed throughout the empire.''

Riktors bowed his head.

Then Mikal turned to the Chamberlain, who looked petrified with fear, though he still clung to his dignity.

''Chamberlain, what would you recommend that I do with my Songbird?''

The Chamberlain was back to being careful. ''My Lord, it is not a matter to which I have given thought. The disposition of your Songbird is not a matter on which I feel it proper to advise you.''

''Very carefully said, my dear Chamberlain.''

Ansset struggled to keep Control as he listened to their discussion of what should be done with him. Mikal raised his hand in the gesture that, by ritual, spared the Chamberlain's life. The Chamberlain's relief was visible, and at another time Ansset would have laughed; but now there was no laughter in him, and he knew that his own relief would not come so easily as it had come to the Chamberlain.

"My Lord," Ansset said, when the conversation paused. "I beg you to put me to death."

"Dammit, Ansset, I'm sick of rituals," Mikal said.

"This is no ritual," Ansset said, his voice tired and husky from misuse. "And this is no song, Father Mikal. I'm a danger to you."

"I noticed," Mikal said dryly. Then he turned back to the Chamberlain. "Have Ansset's possessions put together and ready for travel."

"I have no possessions," Ansset said.

Mikal looked at him in surprise.

"I've never owned anything," Ansset said.

Mikal shrugged, spoke again to the Chamberlain. "Inform the Songhouse that Ansset is returning. Tell them that he has performed beautifully, and I have marred him by bringing him to my court. Tell them that they will be paid four times what we agreed to before, and that it doesn't begin to compensate them for the beauty of their gift to me or to the damage that I did to it. See to it. See to it all."

Then Mikal turned to go. Ansset could not bear to see Mikal leave like that, turning his back and walking out without so much as a farewell. "Father Mikal," Ansset called out. Or rather, he meant to call out. But the words came out softly. They were a song, and Ansset realized that he had sung the first notes of the love song. It was all the good-bye he'd be able to give.

Mikal left without giving any sign that he heard.

19 "They told me you're not a prisoner," the guard said. "But I'm supposed to watch you, me and the others, and not let you do anything dangerous or try to get away. Sounds like a prisoner to me, but I guess they mean I'm supposed to be nice about it."

"Thanks," Ansset said, managing a smile. "Does that mean I can go where I want?"

"Depends on where you want."

"The garden," Ansset said, and the guard nodded, and he and his companions followed Ansset out of the palace and across the broad lawns to the banks of the Susquehanna. All the way there his Control returned. He remembered the words of his first teacher. "When you want to weep, let the tears come through your throat. Let pain come from the pressure in your thighs. Let sorrow rise and resonate through your head." Everything was a song and, as a song, could be controlled by the singer.

Walking by the Susquehanna as the lawns turned cold in the afternoon shade, Ansset sang his grief. He sang softly, but the guards heard his song, and could not help but weep for him, too.

He stopped at a place where the water looked cold and clear, and began to strip off his tunic, preparing to swim. A guard reached out a hand and stopped him. Ansset noticed the laser pointed at his foot. "I can't let you do that. Mikal gave orders you were not to be allowed to take your own life."

"I only want to swim," Ansset answered, his voice heady with trustworthiness.

"I'd be killed if any harm came to you," the guard said.

"I give you my oath that I will only swim. I'm a good swimmer. And I won't try to get away."

The guards considered among themselves, and the confidence in Ansset's voice won out. "Don't go too far," the leader told him.

Ansset took off his underwear and dove into the water. It was icy cold, with the chill of autumn on it, and it stung at first. He swam in broad strokes upstream, knowing that to the guards on the bank he would already seem like only a speck on the surface of the water. Then he dove and swam under the water, holding his breath as only a singer or a pearldiver can, and swam across the current toward the near shore, where the guards were waiting. He could hear, though muffled by the water, the cries of the guards. He surfaced, laughing. God, he could laugh again.

Two of the guards had already thrown off their boots and were up to their waists in water, preparing to try to catch Ansset's body as it swept by. But Ansset kept laughing at them, and they turned at him angrily.

"Why did you worry?" Ansset said. "I gave my word."

Then the guards relaxed, and Ansset didn't play any more games with them, just swam and floated and rested on the bank. The chill autumn air was like the perpetual chill of the Songhouse, and though he was cold, he was, not comfortable, but comforted.

And from time to time he swam underwater for a while, listening to the different sound the guard's quarreling and laughing made when Ansset was distanced from them by the water. They played at polys, and the leader was losing heavily, though he was a good sport about it. And sometimes, in a lull in their game, Ansset could hear the cry of a bird in the distance, made sharper and yet more ambiguous by the roar of the current in his ears.

It was like the muffling of the birdcalls when Ansset had been in his cell on the flatboat. The birds had been Ansset's only sign that there was a world outside his prison, that even though he was caught up for a time in madness, something still lived that was untouched by it.

And then Ansset made a connection in his mind and realized he had been terribly, terribly wrong. He had been wrong and Mikal had to know about it immediately, had to know about it before something terrible happened, something worse than anything that had gone before—Mikal's death.

Ansset swam quickly to shore, splashed out of the water, and without any attempt to dry off put on his underwear and his tunic and started off toward the palace. The guards called out, broke up the game, and chased after him. Let them chase, Ansset thought.

"Stop!" cried the guards, but Ansset did not stop. He was only walking. Let them run and catch up.

"Where are you going!" demanded the first one to reach him. The guard caught at his shoulder, tried to stop him, but Anset pulled easily away and sped up.

"To the palace," Ansset said. "I have to get to the palace!"

The guards were gathered around him now, and some stepped in front of him to try to head him off.

"You were told I could go where I wanted."

"With limits," the leader reminded him.

"Am I allowed to go to the palace?"

A moment's pause. "Of course."

"I'm going to the palace."

So they followed him, some of them with lasers drawn, as he entered the palace and began to lead them through the labyrinth. The doors had not been changed—he could open any that he had ever been able to open. And as the guards accompanied him through the labyrinth of the palace, they grew more and more confused. "Where are we going?"

"Don't you know?" Ansset asked innocently.

"I didn't know this corridor existed, how could I know where it leads!"

And some of them speculated on whether they would ever be able to find their way out alone. Ansset did not smile, but he wanted to. They were passing close to the kitchens, the mess hall, the guards' rooms, the places in the palace most familiar to them. But Ansset was more familiar, and left them utterly confused.

There was no confusion, however, when they emerged in the security rooms just outside Mikal's private room. The leader of the guards instantly recognized it, and in fury planted himself in front of Ansset, his laser drawn. "The one place you can't go is here," he said. "Now move, the other way!"

"I'm here to see Mikal. I have to see Mikal!" Ansset raised his voice so it could be heard in the room, in the corridor outside, in any other security room. And sure enough one of the doorservants came to them and asked, in his quiet, unobtrusive way, if he could be of service.

"No," said the guard.

"I have to see Mikal!" Ansset cried, his voice a song of anguish, a plea for pity. Ansset's pleas were irresistible. But the servant had no intention of resisting. He merely looked puzzled and asked the guards, "Didn't you bring him here? Mikal is looking for him."

"Looking?" the guard asked.

"Mikal wants him in his rooms immediately. And not under guard."

The leader of the guards lowered his laser. So did the others.

"That's right," the doorservant said. "Come this way, Songbird."

Ansset nodded to the guard, who shrugged and looked away in embarrassment. Then, as the doorservant had suggested, Ansset came that way.

20   Ansset fit right into the madness, his hair still wet, his tunic clinging to his damp body. But he wasn't prepared for Mikal and the Chamberlain and Riktors Ashen, the only others in the room. Mikal was oozing joviality. He greeted Ansset with a handshake, something he had never done before. And he sounded incredibly cheerful as he said, "Ansset, my Son, it's fine now. We were so foolish to think we needed to send you away. The Captain was the only one in the plot close enough to have given you the signal. When he died, I immediately became safe. In fact, as you proved today, my boy, you're the best bodyguard, I could possibly have!" Mikal laughed, and the Chamberlain and Riktors Ashen joined in as if they hadn't a care in the world, as if they couldn't possibly be more delighted with the turn of events. But it was all unbelievable. Ansset knew Mikal's voice too well. Warnings laced through everything he said and did. Something was wrong.

Well, something *was* wrong, and Ansset immediately told Mikal what he had realized. "Mikal, when I was imprisoned on the flatboat I could hear birds outside. Birds, and that's all. Nothing else. But when we went down in the boat on the Delaware we heard children laughing on the road and a flesket pass by on the river! I was never kept there! It was a fraud, and the Captain died for it!'' But Mikal only shook his head and laughed. The laugh was maddening. Ansset wanted to leap at him, warn him that whoever had made this plot was more clever than they had thought, was still at large—

But the Chamberlain came to him with a bottle of wine in his hand, laughing just as Mikal was, with songs of treachery in his voice. ''Never mind that kind of thing,'' the Chamberlain said. ''It's time for celebration. You saved Mikal's life, my boy! I brought some wine. Ansset, why don't you pour it!''

Ansset shuddered with memories he couldn't quite grasp.

''I?'' Ansset asked, surprised, and then not surprised at all. The Chamberlain held out the full bottle and the empty goblet.

''For the Lord Mikal,'' the Chamberlain said.

Ansset shouted and dashed the bottle to the floor. ''Make him keep silent!''

The suddenness of Ansset's violent action brought Riktors's laser out of his belt and into his hand. Riktors had come armed into Mikal's private room, Ansset realized with relief. ''Don't let the Chamberlain speak,'' Ansset cried.

''Why not?'' Mikal asked innocently, and the laser sank in Riktors's grasp; but Ansset knew there was no innocence behind the words. Mikal was pretending not to understand. Ansset wanted to fly through the ceiling and escape.

But the Chamberlain had not stopped. He said quickly, almost urgently. ''Why did you do that? I have another bottle. *Sweet Songbird, let Mikal drink deeply!*''

The words hammered into Ansset's brain, and by reflex he whirled and faced Mikal. He knew what was happening, knew and screamed against it in his mind. But his hands came up against his will, his legs bent, he compressed to spring, all so quickly that he couldn't stop himself. He knew that in less than a second his hand would be buried in Mikal's face, Mikal's beloved face, Mikal's smiling face—

Mikal was smiling at him, kindly and without fear. For years Control had come to Ansset to contain emotion. Now it came to express it. He could not, could not, could not hurt Mikal, and yet he was driven to it, he leaped, his hand struck out—

But it did not sink into Mikal's face. Instead it plunged into the floor, breaking the surface and becoming immersed in the gel that erupted from the floor. The impact broke the skin in Ansset's arm; the gel made the pain agonizing; the bone ached with the force of the blow. But Ansset did not feel that pain. All he felt was the pain in his mind as he struggled against the compulsion that still drove at him, to kill Mikal, to kill Mikal.

His body heaved upward, his hand flew through the air, and the back of Mikal's chair shattered and splashed at the impact. The chair shuddered, then sealed itself. But Ansset's hand was bleeding; the blood spurted and splashed and skitted across the surface of the gel spreading across the now-lax floor. But it was his own blood, not Mikal's, and Ansset cried out in joy. It sounded like a scream of agony.

In the distance he heard Mikal's voice saying, "Don't shoot him." And, as suddenly as it had come, the compulsion ceased. His mind spun as he heard the Chamberlain's words fading away: *"Songbird, what have you done!"*

Those were the words that had set him free.

Exhausted and bleeding, Ansset lay on the floor, his right arm covered with blood. The pain reached him now, and he groaned, though his song was as much a song of triumph as of pain. Somehow Ansset had had strength enough, had withstood it long enough that he had not killed Father Mikal.

Finally he rolled over and sat up, nursing his arm. The bleeding had settled to a slow trickle.

Mikal was still sitting in the chair, which had healed itself. The Chamberlain stood where he had stood ten seconds before, at the beginning of Ansset's ordeal, the goblet looking ridiculous in his hand. Riktors's laser was aimed at the Chamberlain.

"Call the guards, Captain," Mikal said.

"I already have," Riktors answered. The button on his belt was glowing. Guards came quickly into the room. "Take the Chamberlain to a cell," Riktors ordered them. "If any harm comes to him, all of you will die, and your families, too. Do you understand?" The guards understood. They were Riktors's men, not the Chamberlain's. There was no love there.

Ansset held his arm. Mikal and Riktors Ashen waited while a doctor came and treated it. The pain subsided. The doctor left.

Riktors spoke first. "Of course you knew it was the Chamberlain, my Lord."

Mikal smiled faintly.

"That was why you let him persuade you to call Ansset back here. To let him show his hand."

Mikal's smile grew broader.

"But, my Lord, only you could have known that the Songbird would be strong enough to resist a compulsion that was five months in the making."

Mikal laughed. And this time Ansset heard real mirth in the laughter.

"Riktors Ashen," Mikal said. "Will they call you Riktors the Great? Or Riktors the Usurper?"

It took Riktors a moment to realize what had been said. Only a moment. But before his hand could reach his laser, which was back in his belt, Mikal's hand held a laser that was pointed at Riktors's heart.

"Ansset, my Son, will you take the Captain's laser from him?"

Ansset got up and took the Captain's laser from him. He could hear the song of triumph in Mikal's voice. But Ansset did not understand. What had Riktors done? This was the man that Esste had told him was as much like Mikal as any man alive—

And Mikal had conquered the galaxy. Oh, Esste had warned him, and he had taken only reassurance from it!

"Only one mistake, Riktors Ashen," Mikal said. "Otherwise brilliantly done. And I really don't see how you could have avoided that mistake either."

"You mean Ansset's strength?" Riktors asked, his voice still trying to be calm and succeeding amazingly well.

"Not even I counted on that. I was prepared to kill him, if I needed to." The words did not hurt Ansset. He would rather have died than hurt Mikal, and he knew that Mikal knew that.

"Then I made no mistakes," Riktors said. "How did you know?"

"Because my Chamberlain, unless he were under some sort of compulsion, would never have had the courage to argue with me, to insist on taking Ansset on his stupid military expedition, to dare to suggest your name when I asked him who ought to become the new Captain of the guard. But you had to have him suggest you, didn't you, because unless you were Captain you wouldn't have been in a position to take control when I was dead. The Chamberlain would be the obvious guilty one, while you would be the hero who stepped in and held the empire together. The best possible start to your reign. No taint of assassination would have touched you. Of course, half the empire would have rebelled immediately. But you're a good tactician and a better strategist and you're popular with the fleet and a lot of citizens. I'd have given you one chance in four of making it. And that's better odds than any other man in the empire."

"I gave myself even odds," Riktors said, but now Ansset could clearly hear the fear singing through the back of his brave words. Well, why not? Death was certain now, and Ansset knew of no one, except perhaps an old man like Mikal, who could look at death, especially death that also meant failure, without some fear.

But Mikal did not push the button on the laser. Nor did he summon the guards.

"Kill me now and finish it," Riktors said, pleading for an honorable death, though he knew he did not deserve it.

Mikal tossed the laser away. "With this? It has no charge. The Chamberlain installed a charge detector at every door to my chambers over fifteen years ago. He would have known if I was armed."

Immediately Riktors took a step forward, the beginning of a rush toward the emperor. Just as quickly Ansset was on his feet, despite the bandaged arm, ready to kill with the other hand, with his feet, with his teeth. Riktors stopped cold.

"Ah," Mikal said. "You never had time to learn from the man who taught Ansset. What a bodyguard you gave me, Riktors."

Ansset hardly heard him. All he heard was Mikal's voice saying, "It has no charge." Mikal *had* trusted him. Mikal had staked his life on Ansset's ability to resist the compulsion. Ansset wanted to weep in gratitude for such trust, in fear at such terrible danger only barely averted. Instead he stood still with iron Control and watched Riktors for any sign of movement.

"Riktors," Mikal went on, "your mistakes were very slight. I hope you've learned from them. So that when an assassin as bright as you are tries to take *your* life, you'll know all the enemies you have and all the allies you can call on and exactly what you can expect from each."

Ansset looked at Riktor's face and remembered how glad he had been when the tall soldier had been made Captain. "Let me kill him now," Ansset said.

Mikal sighed. "Don't kill for pleasure, my son. If you ever kill for pleasure, you'll come to hate yourself. Besides, weren't you listening? I'm going to adopt Riktors Ashen as my heir."

"I don't believe you," Riktors said, but Ansset heard hope in his voice.

"I'll call in my sons—they stay around court, hoping to be closest to the palace when I die," Mikal said. "I'll make them sign an oath to respect you as my heir. Of course they'll sign it, and of course they'll all break it, and of course you'll have them all killed the first moment you can after you take the throne. If any of them is smart at all, he'll be at the other end of the galaxy by then. But I doubt there'll be any that bright. When shall we have you crowned? Three weeks from tomorrow is enough time to wait. I'll abdicate in your favor, sign all the papers, it'll make the headlines on the newspapers for days. I can just see all the potential rebels tearing their hair with rage. It's a pleasant picture to retire on."

Ansset didn't understand. "Why? He tried to kill you."

Mikal only laughed. It was Riktors who answered. "He thinks I can hold his empire together. But I want to know the price."

"Price? What could you give me, Riktors, that you wouldn't take as a gift for you yourself anyway? I've waited for you for sixty years. Seventy years, Riktors. I kept thinking, surely there's someone out there who covets my power and has guts and brains enough to come get it. And at last you came. You'll see to it that I didn't build for nothing. That the wind won't tear away everything the moment I'm not there to hold it up. All I want after you take the throne is a house for myself and my Songbird until I die. On Earth, so you can keep an eye on me, of course. And with a different name, so that I won't be plagued by all the bastards who'll try to get my help to throw you out. And when I'm dead, send Ansset home. Simple enough?"

"I agree," Riktors said.

"How prudent." And Mikal laughed again.

21   The vows were made, the abdication and the coronation took place with a great deal of pomp, and Susquehanna's caterers and hotelkeepers became wealthier than they had ever dreamed of. All the contenders and pretenders were slaughtered, and Riktors spent a year going from system to system to quell all the rebellions with his own mixture of brutality and sympathy. After the first few planets were at peace, the populace happy and the rebels butchered, most of the other rebellions quelled themselves.

It was only the day after the papers announced that Riktors Ashen was coming home when the soldiers appeared at the door of the little house in Brazil where Mikal and Ansset lived.

"How can he!" Ansset cried out in anguish when he saw the soldiers outside. "He gave his word!"

"Open the door for them, my Son," Mikal said.

"They're here to kill you!"

"A year was more than I hoped for. I've had that year. Did you really expect Riktors to keep his word? There isn't room in the galaxy for two heads that know the feel of the imperial crown."

"I can kill most of them before they could come near. If you hide, perhaps——"

"Don't kill anyone, Ansset. That's not your song. The dance of your hands is ugly without the song of your voice, Songbird."

The soldiers began to beat on the door, which, because it was steel, did not give way easily. "They'll blow it open in a minute," Mikal said. "Promise me you won't kill anyone. No matter who. Please. Don't avenge me."

"I will."

"Don't avenge me. Promise. On your life. On your love for me."

Ansset promised. The door blew open. The soldiers killed Mikal with a flash of lasers that turned his skin to ashes. They kept firing until nothing but ashes was left. Then they gathered them up. Ansset watched, keeping his promise but wishing with all his heart that somewhere in his mind there was a wall he could hide behind. Unfortunately, he was too sane.

22 They took twelve-year-old Ansset and the ashes of the emperor to Susquehanna. The ashes were placed in a huge urn and displayed with state honors. Everyone was told that Mikal had died of old age, and no one admitted to suspecting otherwise.

They brought Ansset to the funeral feast under heavy guard, for fear of what his hands might do.

After the meal, at which everyone pretended to be somber, Riktors called Ansset to him. The guards followed, but Riktors waved them away. The crown rested lightly on his hair.

"I know I'm safe from you," Riktors said.

"You're a lying bastard," Ansset said softly, so that only Riktors could hear, "and if I hadn't given my word to a better man than you, I'd tear you end to end."

"If I weren't a lying bastard," Riktors answered with a smile, "Mikal would never have given the empire to me."

Then Riktors stood. "My friends," he said, and the dignitaries present gave a cheer. "From now on I am not to be known as Riktors Ashen, but as Riktors Mikal. The name Mikal shall pass to all my successors on the throne, in honor of the man who built this empire and brought peace to all mankind." Riktors sat amid the applause and cheers, which sounded like some of the people might have been sincere. It was a nice speech, as impromptu speeches went.

Then Riktors asked Ansset to sing.

"I'd rather die," Ansset said.

"You will, when the time comes. Now sing—the song Mikal would want sung at his funeral."

Ansset sang then, standing on the table so that everyone could see him, just as he had stood to sing to an audience he hated on his last night of captivity in the ship. His song was wordless, for all the words he might have said were treason, and would have stirred the audience to destroy Riktors on the spot. Instead Ansset sang a melody, flying unaccompanied from mode to mode, each note torn from his throat in pain, each note bringing a sweeter pain to the ears that heard it.

The song broke up the banquet as the grief they had all pretended to feel now burned within them. Many went home weeping; all felt the great loss of the man whose ashes dusted the bottom of the urn.

Only Riktors stayed at the table after Ansset's song was over.

"Now," Ansset said, "they'll never forget Father Mikal."

"Or Mikal's Songbird," Riktors said. "But I am Mikal now, as much of him as could survive. A name and an empire."

"There's nothing of Father Mikal in you," Ansset said coldly.

"Is there not?" Riktors said softly. "Were you fooled by Mikal's public cruelty? No, Songbird." And in his voice Ansset heard the hints of pain that lay behind the harsh and unmerciful emperor.

"Stay and sing for me, Songbird," Riktors said. Pleading played around the edges of his voice.

"I was placed with Mikal, not with you," Ansset said. "I must go home now."

"No," Riktors said, and he reached into his clothing and pulled out a letter. Ansset read it. It was in Esste's handwriting, and it told him that if he was willing, the Songhouse would place him with Riktors. Ansset did not understand. But the message was clear, the language unmistakably Esste's own. He had trusted Esste when she told him to love Mikal. He would trust her now.

Ansset reached out his hand and touched the urn of ashes that rested on the table. "I'll never love you," he said, meaning the words to hurt.

"Nor I you," Riktors answered. "But we may, nonetheless, feed each other something that we hunger for. Did Mikal sleep with you?"

"He never wanted to. I never offered."

"Neither will I," Riktors said. "I only want to hear your songs."

There was no voice in Ansset for the word he decided to say. He could only nod. Riktors had the grace not to smile. He just nodded in return and left the table. Before he reached the doors, Ansset spoke to him.

"What will you do with this?"

Riktors looked at the urn where Ansset rested his hand.

"The relics are yours. Do what you want." Then Riktors Mikal was gone.

Ansset took the urn of ashes into the chamber where he and Father Mikal had sung so many songs to each other. Ansset stood for a long time before the fire, humming the memories to himself. He gave all the songs back to Father Mikal, and with love he reached out and emptied the urn on the blazing fire.

The ashes put the fire out.

23 "The transition is complete," Songmaster Onn said to Songmaster Esste as soon as the door to the High Room was closed.

"I was afraid," Esste confided in a low melody that trembled. "Riktors Ashen is not unwise. But Ansset's songs are stronger than wisdom."

They sat together in the cold sunlight that filtered through the shutters of the High Room. "Ah," sang Songmaster Onn, and the melody was of love for Songmaster Esste.

"Don't praise me. The gift and the power were Ansset's."

"But the teacher was Esste. In other hands Ansset might have been used as a tool for power, for wealth. Or worse, he might have been wasted. But in your hands———"

"No, Brother Onn. Ansset himself is too much made of love and loyalty. He makes others desire what he himself already is. He is a tool that cannot be used for evil."

"Will he ever know?"

"Perhaps; I do not think he yet suspects the power of his gift. It would be better if he never found out how little like other Songbirds he is. And as for the last block in his mind—we laid that well. He will never find his way around it, and so he will never learn or even search for the truth about who controlled the transfer of the crown.''

Songmaster Onn sang tremulously on the delicate plots woven in the mind of a child of five, of six, of nine; plots that could have unwoven at any time. ''But the weaver was wise, and the cloth has held.''

''Mikal the Conqueror,'' said Esste, ''learned to love peace more than he loved himself. So will Riktors Mikal. That is enough. We have done our duty for mankind. Now we must teach other little singers.''

''Only the old songs,'' sighed Songmaster Onn.

''No,'' answered Songmaster Esste, with a smile. ''We will teach them to sing of Mikal's Songbird.''

''Ansset has already sung that song, better than we could hope to.''

They walked slowly out of the High Room as Songmaster Esste whispered, ''Then we will harmonize!'' Their laughter was music down the stairs.

JOSIF

1 Kya-Kya's arms were too thin. She noticed it again as she touched the keys on her computer terminal; if she ever had to use her arms to lift something quite heavy, they would break. I am not meant to bear burdens, Kya-Kya reminded herself. I don't look like a substantial person, which is why I am forced into such insubstantial work.

It was a rationalization she had tried before and never more than half believed. She had graduated from the Princeton Government Institute with the fourth highest score in the history of the school; and when she tried to find work, instead of being flooded with prestigious job offers, she found herself forced to choose between a computer-pumping job at the Information Center in Tegucigalpa and a city manager's position on some Godforsaken planet she couldn't even find on the starmaps. "It's an apprenticeship," her adviser had told her. "Do well, and you'll rise quickly." But Kya-Kya sensed that even her adviser didn't really believe it. What could she hope to do well in Tegucigalpa? Her job was in Welfare, the Department of Senior Services, the Office of Pension Payments. And it wasn't an imperial office—it was planetary. Earth, of all places, which might be the capital of the universe but was still a provincial backwater at heart.

If Kya-Kya could once convince herself that she had not been given a better position because of some wrong impression she gave, of weakness or incompetence or undependability, she could then believe that, by her proving that she was strong and competent and dependable, her

215

situation might improve. But she knew better. At the Songhouse it had been the Deafs and, not quite so much, the Blinds who had had to take a second- or third-class role in the community. Here on Earth, it was the young, the female, the gifted.

And while youth would take care of itself, there was nothing she particularly wanted to do about being female— changers were even more heavily discriminated against. And her gifts, the very things that could make her the most valuable to government service, made her an object of envy, resentment, even fear.

It was her third week there, and it had finally come to a head today. Her job took, at best, a third of her time— when she slacked. So she began to try (on the assumption that she needed to prove her competence) to find out more about the system, to grasp the overall function of everything, the way all the data systems linked together.

"Who programs the computers?" she innocently asked Warvel, the head of Pensions.

Warvel looked annoyed—he did not like interruptions. "We all do," he said, turning immediately back to his desk, where figures danced across the whole surface, showing him exactly what was going on at every desk in his office.

"But who," persisted Kya-Kya, "set up the way it works? The *first* programming?"

Warvel looked more than annoyed. He stared at her intently, then said savagely, "When I want a research project on the subject, you'll be the person I appoint. But right now your job is taking inflation tables and applying them to classes of pensions for the budget year starting in only six months, and when you're here at my desk, Kyaren, it means that neither you nor I is doing his job!"

Kya-Kya waited for a few moments, watching the slightly balding top of his head as he played with the numbers on his desk, querying the computer on questioning procedures. She could not understand the violence of his outburst, as defensive as if she had asked him whether it was true he had been castrated in a playground accident when he was five. When he noticed she was still standing there, he reached over and pointed to a spot on his desk where no figures appeared at all.

"See that blank spot?" Warvel asked.

"Yes."

"That's you. That's the work you're doing right now."

And Kya-Kya returned to her desk and her terminal and began punching in the numbers with her slender fingers on the end of slender arms, feeling weaker and slighter than she had ever felt before.

It was not just Warvel, not just the work. From the moment she arrived, it seemed that none of her co-workers was interested in making her acquaintance. Conversations never included her; in-jokes left her completely in the dark; people fell silent when she came near a table in the lunchroom or a fountain in the halls. At first—and still—she tried to believe that it was because she was young, she was frail, she did not make friends easily. But actually, right from the start, she knew it was because she was an ambitious woman with remarkable scores from the best school on the planet; because she was curious and wanted to learn and wanted to be excellent, which would threaten all of them, make them all look bad.

Petty bureaucrats with infinitesimal minds, she told herself, jabbing at the keys on the computer. Small minds running a small planet, terrified of someone who smacks of potential greatness—or even potential averageness.

They had all watched her return to her desk from her interview with Warvel. Even the women had looked her up and down in the contemptuous way they had on Earth, as if the act of surveying her body expressed their opinion of her mind and her heart. There wasn't one sympathetic look on anyone's face.

She stopped punching keys and got hold of herself. Think that way, Kyaren, she told herself, and you'll never get anywhere. Must do my best, must try to be good at it, and hope for a change, hope for some opportunity to shine.

Her terminal glowed at her, unwinking, as steady as her ambition, as blinding as her fear, and she could not concentrate on it anymore. And so she punched in her lunchtime, was given clearance—there were enough tables open in the lunchroom—and left her desk to go eat. The eyes followed her again, and after she left, she could hear the buzz of conversation begin. The office was unbearably silent when she was there; when she was gone, everyone was friendly.

It was in the lunchroom that day that she met Josif.

The setting was the good thing about Tegucigalpa. The Information Center was almost invisible from the air—all the roofs were planted with the same jungle growth that was lush on the hills. But in the complex itself, everything was a miracle of green and glass, huge transparent walls on hundreds of buildings rising twenty or forty or eighty meters into the air. The lunchroom was at the edge, on a slope, where it could overlook much of the rest of the complex—even had a view of the village that was all that was left of the ancient city. As Kya-Kya—or Kyaren, as she had taken to calling herself when she first discovered she was going to work on Earth, in an effort to sound more native—took her food from the dispensers and carried it to an empty table, she watched a dazzlingly bright bird float down from the roof of the Income Department and land on a small island in the Chultick River. During its descent, a wild thing living in a perfectly wild habitat, the bird had passed in front of the glass windows where dozens of people worked sucking information out of computers, twisting it around, and spewing it back in. A jungle, with electricity manipulated amid the trees to hold all the knowledge of a world.

It was because she was watching the bird and thinking of the contrasts that Josif was able to set down his tray unnoticed. Of course, Josif was quiet, too—as silent as a statistic, Kyaren would later tell him. But as she watched the bird walking around in a seemingly purposeless dance on the island, she became aware of someone watching her.

She turned, and there was Josif. Deep but open-seeming eyes, delicate features, and a mouth that perpetually smiled as if he knew the joke and would never tell anyone, because it wasn't really funny.

"I hear Warvel ate you alive today."

Gossip travels quickly, Kya-Kya thought—but couldn't help being flattered that this total stranger would even care; couldn't help being pleased that someone was actually speaking to her about something besides business.

"I've been chewed," Kya-Kya said, "but I haven't been swallowed yet."

"I've noticed you," Josif said, smiling at her.

"I've never noticed you," Kyaren answered, though it was not really true. She had seen him around—he worked in Statistics, Department of Vitals, Office of Death, which was on the floor below hers. She just hadn't cared much. Kya-Kya had been raised in the Songhouse, and the close association of the sexes had somewhat numbed her to the attractions of males. She briefly wondered, Is he good-looking? Is he beautiful? She wasn't sure. Interesting, anyway. The eyes that looked so innocent, the mouth that looked so world-wise.

"Yes you have," Josif answered, still smiling. "You're an outcast."

So it was that obvious; she resented hearing it in words.

"Am I?" she asked.

"It's something we have in common. We're both outcasts."

It was a line, then, and Kyaren sighed. She had become expert at deflecting lines—bored students had tried many times to spark up a dull evening with attempts at seducing Kya-Kya. Once or twice she had gone along with it. It was never worth the effort.

"With that little in common, I doubt we have much of a friendship ahead of us." She turned back to her food.

"Friends? We should be enemies," Josif said. "We can help each other, as long as we hate each other."

She couldn't help it. She looked up from her lunch. She told herself that it was because she was tired of the lunchroom's attempts at local color—Honduran food was wretched. She pushed the food away from her and leaned back in her chair, waiting for him to go on.

"You see," Josif went on, assured of an audience, "while you're busy rejecting me, you can have the satisfaction of knowing that you're part of the majority around here. I mean, you may not be *in,* but you sure as hell know who's *out.*"

She couldn't help it. She laughed, and he cocked his head at her.

"So much for the frigid bitch theory," Josif said.

"You should see me in bed," Kyaren said, joking, and then was appalled to realize that instead of averting his attempt at seduction she had brought up the topic instead. He avoided any of the obvious repartee, however, and changed the subject.

"Your big mistake today was asking Warvel about history. How would he know? He could stand in the middle of a war and not know that anything had happened. For him there aren't any events—only trends. It's statistical myopia, a disease endemic to our trade."

"I just wanted to know. How it all works. He blew it up out of proportion. I'm amazed that the word spread so quickly."

Josif smiled at her, reached out and touched her arm. She did not appreciate the intimacy of the gesture, but tolerated it. "I'm awfully bored, aren't you?" he asked. "I mean, bored with the whole business."

She nodded.

"I mean, who the hell cares about any of this? It's, got to be done, like sewage and teaching children how to read and all that, but no one really *enjoys* it."

"I would," Kyaren said. "At least, I would enjoy it at a higher level."

"Higher than what?"

"Higher than punching pension information into a terminal."

"Go up fifteen ranks and they're still all asses."

"I wouldn't be," Kyaren said, then realized she had sounded too intense. Did she really want to confide her ambitions in this boy?

"What are you, immune from asshood? Anybody who presumes to make decisions about the lives of other people is an ass." Josif laughed, only this time he seemed embarrassed, made a gesture as if to draw a mask down his face, and, as if he had actually donned a mask, his face went frivolous and innocent again, with any hint of deep feeling gone. "I'm boring you," he said.

"How could you bore me? You're the first person to talk to me about anything other than statistics in three weeks."

"It's because you reek of competence, you know. A week before you got here, everyone heard about your scores on the Princeton examinations. Pretty impressive. We were all set to hate you."

"Now you say *we*. You *are* part of the group, aren't you?"

Josif shook his head, and his face went serious again. "No. But in the opposite direction from you. You they shut out because you're better than they are, they're afraid of you. Me they shut out because I'm beneath contempt."

When he said it, it occurred to Kyaren that he believed that assessment of himself. It also occurred to her that if she let this conversation go on any longer, she would not be able to get rid of this man easily.

"Thanks for the company at lunch," she said. "Actually, though, you needn't make a habit of it."

He looked surprised. "What did I say? Why are you mad?"

She smiled coldly. "I'm not." Her best you-sure-as-hell-can't-get-in-bed-with-me voice was enough to freeze a tropical river; she imagined the icicles forming on his nose as she turned her back on him, walked away, and instantly regretted it. This was the most human contact she had had in weeks. In years, in fact—he seemed more personally concerned than anyone she had known at Princeton. And she had cut him off without even learning his name.

She did not know he was following her until he caught up with her in the glass corridor that crossed a strip of jungle between the lunchroom and the work buildings. He took her by the arm, firmly enough that she could not easily pull away, but not so firmly that she even wanted to. She didn't slow down, but he matched her pace perfectly.

"Are you sure?" he asked.

"About what?" she answered, coldly again.

"About not being friends. I need a friend, you know. Even a cold-hearted, suspicious, scared-to-death lady like you. While of course your social life is so full that you'd have to look months ahead in your appointment book to find an evening you could spend with me."

She turned to him, prepared more by reflex than by desire to cut him dead, retrieve her arm, and go back to

her office alone. But an inadvertent smile ruined the effect—
she said nothing, just tried to stifle the grin, and he
mimicked her, struggling comically to force his face into a
frown and finally failing. She laughed out loud.

"I'm Josif," he said, "You're Kyaren, right?"

She nodded, trying to get rid of the smile.

"Let's pretend you think I'm worth having around.
Let's pretend you want to see me tonight. Let's pretend
that you give me your room number, and we go walking in
the Zone so that you don't have to worry about me trying
to get you in bed. Let's pretend you trust me."

She pretended. It wasn't hard. "Thirty-two seventeen,"
she said. Then he let go of her arm and she went back to
her office alone, feeling strangely delighted, the humiliation of the morning's reprimand from Warvel forgotten.
For the first time since she had first come to Earth, she
genuinely liked someone. Not a lot, but enough that spending time with him might even be fun. The idea of having
fun appealed to her, though she was not altogether sure
what fun felt like.

To her surprise, she had only been at her desk for a few
minutes when one of her co-workers, a parrot-beaked
woman who did actuarial estimates for the population at
large, came over to her desk and sat on the edge of it.

"Kyaren," the woman said.

"Yes?" Kyaren asked, suspicious and prepared openly
for hostility, though inwardly she hoped vaguely that this
would actually be a friendly overture—she was in the
mood for it, now.

"That bastard from Death, Josif."

"Yes."

"Just a friendly warning. Don't bother with him."

"Why not?"

Parrot-beak's expression grew darker—she was apparently not used to being questioned when she gave unsolic-
ited advice.

"Because he's a whore."

That was so far from her impression of Josif that Kyaren could only look surprised and say, "What?"

"You heard me."

"But—he didn't try anything, didn't offer anything."

"Not to *you*," the woman said, rolling her eyes impatiently heavenward. "You're a *woman*."

And the woman got up and went to her own desk, leaving Kyaren to punch money into the lives of old people while wondering if it was true, insisting that it made no difference, and knowing that the thought of Josif as a homosexual prostitute completely destroyed her delight at the quarter-hour she had spent with him.

She was tempted not to answer his voice at the door. I'm not here, she thought. Not to you.

But when he spoke a second time, she couldn't resist getting up from her bed and opening the door. Just to see him and confirm for herself whether it was true or not.

"Hi," Josif said, grinning.

She did not smile back. "One question. True or false. Are you a homosexual whore?"

His face went ugly, and he didn't answer for a moment. Then he said, quietly, "You see? You don't have to be one of the in-group to get the dirt on someone else."

He hadn't said no, and her contempt for people who sold themselves became dominant. She started closing the door.

"Wait a minute," he said.

"You didn't answer my question."

"You asked two questions."

She digested that. "All right then."

"I'm not a whore," he said. "And the other just guarantees you're safe from me tonight, doesn't it?"

The whole thing was ugly. Today had been fun, but

now she could not think of him except in a sexual context. She knew about homosexuality, of course; the mental picture she had of the act between men was an ugly one, and now she could not stop herself from picturing him performing the act. It made him ugly. His slenderness, the delicacy of his face, the innocence in his eyes—they became deceptive, repulsive to her now.

"I'm sorry," she said. "I just want to be alone."

"No you don't," he said.

"I know what I want."

"No you don't."

"Well, if *I* don't, *you* certainly don't."

"Yes I do." And he pushed the door open carefully, ducked under her arm, and went inside.

"You can get out," she said.

"I can," he agreed amiably, sitting on the edge of her bed, the only large piece of furniture in her room.

She pointedly sat in a chair.

"Kyaren," he said. "You liked me today."

"No I didn't," she said. And because she knew she was lying, she went on: "I didn't like you at all. You were pushy and obnoxious and your attention was completely unwelcome."

"Come now, we're statisticians, aren't we?" he said. "Nothing's complete. Let's say I was seventy percent obnoxious and you sixty percent didn't want me around. Well, I'll be here for only ten percent of the night, so there's plenty of margin. Concentrate on liking me. I mean, I overlooked the fact that you're as mean as the imperial fleet. Surely you can overlook the fact that I do perverted things. I won't do any of them to you."

"Why are you bothering me like this?"

"Believe me, I'm not trying to be bothersome."

"Why don't you leave me alone?"

He looked at her a long time before answering, and then

tears came into his eyes and his face went all innocent and vulnerable and he said, quietly, "Because I keep hoping I won't always be the only human being in this zoo."

"Just think of me," she said, "as one of the animals."

"I can't."

"Why not?"

"Because you aren't."

The way he looked at her, his eyes swimming with tears, was getting through to her. Is it an act? she wondered. Is this just an incredibly complex line? Then it occurred to her that he was probably not interested in the thing that lines usually led to.

"What do you want?"

Perversely, he took the question wrong. Deliberately wrong, Kyaren knew, and yet exactly right.

"I want," he said, "to live forever."

She started to interrupt. "No, I mean——"

But he refused to be interrupted. He spoke louder, and got up from the bed and walked aimlessly around the limited floorspace of the room. "I want to live forever surrounded by the things I love. A million books, and one person. All of humanity in the past, and only a single example of the human race in the present."

"Only one person?" she asked. "Me?"

"You?" he asked in mock startlement. Then, more subdued, he said, "Why not? For a while at least. One person at a time."

"All of humanity in the past," she said. "You like your work in the Office of Death that much?"

He laughed. "History, Kyaren. I'm a historian. I have degrees from three universities. I've written theses and dissertations. Feces and defecations," he amended. "With my specialty, there's not a chance in the world of my getting a job on this planet. Or a really good job anywhere."

He walked up to her, knelt beside her, and put his head

in her lap. She wanted to shove him away, but found that she could not bring herself to do it. "I love all mankind in the past. I love you in the present." And he smiled so crazily, reaching up a clawed hand to paw ineffectually at her arm, that she could not stop herself from laughing.

He had won. And she knew it. And he stayed, talking.

He talked about his obsession with history, which began in the library in Seattle, Westamerica, a town on the site of a great ancient city. "I didn't get along with other children," he said. "But I got along great with Napoleon Bonaparte. Oliver Cromwell. Douglas MacArthur. Attila the Hun." The names meant nothing to Kyaren, but they obviously were rich with memories to Josif. "Napoleon is always in dense forest to me. I read about him among trees, huge trees covering ground so moist you could almost swim in it. While Cromwell is always in a little boat on Pungent Bay, in the rain. The library made me pay for the new printout of the book—the ink ran on the copy I had. I dreamed of changing the world. Until I got old enough to realize that it takes more than dreams to make any kind of impression on events. And a reader of books is not a mover of men."

He was so full of memory, which flooded out of him uncontrollably and yet in marvelously subtle order, that Kyaren also remembered, though she said nothing of it to him. She had been raised amid music, constant songs; but here she found a better song than any she had heard on Tew. His cadences, his melodies and themes and variations were verbal, not musical, but because of that they reached her better, and when at last he finished she felt she had listened to a virtuoso perform. She resisted the temptation to applaud. He would have thought she was being ironic.

Instead she only sighed, and closed her eyes, and remembered her own dreams when she first became a Groan and thought of one day singing before thousands of people who would watch her intently and admire and be moved. The dreams had been stripped from her one by one, until nothing was left of them but a scar that bled often but never reopened. She sighed, and Josif misunderstood.

"I'm sorry," he said. "I thought it would matter to you." And he got up to go.

She stopped him, caught his hand and pulled him away from the door, which was closing again because he had not stepped through it.

"Don't go," she said.

"I bored you."

She shook her head. "No," she said. "You didn't bore me. I just don't know why you told me."

He laughed softly. "Because you're the first person in a long time who looked like she might be willing to hear and capable of understanding."

"Dreams, dreams, dreams," she said. "You've never grown up."

"Yes I have," he said, and the pain in his voice was painful to hear.

"Drink?" she asked.

"Water," he said.

"It's all I have," she answered. "So it's a good thing that's what you want."

She came back in with two glasses, and Josif sipped it as reverently as if it had been wine dedicated on some altar. His eyes were grave as he said to her, "I cheated."

She raised an eybrow.

"I changed the subject."

"When?" He had been through many subjects that night. She glanced at her wrist. It had been more than two hours.

"Right at the first. I started talking about childhood and dreams and history and my private madnesses. While all you wanted to talk about was perversion."

She shook her head. "Don't want to talk about it."

"I do."

"No. I've enjoyed this. I don't want it wrecked."

He drank the rest of the water quickly.

"Kyaren," he said. "They make it ugly, and it isn't."

"I don't want to know if it's ugly or not."

"They call me a whore, and I wasn't."

"I believe you. Let's leave it at that."

"No, dammit!" he said fiercely. "What do you think I've been going through the last couple of hours? You think I go to parties and tell people my life story? I'm attaching to you, Kyaren, like a bloodsucker to a shark."

"I don't like the analogy."

"I'm not a poet. I don't know what kind of pain you've gone through in your life to turn you into what you are, but I like what you are, and I want to be with you for a while, and when I do that I don't just play around at it. I become ubiquitous. You won't be able to get rid of me. I'll be there whenever you turn around. You'll trip on me getting out of bed in the morning and whenever you feel someone tickling your feet at work it'll be me, hiding under your desk. You understand? I plan to *stay* here."

"Why me?" Kyaren asked.

"Do you think I know? A stuck-up Princeton graduate like you?" He hazarded a guess. "Maybe because you listened to me all the way through and didn't fall asleep."

"I thought of it a couple of times."

"I came here as Bant's lover."

"I don't want to hear this."

"Bant loved me and I loved Bant and he came here and brought me with him because he didn't want to be without me and so he got me a job in Death while he was in charge of Vitals. I didn't want to come here. All I wanted to do was stay near a library and read. For the rest of my life, I think. But Bant came here and I came, and then after a year Bant got bored with me. I get boring sometimes."

Kyaren decided not to try to be humorous.

"I got boring, and so he didn't bring me with him when he transferred over to be head of Employment. And he didn't notify me when he moved to better rooms. But he didn't take away my job. He was kind enough to let me keep my job."

And Josif was crying and suddenly Kyaren understood something that nobody had ever bothered to explain to her in all the explanations of homosexuality that she had heard. That when Bant left it was the end of the world for Josif, because when he attached to somebody he didn't know how to let go.

Yet Kyaren was unsure how to react. Josif was, after all, nearly a stranger. Why had he poured out his heart to her tonight? What did he expect her to do? If he thought she was going to respond by baring her soul to him, he was wrong—Kyaren kept all her memories hidden. She didn't want to start talking about her childhood in the Songhouse. What could she say? *I was miserable for years because I simply didn't have the ability to measure up to the Songhouse's minimum standards?* She didn't want pity because of her childhood inabilities. She wanted respect because of her current competence.

Respect didn't enter into this situation, with the man crying softly, his face pressed into his knees as he sat on the floor leaning against the bed. She could think of only one reason for his emotional outpouring. He obviously didn't want to seduce her; therefore, he could only be trying for friendship. She knew how painful her isolation had been. If his had been half so bad, no wonder he was grasping at the first person who showed any sign of liking him.

For that matter, she wondered, why don't *I* feel any desire to take hold of his offer of friendship?

Because she didn't quite trust him, she realized. She

was instantly ashamed of her suspicions. She knelt and then sat beside him, put an arm over his shoulders, tried to comfort him.

Fifteen minutes later he started undressing her. She looked at him in surprise. "I thought——" she said, and he interrupted.

"Statistics," he said. "Trends. I'm sixty-two percent attracted to men, thirty-one percent attracted to women, and seven percent attracted to sheep. And one hundred percent attracted to you."

She had been right to mistrust him, the cynical, beaten part of her mind said sneeringly. It had all been a line.

But she clung to the line and let it draw her in. Because there was another part of her that hadn't had much play lately: she needed his gentle hands and quiet tears, his lies and his affection. And so she pretended to believe that he really did need her even as she said, "I thought it would come to this, eventually." She didn't say that she hadn't thought that when it happened she would be longing for it, that it would not be a question of fun but rather a question of need, that this half-man would be able to do in one night what no one had been able to do in her life—win enough of her trust that she was willing, even for a moment, to let herself want him.

So she comforted him that night, and, strangely enough, she was also comforted, though she had said nothing to him of her loneliness, had told him nothing of her dreams. As she ran her hands over his smooth skin, she remembered the harsh cold stone of the Songhouse and could not think why the one should have reminded her of the other.

2 "I will tour the empire next year," Riktors announced at dinner, and the two hundred prefects gathered at the tables cheered and clapped. It struck Ansset, from his place beside Riktors at the table, that the outburst was largely sincere, an unusual event in the palace. Ansset smiled at Riktors. "They mean it," he said, for Riktors's ears only. Riktors's eyes crinkled a little, enough of a sign that he had heard, had understood. And then the tumult died and Riktors said, "Not only will I tour, and visit at least one world in every prefecture, but also I will bring my Songbird with me, so that all the empire can hear him sing!"

And the cheers were even louder, the applause even more sincere. Riktors looked at Ansset and laughed in delight— the boy looked completely surprised, and Riktors loved to surprise him. It wasn't easy to do.

But when the room was quiet again, Ansset said, softly, "But I won't be here next year."

Enough people heard him that a whisper began along the head table. Riktors tried to keep his expression bland. He knew immediately what the boy meant. It was something that Riktors had forgotten without forgetting. He knew that Ansset was nearly fifteen years old, that the contract with the Songhouse was nearly up. But he had not let himself think of it, had not let himself plan for a future without Ansset beside him.

Riktors looked at Ansset and patted his hand. "We'll

talk about it later," Riktors said. But Ansset looked worried. He spoke louder this time.

"Riktors," the boy said, "I'm nearly fifteen. My contract expires in a month."

Some of the prefects in the audience moaned; most, however, realized that what was being said at the head table was not according to plan. That Ansset was doing what no one dared to do—reminding the emperor of something the emperor did not want to know. They kept their silence.

"Contracts can be renewed," Riktors said, trying to sound jovial and hoping to be able to change the subject immediately. He did not know how to react to Ansset's insistence. Why was the boy pushing the matter?

Whatever the reason, he was still determined to push.

"Not mine," said Ansset. "In two months I get to go home."

And now everyone in the hall was silent. Riktors sat still, but his hands trembled on the edge of the table. For a moment he refused to understand what Ansset was saying; but Riktors did not become emperor by indulging his need to lie to himself. Go home, the boy had said. His choice of words had to be deliberate—in public Ansset had no inadvertent words. *Get to go home*, not *have to go home*, he had said. And suddenly the last few years were all undone; Riktors felt them unwinding inside him, unraveling, all the fabric turning into meaningless threads that he could not put together however much he tried.

There were countless days of conversation, the songs Ansset had sung to him, walks along the river. They had romped together like brothers, Riktors forgetting all his dignity, and Ansset forgetting—or so Riktors had believed—all the enmity of the past.

Do you love me? Riktors had once asked, opening himself as, with any other person, he could not have afforded to open himself. And Ansset had sung to him of love. Riktors had taken this to mean yes.

And all the time Ansset was marking time, watching for his fifteenth birthday, for the expiration of his contract, for home.

I should have known better, Riktors told himself bitterly. I should have realized that the boy was Mikal's, would always be Mikal's, would never be mine. He did not forgive, as I thought he had.

Riktors imagined Ansset returning to the Songhouse on Tew; he pictured him embracing Esste, the hard woman who only looked soft when she looked at the Songbird. Riktors pictured her asking, "How was it, living with the killer?" And he pictured Ansset weeping; no, never weeping, not Ansset. He would remain calm, merely sing to her of the humiliation of singing for Riktors Ashen, emperor, assassin, and pathetic lover of Ansset's songs. Riktors imagined Ansset and Esste laughing together as they talked of the moment when Riktors, weary of the weight of the empire in his mind, had come to Ansset in the night for the healing of his hands, and had wept before the boy sang a note. A weakling, that's what I've been, in front of a boy who never shows an unwitting emotion; he has seen me unprotected, and instead of loving me he has felt only contempt.

It was just a moment that Riktors sat there silently, but in his mind he progressed from surprise to hurt to humiliation and, at last, to fury. He rose to his feet, and there was no hiding the anger on his face. The prefects were alarmed—it is not wise to witness the embarrassment of powerful men, they all knew, and no one was so powerful as Riktors Mikal.

"You are right!" Riktors said, loudly. "My Songbird has reminded me that in a month his contract expires and he goes, as he says, home. I had thought that this was his home, but now I see that I was mistaken. My Songbird will return to Tew, to his precious Songhouse, for Riktors Mikal keeps his word. But the Songbird, since he obviously holds us in little esteem, will never again see his emperor, and his emperor will never again permit himself to hear his lying songs.''

Riktors's face was red and tight with pain when he turned and left the dinner. A few of the prefects made some small effort to touch their food; the rest got up immediately, and soon all were headed out of the hall, wondering whether it would be better to stay around to try to show the emperor that they were still as loyal as ever, or to head quickly for their prefectures, so that he and they could all pretend that they had never come, that the scene with Ansset had never taken place.

As they left, Ansset sat alone at the table, looking at but not seeing the food in front of him. He sat that way, in silence, until the Mayor of the palace (the office of Chamberlain had long since been abolished) came to him and led him away.

"Where am I going?" Ansset asked softly.

The Mayor said nothing, only took him into the maze of corridors. It did not take Ansset long to recognize the place they were going to. When Riktors Ashen changed his name and moved into the palace, he had stayed away from Mikal's old chambers; instead he had established himself in new rooms near the top of the building, with windows that displayed the lawns and forest all around. Now the Mayor led Ansset through doors that once had been guarded by the tightest security measures in the empire, and at last they stood inside the door of a room where an empty fireplace still had ashes on the hearth; where the furniture remained ummoved, untouched; where the years of Mikal's presence still clung to all the features of the place, to all the memories the room inevitably stirred in Ansset's mind.

There was a thin layer of dust on the floor, as in all the unused rooms of the palace, which were only cleaned annually, if at all. Ansset walked slowly into the room, the dust rising at each footfall. He walked to the fireplace; the urn that had held Mikal's ashes still waited beside the opening. He turned back to face the Mayor, who finally spoke.

"Riktors Imperator," the Mayor said, with the formality of a memorized message, "has said to you, since you were not at home with me, you will stay where you are at home, until the Songhouse sends for you."

"Riktors misunderstood me," Ansset said, but the Mayor showed no sign of having heard. He only turned away and left, and when Ansset tried the door, it did not open to his touch.

3   They spent weekend after weekend in Mexico, the largest city in the hemisphere. Josif went to make the rounds of bookstores—the market in old books and rare books was alway hot, and Josif had an eye for bargains, books selling for way under value. He also had an eye for what he wanted—histories that were long out of print, fiction written centuries ago about the author's own period, diaries and journals. "They say there's nothing original to be said about the history of Earth, that all the facts have been in for years," Josif said fiercely. "But that was years ago, and now no one remembers anymore. What it was like to live here then."

"When?" Kyaren asked him.

"Then. As opposed to now."

"I'm more interested," she always told him, "in tomorrow."

But she wasn't. Today was all that interested her in the first weeks they spent together. Today because it was the best time she had ever had, and she wasn't sure that it would last, or that tomorrow would be half as desirable.

Kyaren went to Mexico for the feel of people. Nowhere in Eastamerica, and certainly nowhere in the Songhouse, were there people like those who crowded the sidewalks of Mexico. No vehicles were allowed except the electric carts that brought in goods to the stores; people, individual people, had to walk everywhere. And there were millions of them. And they all seemed to be outside all the time; even in the rain, they sauntered through the streets with the rain sliding easily off their clothing, relishing the feel of it on their faces. This was a city where Kyaren's hunger could be filled. She knew no one, but loved everyone.

"They sweat," Josif said.

"You're too immaculate," Kyaren answered crossly.

"They sweat and they step on your feet. I see no reason to be in a crowd any more than is unavoidable."

"I like the sound of them."

"And that's the worst of it. Largest city in the world, and they insist on speaking Mexican, a language that has no reason to exist."

Kyaren only scowled at him. "Why not?"

"They're only five thousand kilometers from Seattle, for heaven's sake. *We* managed to talk like the rest of the empire. It's just vanity."

"It's a beautiful language, you know," she said. "I've been learning it, and it opens your mind."

"And makes your tongue fall out of your mouth."

Josif had no patience with the eccentricities of his native planet.

"Sometimes I'm embarrassed as hell to be from Earth."

"The mother globe."

"These people aren't real Mexicans. Do you know what Mexicans were? Short and dark! Show me a short dark person out there!"

"Does it matter if they can trace their pedigrees back to the number one Mexican and her husband?" Kyaren demanded. "They *want* to be Mexican. And whenever I come here, *I* want to be Mexican."

It was a friendly argument that always ended either with them going outside—Kyaren to wander and talk to storekeepers and shoppers, Josif to prowl along the shelves, waiting for a title to make a sudden move so he could pounce—or in bed, where their pursuits more nearly coincided.

It was on a weekend in Mexico that they decided to take over the world.

"Why not the universe?"

"Your ambition is disgusting," Josif said, lying naked on the balcony because he liked the feel of the rain, which was falling heavily.

"Well, then, we'll be modest. Where shall we start?"

"Here."

"Not practical. We have no base of operations."

"Tegucigalpa, then. We secretly twist all the programs of the computers to follow our every command. Then we cut off everybody's salaries until they surrender."

They laughed; it was a game. But a game they played seriously enough to do research. They would hunt for possible weaknesses, places that the system could be subverted. They also worked to get an overview of the system, to understand how it all fit together. Josif knew his way around the government library in Mexico, and they both spent time punching up readouts on the establishment of Tegucigalpa only three hundred-odd years before.

"The thing's relatively new. Half the functions have only been installed in the last ten years. *Ten years!* And most other planets have been fully computerized for centuries."

"You're too down on Earth," Kyaren chided him, poring over minutes of meetings, which were so heavily edited at their level of clearance that it was hard to get anything coherent out of them at all.

But it was not in Mexico that they found the scam. It was at home.

Kyaren had been reading a book on demographics, one that she had only been able to skim at Princeton. It set norms for age distributions on a planet; she found the information fascinating, especially the variations that depended on local employment, climate, and relative wealth. She amused herself by plotting the demographic distribution of ages for Earth, based on the easily obtained statistics on employment and the economy. Then she took a few minutes of break time at work to check her figures.

They were wrong.

From birth to retirement age at 80, her figures were actually quite good. It was from 80 to 100 that things didn't work.

Not enough people were dying at those ages.

In fact, she realized, almost *no one* was dying, compared to the normal mortality rates. And then, from 100 to 110, they died like flies, so that from 110 on the statistics were normal.

Surely someone would have noticed this before, Kyaren thought. Certainly the Earth would have gained a reputation for unusually low mortality rates. It had to be common knowledge—the food distribution must certainly be affected by it, and pension expenses must be unusually high. Scientists must be trying to discover the reason for the phenomenon.

And yet she had never heard of it at all.

In the programming manuals they had looked at in the library in Mexico, Kyaren had found some little-known programs that allowed an operator to check a program rather than use it to find and process data. Kyaren talked to Josif about it that night, which they spent in his place because it was larger and had room for both of them without having to petition for extra furniture, which would have made their arrangement public knowledge.

"I've checked my figures again and again, and they're not wrong."

'Well, the only way to solve it is go kill some old people, I guess," Josif said, reading a twenty-third-century mystery—in translation, of course.

"Josif, it's wrong. Something's wrong."

"Kyaren," he said, impatient but trying not to sound like it, "this is a game we were playing. We really don't have any responsibility for the whole world. Just for dead people and the not-quite-dead. And then just as numbers."

'I want to find out if the figures on death are right or not."

Josif closed the book. "Kyaren, the figures on death are right. That's *my* job, isn't it? I do death."

"Then check and see if my figures are right."

He checked. Her figures were right.

"Your figures are right. Maybe the book's wrong."

"It's been the bible of demographics for three centuries. Someone would have noticed by now."

Josif opened the book again. "Damned Earth. The people don't even know when to die."

"You must have noticed it," Kyaren said. "You must have seen that most of your deaths were grouped between a hundred and a hundred and ten."

"I've never noticed anything like that. We deal with individuals, not the aggregate. We terminate files, you know? We don't watch trends."

"I just want to check some things. You know that program we found on checking entries? The error-finder?"

"Yeah."

"Remember the numbers?"

"Kyaren, you're not being very good company."

Together they figured out the numbers and codes; Kyaren left for a few minutes and verified them on the local library terminal by hunting up her last library use. The program worked fine; it was quite simple, in fact, which was why they were able to remember it.

The next day, during a break, Kyaren punched in a date-of-entry query on the solitary death in Quong-yung district—she figured a single death would be simpler, would give her a single readout. What should have flashed on her screen was the date of entry, the name of the operator who entered the death information, the vital statistics entered on that date on that person, and the operation number.

Instead, what flashed on was the bright RESTRICTED sign and what sounded was a loud buzzer at Warvel's desk.

Everyone looked up immediately, watched as Warvel got up quickly, looking alarmed. Kyaren knew that on his desk her area was flashing; sure enough, when he located the culprit he slammed his hand on the desk and charged furiously over to her.

"What the bloody hell are you doing, Kyaren!" he bawled as he came over.

What should she tell him—that she was playing a game of plotting to take over the world? That she was double-checking the figures because they didn't jibe with her own calculations?

"I don't know," she said, letting herself sound as surprised and flustered as she felt. "I was just playing with the thing. Just punching in random numbers and words, I don't know."

"Which random numbers and words?" he demanded, leaning over her terminal.

"I don't remember," she lied. "It was just whimsical."

"It was just *stupid,*" he said back to her. "There are programs here that if you just randomly and *whimsically* happened to stumble on them, they'd freeze the whole operation until the stinking *police* came to find out who's trying to jury the system. You understand? This system is *foolproof,* but we don't need any extra fools trying to prove it!"

She apologized profusely, but as he returned, unmollified, to his desk, she realized that he had seemed not so much angry as afraid. And the others in the room, as Warvel returned to his desk, looked at her sullenly, angrily—and, also, fearfully.

What had she done?

"Kyaren," Warvel said as she left the office at the end of the working day. "Kyaren, your four-month report is coming up in a few days. I'm afraid I'm going to have to give you a negative report."

Kyaren was stunned. "Why?" she asked.

"You haven't been working. You've been obviously loafing. It's bad for morale, and it's downright dishonest."

"When have I loafed?" she asked. A negative report now, on her first job—especially one this easy—could destroy her hope of a government career.

"I have complaints from fourteen people. Every single person in this office except you and me, Kyaren. They're tired of watching you playing games. Studying up on ancient history and playing computer games when you should be trying to help old people cope with inflation and the fluctuations of the economy. We aren't here for fun, Kyaren, we're here to help people. Do you understand?"

She nodded. "That's what I'm trying to do."

"I'll give you a negative report, but I won't fire you

unless there's any more trouble. You understand? Three
years of perfect work and you get the negative report taken
off your record. It's something you can live down—if you
just stick to business in the future.''

She left. At home Josif was appalled.

"Fourteen complaints?"

"That's what he said."

"Kyaren, you could have an intimate sexual relationship
with a lamp in the middle of the lunchroom and you'd
have a hard time getting *three* complaints!"

"What do they have against me?" she asked.

Josif's face grew somber. "Me," he said.

"What?"

"Me. You had problems enough. Adding me to them—do
you know how many women have tried to get me into
bed? There's something about a known homosexual that's
irresistible to a certain kind of woman. They regard him as
a challenge. Me as a challenge. And then you come along
and suddenly we're spending weekends together. The ones
that aren't jealous are probably revolted to think of what
perverted things I must be making you do."

"It isn't you."

"Then what is it?"

"They're afraid."

"Of what?"

"How should I know?"

Josif got up from the bed, went to the door, leaned on
it. "Kyaren, it's me. We've got to stop. When you leave
tonight that's it."

He sounded sincere. She wondered why even the thought
of leaving him and not coming back made her feel as if she
were falling from someplace very high.

"I'm not leaving tonight," she said. "I'm leaving in the
morning."

"No. For your own good."

She laughed incredulously. "My own good!"

He looked at her from the door, his face very serious.

"My own good is to stay right here."

He shook his head.

"Do you really mean this?" she asked, unbelieving. "Just like that, you decide I'm supposed to go because *you* think it'll be better for *me?*"

"Sounds pretty stupid, doesn't it," he said.

And they started laughing and he came back to the bed and suddenly they weren't laughing, just holding each other and realizing that this wasn't something they could simply end when it became inconvenient.

"Josif," she said.

"Mmm?" His face was buried in her hair, and he was sucking on a strand of it.

"Josif, I frightened them. They're afraid of something."

"You're a pretty mean-looking woman."

"There's something pretty funny about it. Why should death-entry information be restricted?"

They couldn't think of a reason.

And so the next day at lunch Josif had a sheet of paper—something little used in the computer center—and on it were ten names and ten numbers. "Can you use this?" he asked.

"What are they?"

"Dead people. Today's first entries. They should be in your computer by now, since I punched them all in. That's their identification numbers, and date of entry is a few hours ago. That's basically all the date-of-entry code would have told you anyway. Can you do anything with them?"

Kyaren didn't dare bring the paper with her to the office—anything as unusual as paper would attract attention, and that was not what she needed. So she memorized the first three and left the list in the lavatory on the floor below. On her first break she came down, but instead of getting three more names she went to Josif.

"Are you sure you copied these down correctly?"

Josif looked at the names and numbers, punched them into his terminal, and the vitals showed up. All definitely dead.

"On my terminal," she said, "they're still very much alive."

Josif got up from his terminal and she followed him to the corridor, where Josif spoke softly.

"We should have guessed it immediately. It's a scam, Kyaren. They're paying those pensions to somebody, but not to these people. Because they're dead."

Kyaren leaned against the wall. "Do you know how much *money* that is?"

Josif was not impressed. "Come on," he said.

"Where?"

"Out of this building, immediately."

He started pulling her along. She came willingly enough, but completely confused. "Where are we going?"

He wouldn't answer. They did not go to either of their rooms. Instead they headed for the airport, which was on the eastern edge of the complex. "This isn't the time for a weekend in Mexico," she said.

"Just punch in sick." They stood before the ticket terminal and she did as he said, using her office code. Then he stood to the terminal and punched out two tickets for himself, charging them to his own account.

"I can pay for my own," she said.

He didn't answer. He just took the tickets and they boarded the flit headed for Maraketch. It was when they were in flight that he finally began explaining.

"It isn't just your office, Kyaren," he said. "It's mine, too. This thing has to involve a lot of people, in Death, in Disbursements, in Pensions, who knows where else. If they caught you on a simple query, they surely have a program to notice that you just queried the names of three people whose deaths were registered *today*, and that immediately afterward *I* queried the same names. The computer knows that somebody knows there is a discrepancy. And I don't know how long we'd live if we stayed there.''

"They wouldn't do anything *violent*, would they?" Kyaren asked.

Josif only kissed her and said, "Wherever you grew up, Kyaren, must be paradise."

"Where are we going?" she asked again.

"To report it, of course. Let the police handle it. Let Babylon do it. They have the power to freeze everything and everyone there while they investigate. We don't have any power at all."

"What if we're wrong?"

"Then we go looking for jobs about a billion lights away from here."

They told their story to five different officials before they finally found someone who was willing to take responsibility for a decision. The man was not introduced to them. But he was the first to listen to them without fidgeting, without looking uncomfortable or worried or distrustful.

"Only three names?" he finally asked, when Josif and Kyaren had explained everything.

They nodded. "We didn't think it was safe to wait around looking for more."

"Absolutely right," the man said. He nodded, as if in imitation of their nods a moment before. "Yes, it warrants an investigation." And they watched as he picked up a phone, stroked in a code, and started giving orders in a jargon that they couldn't understand.

His face fascinated Kyaren, though she was not sure why. He looked unremarkable enough—not a large man, not particularly handsome, but not unusually ugly, either. His hair medium length, his eyes medium brown, his expression medium pleasant. Kyaren was aware of a constant change, not so much in his face as in her perception of his face; like an optical illusion, his face kept switching back and forth between absolute trustworthiness and cold menace. No one had told them his title or even his name—he was just the one they passed a knotty problem to, and he didn't seem to mind.

Finally he was through with his call and turned his attention back to Josif and Kyaren. "Very good work," he said.

Then he began to talk to them, very quietly, about themselves. He told Kyaren things about Josif that Josif had never mentioned: how Josif had attempted suicide twice after Bant left him; how Josif failed four classes at his university in his last term, yet turned in a dissertation that the faculty had no choice but to vote unanimously to accept; how the faculty thereupon booted him out of the school with the worst possible recommendation letters so that it was impossible for him to get work in his field.

"You don't get along well with authority, do you, Josif?" the man asked. Josif shook his head.

The man promptly started in on Kyaren, talking about her upbringing in the Songhouse, her failure to meet even the most minimal standards, her flight from that place where she was known to be inferior, her refusal to even mention the Songhouse to anyone else since then. "You are determined not to let anyone see you fail, aren't you, Kya-Kya?" he asked. Kyaren nodded.

She was acutely conscious of the fact that there was so much that Josif hadn't told her about himself—important things, if she was to understand him. And yet it came more as a relief than as a letdown. Because now he also knew the things she had been deliberately hiding from him; they had no secrets of any importance now.

Was that what the man had been trying to do? Or was he

merely being nasty, pointing out to them that their friendship wasn't all they had thought it was? It hardly mattered. She looked at Josif furtively, saw that he also was avoiding her gaze. That would not do. So she stared at him until the very intensity of her gaze forced him to look back at her. And then she smiled. "Hi, stranger," she said, and he smiled back.

The man cleared his throat. "You two are a little better than the average. You've been artificially, for various stupid reasons, kept in places where you couldn't accomplish all that you are capable of. So I'm giving you an opportunity. Try to use it intelligently."

They would have asked for explanation, but he left them without another word. It was the Chief of Planetary Security who finally told them what was happening to them. "You've been fired from your previous jobs," he said, looking as serene as only a man with a great deal of power can look. "And given new ones."

Josif found himself assistant to the minister of education, with special authority over funds for research. Kyaren was made special assistant to the manager of Earth, where she could get her hands into anything on the planet. Not imperial offices, but about as high as novices could hope to get—work that would give them connections for future advances and all the opportunities they would need to show just what kind of work they were capable of doing.

In a stroke, they had been given a chance to make careers for themselves.

"Who *is* he, an angel? God?" Josif asked the Chief.

The Chief laughed. "Most people put him at the opposite end of things. The Devil. The Angel of Death. But he's nothing like that at all. He's just Ferret. The emperor's ferret, you see. He makes people and he unmakes them, and answers only to the emperor."

They knew how well he could make people. The unmaking they saw when, a few weeks later, they were watching the vids in their apartment. The day in Babylon had been hot and rainy, until at sunset they had stood on their balcony watching the light glisten on waterdrops clinging to a billion blades of grass, with the long shadows of trees interrupting the lush savannah at random yet perfect intervals. An elephant moved lazily through the tall grass. A herd of gazelles bounded north in the distance. Kyaren and Josif felt utterly exhausted from the day's work, utterly at peace from the evening's beauty, a delicious mood of languor. They knew the conviction of the plotters would be cast from Tegucigalpa tonight, and they felt an obligation to watch.

As moments from the trials were presented, with the faces of their former co-workers again and again in the dock, Kyaren began to feel vaguely uncomfortable. Not because she had turned them in—but because she had felt no qualms about doing so. Would she have been so eager to denounce them if they had not so openly excluded her? She imagined what it might have been like if she had come into the Office of Pensions more humbly, not preceded by remarkable tests, not clothed in her perpetual reserve. Would they then have befriended her, gradually admitted her to the plot? Would she *then* have denounced them?

Impossible to know, she realized. For if she had come humbly, she would not have been herself and so who could then predict how she would have acted?

Beside her, Josif gasped. Kyaren looked closely at the vids again. It was just another man in the dock, one she didn't know. "Who is it?" she asked.

"Bant," Josif said, gnawing at his knuckles.

In all their thinking, they hadn't thought of this—that Bant, of course, as head of Vitals, had to be involved. Kyaren had never met him, but felt that she knew him through Josif. Yet what she knew of him was his hilarity, his insistence that lovemaking had to be fun. Kyaren hadn't enjoyed imagining Josif making love with a man, but that much, at least, had been impossible for Josif not to talk about. Apparenty Bant's greed for sex was just a facet of his overall greed; his unconcern for Josif's feelings was part of a general unconcern for anyone.

All those charged were convicted. They were all sentenced to five to thirty years in hard labor, deported, and permanently exiled from Earth, permanently barred from employment. It was a severe sentence. Apparently it was not severe enough.

The announcer began talking about the need to make an example of these people, lest others decide that a group scam on government funds might be worth the risks. As he talked, the vids showed a man from the back, walking toward the line of prisoners. The prisoners all had guards behind them; their hands were bound. They looked toward the man who approached them, and their faces suddenly looked alarmed. The vids backed off so that the viewers could see why. The man held a blade. Not a laser—a blade, made of metal, a frightening thing in part because it was so ancient and barbaric.

"Ferret," Kyaren said, and Josif nodded. The vids didn't show the man's face, but they were quite sure they recognized him.

And then Ferret reached the first of the prisoners, paused before him, then moved to the next, paused. It was not until the fourth prisoner that the hand lashed out; the blade caught the prisoner at the point where the jaw meets the ear, then flashed to the left and emerged at the same point on the other side. For a moment the prisoner looked surprised, just surprised. Then a red line appeared along his throat, and suddenly blood erupted and spurted from the wound, spattering those to either side. The body sagged, the mouth struggling to speak, the eyes pleading for the act to somehow be undone. It was not undone. The guard behind the man held him up, and when the prisoner's head sagged forward, the guard grabbed the hair and pulled the head back, so that the face could be seen. The action also made the wound gape, like the maw of a piranha. And finally the blood stopped pumping and the ferret, his back still to the vids, nodded. The guard let the man drop to the floor.

Apparently the vids had shown this execution in detail because it was the first. As the ferret walked along, snicking the throats of every third, fourth, or fifth prisoner, the vids did not hold close for the dying, as they had with the first; rather the program moved quickly.

Kyaren and Josif did not notice, however. Because from the moment the blade first flashed forward, catching the prisoner in the throat, Josif had been screaming. Kyaren tried to force him to look away from the vids, tried to make him hide his eyes from the man's death, but even as he screamed piteously, Josif refused to take his eyes from the sight of the blood and the agony. And when the prisoner sagged forward, Josif wept loudly, crying, "Bant! Bant!"

Now they knew how Ferret unmade people. He must, Kyaren thought, he must have known how Josif felt about Bant, chose to kill him knowing that, as if to say, "You can denounce a criminal, but you cannot do it without consequences."

Kyaren was sure that his choice of victim had been deliberate, for when he got to the last six people, he slowed down, looking each one of them in the eyes. The prisoners were reacting very differently, some trying to be stoic about their possible death, some trying to plead with him, some near vomiting with fear or disgust. With each person he passed, the next became more sure that he was the victim—the ferret had not skipped more than four people in a row before. And then he came to the last one.

The last one was Warvel, who was utterly certain that he would die—five had already been passed over. And Kyaren, her arms around Josif, who wept softly beside her, found herself inwardly pleased, sickeningly pleased, that Warvel would also die. If Bant, then surely Warvel.

Then Ferret snaked out his hand. But not to kill. For the hand now was empty, and he caught Warvel by the neck, pulled him forward away from the guard. Warvel stumbled, nearly fell, his knees were so weak. But the vids carried the sound of Ferret's voice. "Pardon this one. The emperor pardons this one."

And Warvel's bonds were loosed as the announcer's voice began talking about how the emperor was to be remembered always—because when someone cheated or abused the people, the emperor would be the people's champion and carry out their vengeance. "But always the emperor's justice is tempered with mercy. Always the emperor remembers that even the worst of criminals is still one of the emperor's people."

Warvel.

Bant.

Whatever Ferret wanted to teach us, Kyaren whispered silently, so that even she could hardly hear the thought as her lips moved. Whatever the ferret wanted to teach us, we have learned. We have learned.

And that was why Kyaren and Josif were in Babylon when Ansset was placed there.

4 For the first time in his life, Ansset lost songs.

Up to now, everything that had happened to him had added to his music. Even Mikal's death had taught him new songs, and deepened all the old ones.

He spent only one month as a prisoner, but he spent it songless. Not that he meant to keep his silence. Occasionally, at first, he tried to sing. Even something simple, something he had learned as a child. The sounds came out of his throat well enough, but there was no music in it. The song always sounded empty to him, and he could not bring himself to go on.

Ansset speculated on death, perhaps because of the constant reminder of the urn that had held Mikal's ashes, perhaps because he felt entombed in the dusty room with its constant reminders of a long-gone past. Or perhaps because the drugs that delayed the Songbird's puberty were now wearing off, and the changes came on more awkwardly because of the artificial delay. Ansset awoke often in the night, troubled by strange and unfulfilling dreams. Small for his age, he began to feel restless, an urge to grapple violently with someone or something, a passion for movement that, in the confines of Mikal's rooms, he could not fulfill.

This is what the dead feel, Ansset thought. This is what they go through, shut up in their tombs or caught, embarrassingly, in public without their bodies. Ghosts may long to simply *touch* something, but bodiless they cannot; they may wish for heat, for cold, for even the deliciousness of pain, but it is all denied them.

He counted days. With the poker from the fire he notched
each morning in the ashes in the hearth, in spite of the fact
that the ashes were of Mikal's body—or perhaps because
of it. And, at last, the day came when his contract was
expired and he could finally go home.

How could Riktors have misinterpreted him so? In all
his years with Mikal, Ansset had never had to lie to him;
and in his time with Riktors, there had also been a kind of
honesty, though silences fell between them on certain
matters. They had not been like father and son, as he and
Mikal had been. They were more like brothers, though
there was some confusion as to which of them was the
elder brother, which the rambunctious younger one who
had to be comforted, checked, counseled, and consoled.
And now, simply by being honest, Ansset had touched a
place in Riktors that no one could have guessed was
there—the man could be vindictive without calculation,
cruel even to the helpless.

Ansset had thought he knew Riktors—as he thought he
knew practically everyone. As other people trusted their
sight, Ansset trusted his hearing. No one could lie to him
or hide from him, not if they were speaking. But Riktors
Ashen had hidden from him, at least in part, and Ansset
was now as unsure as a sighted man who suddenly discovered that the wolves were all invisible, and walked beside
him ravening in the night.

On the day Ansset turned fifteen, he waited expectantly
for the door to open, for the Mayor or, better yet, someone
from the Songhouse to come in, to take his hand and bring
him out.

The Mayor did indeed come in. Near evening he came
and wordlessly handed a paper to Ansset. It was in Riktors's
handwriting.

I regret to inform you that the Songhouse has sent us

word that you are not to return to them. Your service of two emperors, they said, has polluted you and you may not go back. The message was signed by Esste. It is unfortunate that this message should have come when you are no longer welcome here. We are currently holding meetings to decide what we can possibly do with you, since neither we nor the Songhouse can find any further justification for maintaining you. This undoubtedly comes as a blow to you. I'm sure you can guess how sorry I am.

Riktors Mikal, Imperator

If Ansset's long silence in Mikal's rooms had ended with a return to the Songhouse, it might have helped him grow, as the silence and the suffering in the High Room with Esste helped him grow. But as he read the letter, the songs drained out of him.

Not that he believed the letter at first. At first he thought it was a terrible, terrible joke, a last vindictive act by Riktors to make Ansset regret wanting to leave Earth and return to the Songhouse. But as the hours passed, he began to wonder. He had heard nothing from the Songhouse in his years on Earth. That was normal, he knew—but it was also distancing him from his memories there. The stone walls had faded into the background, and the gardens of Susquehanna were more real to him. Riktors was more real to him than Esste, though his feelings for Esste were more tender. But with that distance he began to think: perhaps Esste had merely beem manipulating him. Perhaps their ordeal in the High Room had been a strategem and nothing more—her complete victory over him, and not a shared experience at all. Perhaps he had been sent to Earth as a sacrifice; perhaps the skeptics were right, and the Songhouse had given in to Mikal's pressure and sent him a Songbird knowing he was unworthy, knowing that it would destroy the Songbird they sent and they could never bring him home.

Maybe that was why, when Mikal died, the Songhouse did the unthinkable and let him stay with Riktors Ashen.

It fit, and the more Ansset thought about it, the better it fit, until by the time he was able to sleep he had almost despaired. He still harbored a hope that tomorrow the Songhouse people would come in and tell him it was a cruel joke by Riktors, and they had come to claim him; but the hope was slimmer, and he realized that now, instead of being one of the few people on Earth who could regard himself as independent of the emperor, almost his equal, he was utterly dependent on Riktors, and not at all sure that Riktors would feel any obligation to be kind.

That night his Control failed him, and he awoke from a dream weeping out loud. He tried to contain himself, but could not. He had no way of knowing that it was the onset of puberty that was weakening, temporarily, his knowledge of himself. He thought that it was proof that the Songhouse was right—he was polluted, weakened. Unworthy to return and live among the singers.

If he had been restless before, now he was frantic. The rooms were smaller than they had ever been before, and the softness of the floor was unbearable. He wanted to strike it and find it hard; instead it yielded to him. The dust, which his constant walking had pushed to the edges and corners of the room, began to irritate him, and he sneezed frequently. He constantly caught himself on the edge of tears, told himself it was the dust, but knew it was the terror of abandonment. Almost all his life that he could remember he had been surrounded by security, at first the security of the Songhouse, and later the security of an emperor's love. Now, suddenly, both of them were gone, and a long-forgotten abandonment began to intrude into his dreams again. Someone was stealing him away. Someone was taking him from his family. Someone was vanishing his family in the distance and he would never see them again and he woke up in darkness full of terror, afraid to move in his bed, because if he so much as lifted an arm they would cease to forbear; they would take him and he would never be found again, would live perpetually in a small cell in a rocking boat, would always be surrounded by the leering faces of men who saw only his nakedness and never his soul.

And then, after a week of this, his long silence ended. The Mayor came for him.

"Riktors wants to see you," the Mayor said, and because he was not delivering a memorized message his voice was his own, and it was sympathetic and warm, and Ansset trembled as he walked to him and took his offered hand and let himself be led from Mikal's rooms to Riktors's magnificent apartments.

The emperor waited for him standing at a window, looking out over the forest where the leaves were starting to go red and yellow. There was a wind blowing outside, but of course it did not touch them. The Mayor brought Ansset inside and left him alone with Riktors, who showed no sign of knowing the boy had come.

Boy? Ansset was, for the first time, aware that he was growing, that he had grown. Riktors did not tower over him as he had when he took him away from the Songhouse. Ansset still did not come to his shoulder, but he knew that someday he would, and felt a growing equality with Riktors—not an equality of independence, for that feeling was gone, but an equality of manhood. My hands are large, Ansset thought.

My hands could tear his heart out.

He pushed the thought into the back of his mind. He did not understand his lust for violent action; he had had his fill of it, he thought, when he was a child.

Riktors turned to face him, and Ansset saw that his eyes were red from weeping.

"I'm sorry," Riktors said. And he wept again.

The grief was sincere, unbearably sincere. By habit Ansset went to the man. But habit had weakened—where before he would have embraced Riktors and sung to him, he only came near, did not touch him, and certainly did not sing. He had no song for Riktors now.

"If I could undo it, I would," Riktors said. "But you pushed me harder than I can endure it. No one but you could have made me so angry, could have hurt me so deeply."

Truth rang in Riktor's voice, and with a sinking of his heart Ansset realized that Riktors had not defrauded him. He was telling no lies.

"Won't you sing to me?" Riktors pleaded.

Ansset wanted to say yes. But he could not. He hunted inside himself for a song, but he couldn't find one. Instead of songs, tears pressed forward in his mind; his face twisted, and he shook his head, making no sound.

Riktors looked at him bitterly, then turned away. "I thought not. I knew you could never forgive me."

Ansset shook his head and tried to make a sound, tried to say, I forgive you. But he found no sound inside himself right now. Found nothing but fear and the agony of being forsaken.

Riktors waited for Ansset to speak, to deny, to forgive; when it became clear the silence would last forever if it were up to Ansset to break it, Riktors walked. Around the room, touching windows and walls. Finally he came to rest on his bed, which, when it was clear he was not going to lie down, cooperated by flowing up and around his back a little, providing support.

"Well, then, I won't punish you further by keeping you with me here in the palace. You aren't going back to Tew.

I can't just pension you off; I owe you better treatment than that. So I've decided to give you work.''

Ansset was incurious.

"Don't you care? Well, I do," Riktors said to Ansset's silence. "The manager of Earth is due for a promotion. I'll give you his job. You'll report directly to the imperial capital, no prefects between us. The Mayor wanted to give you something smaller, some office where you wouldn't have so much responsibility." Riktors laughed. "But you aren't trained for any lesser office, are you? At least you know protocol. And the staff is very good. They'll carry you until you learn your way. If you need help, I'll see to it you get it."

Riktors studied Ansset's face for any sign of emotion, though he knew better. Ansset wanted to show him something, show him what he was looking for. But it took all Ansset's concentration to maintain Control, to keep from breaking the glass and leaping from the palace to get outside, to keep from weeping until he cried his throat out. So Ansset said and showed nothing.

"But I don't want to see you," Riktors said.

Ansset knew it was a lie.

"No, that's a lie. I must see you, I can't live without seeing you. I found that out clearly enough, Ansset. You showed me how much I need you. But I don't want to need you, not you, not now. And so I can't want to see you, and so I won't see you. Not until you're ready to forgive me. Not until you can come back and sing to me again."

I can't sing to anyone, Ansset wanted to say.

"So I'll have them give you some sort of training— there isn't any school for planet managers, you know. The best they can do, meetings with the current manager. And then they'll take you to Babylon. It's a beautiful place, they tell me. I've never seen it. Once you get to Babylon, we'll never meet again." His voice was painful, and it tore at Ansset's heart. For a moment he wanted to embrace this man who had, after all, been his brother and his friend. He had known Riktors, he thought, and Ansset did not know how not to love someone he so completely understood. But I did not really understand him, Ansset realized. Riktors was hidden from me, and I do not know him.

It was a wall, and Ansset did not breach it.

Instead, Riktors tried to. He got up from the bed and came to where Ansset stood, knelt in front of him, embraced him around the waist, and wept into his hip, clinging desperately. "Ansset, please. Take it back! Say you love me, say that this is your home, sing to me, Ansset!"

But Ansset held his silence, and the man slid down his body until he lay crumpled at Ansset's feet, and finally the weeping stopped and, without lifting his head, Riktors said, "Go. Get out of here. You'll never see me again. Rule the Earth, but you won't rule me any longer. You can leave."

Ansset pulled away from Riktors's slack arm and walked to the door. He touched it; it opened for him. But he had not left when Riktors cried out in agony, "Won't you say anything to me?"

Ansset turned around, hunting for something to break the silence with. Finally he thought of it.

"Thank you," he said.

He meant thank you for caring for me, for still wanting me, for giving me something to do now that I can't sing anymore, now that my home is closed to me.

But Riktors heard it another way. He heard Ansset saying thank you for letting me leave you, thank you for not requiring me to be near you, thank you for letting me live and work in Babylon where I won't be required to sing for you anymore.

And so, to Ansset's surprise, when his voice croaked

out the two words, utterly devoid of music, Riktors did not take them kindly. He only looked at Ansset with a look that the boy could only interpret as cold hatred. The look held for a few minutes, an unbearably long time, before Ansset finally could not stand to see Riktors's hatred any longer. He turned away and passed through the door. It closed behind him. When the door closed, Ansset realized that at last he was no longer a Songbird. The work he had now would require no songs.

To his surprise, he felt relieved. The music fell off him like a burden welcomely shed. It would be some time before he realized that not singing was an even heavier burden, and one far harder to be rid of.

5 Songmaster Onn returned alone to the Songhouse. No one was eager to spread bad news; no one rushed ahead of him to report that, incredibly, his mission had failed.

And so Esste, waiting patiently in the High Room, was the first to hear that Ansset would not come home.

"I was not allowed to come to Earth. The other passengers were unloaded by shuttle, and I never set foot on the planet."

"The message," Esste said. "Was it sent in Ansset's own language?"

"It was a personal apology from Riktors Mikal," Onn said, and he recited it: " 'I regret having to inform you that Ansset, formerly a Songbird, refuses to return to Tew. His contract has expired, and since he is neither chattel nor a child, I cannot legally compel him. I hope you will understand that for his protection no one from the Songhouse will be allowed to land on Earth while he is here. He is busy; he is happy; do not be concerned for him.' "

Esste and Onn looked at each other in silence, but the silence between them sang.

"He is a liar," Esste finally said.

"This much is true: Ansset does not sing."

"What *does* he do?"

Onn looked and sounded pained as he said it. "He is manager of Earth."

Esste sucked in air quickly. She sat in silence, her eyes focused on nothing. Onn's voice had been as kind as possible, his song gentle to her. But there was no gentleness in the message. Riktors might have forced Ansset to stay—that was believable. But how could Ansset have been forced to take a position of such responsibility?

"He is so young," Esste sang.

"He was never young," Onn answered, a descant.

"I was cruel to him."

"You gave him nothing but kindness."

"When Riktors begged me to let them stay together, I should have refused."

"All the Songmasters agreed that he should stay."

And then a cry that was not a song, that came deeper from within Esste than all her music.

"Ansset, my son! What have I done to you, Ansset, my son, my son!"

Onn did not stay to watch Esste lose Control. What she did alone in the High Room was her own affair. He descended the long flight of steps, his body heavy with his own regret. He had had time to get used to the idea of Ansset not returning. Esste had not.

Esste could not, he feared. Not a week had passed since Ansset had left that Esste had not sung of him, either mentioning him by name or singing a melody that those who knew her recognized—a song of Ansset's, a fragment of voice that could only have been produced by the child's throat, or by Esste's, since she knew all his songs so well.

His homecoming had been watched for as no other singer's return. There was no celebration planned, except in the hearts of those who meant to greet him. But there the songs had been waiting, ready to burst the air with rejoicing for the greatest Songbird of them all. The place was ready for Ansset. It was meant that he would begin to teach at once. It was meant that his voice would sing all the hours of the day, would lead the song in the courtyards, would be heard in the evening from the tower. It was meant that, someday, he would be Songmaster, perhaps in the High Room.

Onn had had time to get used to the failure of all these intentions. Yet as he walked slowly down the stairs he heard his footsteps ringing hollowly against the stone, for he still wore his traveling shoes. The wrong wanderer has returned, he thought. In his mind he heard Ansset's last song, years before, in the great hall. The memory of it was thin. It sounded like wind in the tower, and made him feel cold.

6 Ansset had only been in Babylon a week when he got lost.

He had been in the palace too long. It didn't occur to him that he didn't know his way around. And in fact he had learned almost immediately every corner of the manager's building, which he was sharing for two weeks with the outgoing manager, who was trying to acquaint him with his staff and the current problems and work. It was tedious, but Ansset thrived on tedium these days. It kept his mind off himself. It was much more comfortable to immerse himself in the work of government.

He had no training for it, formally. But informally, he had the best training in the world. Hours and hours spent listening to Mikal and Riktors pour their hearts out, discreetly, about the decisions that faced them. He had been the dumping ground for the problems of an empire; it was not strange to him to face the problems of a world.

Yet there were times when they left him alone. There were limits to what anyone could absorb, and though Ansset knew he had no reason to be ashamed of the way he had been learning, he was keenly aware of the fact that they all thought him to be a child. He was small, and his voice had not changed, thanks to the Songhouse drugs. And so they were solicitous, oversolicitous, he thought. "I can do more," he said one day when they quit before sunset.

"That's enough for a day," the minister of education said. "They told me not to go past four and it's nearly five. You've done very well." Then the minister had realized that he was sounding patronizing, tried to correct himself, then gave it up and left.

Alone, Ansset went to the window and looked out. Other rooms had balconies, but this one faced west, and he saw the sun setting over the buildings to the west. Yet below, where the stilts of the building left undisturbed ground, thick grass grew, and Ansset saw a bird rise from the grass; saw a large mammal lumbering under the buildings, heading, he assumed, toward the river to the east.

And he wanted to go outside.

No one went outside, of course, not in this weather. Months from now, when the Ufrates rose and the plain was water from horizon to horizon, then there would be boating parties dodging hippopotamuses and singing from building to building, while work went on in the buildings rooted in bedrock, like herons ignoring the current because their feet had a firm grasp in the mud.

Now, however, the plain belonged to the animals.

But there was no door that did not open to Ansset's hand, no button that did not work when he pushed it. And so he took elevators to the lowest floor, and there wandered until he found the freight elevator. He entered, pushed the only control, and waited as the elevator sank.

The door opened and Ansset stepped out into the grass. It was a hot evening, but a breeze flowed under the buildings. The air smelled very different from the deciduous breezes of Susquehanna, but it was not an unpleasant smell, though it was pungent with animals. The elevator had brought him to the center of the space under the building. The sun was just beginning to become visible between the second building to the west and the ground; Ansset's shadow seemed to stretch a kilometer into the east.

Better than sight or smell, however, was the sound. Distantly he heard the roaring of some indelicate beast; much closer, the cry of birds, a more savage cry than the twitters of the small birds in Eastamerica. He was so enthralled with the novelty of the sound, and the beauty of it, that he hardly noticed that the elevator behind him was rising until he turned to follow the motion of a bird and realized that there was nothing behind him at all. Not just the elevator, but the entire shaft as well had risen into the building, and was just settling into its place, a metal square high above him on the bottom of the first floor.

Ansset had no idea how to get the elevator to come down again. For a moment he was afraid. Then he thought wryly that they would notice he was missing almost immediately, and come looking for him. Someone always came and asked him if he needed anything every ten minutes or so.

As long as he was away from everyone, as long as he was there with his feet in the grass and his ears attuned to new music, he might as well make the most of it. The buildings extended indefinitely to the east; to the west, only two buildings stood between him and the open plain. So he went west.

He had never seen so much space in his life. True, the plain was dotted with trees, so that if he looked far enough, the trees made a thin green line that kept the world from going on forever until it curved out of sight. But the sky seemed to be enormous, and birds disappeared easily into it, they were so small against the dazzling blue.

Ansset tried to imagine the plain in flood, with the trees rising resolutely above the water, so that boaters could dock in the branches and picnic in the shade. The land was unrelentingly flat—there was no high ground. Ansset wondered what became of the animals. Probably they migrated, he decided, though for a moment he imagined thousands of game wardens gathering them up and flying them to safe ground. A vast evacuation; man protecting nature in a reversal of the ancient roles. But it happened only here, in the huge Origins Imperial Park, which stretched from the Mediterranean and Aegean seas to the valley of the Indus River. Here dead land had been brought to life, and only Babylon, and here and there a tourist center, interrupted the animals' reclaimed kingdom.

As the sun touched the horizon, the birds became almost frantic in their calls, and many new birds erupted into song. At dusk all the animals would prowl, some in their last activity before night, others in their first activity after a day of sleep.

The song made Ansset feel at peace. He had thought never to feel that way again, and he felt tension he hadn't known gripped him gradually uncoil and relax. Almost by reflex he opened his mouth to sing. Almost. Because the very length of time between songs called to his attention the novelty of the act. He was instantly aware that this was his First Song. And so as he began so sing, the music was tortured by calculation. What should have been reflex became deliberate, and therefore he faltered, and could not sing. He tried, and of course tones came out. He did not know that much of the awkwardness was simply lack of use, and that much of it was the fact that his voice was now beginning to change. He only knew that something that had been as natural as breathing, as walking, was now totally unnatural. The song sounded hideous in his ears. He shouted, his voice as forlorn as a cormorant cry. The birds near him fell silent, instantly sensing that he did not belong among them.

I don't belong among you, he said silently. Or among anyone else. My own won't have me, and here I'm a stranger.

Only Control kept him from weeping, and gradually, as feeling built inside him, he realized that, songless, he could not keep Control. There had to be an outlet somewhere.

And so he cried out, again and again, screams and howls into the sky. It was an animal sound, and it frightened even him as he made the noise. He could have been a wounded beast, from the sound; fortunately, the predators were not easily fooled, and did not come to the cries.

Someone came, however, and not long after he fell silent and the sun disappeared behind the distant trees, someone touched his elbow from behind. He whirled, frightened, not remembering that he was expecting rescue.

She looked familiar, and in a moment he placed her in his mind. She belonged, oddly, both in the Songhouse and in the palace. Only one person had ever stood both places in his life, besides himself.

"Kya-Kya," he said, and his voice was hoarse.

"I heard your cry," she said. "Are you hurt?"

"No," he said, instantly.

They looked at each other, neither sure what to say. Finally Kya-Kya broke the silence. "Everyone was in a panic. No one knew where you had gone. But I knew. Or thought I knew. Because I come down here, too. Not many of us ever make the descent when it's the dry season. The animals aren't very good company. They just wander around looking powerful and free. Human beings aren't meant to look at power and freedom. Makes us jealous." She laughed, and so did he. Gracelessly, however. Something was very wrong.

"You work here?" Ansset asked.

"I'm one of your special assistants. You haven't met me yet. I'm on your agenda for next week. I'm not very important."

He said nothing, and again Kya-Kya waited, unsure what to say. They had spoken before—angrily, on her part, when they conversed both in the Songhouse and in the palace. But she was damned if she'd let that stand in the way of her career. A terrible thing, having this boy made her direct superior, but she could and would make the best of it.

"I'll show you how to go back. If you want to go back."

He still said nothing. There was something strange about his face, though she couldn't think what it was. It seemed rigid somehow. Yet that couldn't be it—he had been utterly unflinching when she talked to him in his cell in the Songhouse and he sang comfort to her, an inhuman face, in fact.

"*Do* you want to go back?" she asked.

He still didn't answer. Helpless, unsure what to do for this child who had her future in his control—the Songhouse comes back to haunt me no matter what I do, she thought, as she had thought a hundred times since learning he would be manager—she waited.

Finally she realized that what was wrong with his face was that it was *not* rigid. It was only trying to be. The boy was trembling. The most perfectly controlled creature in the Songhouse was shaking, and his voice wavered and sounded awkward as he said, "I don't know where I am."

"You're just two buildings away from your——" And then she realized that he did not mean that.

"Help me," he said.

Her feelings toward the boy suddenly wrenched, turned completely another way. She had been prepared to deal with him as a tyrant, as a monster, as a haughty superior. She had not been prepared to deal with him as a child asking for help.

"How can I help you?" she whispered.

"I don't know my way," he said.

"You will, in time."

He looked impatient, more frightened; the mask was coming off his face.

"I've lost my . . . I've lost my voice."

She did not understand. Wasn't he speaking to her?

"Kya-Kya," he said. "I can't sing anymore."

Of all the people on Earth, only Kya-Kya could possibly understand what he meant, and what it meant to him.

"Not ever?" she asked, incredulous.

He shook his head, and tears came to his eyes.

The boy was helpless. Still beautiful, the face still impossible not to look at, and yet now a real child, which in her mind he had never been before. Lost his voice! Lost the one thing that had made him a success where Kyaren had been a hopeless failure!

She was instantly ashamed of her excitement. She had never had it. He had lost it. And she forced herself to compare his loss to her losing her intellect, on which she depended for everything. It was not imaginable. Mikal's Songbird, without singing?

"Why?" she asked.

In answer a tear came uncontrolled from his eye. Ashamed, he wiped it off, and in the gesture won her to his side. Whatever side that was. Someone had done something to Ansset, something worse than his kidnapping, something worse than Mikal's death. She reached out to him, put her arms around him, and then said words that she had not thought ever to recall to her mind, let alone to her lips.

She spoke the love song to him, in a whisper, and he wept in her arms.

"I'll help you," she said afterward. "All I can, I'll help you. And you'll get your voice back, you'll see."

He only shook his head. Her chest was wet where his head pressed against her.

And then she led him to a stilt and stroked the panel that called the elevator, and as it descended she held him at arm's length from her.

"My first help to you is this. To me you can cry. To me you can show anything and say anything you feel. But to no one else, Ansset. You thought you needed Control before, but you really need it now."

He nodded, and almost immediately his face became composed again. The boy hasn't forgotten all his tricks, she thought.

"It's easier," he said, "when I can let it out somehow." Now that I can't sing it out, he didn't say. But she heard the words all the same, and while he stood alone and walked easily beside her through the buildings, where anyone could see them, in the enclosed bridges that connected the buildings, leading them back to the manager's quarters, he reached to Kya-Kya, and took her hand.

For years she had hated Ansset as the epitome of everyone that had hurt her. It amazed her how easily that hate could dissipate, just because he let himself be vulnerable. Now that she could hurt him, she never would.

The chief of staff was beside himself with joy at Ansset's return; but he spoke to Kya-Kya, not Ansset, as he asked, "Where did you find him? Where was he?"

Coldly Ansset said to the man, "She found me where I chose to be, Calip, and I returned when I chose to come." Deliberately he turned to Kya-Kya and said, "Please meet me at eight o'clock in the morning, Kya-Kya. I would like you to be with me through tomorrow's meetings. Calip, I want supper at once."

Calip was surprised. He had been so much in the habit of giving Ansset his schedule and introducing people to him, it didn't occur to him until now that Ansset would have things his own way. After a moment of embarrassed inaction, Calip nodded his head and left the room.

As soon as the man was gone, Ansset looked at Kyaren with raised eyebrows.

"That was pretty good," Kyaren said.

"Mikal was better at it, but I'll learn," Ansset said. Then he smiled at her, and she smiled back. But in his smile she still saw the traces of his fear, a hint of the expression on his face when he had pleaded for help.

And in her voice, as Kyaren said good-bye, he heard friendship. And he was, to his own surprise, certain that she meant it from the heart. Perhaps, he thought to himself, I may survive this after all.

7 "It's very important," said the minister with the Latin portfolio. "There has been bloodshed. Thirty people killed, that we know of, and ten of those in open combat."

Ansset nodded.

"There's another complication, sir. While the Uruguayans and Paraguayans are willing to speak Imperial in this meeting, the Brazilians insist on speaking Portuguese."

"Which is absurd," the chief of staff said, "because the *Portuguese* don't even speak it anymore."

Ansset had never understood the purpose of multiple languages. He thought of it as an aberration of history, which had luckily been set to rights years before. And here, on the capital of the empire, was a rather large nation that clung to an anachronism to the point of antagonizing those who had power over them.

"Do we have an interpreter?"

The chief of staff nodded. "But he's one of them. No one here speaks Portuguese."

Ansset looked over at Kyaren, who smiled. She sat beside him, but deferentially pulled back from the table, appearing to be a secretary but actually ready to slip him a note. She had been studying this problem for weeks for the outgoing manager—she already had in mind several compromise solutions to the border war, depending on how cooperative they were. Since the Brazilians were currently in control of the land, their cooperation was the key to any solution. But the Brazilians were famous for being uncooperative.

"Bring them in," Ansset said.

Two envoys entered from each nation. Protocol in this case demanded that they enter in order of age of the envoys, so that no nation would seem to get precedence. Ansset noticed, however, that each team included one who was very, very old. Odd, the things nations were willing to invest their pride in.

The chief of staff explained carefully the rules of the discussion. No interruptions would be tolerated. Any envoy who interrupted any other envoy would be summarily dismissed and no replacement would be allowed. They would ask Ansset for permission to speak, and would listen politely to all other speakers. Ansset was surprised that such instructions were necessary. In the imperial court it was all taken for granted.

Then everyone waited while the Brazilian interpreter translated the instructions into Portuguese. Ansset watched carefully. It was as he had suspected. The Brazilian envoys did not pay much attention to the translation—they had understood the Imperial perfectly well.

It was the sound of the language that fascinated Ansset. He had never before thought of shaping his mouth in just that way, using his nose to such good effect. It enticed him. As the interpreter spoke, Ansset formed the sounds in his mouth, felt them in his head. More than the individual sounds, he also sensed cadence, feeling, mood. The language was expressive, and without understanding the intensions of the language, he knew he could use it well enough to accomplish his purpose.

As soon as the interpreter was finished, the envoys all lifted their hands slightly off the table, palms facing Ansset—asking for permission to speak. Ansset impulsively turned to the Brazilian ambassador and began to sing. Not the music he had performed so often before. This was speech considered as song, and Portuguese language used for the sheer sound and power of it. If there were any recognizable words in it, it was an accident. But Ansset spoke on and on, delighted that he had not lost the power of imitation, working carefully to make this simple song touch the Brazilians as he wanted to touch them.

The Brazilians, one ancient man who did not seem altogether alert and a younger man with a look of resolute determination, were startled to hear their own language, then puzzled to try to decipher it. Even to them, it sounded like perfect Portuguese. But it was doubletalk, and the younger one looked angry for a moment, thinking he was being mocked.

By then, however, Ansset's tone had got through to them; they felt that despite the nonsense of his words, he was speaking affection and understanding to them. This is a beautiful language, he seemed to be saying, and I understand your pride in it. What would have been mockery by anyone else was high praise when spoken by Ansset, and when he at last fell silent, looking intently at them, the Brazilians both arose from the table, walked around it, and approached Ansset.

The guards in the room, at least as puzzled by what had happened as anyone else, fingered their weapons. They relaxed, however, when Calip raised his hand, motioned them to relax. The old Brazilian first, and then the young one, embraced Ansset. It was an incongruous sight, the old man clinging to the beautiful boy, and then the tall younger man bending to touch his rough cheek to Ansset's smooth one.

While they were in the embrace, Ansset murmured, in Imperial, "I beg you to speak Imperial so that the others can understand us."

And the man smiled, stepped back from Ansset, and said, "The manager Ansset is too kind. No other governor has troubled to understand us or our love of our country.

He has asked me to speak Imperial, and for his gracious sake I will.''

Kya-Kya, no less surprised than anyone else, could not help but notice the look of consternation on the interpreter's face. She was sure the Brazilians had planned a strategy of using the interpreter as a means of pacing the meeting, controlling it to their own purposes, since whenever anyone spoke, the interpreter would cause a maddening delay. Now that was discarded, and the pretense that Brazilian envoys spoke no Imperial would have to be abandoned for good.

The meeting proceeded, and gradually the envoys laid out their cases. In the troubled Paraná region, the original inhabitants had spoken Spanish, and now, millennia later, they still did. However, in the last four hundred years, Brazilians had asserted hegemony over the region—successfully, since before Mikal made Earth his capital there was little planetary government, and there were few restraints on national governments. Now the veneer of Portuguese was wearing thin, as the Spanish-speaking majority began to resent the greater and greater pressure on them to give up their language. Complicating matters further, the people in the north spoke the Paraguayan version of Spanish, which was unintelligible to the Uruguayans. There had been a lot of talk about self-determination for years, matched by official Brazilian statements about One Nation, Indivisible. The talk had finally turned into bloodshed, and the Uruguayans and Paraguayans were demanding that the Brazilians hand over the territory. Unfortunately, the territory was a hydroelectric paradise, and the Brazilians did not want to turn over fifty percent of their nonsolar energy to other nations.

And when the envoys had finished presenting their case, Ansset asked them to prepare in writing a one-page summary of what they think a just solution would be that would meet the needs of all the parties to the dispute. Then he dismissed them until after he had a chance to read their proposals.

In private, the minister with the Latin portfolio was effusive. "How did you do it? What did you say to them?"

Ansset only smiled and said nothing, turning his attention to Kya-Kya, who had scribbled furiously throughout the meeting. "The disagreement really isn't insoluble. They don't want opposite things," she said. "The Brazilians want to save face, to maintain their borders. They're very tight on this. And they need the energy. But the others are simply asking for preservation of culture. They want the Spanish-speaking citizens to be allowed to dominate in their own country. They don't need and can't really use the hydroelectric energy in the area." The Latin minister nodded, agreeing with her. They began drawing up the proposed compromise even before the envoys' proposals began arriving.

It was evening before the envoys were called back. Kyaren was delighted with the way Ansset looked—as fresh and cheerful as he had in the morning. As if no work had gone on at all, as though the solution to their problems seemed easy. Ansset read his compromise to them, providing them with copies when he was through.

"Let us study this," said the younger envoy from Paraguay.

"I doubt that there's a need," said Ansset, following Kyaren's advice. "This is very little different from your own proposal. Indeed, we were quite pleased with the fairness with which you approached the problem." Ansset began parrying the various objections skillfully. Kyaren and the Latin minister had already gone over with him very carefully which items could be altered and how far. Ansset's voice was reasonableness itself, gentle and friendly and warm, speaking love and appreciation to the envoys. Thank you for being willing to give a little on this point, in the interest of peace. And on this point, you can see why I cannot give in, because it would be intolerable to the others, and justly so. But we can give *here*, would that help? Ah, I thought it would.

Each envoy was completely convinced that Ansset was their advocate in the discussion, and when it was finished, late at night, the clerks prepared a fair copy of the new agreement and all the envoys and Ansset signed it.

And then, with peace looking quite possible, Ansset carefully looked around the table. He still did not seem tired; Control, Kyaren thought. "My friends," Ansset said, "I have come to respect you very much today. You have acted quickly and fairly and wisely. Now, I know that some of your governments will look at these compromises and want to change them. I don't want you to have to quarrel with your own governments. And I certainly don't want to see you or other envoys back again with the same dispute. So you may tell your governments as apologetically as you like that if they do not accept this compromise exactly as it is written here, within five days, I will rewrite the agreement to exclude that government entirely from the solution, and if after that there is any further resistance, I will remove the government from power. I mean to have this reasonable document treated as law. Do you understand?"

They understood.

"But there is no reason to tell them how intransigent I intend to be unless they bring up objections. I trust to your discretion and good judgment, which I have learned to respect today better than I respect my own. And now let's go to bed; I'm sure you're all as tired as I am."

When Ansset arose to leave, the envoys spontaneously applauded him.

The evening was not over yet, however. Ansset, Kyaren, and the Latin minister went from the meetingroom to a small chamber where the outgoing manager waited for them. He had been watching everything by vids all day. And now he was supposed to criticize Ansset's actions and statements, helping him to learn from his mistakes.

"But you made no mistakes," the manager said, with a smile that did not, to Kyaren's eyes, look sincere. "And so I can leave with an easy heart."

And he left.

"He can talk about an easy heart all he likes," Ansset said to Kyaren when the man was gone. "But he didn't like me."

She laughed. "Can you tell Ansset why?" she asked the Latin minister.

The minister did not laugh. "I don't wish to sound disrespectful of the former manager, Ansset, but no one has ever been able to deal reasonably with the Brazilians. This is the first time I've ever seen a conference end without the manager having to threaten to send in troops against them."

Ansset smiled. "They're proud people," he said. "I liked them."

Then the minister left, and Ansset sat down. The weariness finally showed in his face, and he was trembling. 'This is the hardest thing I've ever done in my life," he said softly.

"It should get easier," Kyaren answered, still surprised to see him showing weakness.

"Look," Ansset said. "I'm shaking. I never shake."

Because you used to sing, Kyaren did not say. They were both well aware of the reason why Ansset could not maintain perfect Control anymore. She helped him up from the bench where he sat.

"Are you going to bed now?" Kyaren asked.

Ansset shook his head. "I doubt it. I couldn't sleep. Or if I forced myself to, I'd pay for it tomorrow. Break a window and chew the glass, or something." Ansset was obviously ashamed of his new weakness.

"Will you come with me, then?" Kyaren asked. "I haven't had supper, and we could eat together and relax a little. If you don't mind."

Ansset did not mind.

8 Josif woke up more from the smell than the sound. At least the smell was the first thing he was aware of, real food cooking in the kitchen instead of the bland smell of machine food. He looked at the clock. One in the morning. He had gone to bed three hours before, knowing Kyaren would not be home until late. But real food was cooking in the kitchen, and while they had real food often—one of the luxuries they indulged in on their newly expanded salaries—they always ate it together.

He then became aware of the voices. They were not loud. Kyaren's voice he knew from the cadences. The other voice he did not know. It sounded like a woman. Inwardly Josif relaxed, got out of bed, put on a robe, and walked sleepily into the front room.

In the kitchen Kyaren was making a salad, while talking to a boy who looked to be about twelve or thirteen. Their backs were to him.

"Still, you handled them masterfully," Kyaren was saying.

The boy shrugged. "I heard their songs and sang them back. It's easy."

"For you," Kyaren said. "But then, you *were* singing."

The boy laughed. To Josif the sound was received not so much by his ears as by his spine, tingling with the music of it. He knew now who the child was—the only person so young whose voice would have that kind of power to it. Ansset. Josif had never met him, had only seen pictures. But he did not want the boy to turn around. Instead he watched him from the back, the way his hair curled gently onto his neck, clinging with sweat from the heat of the kitchen; the way his chest sloped into his waist, which was lithe, and then did not flare at all as the lines of his body went smoothly down narrow hips to strong, well-shaped legs. His movement was graceful as he alternately leaned in to watch Kyaren's hands working and leaned out to look at her face as they talked.

"Singing?" the boy was asking. "If that was singing, then a parrot speaks."

"It was singing," Kyaren said. "But then, I never had an ear."

The Songhouse, of course. Josif knew from what Ferret had said that Kyaren came from the Songhouse. But they had never talked about it. It was clearly on the list of things that Josif may know, but that Kyaren was not able to discuss. It had not really occurred to Josif, not seriously, anyway, that Kyaren might know Ansset. It was like being from a city on Earth. Even being from Seattle, far from a large town, it always seemed absurd to him when people asked, "From Seattle? Why then, do you know my cousin?" The name never meant anything to him. But the Songhouse wasn't so much a town as a school, was it? And Kyaren knew this boy. Who also happened to be the planet manager, and therefore the key to their advancement.

It occurred to Josif that Ansset might be helpful to them. But that thought was buried in far stronger thoughts and feelings. For then Ansset turned around and looked at him.

The pictures were poor imitations. Josif was not prepared for the eyes, which found his face as if Ansset had been looking for him for a long time; the lips that were parted just slightly, that hinted of smiles and passion; the translucence of the skin, which seemed smooth as marble yet deep and warm as soil in sunlight. Josif had been beautiful as a boy, but this child made him feel ugly by contrast. Josif's hands longed just to touch his cheek—it could not be as perfect as it looked.

"Hi," Ansset said.

Kyaren turned around, startled. When she saw it was Josif, she was relieved. "Oh, Josif. I thought you were asleep."

"I was," Josif said, surprised that he could speak.

"How long have you been standing there?"

It was Ansset who responded: "A few minutes. I heard him come in."

"Why didn't you say something?"

And again Ansset answered, though the question had been directed to Josif. "I knew he was no danger to us. He came from the bedroom. I assume he's Josif, your friend."

"Yes," Kyaren said. Her tone sounded tentative. Josif realized that she had never mentioned him to Ansset—she was surprised that Ansset knew about him.

Apparently Ansset caught her hesitation, too. "Oh, Kyaren, you didn't think they'd let me be friends with you without a security check, did you?" He sounded amused. "They're so thorough. I'm sure they know exactly where I am right now, and what we're doing."

"Are they listening to us?" Kyaren asked, appalled.

"They aren't allowed to," Ansset said, "but they probably are. If not the locals, then the imperial snoops. No, don't worry about it. They're probably just monitoring heartbeats and the number of people present, that kind of thing. I'm allowed some privacy. I can insist on it, and I will." His voice radiated calm. Both Josif and Kyaren visibly relaxed.

The salad was done, and Kyaren sprinkled hot mushrooms over the top of it.

"I didn't expect real food," Ansset said.

"We usually eat out of the machines," Kyaren answered, and they spent a while during the meal talking about the virtues and dangers and expenses and inconveniences of eating real. Of course, in the palace Ansset had never tasted machine food; there are benefits to eating with the emperor.

Josif said little, however, and ate little. He tried to convince himself that it was because he was tired. Actually, however, his eyes were wide open and his attention never flagged. He watched both Kyaren and Ansset, but mostly Ansset, as his hands described graceful patterns in the air, as his eyes danced with delight at flavors, at wit, and sometimes at nothing at all, just sheer enjoyment of being where he was, doing what he was doing.

Ansset's every word was love, and Josif's silence answered him.

"Don't you think so, Josif?" Kyaren asked, and Josif realized that he had not been listening to the conversation.

"I'm sorry," Josif said. "I think I dozed off."

"With your eyes wide open?" Kyaren laughed. She sounded tired.

Ansset looked carefully at Josif. Josif thought that the boy was trying to tell him something; trying to tell him that he knew Josif had lied, that Josif had not been dozing. "Why don't you go to bed?" Ansset asked. "You're tired."

Josif nodded. "I will."

"And I'd better leave, too," Ansset said. "It was wonderful. Thank you."

Ansset got up and went toward the door. Kyaren went with him, talking all the way. Josif, however, ignored courtesy and returned to the bedroom. It took no thought at all. He knew what he had to do. Ansset was obviously not just a casual friend, not just a superior officer in government. Kyaren would have him back, again and again. And so Josif started taking his clothing from the shelves and putting it in his duffel.

But he was tired, and soon sat down on the edge of the bed, holding the edges of his half-full duffel and wondering what good it would do. The thought of leaving Kyaren was terrifying. The thought of not leaving her was worse.

I have done this before, he thought. This has all happened before, and what good does it do?

He remembered Pyoter, and then it was impossible for him to get up, to finish packing, to leave. It was Pyoter he had first loved, who had taken Josif as a shy child of unusual beauty and shown him love and loving. Josif then discovered what he had not known about himself. That when he trusted, he held back nothing. That when he loved, he could not love anyone else. He and Pyoter had been everywhere together, done everything together. They had both said *we* so often that the word *I* came only with difficulty to their lips. Only a year apart in age, their friendship had been so boyish and exuberant that no one had thought there was anything sexual in it; but Josif also learned that he could not love without lovemaking, that it was a part of it, the center of the yearning. And so he and Pyoter had shared everything and it seemed it would go on forever.

Until Bant. Bant had known at once. Josif never knew what made the difference or why he changed. Just that one day everything had been the same; Bant a friend of sorts, but very distant, Pyoter the beginning and end of the world to him. And then the next day, it had all been changed. Pyoter was a stranger, and Bant, who had finally taken Josif to his bed, had completely replaced him.

It horrified Josif that he could change that quickly, that overnight his attitudes could change. He refused to think it might be just the sex; he reconstructed events and saw the seeds of the change months before, when Bant had first hired him as his secretary and they had begun their friendly banter in the office. Josif now remembered the touches, the smiles, the warmth; he had been changing all along, and only noticed it all at once.

He could not bear to be disloyal to Pyoter. He had tried, for weeks, to keep things the same between them. It was impossible. Pyoter wasn't a fool, and Josif watched him getting more and more hurt as it became clearer and clearer that Josif no longer belonged to him as he had. And finally Pyoter said, "Why didn't you just leave at once, instead of tearing me up bit by bit like this?"

This time, Josif thought, this time I *must* leave. Before I destroy Kyaren. Because this boy I cannot resist, and sooner or later the change will come, if he's here often. Sooner or later it will not be Kyaren I come to with my thoughts and my feelings; or, even if the boy never becomes my friend, it will get to a point where I will be so obsessed by him, as I was obsessed by Bant, that I cannot bear to be with Kyaren anymore.

The duffel lay at his feet, half full. Why don't I go? Josif asked himself. Why am I still here? I know what I have to do, I know why, it's the way I am and the only way to stop myself is to stop everything, and yet here I sit and I haven't packed and I'm not leaving and why not?

The answer stood in the door, her face surprised, uncomprehending.

"What are you doing?" Kyaren asked.

"Packing," Josif answered, but he knew even then that he would not leave. He had never been able to leave Pyoter or Bant willingly; he would not be able to leave Kyaren either. I am not in control of myself, Josif realized. I gave myself to her, and I can't just decide to take myself back.

"Why?" Kyaren asked, already hurt because she could not comprehend what he was doing.

If I stay, I'll destroy her as I destroyed Pyoter.

"We'll still be friends," Josif answered.

"What brought this on? Why now, at three o'clock in the morning? What did I do?"

"Ansset," Josif said.

She misunderstood. "How can you possibly be jealous of him? He's only fifteen! They give them drugs in the Songhouse, he's sterile, puberty is put off for years—he hardly even has a sex, Josif——"

"I'm not jealous of him," Josif answered.

She stood regarding him for a while, and then realized what he meant.

"Still the old sixty-two percent, is it?" she asked.

"No," he answered, "I just see the potential. I want to avoid it."

"There is no potential," she said.

"You don't understand."

"Damn right I don't. You mean that all this time, I've just been filling your bed until you could find a beautiful boy to fill it?"

Maybe postponing it would have been better, Josif thought. Postponing is definitely better. I can't do this tonight. Because Ansset is only potential, and Kyaren is real, Kyaren I love *now*, and I can't bear the hurt and anger in her voice. "No," he said softly, fervently.

"Kyaren, you don't understand. I didn't *choose* you. I didn't *choose* Bant. Things like this happen. They just happen, and I don't have any control over it."

"You mean that in just one evening you suddenly forget that you love me—"

"No!" he cried out, in agony. "No! Kyaren, I just know that it's possible, it's possible and I don't want it to happen, don't you see?"

"I don't," she said. "If you love me, you love me."

Josif got up, walked to her, knocking over the duffel in the process. "Kyaren, I don't want to leave you."

"Then don't."

"It's because I love you that I want to leave."

"If you love me, you'll stay," she said.

He had known it, from the moment she appeared in the door. He couldn't leave her. When the change came, it would come, and then it would be irreversible, and then he would leave because he loved someone else and there was something in him that made it impossible for him to love two people at once. But now the one person was Kyaren, and he could not leave her because she wanted him to stay.

"I'll hurt you," he said.

"You could not hurt me worse than leaving me now, for no reason."

He wondered if she was right, or if it was easier for no reason than for the reason that there would be in the future. Surely it was. Surely it was easier to bear if you didn't have to know who it was who took your lover's heart from you. But maybe not; she was a woman, and Josif did not understand women. Maybe she was right, and it would be better this way.

"Besides, Josif, what makes you think Ansset would ever have you? He didn't have two emperors, you know."

She was right. She was right and he knew it and he went

to the duffel and unpacked it and put the clothing away. "He never will," Josif said. "I was a fool. I'm just tired." And he undressed and got into the bed.

They made love in silence, and several times Kyaren seemed surprised by the force of his passion tonight. She did not realize that in spite of his best efforts he kept seeing the curls clinging to Ansset's neck, the soft cheek that he had not touched except in his mind but that was all the softer because of that. He tried to take Ansset's face out of his mind. And failed.

Kyaren sighed contentedly afterward, and kissed him. She thinks it's all better now, Josif thought bitterly. She thinks she's kept me. She would have kept me better if she had let me go now.

And when her breathing became heavy and regular, he leaned up on his arm and looked at her face, which she always turned away from him in sleep. He stroked her cheek softly; her mouth moved, almost like the sucking instinct of a baby.

"I warned you," he said softly, so softly that perhaps the words did not even find voice. I warned you.

Then he gave up and lay back and tried to sleep, sour at heart because he had tried to control his life just once and could not do it after all.

Kyaren was not asleep, however, or she had been wakened by his touch. "Josif," she said. "I'm going to have your baby."

"No," he said softly.

"Please," she said. And because he was tired and not disposed to deny her anything, and because he knew that soon enough he would deny her everything, he let himself cool, and they made love again. And sometime in the next week she conceived, and when Josif saw how happy it made her and how concerned for her it made him, he began to think that maybe he had been wrong, that maybe Ansset would mean nothing to him.

For the child's sake, and because he wanted to bind himself to Kyaren even tighter, Josif insisted and they married. Now I will never let go of you in my heart, Josif thought. I will love you forever, he thought.

I am lying, he thought, and this time he was right.

9　The tour was Ansset's idea. Riktors had just returned from his tour of the prefects, and the results had been splendid. "Well, why not me?" Ansset asked, and the more he talked about it, the better his advisers liked it. "There are always differences from region to region on a planet," Ansset said, "and most planets develop dialects, some even languages. But Earth has nations. If it makes sense for the emperor to have contact with every prefect, it makes sense for the manager of Earth to have contact with every nation."

To Kyaren he also explained. "The statistics and figures you and the others play with all the time, they mean nothing to me. I can't think that way. You tell me what you've concluded and I don't understand why. But when I meet them, when I hear them speak, when I hear the songs of the people and their leaders, I'll be able to understand better."

"Better?"

"Than I do now. And in some ways, better than you understand them, for all that the computers even keep track of the number of old fleskets returned to the pots for scrap."

So they took the tour, and Ansset brought all his top advisers with him, and allowed them to bring their spouses, those who had contracts. That was why Josif came along, though he was not an adviser to the manager.

The tour began in the Americas, with visits to Uruguay, Paraguay, Brazil, Titicaca, Panama, Mexico, Westamerica, Eastamerica, and Quebec. In Mexico Josif and Kyaren stayed three extra days, revisiting the places and redoing the things seen and done when they first loved each other. They had their son with them, of course, little Efrim— Josif chose the name because an earlier Josif, thousands of years before, had given his favorite son that name. "History," Kyaren had snorted. "A ridiculous name." She actually liked it quite a bit.

Efrim was only a year old, but thought of himself as an accomplished athlete. He was unusually well coordinated for his age, but not so adroit as he thought, and he broke his arm in a fall from a ledge in the ruins of the Olympic Stadium.

"Efrim is doing fine," Kyaren complained. "It's you that's driving me out of my mind, Josif."

"I get worried."

"You get worried obnoxiously," Kyaren said. "It just takes two weeks' rest, and then he's fine. I'm taking care of him. You're just making him nervous."

"I can't stand sitting around doing nothing," Josif said.

And so they decided that Josif should rejoin the manager's tour in Quebec, and they would meet again when Efrim was well, in Europe. "Shouldn't *you* go, and *I* stay? After all, you're the personal adviser. I'm just a spouse."

"He doesn't need me with him. And Efrim doesn't need you with him. Just see the sights and study the history and let Efrim keep busy healing instead of trying to constantly entertain his father. He had the hiccoughs for half an hour yesterday, you got him laughing so hard.''

"I'm going, then, if you want to be rid of me."

She kissed him. "Get out of here," she said. He got out, sorry in a way to be leaving her, but delighted not to be missing the weeks in old Europe, which, more than any other region, had preserved the ancient nations intact.

Ansset noticed him almost as soon as he returned. "Back with us already?"

"Kyaren's staying with the baby. She kicked me out. I was impossible."

"I hope the boy heals fast." And then busy again, meeting with the self-styled king of Quebec, a title only barely tolerated by the emperor because the kings of Quebec were properly subservient and remarkably hated by their people. No danger of rebellion, and therefore not a problem needing to be corrected.

Over the next several days, however, Ansset and Josif were thrown together more and more. Ansset thought at first that the meetings were accidental. Then he realized that he himself was setting them up, deliberately going to places where he knew Josif would be. He and Josif had had little contact over the months—while Ansset knew from his voice that Josif didn't dislike him, Josif still avoided him, rarely staying in a conversation very long, leaving Ansset always alone with Kyaren. Josif's shyness needed no explanation to Ansset. He respected it. But now his closest confidante and friend, Kyaren, was gone, and he needed to talk to someone. So he didn't stop himself from meeting with Josif. In fact, he began to make it more obvious. He invited him to meals, asked him along on walking tours, talked to him at night. Ansset couldn't understand why Josif always seemed reluctant to accept, yet never refused an invitation. And gradually, over the days, through Paris, Vienna, Berlin, Stratford, Baile Atha Cliath, with rain always making the air deliciously cool and comfortably dim, Josif lost his reticence, and Ansset began to understand why Kyaren was so devoted to him.

Ansset also began to notice that Josif was sexually attracted to him. Hundreds of men and women had been before. Ansset was used to it, had had to put up with it through all his years in the palace. Josif was different, though. His desire seemed not so much lust as affection, part of his friendship. It intrigued Ansset, where years before such things had repelled him. He was curious. He had grown seventeen centimeters since his appointment to Babylon, and his voice was deepening all the time. There were other changes, and he found himself with longings he did not know how to satisfy, with questions he did not dare to ask only because he already knew the spoken answer, and the other answer he was afraid of.

At the Songhouse little was said of the drugs that singers and Songbirds were given. Just that they put off puberty, and that there were side effects. There were also whispers that it was worse for men than for women, but how it was worse, or even how it was bad, was never said. The drugs gave them five more years as children, five more years with the beautiful voices of childhood.

Well, Ansset had lost his songs and so didn't need his voice, except for the coarse singing involved in making every national leader completely devoted to him, easy tricks that he was ashamed of even as he used them. His five extra years of childhood were over, and he wanted to know what happened next.

After the meeting with the Welsh chief, who affected coarse manners but whose Gaelic was beautiful to Ansset, the planet manager and the assistant minister of colonization went to Caernarvon Castle together. It had been domed

thousands of years before, the last castle of Britain to
survive with some of the original stones in place. They
walked together on the walls, overlooking the dense green
of the grass and the trees and the blue of the water that
spread between the castle and the island of Angelsea. The
only sign of modern life was the flesket and the guards
beside it, and the trail where the grass grew lower because
of the vehicles that passed over it. There were others in the
castle, of course—it was maintained as a luxury hotel, and
they would spend the night there. Security guards were
going through the place on a final check. But where
Ansset and Josif stood, there was no one. Birds skimmed
back and forth over the sea.

"What is this place?" Ansset asked. "Why is it kept
like this?"

"A castle was like a battleship," Josif answered. "All
the men would come in here when their enemies attacked,
and the walls kept them out."

"This was before lasers, then."

"And before bombs and artillery. Just bows and arrows,
spears. And a few more choice things. They used to pour
boiling oil over the walls to kill men trying to climb
them."

Ansset looked down, hiding his revulsion easily, curious
to see how far the drop was to the ground. "It seems
dangerous enough just to stand up here."

"They lived in violent times."

Ansset thought of his own violent times. "We all do,"
he said.

"Not like then. If you had a sword, you had power.
You ruled over everyone weaker than you. They were
always at war. Always trying to kill each other. Fighting
over land."

"Mikal ended wars," Ansset said.

Josif laughed. "Yes, by winning all of them. It's probably the only way ever to have peace. Other ways have been tried. They never worked." Josif's hand rubbed along the rough stone.

"I lived in a place like this once," Ansset said.

"The Songhouse? I didn't think that was a castle."

"No one poured down boiling oil, if that's what you mean. And it wouldn't have stopped a determined army for more than, say, half an hour. But it's stone, like this."

Ansset sat down, took the shoes off his feet, and let his bare soles touch the stone.

"I feel like I've come home." And he ran lightly along the stone into one of the turrets, where he climbed a winding staircase to the top. Josif followed him. Ansset stood at the edge, the highest point of the castle, feeling giddy. It reminded him of the High Room, only here it would never be cold and the wind would never blow, because of the almost transparent dome that protected the rock. He began to get a sense of the age of the thing. The Songhouse was a thousand years old. And men had lived on Tew for two thousand years before the Songhouse had been built. And when Tew was first settled, three thousand years ago, this castle had already been sixteen thousand years old, had already spent ten thousand of those years under the dome.

"We are so old," Ansset said.

Josif nodded. "We've forgotten nothing in all that time. And learned nothing."

Ansset smiled. "Maybe we have."

"Some of us."

"You're so dour."

"Maybe," Josif said. "We don't build things like this anymore. We're far too sophisticated. We just put a fleet in orbit around the planet, so that instead of a fortress sitting like this on the edge of the sea, the fortresses cast their shadows over every centimeter of the soil. It was a frightening time then, Ansset, but there were advantages.''

''I understand they defecated and kept it.''

''They didn't have converters.''

''In piles. And put it in the fields so the crops would grow better.''

''That's China.''

''Oh.''

''It was better then in one way. There were places a person could hide.''

Josif sounded so wistful that Ansset became concerned. ''Hide?''

''Countries that were still undiscovered. Just crossing the water to Eire would have been enough. A man could have hidden from his enemies.''

''Do you,'' Ansset asked, ''have enemies?''

Josif laughed bitterly. ''Only me. I'm the only one.''

And more than ever since he had been imprisoned in Mikal's room in the palace, Ansset longed for his songs. But he had no song, could not sing comfort for whatever fears haunted Josif. He knew that, in part, Josif was afraid of *him;* he wanted to sing the love song, to tell the man that Ansset would never do him any harm, that in the last few months, and especially in the last few days, Ansset had come to love him as he also loved Kyaren, the two of them, in different ways, filling part of the huge gap left inside Ansset with the loss of his songs.

But he could not sing it, and he could not say it, and so Ansset reached out and stroked Josif gently on the shoulder and down the arm.

To his surprise, Josif immediately pulled away from him, turned and ran down the stairs. Ansset followed almost immediately, and almost ran into Josif where he had stopped, at the door leading onto the walkways atop the walls. Josif turned to face Ansset, his face twisted and strange.

"What's wrong?" Ansset asked.

"Kyaren's coming here tomorrow."

"I know. I'm looking forward to it. I've missed her."

"So have I."

"But I'm glad she was gone," Ansset said. "Or I would never have come to love you."

Josif walked away then, and Ansset, not understanding, did not follow.

All the rest of the afternoon and into the evening, Ansset puzzled over it. He knew Josif loved him, and he knew Josif loved Kyaren—such things couldn't be lied about. Why should there be anything difficult about it? Why should Josif be in such pain?

He went to the room where Josif was supposed to be, and found someone else in it. "Where's Josif?" he asked, and the security guard who had been assigned those sleeping quarters shrugged. "I just sleep where they tell me, sir," he said.

Ansset went straight to Calip, who was responsible for room assignments. "Where's Josif?"

Calip looked surprised. "Don't you know? He said that you had asked him to move to another room. So he'd be closer to the library."

"What room?"

Calip didn't answer immediately. Instead he fidgeted, then said, "Sir, did you know that Josif is a homosexual?"

"Hardly an exclusive one," Ansset answered. "Do you have special rooms assigned for homosexuals?"

"I wasn't sure if you knew. We thought—we thought he looked so agitated because he had made advances. And you had objected."

"When I object to something, *I'll* tell you. He didn't

make advances. He's my friend, I want to know where his room is.''

"He asked us not to tell you. He wanted to be alone, he said."

"Do you work for him or for me?"

"Sir," Calip said, looking very upset. "We thought he was right. Your friendship with him is good, but it's gone far enough."

"Am I, or am I not, planet manager?" Ansset asked, his voice icy.

Calip was immediately afraid—Ansset's voice could still do that, especially when he was imitating Mikal's most terrifying command voice.

"Yes, sir," Calip said. "I'm sorry."

"Has anyone told you not to take orders from me?"

Summoning his courage, Calip said, "Sir, it's only proper for me to advise you when I think you're making a mistake."

"Do you think I'm a fool?" Ansset asked. "Do you think I lived in the palace all those years without learning how to take care of myself?"

Calip shook his head.

"When I ask for something, your only duty, Calip, is to find the quickest way to do it. What room is Josif in?"

And Calip told him. But his voice was trembling with anger. "You listen to the wrong people too often, sir," Calip said. "You should listen to me from time to time."

It occurred to Ansset that Calip might be right. After all, Mikal and Riktors had listened to all their advisers, all the time, before making important decisions. While Ansset had gradually been closing himself off to everyone but Kyaren and, in the last few days, Josif. But in this case Calip's advice was unwelcome and inappropriate. Legally Ansset was an adult. It was none of Calip's business—it was a matter for friends.

He found the room with no trouble, but hesitated before knocking, trying again to understand Josif's motives, his reasons for shutting Ansset out so abruptly. He could think of none. Josif's emotions were not concealed from Ansset— the boy knew perfectly well everything that the man wanted and did not want. Josif wanted Ansset, and did not want to, and Ansset did not know why. It could not be because Kyaren would be jealous—she was not prone to that sort of thing, and if Josif wanted to make love to Ansset, she would not mind. Yet Josif acted as if Ansset's very touch were poisonous, though Ansset knew Josif had been wanting that touch.

He did not understand, had to understand, and so he knocked on the door and it opened.

Josif immediately tried to shut the door again, but Ansset slipped inside. And when Josif then tried to leave, Ansset shut the door, and stood there, looking Josif in the eyes.

"Why are you at war with yourself?" he asked the man.

"I want things," Josif said thickly, "that I do not want to want. Please leave me."

"But why shouldn't you have what you want?" Ansset asked, reaching up and touching Josif's cheek.

The struggle was clear on Josif's face. He wanted to hurl Ansset's arm away, but did not. Instead he did what he wanted more. As Ansset's fingers reached along Josif's neck, Josif's own hand moved, glided along Ansset's face, outlined his lips and his eyes.

And then, abruptly, Josif turned away, walked to the bed and threw himself on it.

"No!" he cried out. "I don't love you!"

Ansset followed him, sat beside him on the bed, ran his hands along Josif's back. "Yes you do," Ansset said. "Why do you want to deny it?"

"I don't. I can't."

"It's too late, Josif. You can't lie to me, you know."

Josif rolled back, away from Ansset, and looked up into the boy's face. "Is it?"

"I know what you want," Ansset said, "and I'm willing."

And the war in Josif's face and voice ended, and he surrendered, though Ansset still could not figure out why the war had been fought at all, or what fortress had fallen. Josif had won, but Josif had also lost; and yet Josif was getting what he longed for.

Josif's touch was not like the touch of the guard who had lusted for Ansset when he first came to Earth. His eyes were not like the eyes of the pederasts who visited the palace and hardly heard Ansset's song for looking at Ansset's body. Josif's lips on his skin spoke more eloquently than they had ever spoken when only air could receive their touch. And Ansset's questions began to be answered.

And then, suddenly, when his feelings were most intense, Ansset was startled by a sudden pain in his groin. He had not been exerting Control—he made a soft, inadvertent cry. Josif did not notice it, or misunderstood it if he did. But the pain increased and increased, centering in his loins and spreading in waves of fire through his body. Surely this pain was not normal, Ansset thought, terrified. Surely they don't always feel this, every time. I would have heard of this. I would have known it.

And climax came to Ansset, not as ecstasy, but as exquisite pain, more than his Control could contain, more than his voice could express. Silently he writhed on the bed, his face twisting in agony, his mouth open with screams far too painful to become sound.

Josif was horrified. What had he done? Ansset was obviously in terrible pain; he had never seen the boy show pain before. Yet Josif knew that there should be no pain, not with the gentle way that Josif had been teaching.

"What is it?" he asked.

Ansset could not find any voice at all, just convulsed so violently that he was thrown from the bed.

"Ansset!" Josif cried out.

Ansset's head struck the wall. Once, again, again. He seemed not to notice. Spittle came from his mouth, and his naked body arched upward, then slammed brutally against the floor. Josif had known Ansset was on the verge of orgasm, but instead of the gift he had meant to give the boy, there had been this. Josif had never desired to cause pain to anyone in his life; when he did, it nearly destroyed him. And he had never seen such pain as Ansset's. Every shudder of the boy's body struck Josif like a blow.

"Ansset!" he screamed. "Ansset, I only meant to love you! Ansset!"

With Josif's voice ringing in his ears, Ansset finally struck his head hard enough to bring unconsciousness, the only relief he could find from the pain that had long since ceased to be unbearable, that had come to be infinite and eternal, the only reason for Ansset to exist. The pain *was* Ansset, and then, as the room went black and the screams went silent, Ansset was finally able to remove himself from the agony.

He awoke with the dim light of morning coming in through a window. The walls were stone, but not thick; he was still in the castle, but in one of the buildings in the courtyard. He became aware of movement in the room. He turned his head. Calip and two doctors stood by him.

"What happened?" Ansset asked, his voice weaker than he had expected.

The three men immediately became alert. "Is he awake?" Calip asked one of the doctors.

"I'm awake," Ansset said.

Calip rushed to his side. "Sir, you've been delirious all

night. It took us two hours to find out enough about what had happened to you to know how to relieve the pain.''

''It might have killed you,'' one of the doctors said. ''If your heart had been any weaker, it would have.''

''What was it?'' Ansset asked dully.

''The Songhouse drugs. Nothing should do what they did to you. But we found a combination that might, and since it was our best chance at saving your life, we tried the contra-treatment, and it worked, after a fashion. It's incredible to me that they would have let you stay here past the age of fifteen without letting us know the treatment formulas.''

''What caused it?'' Ansset asked.

''You should have listened to me,'' Calip answered.

''Do you think I don't know that by now?'' Ansset said, impatiently.

''The Songhouse drugs make orgasm torture for you. Whoever your lover was, sir,'' said the doctor, ''she set you up for a good one.''

''Will it happen every time?''

''No,'' the doctor said, glancing at his colleague and then at Calip. Calip nodded.

''Well, then,'' said the doctor. ''Your body feeds back on itself. Like birth control, only stronger. It will never happen to you again, because you're permanently impotent, or will be at the slightest sign of pain. Your body isn't willing to go through this again.''

''He's only seventeen,'' the other doctor said to Calip.

''Will he be all right now?'' Calip asked them.

''He's exhausted, but there's no physical damage except a few bruises. You may have headaches for a few days.'' The doctor brushed hair out of Ansset's eyes with his hand. ''Don't worry, sir. There's worse that could have happened to you. You won't miss it.''

Ansset managed a wan smile. It didn't bother him too

much—he didn't really know what he was missing. But as the doctors left, he remembered Josif's touch, and realized that the way he felt before the pain began—that would never come back again. Still, he wanted Josif by him. Wanted to assure Josif that it hadn't been his fault. He knew Josif well enough to imagine the terrible guilt he was feeling, the certainty that he had caused pain where he had meant to bring joy. "I must talk to Josif."

"He's gone," Calip said.

"Where?"

"I don't know," Calip said. "He wasn't here this morning, and I haven't bothered putting out a search order. I really don't give a damn where he is." And Calip left the room, and Ansset, wearier than he had thought, slept again.

He awoke again with Kyaren beside him, looking worried.

"Kyaren," he said.

"They told me," she answered. "Ansset, I'm sorry."

"I'm not," Ansset said. "Josif couldn't have known. And I didn't know. It was the Songhouse. They could have told me."

Kyaren nodded, but her mind was on something else. "Calip won't authorize a search for Josif. He keeps saying that he hopes he falls off a cliff. It's raining out there. You don't know, Ansset. Josif tried to commit suicide before. It's been years, but he might do it again."

Ansset was instantly alarmed. He sat up, and was surprised to find that his head did not hurt very badly, and that he was only languid, not incapacitated. "Then we have to find him. Call the Chief of Security."

She called him; he came in a matter of moments.

"We have to organize a search for Josif," Ansset said. "I find it hard to believe no search has been organized up to now."

The Chief looked at the floor. "Not really," he said.

"He may be suicidal," Ansset said, letting the outrage pour into his voice.

"Calip didn't ask for a search, sir, but I wouldn't have organized one anyway."

Ansset could not believe the insubordination from these men, who in the last two years he had thought were dependable. "Then you would have been removed from office, as you are right now."

"As you wish, sir. But I wouldn't have organized a search for Josif because I know where he is."

His voice was still uncertain—he may know where Josif is, Ansset thought, but he certainly doesn't know *how* Josif is.

"Who has him? Where is he?"

"Imperial Security, sir. It was only natural. We didn't know what had happened to you. We suspected an attempt had been made on your life. It was only three hours after we got to you that we found what was wrong. And in the meantime, we had notified the emperor. He left standing orders with me to let him know if anything happened to you."

"Imperial Security has Josif," Kyaren said numbly.

"Why didn't you tell me?"

"The Ferret told me not to tell you until you asked."

"The Ferret gives orders that you aren't to notify me of something this important?"

The Chief looked uncomfortable. "The emperor always backs Ferret up in what he says. And you must understand, sir, finding you the way we did, with Josif the way he was——"

"How was he?" Kyaren demanded.

"Stark naked," the Chief said blandly. "And screaming his lungs out. We thought he'd tried to bugger you with something, sir. We had no idea what was going on. You never know, with homosexuals.''

Kyaren slapped the Chief, which he took calmly. ''You don't deal with them like I do,'' he said. ''This sort of thing happens a lot.''

''What sort of thing,'' Ansset said, taking Kyaren's hands and holding them. She was trembling. ''It happens all the time that the Songhouse drugs nearly kill someone?''

''I mean violence. Homosexuals are like that.''

''Josif isn't,'' Ansset said. ''Josif isn't at all. And therefore your theory isn't worth shit.'' He made his voice as ugly as possible; he saved vulgarity for times when he needed it, and it pleased him that the Chief winced. ''Now get us a direct flight to Susquehanna.''

''There isn't any from Caernarvon.''

''There is now. And it will take off in fifteen minutes.''

It took off in fifteen minutes, and Ansset and Kyaren sat together in the empty commercial jet. There was only one steward—they dismissed him immediately. The security guards, much against standard procedure, were following in another plane. Ansset was still weak, but the tension had helped him keep going during the rush to the port. Now he relaxed, not sleeping but not wholly awake, lost in his thoughts.

After a while, however, he realized that Kyaren might need company more than he needed rest. She stared out the window at the ocean below, motionlessly; but her hands were white from gripping the armrest on the seat, which was rigid to match her tension.

''Kyaren,'' he said. ''He'll be all right. I can clear this up with Riktors in a short time.''

She nodded, but said nothing.

''That isn't all, is it?''

She shook her head.

"Does it bother you that Josif and I were together? I didn't think it would, but he acted as if he thought it might."

"No," she said. "I don't mind you being together."

"But."

"But what?" she asked.

"You were thinking, *but*. You don't mind, *but*."

She looked down at her lap, and intertwined her fingers nervously. "Ansset, the first time you and he met. Two years ago, when you came home with me for a salad."

Ansset smiled. "I remember."

"Josif told me. That he thought he was going to fall in love with you."

"Did you mind?"

"Why should I mind?" she answered, her voice jumpy with emotion. "There's plenty of love, what should I care? I love both you and him, you know, and you love both of us, but he kept talking as if it were something that could only—As if once he loved you, he would have to stop loving me. He said that. He said that if he ever made love to you, it would be."

"It would be what?"

"It would be after he stopped loving me."

It sounded like nonsense to Ansset. But then he realized that, whether he meant to or not, he had so far loved serially. Esste and *then* Mikal and *then* Riktors and *then* Kyaren. But did he love Kyaren less for having loved Josif? Of course not.

Yet now Josif's actions made sense. If he really believed that, then it made a perverse sort of sense for him to have resisted his own desire for Ansset for so long, for him to have avoided becoming friends with Ansset, knowing what it would cost him if it ever became more than friendship.

"Where's Efrim?" Ansset asked.

"I left him in Caernarvon with the wife of the minister of information."

"Josif still loves you," Ansset said.

She looked at him and tried to smile in agreement. But her heart wasn't in it. Josif was in the custody of Imperial Security, and it had happened because he had done the thing he had said would mean the end of them. And what about Efrim?

"There's always the contract," Kyaren said, and wept. Ansset put his arms around her, held her head against his chest. He was surprised to realize that he was taller than Kyaren now. He was growing up. Soon he would be a man. He wondered what that would mean. Surely he could not have more required of him as an adult than had been required of him as a child. There could not be more.

10 Riktors received them in the great hall.

There were no guards. Only Ferret. But Ansset and Kyaren knew that he was guard enough.

The Mayor of the palace brought them in, but at Riktors's nod, he left. Kyaren was keenly aware of the tension in the air. None was visible from Ansset, but Kyaren knew that didn't mean anything. Control still served him when he needed it, usually. And the tension in Riktors was clear. Kyaren had not seen the man close up. He had the imperial presence, the mood about him so that no one dared oppose him. Yet he also seemed afraid. As if Ansset held a weapon that could hurt him, and he was terrified that it would be used.

She knew they had not seen each other in two years. Knew also from her conversations with Ansset that they had not parted on friendly terms. Yet they outwardly seemed pleased to see each other, and Kyaren did not think it was a sham.

"I've missed you," Riktors said.

"And I you," Ansset answered.

"My servants tell me that you've done very well."

"Better than I had expected, not as well as I had hoped," Ansset said.

"Come here," Riktors said.

Ansset walked forward, came within a few meters of the throne, and knelt, touching his head to the floor. Impatiently, Riktors motioned for him to arise and come closer. "You don't need to do that kind of thing, not when there's no audience."

"But I've come to ask a favor from the throne."

"I know you have," Riktors said, and his face darkened. "We'll discuss that later. How have you been?"

"Reasonably good health, surrounded by reasonably helpful people. I've come for Josif. He's innocent of any crime."

"Is he?" Riktors asked.

And Kyaren's heart suddenly grew heavy in her chest, and she felt something go out of her. She identified it a moment later as confidence. She had been expecting no resistance—just an error, to be rectified as soon as there was an explanation. What crime had Josif committed? Why was the emperor delaying and arguing?

She knew the answer as she asked the question. Josif had been making love to Mikal's Songbird. Even the emperor had not made love to Mikal's Songbird. Josif had had what the emperor had not even asked for. But had he wanted it? Was that the reason for his anger and delay?

"He is innocent," Ansset said slowly, but danger crept into his voice. "I want to see him."

"Is this Josif all you can think of?" asked Riktors.

"There was a time when you would have sung for me first. When you would have come to me full of songs."

Ansset said nothing.

"Two years!" cried Riktors, the emotion taking control of his voice. "In two years, you haven't visited, you haven't tried to visit!"

"I didn't think you'd want me."

"Want you," said Riktors, getting some of his dignity back. "Ever since I came here, this place was full of your music. And then gone. For two years, silence. And the babble of fools. Sing for me, Ansset."

And Ansset was silent.

Riktors watched him, and Kyaren realized this was the price that Riktors expected to be paid. A song in exchange for Josif's freedom. A cheap price, if only Ansset still had any songs in him. And Riktors didn't know. How could he not have known?

"Sing for me, Ansset!" Riktors cried.

"He can't," Kyaren answered. She glanced at Ansset, but he was standing quietly, regarding Riktors impassively. Control. Just another thing that she had been unable to master in the Songhouse.

"What do you mean, he can't?" asked Riktors.

"I mean that he's lost his songs. He hasn't sung anything, not since he left you. Not since you—"

"Not since I what?" He dared her to go on, dared her to condemn him.

"Not since you locked him in Mikal's rooms for a month." She dared.

"He can't lose his songs," Riktors said. "He was trained since he was three."

"He can and he did. Don't you realize? He doesn't *learn* songs. He learns how to discover them. Inside himself, and bring them out to the surface. Do you think he memorized them all, and chose the right one for the proper occasion? They came from his soul, and you broke him, and now he can't find them anymore." Her anger surprised her. She had listened sympathetically to Ansset. It had never occurred to her how much she had come to hate Riktors for Ansset's sake. Which was odd, for Ansset had never even hinted at hatred for Riktors. Only hurt.

Riktors seemed not to notice the impertinence of her tone. He only looked wonderingly at Ansset. "Is it true?" Ansset nodded.

Riktors dropped his head into his hands, which rested on the arms of the throne. "What have I done," he said. His hands twisted in his hair.

He really grieves for Ansset's loss, Kyaren thought, and realized that despite all he had done to hurt Ansset, he still loved him. And so, fumbling, she offered some words to assuage the blow that had just struck him. "It wasn't just you," she said. "It was the Songhouse, really. What the Songhouse did. Cutting him off here. You don't know what the Songhouse means to—to people like him." She had almost said *us*. "*I* knew they were bastards there, who didn't care for any of us, but they get chains on you and never let go."

Beside her, Ansset was shaking his head.

"It's true, Ansset. It was bad enough for them to strand you here without warning, but when they didn't even prepare you for—what happened, what the drugs would do to you—" She didn't finish. She merely turned to Riktors, who did not seem to be listening, and said, "It's the Songhouse that hurt him most."

He did hear. He sat up, and looked much relieved, though there was still tension in him, even for Kyaren to see, who did not know him.

"Yes," he said. "It's the Songhouse that hurt him most."

Suddenly Ansset stepped forward, toward the throne. He was angry. Kyaren was surprised—she had been the one speaking, and yet he seemed angry at Riktors.

"That was a lie," Ansset said.

Riktors only looked at him, startled.

"I know your voice, Riktors, know it as well as I know my own, and that was a lie, and not just a small one, Riktors, that was a lie that matters to you right to the core and I want to know why it's a lie!"

Riktors did not answer. But after a few moments he looked away from Ansset, glanced toward Ferret, who immediately came forward.

"Stay where you are!" Ansset commanded, and Ferret, surprised by the ferocity of his voice, obeyed. Ansset spoke again to Riktors. "It was not the Songhouse that hurt me most, then?"

Riktors shook his head.

"Where is the lie, Riktors? I was cut off from the Songhouse, and that has cost me more than any other loss I have ever sustained, even the loss of Mikal, even the loss of your friendship. And you say that it was not the Songhouse that hurt me most? Who was it, then? Who was it who cut me off from them?"

Again Riktors appealed to Ferret. "He's dangerous, Ferret."

Ferret shook his head. "When he plans to attack you, I'll know it."

It was obvious to Kyaren that Riktors did not share his confidence. But any pity or understanding she had had for the man was gone now; yet she found it hard to believe that anyone could have been as cruel as Riktors was. "It was all a lie, then," she said into the silence. "The Songhouse didn't refuse him. The Songhouse wanted him back."

Riktors said nothing.

"You were clever," Ansset said to him. "In all our conversation, that last day, you never once told me a lie. Not once. And I thought all your tension was because you were sad to see me go."

Riktors spoke at last, his voice husky. "I was sad to see you go."

"Anywhere. To anyone. I was yours, is that it? I had to love you most, is that it? If I thought of the Songhouse as home, you couldn't bear that, could you? If I loved the Songhouse more than I loved this palace, then you'd take the Songhouse away from me, wouldn't you? Only you had to twist it, so I'd hate them in the process, and not you at all. You couldn't have me hate you."

The words seemed to slam visibly into Riktors, and he gasped at the end of Ansset's speech. Ansset may have no songs, but his voice was still a potent tool, and he was using it to savage Riktors.

"I wanted your songs," Riktors said.

"You wanted my songs," Ansset answered, bitterly, "more than you wanted my happiness. So you took my happiness, and stole my songs."

And then Kyaren made a connection in her mind, and realized that Riktors was not holding Josif ransom against a song.

"Ansset," Kyaren said. "Josif."

Ansset remembered, and the mask of Control appeared again on his face. Time enough for hatred when Josif was free.

"I want Josif. Now," Ansset said.

"No," Riktors said.

"Aren't you through?" Ansset asked. "Do you think you can still save something? Or are you determined that if you can't have my love—and you can't, Riktors, you can't—then no one can. If you ever loved me, Riktors, you will let me have Josif. Now."

You can't, Riktors, you can't.

If you ever loved me, Riktors.

The words struck Riktors hard; his face worked, though whether with anger or grief Kyaren couldn't tell.

"Call a guard," Riktors said.

"No," Ferret said.

Riktors arose from his throne. "Call a guard!" he roared, and Ferret left, returning a moment later with two guards.

"Take them to the prisoner. To Josif."

The guards looked at each other, then at Ferret, who nodded and whispered something. The guards looked doubtful, but they led the way. Ansset and Kyaren followed.

"He won't do anything to us, will he?" Kyaren whispered.

Ansset shook his head. "Riktors will never hurt me directly, or you, as long as you're with me. And as long as you're with me, no one can take you away." She looked at his face. Control was lagging. She saw the killer there, and was afraid. This should never have happened to Ansset, none of this.

"How did they keep the Songhouse people from coming for you?" she asked. "If they really wanted you back—"

"The empire controls the spaceports. Besides, if he could lie to me, he could lie to them. But that's past now. Time enough to set things right once we have Josif back."

Kyaren was baffled by the labyrinth of the palace, lost all sense of direction. But they went generally downward. Into the prison, she assumed. But they made a certain turn that Ansset had not been expecting—he was taken by surprise and had to retrace a few steps.

"What's wrong?" she asked.

"He isn't in the prison," he said.

"Then where?"

"Hospital," Ansset answered.

The guards stopped outside a door.

"He's fairly drugged up. He isn't pretty right now, but Ferret said to let you see him as he is. I'm sorry."

Then the guard opened the door, and they walked in, and they saw Josif.

At first nothing seemed wrong with him, except the drugs. Josif saw them, but his eyes showed no recognition, and his jaw hung partly open. He sat on a narrow bed, leaning against the wall. His legs were loosely apart, and his arms hung slackly beside him. He looked as if he never planned to move.

Then Kyaren looked down, between his legs, just as Ansset saw and turned to try to block her sight. He was too late.

She screamed, shoved past him, and, still screaming, took Josif by the shoulders and pulled him toward her, embraced him in an agony of grief. He slumped against her, and with his head tilted down, he drooled. She still heard herself shouting hysterically; gradually she was able to stop, until finally even her spasmodic sobbing ended and all was silent in the room again. She looked at Ansset. His face was terrible, not because of the emotion on it, but because there was nothing on his face at all.

Carefully she leaned Josif back against the wall. His head moved to the right, so that he could not see her, but merely stared at the wall. He did not attempt to move. The drugs had him well in hand.

"They plan to fit him with a permanent tube tomorrow," said one of the guards.

Ansset ignored him, and Kyaren tried to. They started to push past him, but the guard raised a gun. It wasn't a laser—it was a tranquilizer. "Ferret said that after you saw, you weren't to be allowed back to the great hall."

Ansset didn't pause, simply brought up his foot. The man's hand broke at the wrist; the gun dropped to the floor as the hand went slack and hung perpendicular to the floor. A moment for the pain to register, and the guard reeled out of the way. The other was too slow—Ansset took his face off with both hands, and Kyaren raced to follow the Songbird as he shoved past the screaming guard, who knelt with his hands in front of his face, blood streaming down his arms.

This was not the way they had come, Kyaren was sure. But Ansset seemed sure of where he was going, and it occurred to her that he would want to avoid the ways where guards might be waiting. Also, he avoided any doors, finally coming to the great hall through the main entrance, which stood wide.

Kyaren reached the doors a moment after Ansset passed through them, but already he was halfway across the floor, heading, not for Riktors, but for Ferret. Suddenly Ansset was in the air, and Kyaren was expecting him, in his fury, to destroy the emperor's assassin.

But a moment later Ferret and Ansset were grappling. None of Ansset's movements could penetrate the man's defenses; Ferret was unable to land a blow or a cut on Ansset's body.

Finally, exhausted, they held each other firmly, neither able to move for fear the other would be able to use the movement against him. Ansset's mouth was near Ferret's ear. He moaned softly, and the moan was his agony of being unable to express what was in him, either with his body or with his voice. He could not kill, he could not sing, and he could not find another way to open what demanded to be opened inside him.

Ferret whispered triumphantly in his ear, "You've forgotten nothing."

Riktors spoke from the throne, where he was sitting again, relieved that Ansset's attack was not against him, relieved that neither fighter had been able to win. "Who do you think taught you how to kill that way, Ansset?"

"I killed my teacher," Ansset said.

"You were told you were killing your teacher," Riktors answered. "It was a lie."

"You can't match me," said Ferret.

"You were Mikal's servant, sworn to him," Ansset said.

"I am the emperor's servant," Ferret answered. "Mikal was old."

It was one betrayal, one injury too many. It tore something inside Ansset. The barrier broke, and all the hurt of the years he had thought the Songhouse did not want him, all the grief at Josif's mutilation, all the rage at Riktors's lies, all the vengeance and hatred that had built within him, unable to be expressed—it all came out at once.

Ansset sang again.

But it was not a subtle song, as all of his had been. Much of his technique had been lost in the years of songlessness, and there was no attention to filling the room or displaying nuances of melody. It was an instinctive song, one that depended not on the veneer the Songhouse had put on Ansset's ability, but rather on the powers within him that the Songhouse had only gradually discovered, the power to comprehend exactly what was in other people's hearts and minds, reshape it, manipulate it, and change it until they felt what Ansset wanted them to feel.

The song was terrible, even to Kyaren, who was at the edge of the room, and who could not understand it all because it was not sung to her.

But to Riktors, who understood almost all of it, it was the end of the world. It was all his crimes held up to him, and against his will he felt guilt for them, a terrifying guilt like the eyes of God staring down his soul, like the devil's teeth gnawing at his heart; the Furies fluttered passionately at the edge of his vision; he lifted up his voice in a vast scream that would have overshadowed any other sound, but not the sound of Ansset's song.

For it went on.

It went on, filled with the colors of Ansset's love for Riktors, betrayed; Mikal's love for Ansset, destroyed; and the timidity, the gentleness and passion of Ansset's night with Josif, forever out of reach. It was shaded by the darkness of Ansset's pain as the best joy the body can receive was torn from him and replaced by the worst pain the body can endure. And as all those griefs and agonies filled the air, they were intensified by Ansset's long, long months of silence, with his songs stolen from him, his Control partly broken. Now there was no Control. Now there was nothing holding him in.

The Mayor of the palace heard Ansset's song like the death of some forest animal, but it would have been impossible to hear the sound inside. And then he heard Riktors's scream. He shouted for guards; he raced for the great hall; he burst in; he saw:

Ansset, his face tipped upward toward the ceiling, the song still pouring from his throat like a volcano's eruption, seemingly endless, seemingly the death of the world. His arms were spread out, his fingers distended, his legs standing wide, as if the world were shaking and he was barely able to stay upright.

Kyaren, leaning against the door, weeping for the parts of the song that she could understand.

Riktors Mikal, emperor of all mankind, lying on the floor crying out again and again, begging for forgiveness, writhing to try to find a place where the sound wouldn't go. It had found him, almost all the song had touched him, and he was insane, tearing at his clothing, blood coming from his face where his own nails had raked him. Hours before, he had been serene and untouchable; now he had been felled by a song.

But not all the song. There were parts of the song that Riktors Mikal could not understand. Esste had been right about Riktors, when she felt that, like Mikal before him, he was cruel but not without limits. Riktors, like Mikal, had a love for, a sense of responsibility for, mankind. What killing he might do, he did because it was needed, because of the goal he had in mind. And when the goal was achieved, he did not kill. Riktors did not understand all the song because, while he was crueler than Esste had thought he was, he was also, in the end, partly kind.

For there was a part of the song that spoke of death, and loved death; that spoke of killing, and loved killing. There was a part of the song that proclaimed that there must be expiation for the crimes, and the only payment that could be made was death, and that only he who loved death could pay that price.

Only one person in the room understood that part of the song.

The Mayor of the palace looked last at Ferret, who alone was silent. He had torn his stomach open with his own hands; with his own hands he was throwing his bowels onto the floor. Again and again, with gushes of blood, he spilled himself. His face was in ecstasy; he alone in the room had found an outlet adequate for the pressure of the song.

He kept on rhythmically destroying himself until at last he had found his heart; with the last of his strength he tore it from his chest, held it in his hands. Only then did he look down. And he watched his hands as they crushed the organ. It was his benediction. He could die.

And as he fell to the ground, the song ended, and Riktors's screams ended, the only sound in the hall was the Mayor's heavy breathing and the soft crying of Kyaren at the other end of the hall.

KYAREN

1   It could have been chaos. Word could have gone out, and a thousand soldiers and managers and prefects and rebels of every stripe could have plunged the empire into a civil war that would have undone every work that Mikal had built and Riktors had maintained.

Could have.

But did not. Because the Mayor of the palace was a man who knew he was not adequate to handle the responsibility thrust on him. Because Kyaren was a woman of great presence of mind, who could set aside grief until she needed it.

Riktors Ashen fell into a coma, and when he came out of it, he refused to talk; though his eyes registered that he could see light, he would not blink when something was thrust at his eyes; he would not answer; when his arms were raised, they stayed raised until someone put them down. There was no question of his continuing to govern the empire. No one knew when he would recover, if he ever would.

But few people knew there was anything wrong at all. The Mayor of the palace immediately put tight security on the places in the palace where the truth could not be concealed. Riktors's chambers, where he lay attended by two doctors who suspected that unless something happened they would never get out of the room alive. Ansset's room, where the boy with perfect Control, now nearly a man in stature and old in grief, lay weeping hysterically when he was awake. The prison cell, where Josif came out of his drugged stupor and killed himself by stuffing a sheet down his throat until he suffocated. And the rooms where the Mayor of the palace and Kyaren met with imperial officials and gave them Riktors's instructions, as if Riktors were merely busy elsewhere. Those ministers and advisers who usually had close access to the emperor were sent on assignments that kept them out of reach, so they would not wonder why they were denied his presence. One of them was assigned to replace Ansset as manager of Earth. And when anyone asked why Riktors had not held court for so long, the Mayor replied, "Riktors has brought his Songbird home again, and they wish to be alone." Everyone nodded, and thought they understood.

But they could not keep it up indefinitely, they knew. Some decision had to be reached, and it was too hard for them. They were both gifted at government, the Mayor and Kyaren, and because they needed help desperately, they depended on each other, and were not jealous, and gradually began to think as one on almost all the issues; when one made a decision alone, it was invariably the decision the other would have made in the same situation. Yet they needed help, and after only two weeks, Kyaren decided to do what she had known she would have to do almost from the start.

With the Mayor's consent, she sent a message to Tew, asking Esste to leave the High Room and come cure the ills of the empire.

2   It is quiet, a silence as black as the dark beyond the farthest star. But in the silence Ansset hears a song, and he wakes. This time he does not wake to weeping; he does not see Josif always before him, smiling shyly and carefully, as if he did not feel the mutilation of his body; he does not see Mikal crumbling to ash; he does not see any of the visions of agony from his past. This time the song controls his waking, and it is a sweet song of a room in a high stone tower with fog seeping in at the shutters. It is a song like the caress of a mother's hand in her child's hair; the song holds him and comforts him, and he reaches out his hand, groping in the darkness for a face. And he finds the face, and strokes the forehead.

"Mother," he says.

And she answers, "Oh, my child."

And then she talks in song, and he understands every word, though it is wordless. She tells him of her loneliness without him, and sings softly of her joy at being with him again. She tells him that his life is still rich with possibility, and he is not able to doubt her song.

He tries to sing back to her, for once he knew this language. But his voice has been tortured, and when he sings it does not come out as it ought to. He stumbles, and the song is weak and pitiful, and he weeps at his failure.

But she holds him in her arms and comforts him again, and weeps with him into his hair, and says, "It's all right, Ansset, my son, my son."

And, to his surprise, she is right. He goes to sleep
again, rocking in her arms, and the blackness goes away,
both the blackness of light and the blackness of sound. He
has found her again, and she loves him after all.

3 Esste stayed for a year, working quiet miracles.

"I never meant to involve myself directly in these things,"
she said to Kyaren, when it was time for her to leave.

"I wish you wouldn't go."

"This isn't my real work, Kya-Kya. My real work waits
for me in the Songhouse. This is *your* work. You do it
well."

In the year that she was there, Esste healed the palace
while holding the empire at bay. Humanity had been disor-
ganized for more than twenty thousand years, knit together
in an empire for less than a century. It could have come
apart easily. But Esste's deft voice was confident and
forceful; when it was time to announce that Riktors was
ill, she already had the trust or respect or fear of those she
had to depend on. She made no decisions—that was for
Kyaren and the Mayor, who knew what was going on. She
only spoke and sang and soothed the million voices that
cried to the capital for guidance, for help; that searched in
the capital for weakness or sloth. There were no holes for
the knives to go in. And by the end of the year, the
regency was secure.

Esste, however, regarded as far more important the
work she did with Ansset and with Riktors. It was her
song that at last brought Riktors out of catalepsia. She was

the antidote to Ansset's rage. And while Riktors did not speak for seven months, he did become attentive, watched as people walked around the room, ate decently, and took care of his own toilet, much to the relief of his doctors. And after seven months, he finally answered when spoken to. His answer was obscene and the servant he spoke to was mortified, but Esste only laughed and came to Riktors and embraced him. "You old bitch," he said, his eyes narrow. "You've taken my place."

"Only held it for you, Riktors. Until you're ready to fill it again."

But it soon became clear that Riktors would never be ready to fill his place. He became cheerful enough, after a time, but he was often overcome by great melancholy. He was taken by whims, and then forgot them suddenly in the middle—once he left thirty hunters beating the forest and walked back to the palace, causing a terrible panic until he was found swimming naked in the river, trying to sneak up on the geese that landed in the eddies near the shore. He could not concentrate on matters of state. And when decisions were brought to him, he acted quickly and rashly, trying to get rid of problems immediately, uncaring whether they were solved right nor not. He had lost no memory. He remembered clearly that he had once cared about these things very much.

"But it weighs on me now. It chafes me, like a bad-fitting uniform. I'm a terrible emperor, aren't I?"

"You're good enough," answered Esste, "so long as you don't interfere with those who *are* willing to bear the burdens."

Riktors looked out the window to where the clouds were coming in over the forest.

"Already my shoes are full?"

"They aren't your shoes, Riktors," Esste said. "They're Mikal's. You filled them, and walked awhile in them.

But now they don't fit—as you said. You can still serve. By staying alive and putting in an appearance now and then, you can keep the empire unified. While the others make the decisions you don't care to make anymore. Isn't that fair enough?"

"Is it?"

"What use do you have for power now? You used it once, and nearly killed everything you loved."

He looked at her in horror. "I thought we didn't discuss that."

"We don't. Except when you need a reminder."

And so Riktors lived in his rooms in the palace, and amused himself as he pleased, and put in public appearances so the citizens would know he was alive. But all the business was carried on by underlings. And gradually, as the year went on, Esste withdrew herself from the business, failed to attend the meetings, and the Mayor and Kyaren ruled together, neither of them strong enough yet to rule alone, both of them glad that ruling alone wasn't necessary.

Healing Riktors as much as he could be healed was only part of Esste's work. There was Efrim, in a way the easiest; in a way the hardest.

He was only a year old when his father was taken from him and killed, but that was young enough to feel the loss. He cried for his father, who had been tender and playful with him, and Kyaren could not comfort him. So it was Esste who took him, and sang to him until she found the songs that filled the boy's need. "But I won't be here forever," said Esste, "and he must have someone to replace his father."

The Mayor was not slow to catch on, and he turned to Kyaren. "He's around the palace, and so am I. I'm convenient, don't you think?" So that before Esste had been there six months, Efrim was calling the Mayor *Daddy,* and before Esste left the palace, Kyaren and the Mayor had signed a contract.

"I always call you Mayor," Esste said one day. "Don't you have a name?"

The Mayor laughed. "When I took on this duty, Riktors told me that I had no name. 'You've lost your name,' he said. 'Your name is Mayor, and you are mine.' Well, I'm not really his now, I suppose. But I've got used to having no other name."

So Efrim was healed, and Kyaren with him, almost by accident. Oh, there was none of the passion she had known with Josif. But she had had enough of passion. There was something just as strong and just as comforting in shared work. There was not a part of her life that she didn't share with the Mayor, and there was not a part of his life that he did not share with her. They periodically got quite irritated with each other, but they were never alone.

But all these healings, of Riktors, of Efrim, of Kyaren, of the empire—they were not Esste's most important work.

Ansset refused to sing.

As soon as the hysteria had ended, and he was rational again, she had tried to hear his voice. "Songs can be lost," she said, "but songs can be regained."

"I have no doubt of it," he said. "But I have sung my last song."

She did not try to persuade him. Just hoped that, before she left, she could see a change in his view.

There were changes, certainly. He had always been kinder than Riktors, and so the suffering that purged him of all his hatred did not strip him of his personality. He laughed quite soon, and played happily with Efrim as if he were a younger brother, imitating Efrim's baby speech perfectly. "I feel like I have two children," Kyaren said one day, laughing.

"The one will grow up sooner than the other," Esste predicted, and Ansset did. In only a few months he was interested in the matters of government. He was one of the few people in the palace who had been there under both Riktors and Mikal. He knew many people that the Mayor and Kyaren did not. More important, he was much better than Esste in understanding what people had to say, what they really meant, what they really wanted, and he was able to answer them the way they needed in order to leave satisfied. It was the remnant of his songs that had made him a good manager of Earth. Now, in the absence of the emperor and as Esste withdrew herself more and more from government, Ansset began to take the public role, meeting the people Riktors could not be trusted to meet, the dangerous ones that Kyaren and the Mayor were not sure they could handle.

And it worked well. While Kyaren and the Mayor remained virtually unknown to the rest of the empire, Ansset was already as famous as Riktors and Mikal themselves had been. And though no one ever again heard him sing in the palace as he had before, he was still called the Songbird, and the people loved him.

Yet he was not really happy, despite his cheerfulness and hard work. The day that Esste left, she took him aside, and they spoke.

"Mother Esste, let me go with you," he said.

"No," she answered.

"Mother Esste," he repeated, "haven't I stayed on Earth long enough? I'm nineteen. I should have gone home four years ago."

"Four years ago you could have gone home, Ansset, but today you can't."

He pressed his face into her hand. "Mother, I found you only days before I left the Songhouse; this is the first year I've spent with you. Don't leave me again."

She sighed, and the sigh was a song of regret and love that Ansset heard and understood but did not forgive. "I don't want regret. I want to go home."

"And what would you *do* there, Ansset?"

It was a question he had not thought of, probably because he knew in secret that the answer would hurt, and he tried to avoid pain these days.

What would he do there? He could not sing, and so he could not teach. He had governed a world and helped to rule an empire—would he be content as a Blind, running the small business affairs of the Songhouse? He would be useless there, and the Songhouse would be a constant reminder to him of all that he had lost. For in the Songhouse there was no escaping the songs: the children sang in all the corridors, and the songs came from the windows into the courtyard, and whispered in the walls, and vibrated gently in the stone underfoot. Ansset would be worse off than even Kyaren had been, for she at least had never sung and did not know what it was she lacked. Better for the mute to live among other mutes, where no one would notice his silence and he would not miss his lost voice.

"I would do nothing there," Ansset said. "Except love you."

"I'll remember that," she said. "With all my heart."

And she held him close and cried again because she was leaving—in front of Ansset she had no need of Control.

"Before I go, there's something I want you to do for me."

"Anything."

"I want you," she said, "to come with me to see Riktors."

His face set hard, and he shook his head.

"Ansset, he isn't the same man."

"All the more reason not to go."

"Ansset," she said sternly, and he listened. "Ansset, there are places in you that I can't heal, and there are places in Riktors that I can't heal. His wounds were torn by your song; your injuries were made by his interference in your life. Don't you think that what I can't heal, you might be able to heal?"

Ansset did not answer.

"Ansset," she said, meaning to be obeyed. "You know that you still love him."

"No," Ansset said.

"Ansset, your love was never slight. You gave without bar, and received without caution, and just because it brought pain doesn't mean that it is gone."

And so she led him slowly up to Riktors's rooms. Riktors was standing at the window, looking out as he usually did, watching the birds settle on the lawns. He did not turn until they had been there for several minutes. At first he saw only Esste, and smiled. Then he saw Ansset, and grew sober.

They studied each other in silence, both waiting for the terrible emotions to come back. But they did not come. There was wistfulness, and sorrow, and a memory of friendship and pain, but there was no pain itself, and grief and guilt had faded. Ansset was surprised to discover how much hate he did not feel, and so he walked closer to Riktors even as Riktors walked closer to him.

I will not be your friend as I was, Ansset said silently to the man who was now his height, for Riktors bent a little and Ansset had grown. But I will be your friend as I can be.

And in the silence between them Riktors's eyes seemed to say the same things.

"Hello," Ansset said.

"Hello," Riktors answered.

They said little else, for there was little enough to say. But when Esste left the room, they stood together at the window, looking out, watching the hawks hunting and shouting instructions at the birds desperately trying to survive.

4 Riktors died three years afterward, in the spring, and in his will he asked the empire to accept Ansset as his heir. It seemed the natural thing to do, since Riktors had no children and their love for each other was legendary. So Ansset was crowned and reigned for sixty years, until he was eighty-two years old, always with the help of Kyaren and the Mayor; privately they regarded each other as equals, though it was Ansset's head that wore the crown.

They became beloved, all of them, as Mikal and Riktors, who had made many enemies, could never have been loved. The stories gradually came out, about Ansset and Mikal and Riktors and Josif and Kyaren and the Mayor; they became myths that people could cling to, because they were true. The stories were told, not in public meetings, where it might be politic to praise the rulers of the empire, but in private, in homes where people marveled at the things the great ones suffered, while children dreamed of being Songbirds, loved by everyone, so that someday they could become emperors on the golden throne at Susquehanna.

The legends amused Ansset because they had grown so in the telling, and touched Kyaren because she knew it was a reflection of the people's love. But it changed nothing. In the middle of the government, surrounded by work for a hundred thousand worlds, they managed to make a family of it. Every night they would come home together, Mayor and Kyaren as husband and wife, with Efrim the oldest of their children; and Ansset was the uncle who never took a wife, who acted more like the older brother to everyone, who played with the children and talked with the parents but then, in the end, went alone to his bedroom where the noise of the family penetrated softly, as if from a great distance.

You are mine, but you are not mine, Ansset said. I am yours, but you hardly know it.

He was not unhappy.

But he wasn't happy, either.

5 "This is a hell of a thing to spring on us," Kyaren said crossly.

"If you expect either of us to take the crown, you're going to be disappointed," the Mayor said.

"I wouldn't give you the crown if you wanted it," Ansset said smiling. "I'm getting old, and you're even older. So to hell with you." He turned and called across the room, where Efrim was talking to two of his brothers while he held his youngest grandson in his arms. "Efrim," Ansset called. "Are you ready to be emperor?"

Efrim laughed, but then saw that Ansset was not laughing. He came to the table where his parents and his uncle sat. "You're joking?" he asked.

"Are you ready? I'm leaving."

"Where?"

"Does it matter?"

"Don't make it such a mystery," Kyaren said, cutting in. "He has some crazy idea that the Songhouse is aching to have him come home."

Ansset was still smiling, still watching Efrim's face.

"You're really abdicating?"

"Efrim," Ansset said, letting himself sound impatient, "you knew damn well you'd be emperor someday. How many of *my* children do you see crowding around? Now I ask you, are you ready?"

"Yes," Efrim answered seriously.

"When Mikal abdicated, it took him only a couple of weeks. I won't dally so long. Tomorrow."

"Why so quickly?" Kyaren asked.

"I've made up my mind. I want to do it. I'm wasting time waiting here."

"If you just want to visit, Ansset, visit," the Mayor said. "Stay on Tew for a few months. Then decide."

"You don't understand," Ansset said. "I don't want to go there as emperor. I want to go there as Ansset. Not even Ansset the former Songbird. Just Ansset who's willing to sweep or clean stables or any damn thing they have for me to do, but don't you understand? This is home for you, and for me too, in a way—"

"In every way—"

"No. Because you belong here. But this isn't what I was born for. I'm not right here. I was raised among songs. I want to die among them."

"Esste's dead, Ansset. She died years ago. Will you even know anyone there? You'll just be a stranger." Kyaren looked worried, but Ansset reached out and playfully smoothed the wrinkles on her forehead. "Don't bother," she said, brushing his hand away. "They've been permanently engraved."

"It's not Esste I'm going back to see. It's not anyone."

And Efrim put his hand on his uncle's shoulder. "It's Ansset you want to find, isn't it? Some little boy or girl with a voice that moves stones, isn't it?"

Ansset clapped his hand over Efrim's and laughed. "Another me? I'll never find another Ansset, Efrim! If I go there looking for that, I'll never find it. I may not have sung long, but no one will ever sing like that again."

And Kyaren realized that out of all the achievements of his life, out of all that he had done, Ansset was still proudest of what he had done when he was ten years old.

The legends would have been good enough just with the stories that were current before Ansset abdicated. But there was one more story to add, and for this one Ansset left Earth, left his office, left the last of his money at the station, and arrived penniless at the Songhouse door.

They let him in.

RRUK

1   Ansset had been emperor for only thirty years when Esste's work came to an end. She felt the end coming in summer; felt the ennui of doing again and again work that she had mastered long before. There were no students who interested her. There were no teachers left who were her close friends, except Onn. She was more and more distant from all the life of the Songhouse, though from the High Room she still directed that life.

In the fall, Esste began to long for things she could not have. She longed for her childhood. She longed for a lover in a crystal house. She longed for Ansset, the beautiful boy whom she had held in her arms and loved as she had loved no one else.

But the longings could not be fulfilled; the crystal house was filled with other loves by now, surely; the girl Esste had died, shedding younger skins until now the hard-faced woman in dark robes was her only relic; and Ansset was emperor of mankind, not a child anymore, and she could not embrace him now.

Oh, she toyed with the idea of journeying to Susquehanna again. But before, she had gone in answer to the empire's need. She could not justify such a journey merely to satisfy her own, especially when she knew that, in the end, her real need would be unsatisfied.

All songs must end, said the maxim, before we can know them. Without borders on a thing it cannot be comprehended as a whole. And so Esste decided to put the final border on her life, so that all her works and all her days could be viewed and understood and, perhaps, sung.

It was winter, and snow fell heavily outside the windows of the High Room. Esste had not decided beforehand that this day above all others would be the day. Perhaps it was the beauty of the snow; perhaps it was the knowledge that the cold would take her quickly, in a storm like this. But she sent on errands those likely to discover her too soon. Then she opened all the shutters and let the wind pour in, took off her clothing, and lay on stone in the center of the room.

As the wind swept over her, covering her with snowflakes that melted more and more slowly, Esste hid behind her Control and wondered. She had sung many songs in her life, but which should she sing last? What song should the High Room hear as her own funerary?

She was indecisive too long, and sang nothing as she lay on the High Room floor. In the end her Control failed her, as in extremity it must always fail; but as she crawled feebly under her robes and blankets, a part of her noticed with satisfaction that the work was already done. Blankets alone would do nothing. The snow was two inches deep in the High Room. Tomorrow a new Songmaster would come here and the Songhouse would be taught new songs.

2　Onn was busy.

There was much to be done, and several key Deafs and Blinds had been sent on errands at once, which sometimes happened but was damned inconvenient.

"Sometimes," Onn had confided to a young master, "I feel like I might as well be deaf, for all the time I get to spend with music."

But he didn't mind. He was a good singer, a good teacher, worthy of respect. Yet unlike many of the high masters and Songmasters who had the responsibility of seeing that the Songhouse ran smoothly, he was also a good administrator. He got jobs done. He remembered details. So that where most masters were willing to see almost all the work and decisions taken care of by the Blinds, Onn made it a point to know as much about all the operations of the Songhouse as he could, and help Esste as much as possible.

More important, he did it without being obnoxious. And so it was only reasonable for him and everyone else to assume that he would be the next Songmaster in the High Room, when Esste decided she was finished. And he would have been, too, if he hadn't been so busy.

When the Songmaster of the High Room did not wish to be disturbed, he or she simply did not answer a knock on the door. This was accepted practice. The only ones who could defy this were Deafs and Blinds going about their business, because, according to the etiquette of the place, they were generally regarded as nonexistent. A Deaf whose routine called for him to sweep out a room would simply sweep out the room, and the person who had sought privacy there would not mind—though if a student or a teacher were to enter without permission, it would be quite rude.

All this was simply taken for granted. But Onn had to consult the computer for an answer to a question, and that meant conferring with Esste. The problem seemed urgent at the time, though a few hours later he could not even remember what it was. He went to the High Room and knocked on the door.

There wasn't an answer.

If Onn had been ambitious instead of dedicated, he would have thought of the possibility that Esste did not answer because she had decided to quit her work, and he would have tiptoed away and been patient. Or if Onn had been less confident of himself, he would not have dared to open the door. But he was dedicated and confident, and he opened the door, and so it was he who found Esste's corpse cold under a thick layer of snow.

Esste's loss grieved him, and he sat in the cold (after having closed the shutters and turned on the heat) with her corpse for some time, mourning the loss of her friendship, for he had loved her very much.

But he also knew his responsibility. He had found the body. Therefore he had to inform the person who would be the next Songmaster in the High Room. Yet he himself was the only logical choice for the position. And custom forbade him to name himself. It could not be done.

It occurred to him—he was human, after all—to leave the room immediately with all as he had found it and go wait patiently for some Deaf or Blind to find the body, which was as it should be anyway.

But he was honest, and knew that the very fact that he had defied custom already and entered without permission was reason enough for him to be denied the office. If he could flout courtesy and enter when a person wanted privacy, he was too thoughtless to be Songmaster of the High Room.

But who else? It was not an accident that he was the most obvious choice for the High Room—it was not just because he was outstanding, but also because no one else was particularly suited for the work. There were many gifted singers and teachers among the Songmasters and high masters—after all, it was singing and teaching they were selected for. But a person of such strong will, such dedication, such wisdom that the Songhouse would be safe if guided by that will and that wisdom?

In all the years of the Songhouse's existence, there had always been someone, an easy choice, or at least an

understandable one. Always one of the Songmasters had
been ready, or if not one of them, then an outstanding
young high master whose choice was clearly right.

This time there was no one. Oh, there were two or three
who might have done passable work, but Onn could not
have borne to work under them, for one was prone to
make whimsical decisions, and another often got involved
in petty quarrels, and the third was too absentminded to be
depended on. Someone would always be cleaning up after
their errors. That was not the way it ought to be.

By evening, Onn was getting desperate. He had barred
the door—no sense in letting the rumor get out if a chance
Deaf should enter—and with the snow forming puddles on
the ground, he was feeling quite damp and uncomfortable.
He resolved not to leave the room until he had decided.
But he could not decide.

And so, early in the morning, after a fitful sleep, he got
up, keyed the door to open to his hand, locked it behind
him, and began prowling the Stalls and Chambers, the
Common Rooms and the toilets and the kitchens, hoping
that some startling idea would occur to him, or that his
indecision would be resolved, so that he could choose
someone to replace Esste.

It was afternoon when, despondent, he stepped into a
Common Room where a group of Breezes were being
taught. He came just for solace; the young voices were
unskilled enough that their singing did not force him to
pay attention, yet they were good enough that their harmo-
nies and countermelodies were a pleasure to hear.

As he sat at the back of the room, he began to watch the
teacher, began to listen to her. He recognized her immediately, of course. She had enough ability that she ought to
have been teaching in Stalls and Chambers—her own voice
was refined and pure. But she was not young, and never
likely to be advanced to be a high master or Songmaster,

and so she had asked to remain in the Common Room,
since she loved the children and would not be ashamed or
disappointed to end her life teaching them. Esste had
immediately given consent, since it was good for children
to learn from the best possible voices, and this woman was
the best singer of any of the teachers in the Common
Room.

Her manner with the children was loving but direct,
kind but accurate. It was plain that the children were
devoted to her; the normal squabbles that were bound to
break out in a class this age were easily handled, and they
were touchingly eager to sing well for her approval. When
a song was especially good, she would join in, not loudly,
but in a soft and beautiful harmony that would excite the
children and inspire them to sing better.

Onn had made up his mind before he realized it. Suddenly he found himself protesting a decision he had not
known that he had made. She's too inexperienced, he told
himself, though in fact there was no one but him who
really had experience in doing some of the work of the
High Room. She's too quiet, too shy to work her will in
the Songhouse, he insisted, but knew that as she guided
the children with love, not power, she would be able to
guide the Songhouse as well.

And finally all his objections came down to the last one:
pity. She loved teaching the little children, and in the High
Room she would only have time for one or two children,
and those would have to be in Stalls and Chambers. She
would not be happy to give up a work she so enjoyed
doing to accept a task that she herself and most others
would think was beyond her.

Onn was certain, however. Watching her he knew that
she should take Esste's place. And if it was hard for her,
and she had to give up something to do it—well, the
Songhouse exacted high prices from its children, and she

would do her duty willingly, as all the people of the Songhouse would.

He arose, and she ended the song to ask him what he wanted.

"Rruk," he said, "Esste has died."

He was pleased that it did not occur to her that she was being called to replace Esste. Instead her dismay was heartfelt, and nothing but mourning for her beloved Songmaster Esste. She sang her grief, and the children tentatively joined in. Her song had begun with all the technique she had, but as the children tried to join her, she simplified almost by habit, put her music within their reach, and together they sang touchingly of love that had to end with death. It moved Onn greatly. She was a generous woman. He had chosen well.

When her song ended, he said the words that would cause her, he knew, much misery.

"Rruk, I found her body, and I ask you to make the funeral arrangements."

She understood instantly, and her Control held, though she said softly, "Songmaster Onn, the chance that led you to find her body was cruel, but the chance that brought you to me was madness."

"Nevertheless, it is your task."

"Then I will do it. But I think I will not be the only one to mourn the fact that for the first time, our custom has failed to choose the one best-suited for that duty."

They were singing to each other, their voices controlled but beautiful with emotions that the children were hardly experienced enough to comprehend.

"Our custom has not failed," Onn said, "and you will be sure of that in time."

She left her class then, and the students scurried away to tell everyone the news, and all over the Songhouse songs of mourning for Esste began, along with whispers of amazement that Onn was not the successor, that he in fact had for the first time in history chosen a Songmaster for the High Room who was not even a master, who was merely a teacher of Breezes.

Onn and Rruk carefully tended to Esste's body. Naked, the old woman looked incredibly frail, nothing like the image of power she had always presented. But then, she had lived among those to whom the body meant nothing and the voice was the key to what a person was, and by that standard no one more powerful had been known in the Songhouse in many lifetimes. Onn and Rruk sang and talked as they worked, Rruk asking many questions and Onn trying to teach her in a few hours what had taken him many years to learn.

Finally, in frustration, she said, "I cannot learn it."

And he answered, "I will be here and help you all you need."

She agreed, and so, instead of immediately trying to assert her authority as Songmaster, she began merely as a mouthpiece for Onn's decisions. Such a thing could not be kept hidden, and there were those who thought Onn might have done better to choose them, but that he had chosen Rruk because she was so weak he could rule the Songhouse through her.

Gradually, however, she began to perform her duties alone, and slowly the people of the Songhouse came to realize that she had made them all, somehow, happier; that while the music had not noticeably improved or got worse, the songs had all become somehow happier. She treated all the children with as much respect as any adult; she treated all the adults with as much patience and love as any child. And it worked. And when Onn died not too many years afterward, there was no doubt that he had chosen correctly—in fact, there were many who said that chance had been kind to the Songhouse, by making Rruk and not

Onn Songmaster in the High Room. For the Songhouse had not lost his expertise, and had gained Rruk's understanding as well.

This is why Rruk was the Songmaster in the High Room when Ansset came home.

3   The doorkeeper did not recognize him, of course. It had been too many years, and though the doorkeeper had been a Groan when Ansset was in Stalls and Chambers, there was no way to connect that aging face and the shock of white hair with the beautiful blond child whose songs had been so pure and high.

But the Songhouse was not unkind, and it was obvious that the old man at the door was not overburdened with wealth—his clothing was simple and he carried no purse and wore no ornaments. He refused to state his business, only that he wanted to see the Songmaster in the High Room, which was out of the question, of course. But as long as he wanted to wait in the door-room, he was welcome to wait, and when the doorkeeper saw that he had brought no food, she led him to the kitchens and let him eat with a group of students from Stalls and Chambers.

He did not take any unfair advantage of the kindness, either. When the meal was over, the old man was led back to the door-room, and there he stayed until the next meal was served.

The old man did not speak to any of the children. He just ate slowly and carefully, and watched his own dish. The children began to feel at ease around him and talked and sang. He never joined in or showed any reaction.

Having the old man in the kitchen actually became a point of pride with them. After all, they had been in the Songhouse for at least five or six years, and they knew all the adults, particularly the old ones; the only new ones were usually singers and Songbirds coming home when they turned fifteen and seekers coming back with new ones for the Common Room. To have someone old be new was unheard of.

And he was a mystery among the children. Stories were told about him, how he had committed terrible crimes in some far-off world and was coming to the Songhouse to hide; how he was the grandfather of a famous singer and he was coming to spy on his child; how he was a deaf mute who felt their songs through the vibrations on the table (which had several children putting cotton in their ears and feeling the tables during meals, trying to sense something); how he was a Songbird who had failed and was now trying to gain a place in the Songhouse. Some of the stories were rather close to the mark in detail. Some were so magic and fantastical that they could not be believed even by the most credulous of the children, though of course they were repeated all the same. Yet in all the telling and retelling of the stories of the old man in the Rainbow Kitchen, not one of the stories was ever told to an adult.

So it was only by chance that Rruk ever learned the old man was there. He had taken to helping clean up after the meal. The Rainbow cook was a Blind, helped by two young Deafs who circulated from kitchen to kitchen. The Deafs were late for cleanup one day, and so the old man got up and began to wash the dishes. The cook was an observant woman, and she realized that while the hands of the old man were strong, they had never done any kind of rough work at all—they were soft on the palms as a baby's hand. But the old man was careful and the dishes got clean, and pretty soon the two young Deafs discovered that if they were later and later for cleanup in the Rainbow Kitchen, they wouldn't have to clean up at all.

The cook mentioned this to the doorkeeper when she led the old man to the kitchen one day, and the doorkeeper shrugged. "Why not? Let him feel that he's earning his keep." The cook still believed that someone higher than the doorkeeper had authorized the old man to stay.

It was when the old man carelessly touched a pot that had stayed in the fireplace instead of being put on the table that the cook realized something was wrong. The old man was obviously severely burned. But he made absolutely no sound, showed absolutely no pain. He merely went on about his work after supper, washing dishes, though the pain must have been very annoying. The cook got worried. Because she could think of only two reasons the old man might have touched the pot without even wincing.

"Either he's a leper and doesn't feel it, which I doubt, since he has no trouble handling pots and pans, or he's got Control."

"Control?" asked the head cook. "Who is he, anyway?"

"Someone the doorkeeper brings up. As a kindness, I suppose."

"It should have been cleared with me. An extra mouth eating the food, and I'm not told so I can allow for it in my budget?"

The Rainbow cook shrugged. "We've never run out."

"It's the principle of the thing. Either we're organized or we aren't."

So the head cook mentioned it to the purchaser, and the purchaser mentioned it to security, and security asked the doorkeeper what the hell was going on.

"He's hungry and obviously very poor."

"How long has this been going on?"

"Three months, more or less. More."

"We don't run a hotel. The man should be asked, kindly, to leave. Why did he come?"

"To see the Songmaster in the High Room."

"Get rid of him. No more meals. Be kind, but firm. That's what a doorkeeper's *for*."

So the doorkeeper very kindly told the old man that he would not be able to eat in the Songhouse anymore.

He said nothing. Just sat in the door-room.

Five days later, the doorkeeper came to the head of security. "He plans to starve to death in the door-room."

The head of security came down to meet the old man.

"What do you want, old man?"

"I've come to see the Songmaster in the High Room."

"Who are you?"

No answer.

"We don't let just anybody go see her. She's busy."

"She'd be glad if she saw me."

"I doubt it. You have no idea of what goes on here."

Again no answer. Did he smile? The head of security was too irritated to know or care.

If the old man had been violent or obtrusive, they might have expelled him forcibly. But force was avoided if it was at all possible, and finally, because he intended to stay until he died of starvation, the head of security went to the High Room and talked to Rruk.

"If he's that determined to see me, and he looks harmless, then certainly he should see me."

And so Rruk went down the stairs and through the labyrinth and came to the door-room, where the old man waited.

To her eyes, the old man was beautiful. Wrinkled, of course, but his eyes were innocent and yet wise, as if he had seen everything and forgiven it all. His lips, which opened in a smile the moment he saw her, were childlike. And his skin, translucent with age and yet harsh by comparison with his white, white hair, was unblemished. The wrinkles had been made more by pain than by joy, but the old man's expression transcended all the history of his face, and he reached out his arms to Rruk.

"Rruk," he said, and embraced her.

And in the embrace she startled the doorkeeper and the head of security by saying, "Ansset. You've come home."

There was only one Ansset who could come home to the Songhouse. To the doorkeeper, Ansset was the child who had sung so beautifully at his leavetaking. To the head of security, who had never known him, Ansset was the emperor of the universe.

To Rruk, Ansset was a well-beloved friend that she had sorely missed and grieved for when he did not come home more than sixty years ago.

4 "You've changed," Rruk said.

"So have you."

Rruk compared herself now to the awkward child she had been. "Not so much as you might think. Ansset, why didn't you tell them who you were?"

Ansset leaned against a shuttered window in the High Room. "I tell the doorkeeper who I am, and in ten minutes the entire Songhouse knows I'm here. You might let me visit, and then after a few days you would take me aside and say, 'You can't stay here.' "

"You can't."

"But I have," Ansset said. "For months. I'm not that old yet, but I feel like I'm living in my own childhood again. The children are beautiful. When I was their age and size, I didn't know it."

"Neither did I."

"And neither do they. They throw bread at each other when the cook isn't looking, you know. Terrible breach of Control."

"Control can't be absolute in children. Or most children, anyway."

"Rruk, I've been away so long. Let me stay."

She shook her head. "I can't."

"Why not? I can do what I've been doing. Have I caused any harm? Just think of me as another Blind. It's what I am, you know. A Songbird who came back and can't be used as a teacher."

Rruk listened to him and her outward calm masked more and more turbulence inside. He had done no harm in the months he had been in the Songhouse, and yet it was against custom.

"I don't care much about custom," Ansset said. "Nothing in my life has been particularly customary."

"Esste decided—"

"Esste is dead," he said, and while his words were harsh, she wondered if she could not detect a note of tenderness in his voice. "You're in the High Room now. Esste loved me, but compassion was not her style."

"Esste heard you try to sing."

"I can't sing. I don't sing."

"But you do. Unwittingly, perhaps, but you do. Just speaking, the melodies of your voice are more eloquent than many of us can manage when we're trying to perform."

Ansset looked away.

"You haven't heard your own songs, Ansset. You've been through too much in the last years. In your first years, for that matter. Your voice is full of the worlds outside. Full of too much remembered pain and heavy responsibilty. Who could hear you and not be affected?"

"You're afraid I'd pollute the children?"

"And the teachers. And me."

Ansset thought for a moment. "I've been silent so far. I can keep being silent. I'll be mute here in the Songhouse."

"How long could you keep that up?"

"Aren't there retreats? Let me come and go as I like, let me wander around Tew when I feel the need to speak, and then come back home."

"This isn't your home anymore."

And then Control slipped away from Ansset and his face and his voice pled with her. "Rruk, this is my home. For sixty-five years this has been my home, though I was barred from ever returning. I tried to stay away. I ruled in that palace for too many years, I lived among people I loved, but Rruk, how long could you survive being cut off from this stone?"

And Rruk remembered her own time as a singer, the years on Umusuwee where they loved her and treated her well, and she called her patrons Father and Mother; and yet when she turned fifteen she fairly flew all the way home because the jungle could be beautiful and sweet, but cold stone had formed everything inside her and she could not bear to be away from it longer than she must.

"What do they put in these walls, Ansset, that makes them have such a hold on us?"

Ansset looked at her questioningly.

"Ansset, I can't decide fairly. I understand what you feel, I think I understand, but the Songmaster in the High Room can't act for pity."

"Pity," he said, his Control again in force.

"I have to act for the good of the Songhouse. And your presence here would introduce too many things that we couldn't control. The consequences might be felt for centuries."

"Pity," Ansset said again. "I misunderstood. I thought I was asking you to act for love."

It was Rruk's turn to be silent, watching him. Love. That's right, she thought, that's what we exist for here. Love and peace and beauty, that's what the Songhouse is for. And one of our best children, one of the finest—no, the finest Songbird the house has ever produced—asks for love and out of fear I can't give it to him.

It did not feel right to Rruk. Making Ansset leave did not sound right in her mind, no matter what logic might demand. And Rruk was not Esste; she was not governed by logic and good sense.

"If it were right for the decision in this case to be a sensible one, there would be a sensible Songmaster in the High Room," she said to him. "But I don't make my decisions that way. I don't feel good about letting you stay, but I feel much worse about making you go."

"Thank you," he said softly.

"Silence within these walls. No child is to hear your voice, not even a grunt. You serve here as a Deaf. And when you can't bear the silence anymore, you may leave and go where you like. Take what money you need—you could spend forever and not use up what the Songhouse was paid for your services when you went to Earth."

"And I can come back?"

"As often as you still want to. Provided you keep your silence here. And you'll forgive me if I forbid the Blinds and Deafs to tell any of the singers who you are."

He cast aside Control and smiled at her, and embraced her, and then sang to her:

I will never hurt you.
I will always help you.
If you are hungry
I'll give you my food.
If you are frightened
I am your friend.

I love you now
And love does not end.

The song broke Rruk's heart, just for a moment. Because it was terrible. The voice was not even as good as that of a child. It was the voice of an old man who had talked too much and sung not at all for too many years. It was not controlled, it was not shaped, the melody was not even perfectly true. What he has lost! she cried out inside herself. Is this all that's left?

And yet the power was still there. The power had not been given to Ansset by the Songhouse, it had been born in him and magnified in him by his own suffering, and so when he sang the love song to her, it touched her deeply. She remembered her own weak voice singing those words to him what seemed a million years before, and yesterday. She remembered his loyalty to her when he had not needed to be loyal. And her last misgivings about letting him stay disappeared.

"You may talk to *me*," she said. "To none of the others, but you cannot be a mute to me."

"I'll pollute your voice as surely as the others."

She shook her head. "Nothing that comes from you can do any harm to me. When I hear your voice I'll remember Ansset's Farewell. There are still quite a few of us who remember, you know. It keeps us humble, because we know what a voice can do. And it will keep me clean."

"Thank you," he said again, and then left her, going down the stairs into the parts of the Songhouse where he had just promised that his voice would never be heard again.

5   After a few days' hiatus, the old man returned again to Rainbow Kitchen. The children were excited. They had been afraid this man of mystery would be gone forever. They watched carefully for some clue as to the reason for his disappearance. But he behaved as if nothing unusual had happened. And helped the cook afterward just as he had before.

Now, however, the old man did not disappear after meals. He began to appear in the corridors, in the Stalls, in the Common Room. He was doing jobs usually performed by young Deafs—sweeping, cleaning, changing bedding, washing clothing. He would appear silently, without knocking, as Deafs were allowed to do, but unlike Deafs he was not ignored. No one spoke to him, of course, but eyes followed him around the rooms, surreptitiously watching him, though he did nothing particularly unusual. It was himself that was unusual—for either the Songhouse had broken a thousand-year rule and let someone work inside the Songhouse who had never sung there as a child, or the old man had once been a singer, and there was a story behind his late appearance and his degradation.

There were speculations among the teachers, too, of course. They were not immune, and they soon learned that the Deafs and Blinds would not, under any amount of persuasion and wheedling, discuss the old man. Rruk quickly made it clear that she would not tolerate inquiry. And so they speculated. Of course, the name of Ansset came up with all the other names they knew of singers who had failed to return or who had not found a place within the Songhouse, but none of the names was agreed on as even probable, and Ansset's was far from being the most common suggested. When a man had been emperor, they could not imagine him sweeping floors.

Only two people were sure, besides Rruk and the Deafs and Blinds.

One was a new songmaster named Ller, who had been away as a seeker for many years and returned to find the old man wandering through the Songhouse, ubiquitous and silent as a ghost. He had recognized him instantly—years could not conceal from Ller the features of a face he had memorized in childhood. He toyed with the idea of finding Ansset alone sometime, approaching him, and greeting him with the love and honor he felt toward the man. But then he thought better of the idea. If Ansset was silent and unknown in the Songhouse, it was because of a good reason, and until Ller was given permission to violate that silence and anonymity, he would keep his peace. However, whenever he saw the old man he could not help feeling a rush of childhood sweeping over him, and a sadness to see the greatest of all the singers brought so low.

The other who recognized him had never heard him sing, had never seen his face before, and yet was as certain in her heart as Ller. Her name was Fiimma, and she had heard the legends of Ansset and fixed on them as her ideal. Not in a competitive sense—she had no thought of surpassing this long-gone Songbird. But she longed to be able to touch people's hearts so irrevocably that she would be remembered as long and as happily as Ansset was remembered. She was very young to be longing for immortality, but she knew more of death than most children in the Songhouse. She had seen her parents killed when she was not yet two, and though she never spoke of it, the memory was clear to her. It did not give her nightmares; she handled the weight of memory with relative ease. But she did not forget, and often saw before her the moment of death and knew that it was only chance that had saved her from the thieves.

So she longed to live forever in legend as Ansset did, and took pains to remember everything she ever heard about him. She had asked teachers who had known him years before about his mannerisms, his expressions. They had been little help. So she had imagined the rest. What would a man feel like, act like, look like, having done what Ansset had done? Why hadn't he returned to the Songhouse? What would he desire in his heart?

And gradually, seeing the old man in Rainbow Kitchen and hearing all the speculation about him, she began to wonder if he might *be* Ansset. At first the idea was only appealingly mysterious—she did not believe it. But as days and weeks went by, she became more certain. Ansset, who had become emperor, might come home just this way, silently and unknown. Who knows what barriers there might be to his return? Then he disappeared for a few days and then returned as a Deaf, fully able to wander the corridors of the Songhouse. A decision had been reached, she realized, but it had not been an easy one, and the old man's silence had not been lifted even though he had been allowed to stay. Would Ansset accept such silence as a condition for remaining?

Fiimma thought he would.

And finally she was so certain of him that at supper in Rainbow Kitchen she deliberately sat next to him. Usually he sat alone, but if he was surprised to see her beside him, he gave no sign, merely continued to break bread into his stew.

"I know you," she whispered.

He did not respond, and he did not stop breaking bread.

"You are Ansset, aren't you?"

Again, no sign that he had heard her.

"If you are Ansset," she said, "then keep on breaking bread. If you are not Ansset, take a bite directly from the loaf." She had thought she was clever, but the old man merely responded by setting the rest of the bread into the stew all at once.

And he ate, ignoring her as if she did not exist. Several other children had noticed her there, were commenting among themselves. She was afraid that she was breaking some rule by being with the old man; certainly she had accomplished nothing by trying to get him to talk to her.

But she couldn't let the moment pass so ineffectively. She pleaded with him. "Ansset, if it *is* you, I want you to teach me. I want to learn all your songs."

Did he falter in the rhythm of his eating? Did he pause for a moment to think? She was not sure, but still felt hope.

"Ansset, I *will* learn your songs! You *must* teach me!"

And then, her daring entirely exhausted, she left him and sat with the other children, who begged her to tell them what she had said and if the old man had answered. She told them nothing. She sensed that the old man might be angry with her if she told anyone of her certainty that he was Ansset. *Was* he Ansset? She refused to let herself have any doubts.

The next day the old man did not come to Rainbow Kitchen, and never came there again as long as Fiimma ate there.

6   The silence became unbearable far sooner than Ansset had expected. Perhaps it was lingering memories of the silent days of imprisonment in Mikal's rooms when he was fifteen. Perhaps it was just that like so many old men he had grown garrulous, and the confinement of his promise of silence weighed more heavily than it would have in his youth. Whatever the reason, he found himself longing to give voice, and so he quietly went to Rruk, got her consent, and traveled for the first of his liberties, as he called them in his mind.

The first few liberties, he did not leave the Songhouse lands. There was no need, since the Songhouse owned more than a third of the planet's single continent. He spent weeks wandering the forests of the Valley of Songs, dodging the few expeditions bringing children from the Songhouse. He walked to the lake ringed by mountains, where Esste had first told him that she loved him, had first taught him the true power of Control.

And he was surprised to find the path was gone. Were none of the children taken to this spot anymore? He was sure they were—there were still flesket roads cut through the woods, and the grasses still grew low, a sure sign that visitors still came from time to time. But from the base of the waterfall there was no path coming easily to the top. He remembered as best he could, and finally, very tired, he reached the top and looked out over the lake.

Time had not touched it. If the trees were older, he saw no sign of it. If the water had changed, he could not remember how it was before. The birds still came to the water to dive for fish; the wind still sifted through the leaves and needles with inexpressible music.

I am old, Ansset thought, lying beside the water. I remember the distant past far more easily than I remember yesterday. For if he closed his eyes, he could imagine Esste near him, could hear her voice. Relaxing all Control because he was alone, he let the tears of memory come; the hot sun warmed the tears as they seeped out of the corners of his eyes. But weeping, however gently it was done, could not soothe what was in him.

And so he sang.

After so long being silent, his voice was pathetic. The humblest Groan could do better. Age was playing tricks with pitch, and as for tone, there was none. Just the rough timbre of an old voice overused when young.

Once he had been able to sing with birds and improve on their work. Now the birds fell silent when he sang, and his voice was an interloper in this place.

He wept in earnest then, and vowed never to humiliate himself again.

But he had gone too long without songs in the palace and the Songhouse. There had been too many years when he did not sing because others would have heard his emptiness and his failure. Here, alone in the forest, there were no others, and if he sang badly no one heard but him. So the same day he made that vow, he broke it, and sang again. It was no better, but he did not feel so badly this time.

If this is all the voice I have, he thought, it is still a voice.

No other person would ever hear him sing, of that he was certain. But he would hear himself, and sing out what had been held inside for far, far too long. It was ugly, it was never quite what he wanted it to be, but it served its purpose. It emptied him when he was too full, and in his raucous songs he found some comfort.

On his first liberty he learned the Valley of Songs as few knew it, for no one came here for pleasure, without supervision. But too many memories came with it, and it was too solitary—solitude was good, but he could not bear it for too long.

His second liberty took him to one of the Songhouse's three retreats.

He could not go to the one called Retreat, on the shores of the largest lake in the world, for that was where teachers and masters came from the Songhouse, when they needed ease from their labors. His vow of silence would still be in force there.

The other two were open to him, however.

Vigil, far in the south, was an island of sand and rock lapped by the water of a shallow sea. It was beautiful in a fierce way, and the stone city of Vigil that stood on its northernmost tip was a comforting place, an island of green in the wasteland. Once Vigil had been a fortress, in the days when the Songhouse had been a village and the world was wracked by war. Now it was where the failures went.

Hundreds of singers went out from the Songhouse every year, to do service until they were fifteen years old. Only a few in a decade were Songbirds, but singers were also highly prized, and all were welcomed home when they came.

Some singers became so well adapted to the world they served on that they did not want to come home. The seeker sent for them would try to persuade for several days, but if persuasion did not work, there was no force, and the Songhouse paid for their education until they were twenty-two, just as if they had been Deafs.

Some singers came home to the Songhouse and quickly found happiness in teaching, and were good at it, and remained in the Songhouse for the rest of their lives, except for retreats to Retreat. They could become Song-masters, in time, and if they had the ability. And they ruled the Songhouse.

But there were other variations. Not all who came back to Tew were fit to be teachers, and a place had to be found for them. And not all the singers finished their time. There were some who could not bear the outside worlds, who needed the comfort of stone walls and seclusion and rigor-ous living and routine. There were those who went mad. "The price of the music," the leaders of the Songhouse called it, and took tender care of those who had paid most dearly, gaining their voices but losing their minds.

These were the ones who came to Vigil, and Ansset could talk to them, for they would never come back to the Songhouse.

The sea between the Desert of Squint and the Island of Vigil was shallow, rarely more than two meters deep, with sandbars frequently shifting, so that the passage could almost be made on foot, if the sun were not so dangerously hot and the bottom so unpredictable. As it was, the pas-sage was uncomfortable in a shallow-draft barge, though a canopy kept the voyage in the shade. Ansset was piloted by a young Deaf who spent three months a year here, running the ferry. The Deaf talked eagerly—visitors were few—and Ansset heard in his voice the peace of the place. For all that the land was dry and the water was not deep, there was life here. Fish moved lazily under the water. Birds dove for them and ate them on the wing. Large insects walked along the surface or lived just under it, sucking air from above.

"This is where all the life is," the boy said. "The fish couldn't live underwater without the insects that live on or just under the surface. The birds couldn't live without diving through to get the fish. And the insects eat the surface plants. All the life exists because there's just that thin layer of water that touches the air." The boy had studied. He had no voice, but he had a mind and a heart, and had found a place for himself out here. If he couldn't live in the water, he would live in the air.

He said as much. "You know, the Songhouse couldn't live without sending singers to the outside world."

And Ansset told him, "And the outside world, all the outside worlds, I wonder if they could really live without the Songhouse."

The boy laughed. "Oh, I think the music's just a luxury, that's what I think. Lovely, but they don't need it."

Ansset kept his disagreement to himself. And wondered a little if maybe the boy was right.

There were only seven people living in Vigil, so there was no lack of room for Ansset. Three of them were Blinds, so that only four were mad.

One of the mads was a girl, not more than twenty, who walked every day from the cool of the towers to the sea, where she would lie naked, her body half in the water, half out. At the tides moved, so would she. And whenever a breeze would blow, she would sing, a plaintive, beautiful melody that was never twice the same, but that seemed never to vary, a song of loneliness and a mind as placid and seemingly empty as the sea. When the wind died, so did her song, so that most of the time she lay in silence. She talked to no one, and seemed not to notice that anyone existed, except that she ate what was placed before her and never disobeyed the few orders she was given.

Another mad was an old man, who had spent almost all his life in Vigil. He took long excursions from the town, and in fact seemed not to be insane at all. "I was cured long ago," he said, "but I prefer it here." He was brown from the sun, and collected shellfish from the edge of the water, which formed an important part of the menus at

Vigil. The man told the same stories over and over, and, if
he was left uninterrupted, he would repeat them one after
another to the same person all day and far into the night.
Ansset did it once, letting him have his audience. The old
man finally fell asleep. He had never varied the stories
once. Ansset asked one of the Blinds, "No," the Blind
answered. "None of his stories is true."

And the other two were kept safely in rooms where their
madness was seen only by the Blinds who cared for them.
Sometimes Ansset could hear them singing, but the songs
were always too distant for him to hear well.

Ansset visited Vigil only the once; it was more than he
could bear. There were those, he realized, who had paid a
higher price than he for their songs, and who had been
given less. Alone in the rocky hills behind the towers, he
sang, and learned new echoes and new emotions for his
song.

And he sang with the girl who lay partly in the sea, and
his voice did not silence hers. Once she even looked at
him, and smiled, and he felt that his voice might not be so
hateful, after all. He sang her the love song, and the next
day he left Vigil.

The other retreat was Promontory, and it was by far the
largest. Here was where most of the Blinds lived, singers
who returned and discovered that they did not really enjoy
teaching, that they weren't really good at it. Promontory
was a city of people who sang constantly, but spent their
lives doing other things than music.

Promontory also coasted on a sea, the huge stone buildings (for the Songhouse children could never be long away
from stone) towering over a choppy, frigid sea. There
were no children there, by age, but the games played in
the woods, in the fields, and in the cold water of the bay
were all children's games. As Rruk had explained to him
before he came to Promontory, "They gave up most of

their childhood singing for other people's pleasure. Now they can be children all they like.''

It was not all play, however. There were huge libraries, with teachers who had learned what the universe had to teach them and were passing their knowledge on down to ever younger Blinds until finally they died, usually happy. They never called themselves Blinds here, of course—here they were just people, as if everyone lived this way. Those who showed exceptional ability at government and administration were brought to the Songhouse to serve; the rest were content most of the time at Promontory.

Ansset wasn't, however. The setting was beautiful and the people were kind, but it was too crowded, and while there was no restriction on his speaking to them, he found that they looked at him oddly because he never sang. Soon enough they knew who he was—his identity was no secret among the Blinds—and while they treated him with deference, there was no hope of friendship. His strange life was unintelligible to most of them, and they left him alone.

Inevitably, then, though he visited Promontory several times, he came back to the Songhouse after only a week or so. Speech to the Blinds and solitary songs in the forest or desert were not enough to attract him away from the songs of the children.

And, after a while, there was another reason for him to return. He had never meant to break his vow of silence; he was ashamed when he realized that Rruk could not trust him after all, that his Control was not enough to stop him. But some promises cannot be kept, he knew. And some should not be kept. And so, in one quiet room in the Songhouse, where Esste once had taught him to sing until he touched the edges of the walls, he sang.

7 If Ller had not been Fiimma's Songmaster, it might have gone undiscovered. And if Fiimma had been a worse singer, it might not have worried Ller enough to report it. But Fiimma was obviously going to be a Songbird. And the changes in her songs, which might have been mysterious to another Songmaster, were easily explained to Ller. For he knew that Ansset was in the Songhouse. And he recognized his music in Fiimma's strange new songs.

At first he thought it was just a momentary lapse—that Fiimma had overheard Ansset somehow and incorporated what she heard into her music. But the themes became persistent. Fiimma sang songs that required experiences she had never had. She had always sung of death, but now she sang of killing; she sang of passion she could not possibly have felt; her melodies bespoke the pain of suffering she could not have gone through, not in her few years.

"Fiimma," Ller said. "I know."

She had Control. She showed nothing of the surprise, the fear she must have felt.

"Did he tell you he made an oath of silence?"

She nodded.

"Come with me."

Ller took her to the High Room, where Rruk let them in. Rruk had often heard Fiimma sing before—the child had showed promise from the start. "I want you to hear Fiimma sing," Ller told Rruk.

But Fiimma would not sing.

"Then I'll have to tell you," Ller said. "I know that

363

Ansset is here. I thought I was the only singer who knew. But Fiimma has heard him sing. It has distorted her voice."

"It has made my voice more beautiful," Fiimma said.

"She sings things she shouldn't know anything about."

Rruk looked at the girl, but spoke to Ller. "Ller, my friend, Ansset used to sing things he didn't know. He would take it from the voices of the people who spoke to him, as no singer has ever been able to do."

"But Fiimma has never shown that ability. There isn't any doubt, Rruk. He has not only been singing in the Songhouse, he has been teaching Fiimma. I don't know what conditions you imposed on Ansset, but I thought you should know this. Her voice has been polluted."

It was then that Fiimma sang to Rruk, removing all doubt of Ansset's influence. She must have been holding back on the things she learned from Ansset when she sang for Ller before. For now her voice came out full, and it was not at all the voice that Fiimma had had only months ago.

The song was more powerful than it had a right to be. She had learned emotions she had no reason ever to have felt. And she knew tricks, subtle and distorted things she did with her voice that were irresistibly surprising, that could not easily be coped with, that Rruk and Ller could hardly bear without breaking Control. The song was beautiful, yet it was also terrible, something that should not be coming out of the mouth of a child.

"What has he done to you?" Rruk asked, when the song was through.

"He has taught me my most beautiful voice," Fiimma said. "Didn't you hear it? Wasn't it beautiful?"

Rruk did not answer. She only summoned the head of housekeeping, and had him call for Ansset.

8 "I trusted you," Rruk said to Ansset.

Annset did not answer.

"You taught Fiimma. You sang to her. And you consciously taught her things she had no business learning."

"I did," he said softly.

"The damage is irreparable. Her own voice will never be restored to her, her purity is gone. She was our finest voice in years."

"She still is."

"She isn't herself. Ansset, how could you? Why did you?"

He was silent for a moment, then made a decision. "She knew who I was," he said.

"She couldn't have."

"No one told her. She just knew. When I realized it, I kept away from her as much as I could. For two years, whenever I saw her I would leave. Because she knew."

"Why couldn't you have kept it up?"

"She wouldn't let me. She followed me. She wanted me to teach her. She had heard of me ever since she came here, and she wanted to know my voice. So one day she followed me into a room that no one uses, where I sometimes went because—because of memories. And she begged me."

Rruk stood and walked away from him. "Tell me the coercion she used. Tell me why you didn't just go out the door."

"I wanted to. But Rruk, you don't understand. She wanted to hear my voice. She wanted to hear me sing."

"I thought you couldn't sing."

"I can't. And so I told her that. I broke the vow and said to her, 'I don't have any songs. I lost them all years ago.'"

And as he said it, Rruk understood. For his speech was a song, and that was enough to have broken all the barriers.

"She sang it back to me, you see," Ansset said. "She took my words and my feelings and she sang them back. Her voice was beautiful. She took my wretched voice and turned it into a song. The song I would have sung, if I had been able. I couldn't help myself then. I didn't want to help myself."

Rruk turned to face him. She was Controlled, but he knew, or thought he knew, what she was thinking. "Rruk, my friend," Ansset said, "you hear a hundred children singing your songs every day. You've touched them all, you sing to them all in the great hall, you know that when these singers go out and come back, and in all the years to come, your voice will be preserved among their voices.

"But not mine! Never mine! Oh, perhaps my childish songs before I left. But I hadn't lived then. I hadn't learned. Rruk, there are things I know that should not be forgotten. But I can't tell anyone, except by singing, and only someone who sings could understand my voice. Do you know what that means?

"I can't have any children. I lived with a family that loved me in Susquehanna, but they were never my children. I couldn't give them anything that was very deep within me, because they couldn't hear the songs. And I come here, where I could speak to everyone and be understood, and I must be silent. That was fine, the silence was my price, I know about paying for happiness, and I was willing.

"But Fiimma. Fiimma is my child."

Rruk shook her head and sang softly to him, that she

regretted what she had to do, but he would have to leave. He had broken his word and damaged a child, and he would have to leave. What should be done with the child she would decide later.

For a moment it seemed he would accept it in silence. He got up and went to the door. But instead of leaving, he turned. And shouted at her. And the shout became a song. He told her of his joy at finding Fiimma, though he had never looked for her. He told her of the agony of knowing his songs were dead forever, that his voice, no matter how much it improved in his solitary singing in the forest and the desert, would be irrevocably lost, unable to express what was in him. "It comes out ugly and weak, but she hears, Rruk. She understands. She translates it through her own childishness and it comes out beautiful."

"And ugly. There are ugly things in you, Ansset."

"There are! And there are ugly things in this place, too. Some of them are living and breathing and trying pitifully to sing in Vigil. Some of them are playing like lost children at Promontory, pretending that there's something important in the rest of their lives. But they know it's a lie! They know their lives ended when they turned fifteen and they came home and could not be teachers. They live all their lives in fifteen years and the rest, the next hundred years, they're nothing! That's beautiful?"

"You did more than fifteen years," Rruk answered.

"Yes. I have felt everything. And I survived. I found the ways to survive, Rruk. How long do you think someone as frail and gifted as Fiimma would have lasted out there? Do you think she could survive what I came through?"

"No."

"Now she could. Because now she knows all my ways. She knows how to keep hope alive when everything else is dead. She knows because I taught her, and that's what is coming out in her songs. It's raw and it's harsh but in *her* it will be beautiful. And do you think it will hurt her songs? They'll be different, but the audiences out there—I know what they want. They want her. As she is now. Far more than they would ever have wanted her before.''

''You learned to make speeches in Susquehanna,'' Rruk said.

He laughed and turned back toward the door. ''Someone had to make them.''

''You're good at it.''

''Rruk,'' he said, his back still to her. ''If it had been anyone but Fiimma. If she had not been such a perfect singer. If she hadn't wanted my voice so much. I would never have broken my oath to you.''

Rruk came to him where he stood by the door. She touched his shoulder, and ran her fingers down his back. He turned, and she took his face in her hands, and drew close, and kissed him on the eyes and on the lips.

''All my life,'' she said, ''I have loved you.''

And she wept.

9 The word spread quickly through the Songhouse, carried by the Deafs. The children were to return to the Common Room and the Stalls, where the Blinds would watch them and take them to meals, if necessary. All the teachers and tutors and masters, all the high masters and Songmasters and every seeker who was at home—they were called to the great hall, for the Songmaster of the High Room had to speak to them.

Not sing. Speak.

So they came, worried, wondering silently and aloud what was going to happen.

Rruk stood before them, controlled again so that none would know that she had lost Control. Behind her on the stone stage sat Ansset, the old man. Ller alone of all the teachers recognized him, and wondered—surely he should have been quietly expelled, not brought before them all like this. And yet Ller felt a thrill of hope run through him. Perhaps Mikal's Songbird would sing again. It was absurd—he had heard the terrible changes his songs had wrought in Fiimma's voice. But still he hoped. Because he knew Ansset's voice and, having heard it, could not help but long for it again.

Rruk spoke clearly, but it was speech. She was not trusting this to song.

"It was the way of things that made me Songmaster of the High Room," she reminded them. "No one thought of me except Onn, who should have held the place. But chance shapes the Songhouse. Years ago the custom was established that in ruling the Songhouse we must trust to chance, to who was and was not fit when the Songmaster of the High Room died. And that chance has put me in this place, where it is my duty to safeguard the Songhouse.

"But I am not just meant to safeguard it. The Songhouse walls are not made of rock to make us soft within them. They are made of rock to teach us how to be strong. And sometimes things must change. Sometimes something must happen, even though it can be prevented. Sometimes we must have something new in the Songhouse."

It was then that Ller noticed Fiimma, sitting in a far corner of the great hall, the only student there.

"Something new has happened," Rruk said, and she beckoned to the girl who waited, looking terribly afraid, not because she showed fear, but because she showed nothing as she slowly got up and walked to the stage.

"Sing," Rruk said.

And Fiimma sang.

And when the song was over, the teachers were overcome. They could not contain themselves. They sang back to her. For instead of a child's song of innocence and simplicity, instead of mere virtuosity, Fiimma sang with depth beyond what most of them had ever felt. She tore from them feelings that they had not known they had. She sang to them as if she were as ancient as the Earth, as if all the pain of millennia of humanity had passed through her, leaving her scarred but whole, leaving her wise but hopeful.

And so they sang back to her what they could not keep within themselves; they sang their exultation, their admiration, their gratitude; most of all, they sang their own hope, rekindled by her song, though they had not known they needed hope; had not known that they had ever despaired.

Finally their own songs ended, and silence fell again. Rruk sent Fiimma back to sit in the corner. The girl stumbled once on her way—she was weak. Ller knew what the song had cost her. Fiimma had obviously figured out that Ansset's fate was somehow in her hands, and she had sung better than she had thought she could, out of her own need for Ansset, out of her own love for the old, old man.

"Singers," Rruk said, speaking again, her unsung voice sounding harsh in the silence. "It should be clear to you that something has happened to this child. She has experienced something that children in the Songhouse were never meant to experience. But I don't know. If it has hurt her. Or if it has helped her. What was her song? And the thing that changed her, should it be given to us all, and to all the children?"

Ller did not speak. He knew the importance of a child

finding his own voice. But Fiimma's voice, as she sang, had still been her own. Not the child's voice of a few months before. But not Ansset's voice, either. Still her own; but richer, darker. Not black, however. For as the darkness of her voice had increased with Ansset's teaching, the brightness had also grown brighter.

No one spoke. They were not prepared—either for Fiimma's song or for the dilemma Rruk had given them. They did not know enough. The strangeness of Fiimma's song had obviously come from suffering, but Rruk's voice did not hint of any suffering she planned to cause them. It was plain enough, even though she spoke instead of singing, that she herself favored yet feared the course that she proposed. So they held their silence.

"You are not kind," Rruk told them. "You are leaving the decision up to me. So that if I decide wrong, it will be entirely my own fault to bear."

It was then that Ller stood and spoke, because he could not leave her alone.

"I am Fiimma's teacher," he explained, though everyone knew that already. "I should be envious that her song has been changed by someone else. I should be angry that my work with her has been undone. But I am not. Nor would any of you have been. If I came to you and told you that I had a way to double the range of all your children, would you not accept it? If I came to you and told you that I had a way to help your children sing twice as loudly and even softer than they do now, would you not seize the opportunity? You all know that the emotion behind the song is the most important thing. What happened to Fiimma was the increase of the range of her emotions, not just double, but a thousandfold. It changed her songs. I know better than any of you how much it changed them, and not all the changes are happy ones. But is there anything this child is not prepared to sing? Is there anything this child is not prepared to suffer, and endure? I'm aware of the dangers of what Rruk proposes, but those dangers are the price. And the price may bring us power that we have never had before.''

By the end of his speech, Ller was singing, and when his song was done there were many low murmurs of approval, though all of them were tinged with fear. It was enough, though. Rruk spread her arms and cried. ''Thank you for sharing this with me!''

Then she sent them to get their children and bring them to the great hall.

10 Ansset sang to them.

At first they could not understand why they had been brought to hear this old man. They had not coveted the sound of his voice as Fiimma had. It was harsh to them. His pitch was untrue. His voice was not strong. His songs were crude and unpolished.

But after a while, after an hour, they began to understand. And, understanding, they began to feel. His crude melodies were just intentions—they began to glimpse the music he *meant* to sing them. They began to understand the stories his voice told them, and feel with him exactly what he felt.

He sang them his life. He sang them from the beginning, his kidnapping, his life in the Songhouse, his silence and the agony that finally was broken and healed by Esste in their ordeal in the High Room. He sang them of Mikal. He sang them songs of his captivity, of his killings, and of the grief at Mikal's death. He sang to them of Riktors Ashen and he sang to them of his despair when the Songhouse would not take him back. He sang to them of Kyaren, who was his friend when he most needed one; he sang to them of governing the Earth. As he relived each event, his emotions were nearly those that he had felt at the time. And because he felt that strongly, his audience felt that strongly, for if Ansset had lost his voice, he had only gained in power, and he could touch hearts as no other singer could, despite his weaknesses.

And when he sang of his love for Josif and Josif's death, when he sang of the terrible song that destroyed Riktors's mind and killed Ferret, it was more than anyone could bear. Control broke all over the hall.

They had been worn down not just by his voice, but also by exhaustion. Ansset did not sing quickly, for some songs cannot be sung without time. It was on his fourth day of singing, with his voice often breaking from weariness and sometimes whispering because he could not make a tone at all, that he brought them to the edge of madness, where he himself had been.

For a frightening hour Ller and Rruk both feared that it had been a mistake, that what Ansset was doing could not be endured, that it would be a blow from which the Songhouse would never recover.

But he went on. He sang the healing of Esste's songs; he sang the gentle love of Kyaren and the Mayor and their family; he sang of reconciliation with Riktors; he sang of years of serving the empire and loving, finally, everyone he met.

And he sang of coming home again.

At the end of the sixth day his voice fell silent, and his work was done.

It took time for the effects to be felt. At first all the songs in all the Common Rooms and Chambers were worse; all the children staggered under the weight of what had been given them. But after a few days some of the children began to incorporate Ansset's life into their songs. After a few weeks, to one degree or another, all the children had. And the teachers, too, were colored by the experience, so that a whole new depth sang through the halls of the Songhouse.

And that year even the singers who left the Songhouse sounded like Songbirds to the people they went to serve. And the Songbirds were so strong, so beautiful, that people all over the empire said, "Something has happened to the Songhouse." Those who had heard Ansset sing when he was still a child in the palace sometimes realized where they had heard such songs before. "They sing like Mikal's Songbird," they said. "I never thought to hear such things again, but they sing like Mikal's Songbird."

11 After Ansset sang his life to the children of the Songhouse, he felt a great weight leave him. He went with Rruk to the High Room, and tried to explain to her how it felt. "I didn't know that was what I wanted to do. But that was why I came home."

"I know," Rruk said.

He did not bother with Control now. She had seen all of him, all of his life, as he revealed it to the deepest places in her from the stage in the great hall. There were no secrets now. And so he wept out his relief for an hour, and then sat in silence with her for another hour, and then:

"What do you want to do now?" Rruk asked. "There's

no reason for silence now. You're free to live here as you choose. Do whatever you want to do.''

Ansset thought, but not long.

"No," he said. "I did everything I came here to do."

"Oh," she answered. "But what else is there? Where will you go?"

"Nowhere," he said. And then, "Have I done a Work?"

"Yes," she answered, knowing as she did that she was giving him permission to die.

"Have I done a Work worthy of this room?" he asked.

And again, though no one had ever been granted such a thing before, she said, "Yes."

"Now?" he asked.

"Yes," she said, and as she left the room, he was opening all the shutters, letting the cold air of late autumn pour in. Only Songmasters of the High Room had been allowed to choose the time when their work ended, until now. But it would be absurd, Rruk thought, to deny the greatest Songbird of them all the death granted to others far less worthy of the honor.

As she walked out the door, he spoke to her. "Rruk," he said.

She turned to face him.

"You were the first to love me," he said, "and you're the last."

"They all love you," she said, not bothering not to cry.

"Perhaps," he said. "I thought I would die and disappear from the universe, Rruk. But thanks to you, they're all my children now." He smiled, and she managed to smile back; she ran back into the room, embraced him one more time as if they were still children instead of an old man and an old woman who had known each other too well, and yet hardly at all. Then she turned and left him, and closed the door after her, and three days later the cold and the hunger had done their job. He was so ready to go that he had never wavered, had never in the last extremity sought the comfort of the blankets. He died naked on the stone, and Rruk thought afterward that she had never seen anyone look as comfortable as he did, with rocks pressing into his back and the wind blowing mercilessly over his body.

They delayed the funeral until the emperor could come, with Efrim's parents, Kyaren and the Mayor, the first to arrive. Kyaren did not weep, though she nearly broke when she confided to Rruk privately, "I knew he would die, but I never thought it would be so soon, or without my seeing him again." And, breaking precedent again, though broken taboos were becoming quite common in the Songhouse, Efrim, Kyaren, and the Mayor attended the funeral and heard the songs; and they were not resented when they wept uncontrollably at Fimma's funeral song.

Only Rruk went to the burial, however, of all the people in the Songhouse, except for the Deafs who actually did the work. "It's not a sight much conducive to song," she told Kyaren as they stood together by the grave, "to watch death carry someone into the ground. The dirt closes over him so finally."

And the two women who were the only ones left who had loved him in his childhood stood each with an arm around the other's waist as the Deafs tossed dirt into the grave. "He's not dead, you know," said Kyaren. "He'll never be forgotten. They'll always remember him."

But Rruk knew that memories, however long they are, grow dim, and eventually Ansset would just be a name lost in the books, to be studied by pedants. Perhaps his stories would survive as folk tales, but again his name would be linked to a life that was scarcely his anymore—already the stories of Mikal's Songbird were far grander than the real events had been. Nobler, and so less painful.

Part of Ansset would live, however. Not that anyone

would know it was Ansset. But as singers and Songbirds left Tew and went throughout the galaxy, they would take with them what they had learned from the voices of the singers in the Songhouse. And now a powerful undercurrent in those voices would be Ansset's life, which he had given them irrevocably, forever theirs and forever powerful and forever full of beauty, pain, and hope.

A Selection of Legend Titles

☐	Eon	Greg Bear	£3.50
☐	Forge of God	Greg Bear	£3.99
☐	Falcons of Narabedla	Marion Zimmer Bradley	£2.50
☐	The Influence	Ramsey Campbell	£3.50
☐	Wyrms	Orson Scott Card	£3.50
☐	Speaker for the Dead	Orson Scott Card	£2.95
☐	Seventh Son	Orson Scott Card	£3.50
☐	Wolf in Shadow	David Gemmell	£3.50
☐	Last Sword of Power	David Gemmell	£3.50
☐	This is the Way the World Ends	James Morrow	£4.99
☐	Unquenchable Fire	Rachel Pollack	£3.99
☐	Golden Sunlands	Christopher Rowley	£3.50
☐	The Misplaced Legion	Harry Turtledove	£2.99
☐	An Emperor for the Legion	Harry Turtledove	£2.99

Prices and other details are liable to change

ARROW BOOKS, BOOKSERVICE BY POST, PO BOX 29, DOUGLAS, ISLE OF MAN, BRITISH ISLES

NAME...

ADDRESS...

....

....

Please enclose a cheque or postal order made out to Arrow Books Ltd. for the amount due and allow the following for postage and packing.

U.K. CUSTOMERS: Please allow 22p per book to a maximum of £3.00.

B.F.P.O. & EIRE: Please allow 22p per book to a maximum of £3.00.

OVERSEAS CUSTOMERS: Please allow 22p per book.

Whilst every effort is made to keep prices low it is sometimes necessary to increase cover prices at short notice. Arrow Books reserve the right to show new retail prices on covers which may differ from those previously advertised in the text or elsewhere.